The Shadow of the Cathedral

by Vicente Blasco Ibáñez

Copyright © 6/23/2015
Jefferson Publication

ISBN-13: 978-1514673225

Printed in the United States of America

Contents

INTRODUCTION

There are three cathedrals which I think will remain chief of the Spanish cathedrals in the remembrance of the traveller, namely the Cathedral at Burgos, the Cathedral at Toledo, and the Cathedral at Seville; and first of these for reasons hitherto of history and art, and now of fiction, will be the Cathedral at Toledo, which the most commanding talent among the contemporary Spanish novelists has made the protagonist of the romance following. I do not mean that Vincent Blasco Ibañez is greater than Perez Galdós, or Armando Palacio Valdés or even the Countess Pardo-Bazan; but he belongs to their realistic order of imagination, and he is easily the first of living European novelists outside of Spain, with the advantage of superior youth, freshness of invention and force of characterization. The Russians have ceased to be actively the masters, and there is no Frenchman, Englishman, or Scandinavian who counts with Ibañez, and of course no Italian, American, and, unspeakably, no German.

I scarcely know whether to speak first of this book or the writer of it, but as I know less of him than of it I may more quickly dispatch that part of my introduction. He was born at Valencia in 1866, of Arragonese origin, and of a strictly middle class family. His father kept a shop, a dry-goods store in fact, but Ibañez, after fit preparation, studied law in the University of Valencia and was duly graduated in that science. Apparently he never practiced his profession, but became a journalist almost immediately. He was instinctively a revolutionist, and was imprisoned in Barcelona, the home of revolution, for some political offence, when he was eighteen. It does not appear whether he committed his popular offence in the Republican newspaper which he established in Valencia; but it is certain that he was elected a Republican deputy to the Cortes, where he became a leader of his party, while yet evidently of no great maturity.

He began almost as soon to write fiction of the naturalistic type, and of a Zolaistic coloring which his Spanish critics find rather stronger than I have myself seen it. Every young writer forms himself upon some older writer; nobody begins master; but Ibañez became master while he was yet no doubt practicing a prentice hand; yet I do not feel very strongly the Zolaistic influence in his first novel, *La Barraca*, or The Cabin, which paints peasant life in the region of Valencia, studied at first hand and probably from personal knowledge. It is not a very spacious scheme, but in its narrow field it is strictly a *novela de costumbres*, or novel of manners, as we used to call the kind. Ibañez has in fact never written anything but novels of manners, and *La Barraca* pictures a neighborhood where a stranger takes up a waste tract of land and tries to make a home for himself and family. This makes enemies of all his neighbors who after an interval of pity for the newcomer in the loss of one of his children return to their cruelty and render the place impossible to him. It is a tragedy such as naturalism alone can stage and give the effect of life. I have read few things so touching as this tale of commonest experience which seems as true to the suffering and defeat of the newcomers, as to the stupid inhumanity of the neighbors who join, under the lead of the evillest among them, in driving the strangers away; in fact I know nothing parallel to it, certainly nothing in English; perhaps *The House with the Green Shutters* breathes as great an anguish.

At just what interval or remove the novel which gave Ibañez worldwide reputation followed this little tale, I cannot say, and it is not important that I should try to say. But it is worth while to note here that he never flatters the vices or even the swoier virtues of his countrymen; and it is much to their honor that they have accepted him in the love of his art for the sincerity of his dealing with their conditions. In *Sangre y Arena* his affair is with the cherished atrocity which keeps the Spaniards in the era of the gladiator shows of Rome. The hero, as the renowned *torrero* whose career it celebrates, from his first boyish longing to be a bull-fighter, to his death, weakened by years and wounds, in the arena of Madrid, is something absolute in characterization. The whole book in fact is absolute in its fidelity to the general fact it deals with, and the persons of its powerful drama. Each in his or her place is realized with an art which leaves one in no doubt of their lifelikeness, and keeps each as vital as the *torrero* himself. There is little of the humor which relieves the pathos of Valdés in the equal fidelity of his *Marta y Maria* or the unsurpassable tragedy of Galdós in his *Doña Perfecta*. The *torrero's* family who have dreaded his boyish ambition with the anxiety of good common people, and his devotedly gentle and beautiful wife,—even his bullying and then truckling brother-in-law who is ashamed of his profession and then proud of him when it has filled Spain with his fame,—are made to live in the spacious scene. But above all in her lust for him and her contempt for him the unique figure of Doña Sol astounds. She rules him as her brother the marquis would rule a mistress; even in the abandon of her passion she does not admit him to social equality; she will not let him speak to her in thee and thou, he must address her as ladyship; she is monstrous without ceasing to be a woman of her world, when he dies before her in the arena a broken and vanquished man. The *torrero* is morally better than the aristocrat and he is none the less human though a mere incident of her wicked life,— her insulted and rejected worshipper, who yet deserves his fate.

Sangre y Arena is a book of unexampled force and in that sort must be reckoned the greatest novel of the author, who has neglected no phase of his varied scene. The *torrero's* mortal disaster in the arena is no more important than the action behind the scenes where the gored horses have their dangling entrails sewed up by the primitive surgery of the place and are then ridden back into the amphitheatre to suffer a second agony. No color of the dreadful picture is spared; the whole thing passes as in the reader's presence before his sight and his other senses. The book is a masterpiece far in advance of that study of the common life which Ibañez calls *La Horda*; dealing with the horde of common poor and those accidents of beauty and talent as native to them as to the classes called the better. It has the attraction of the author's frank handling, and the power of the Spanish scene in which the action passes; but it could not hold me to the end.

It is only in his latest book that he transcends the Spanish scene and peoples the wider range from South America to Paris, and from Paris to the invaded provinces of France with characters proper to the times and places. *The Four Horsemen of the Apocalypse* has not the rough textures and rank dyes of the wholly Spanish stories, but it is the strongest story of the great war known to me, and its loss in the Parisian figures is made more than good in the novelty and veracity of the Argentinos who supply that element of internationality which the North American novelists of a generation ago employed to give a fresh interest to their work. With the coming of the hero to study art and make love in the conventional Paris, and the repatriation of his father, a cattle millionaire of French birth from the pampas, with his wife and daughters, Ibañez achieves effects beyond the art of Henry James, below whom he nevertheless falls so far in subtlety and beauty.

The book has moments of the pathos so rich in the work of Galdós and Valdés, and especially of Emilia Pardo-Bazan in her *Morriña* or *Home Sickness*, the story of a peasant girl in Barcelona, but the grief of the Argentine family for the death of the son and brother in battle with the Germans, has the appeal of anguish beyond any moment in *La Catedral*. I do not know just the order of this last-mentioned novel among the stories of Ibañez, but it has a quality of imagination, of poetic feeling which surpasses the invention of any other that I have read, and makes me think it came before *Sangre y Arena*, and possibly before *La Horda*. I cannot recall any other novel of the author which is quite so psychological as this. It is in fact a sort of biography, a personal study, of the mighty fane at Toledo, as if the edifice were of human quality and could have its life expressed in human terms. There is nothing forced in the poetic conception, or mechanical in the execution. The Cathedral is not only a single life, it is a neighborhood, a city, a world in itself; and its complex character appears in the nature of the different souls which collectively animate it. The first of these is the sick and beaten native of it who comes back to the world which he has never loved or trusted, but in which he was born and reared. As a son of its faith, Gabriel Luna was to have been a priest; but before he became a minister of its faith, it meant almost the same that he should become a Carlist soldier, and fight on for that cause till it was hopeless. In his French captivity he loses the faith which was one with the Carlist cause, and in England he reads Darwin and becomes an evolutionist of the ardor which the evolutionists have now lost. He wanders over Europe with the English girl whom he worships with an intellectual rather than passionate ardor, and after her death he ends at Barcelona in time to share one of the habitual revolutions of the province and to spend several years in one of its prisons. When he comes out it is into a world which he is doomed to leave; he is sick to death and in hopeless poverty; he has lost the courage of his revolutionary faith if not his fealty to it; all that he asks of the world is leave to creep out of it and somewhere die in peace. He thinks of an elder brother who like himself was born in the precincts of the Cathedral where generations of their family have lived and died, and his brother does not deny him. In fact the kind, dull gardener welcomes him to a share of his poverty, and Gabriel begins dying where he began living. The kindness between the brothers is as simple in the broken adventurer whose wide world has failed him as in the aging peasant, pent from his birth in the Cathedral close, with no knowledge of anything beyond it. All their kindred who serve in their several sort the stepmother church, down to the gardener's son whose office is to keep dogs out of the Cathedral and has the title of *perrero*, are good to the returning exile. They do not well understand what and where he has been; the tradition of his gifted youth when he was dedicated to the church and forsook her service at the altar for her service in the field, remains unquestioned, and he is safe in the refuge of his family who can offer mainly their insignificance for his protection. The logic of the fact is perfect, and Gabriel's emergence from the quiet of his retreat inevitably follows from the nature of the agitator as the logic of his own past and has the approval at least of the *perrero* and the allegiance of the rest. What is very important in the affair is that most of the inhabitants of this Cathedral-world, rich and poor, good, bad, and indifferent, mean and generous, are few of them wicked people, as wickedness is commonly understood; they all have their habitual or their occasional moments of good will.

The refugee is tired of his past but he does not deny his faith in humanity; his doctrine only postpones to a time secularly remote the redemption of humanity from its secular suffering. He begins at once to do good; he rescues his kind elder brother from the repudiation of the daughter whom he has cast off because her seduction has condemned her to a life of shame; he wins back the poor prostitute to her home, and forces her father to tolerate her in it.

Most of the Cathedral folk are of course miserably poor, but willing to be better than they are if they can keep from starving; the fierce and prepotent Cardinal who is over them all, has moments of the common good will, when he forgives all his enemies except the recalcitrant canons. He likes to escape from these, and talk with the elderly widow of the gardener whom he has known from his boyhood, and to pity himself in her presence and smoke himself free from, his rancor and trouble. He is such a prelate as we know historically in enough instances; but he is pathetic in that simplicity which survives in him and almost makes good the loss of innocence in Latin souls. He keeps with him the young girl who is the daughter of his youth, and whom it cuts him to the soul to have those opprobrious canons imagine his mistress. He is one out of the many figures that affirm their veracity in the strange world where they have their being; and he is only the more vivid as the head of a hierarchy which he rules rather violently though never ignobly.

But the populace, the underpaid domestics and laborers of the strange ecclesiastical world in their wretched over-worked lives and hopeless deaths are what the author presents most vividly. There is the death of the cobbler's baby which starves at the starving mother's breast which the author makes us witness in its insupportable pathos, but his art is not chiefly shown in such extremes: his affair includes the whole tragical drama of the place, both its beauty and its squalor of fact, but he keeps central the character of the refugee, Gabriel Luna, in the allegiance to his past which he cannot throw off. When he begins to teach the simple denizens of the Cathedral, some of them hear him gladly, and some indifferently, and some unwillingly, but none intelligently. He fails with them in that doctrine of patience which was his failure, as an agitator, with the proletariat wherever he has been; they could not wait through geological epochs for the reign of mercy and justice which he could not reasonably promise the over-worked and underfed multitude to-morrow or the day after. His brother, who could not accept his teachings, warns him that the people of the Cathedral will not understand him and cannot accept his scientific gospel, and for a while he desists. In fact he takes service in the ceremonial of the Cathedral; he even plays a mechanical part in the procession of Corpus Christi, and finally he becomes one of the night-watchmen who guard the temple from the burglaries always threatening its treasures.

The story is quite without the love-interest which is the prime attraction of our mostly silly fiction. Gabriel's association with the English girl who wanders over Europe with him is scarcely passionate if it is not altogether platonic; his affection for the poor girl for whom he has won her father's tolerance if not forgiveness becomes a tender affection, but not possibly more; and there is as little dramatic incident as love interest in the book. The extraordinary power of it lies in its fealty to the truth and its insight into human nature. The reader of course perceives that it is intensely anti-ecclesiastical, but he could make no greater mistake than to imagine it in any wise Protestant. The author shares this hate or slight of ecclesiasticism with all the Spanish novelists, so far as I know them; most notably with Perez Galdós in *Doña Perfecta* and *Lean Rich*, with Pardo-Bazan in several of her stories, with Palacio Valdés in the less measure of *Marta y Maria*, and *La Hermana de San Sulpicio* and even with the romanticist Valera in *Pepita Jimenez*. But it may be said that while Ibañez does not go any farther than Galdós, for instance, he is yet more intensively agnostic. He is the standard bearer of the scientific revolt in the terms of fiction which spares us no hope of relief in the religious notion of human life here or hereafter that the Hebraic or Christian theology has divined.

It is right to say this plainly, but the reader who can suffer it from the author will find his book one of the fullest and richest in modern fiction, worthy to rank with the greatest Russian work and beyond anything yet done in English. It has not the topographical range of Tolstoy's *War and Peace*, or *Resurrection*; but in its climax it is as logically and ruthlessly tragical as anything that the Spanish spirit has yet imagined.

Whoever can hold on to the end of it will find his reward in the full enjoyment of that "noble terror" which high tragedy alone can give. Nothing that happens in the solemn story—in which something significant is almost always happening—is of the supreme effect of the socialist agitator's death at the hands of the disciples whom he has taught to expect mercy and justice on earth, but forbidden to expect it within the reach of the longest life of any man or race of men. His rebellious followers come at night into the Cathedral where Gabriel is watching, to rob an especially rich Madonna, whom he has taught them to regard as a senseless and wasteful idol, and they will not hear him when he pleads with them against the theft. The inevitable irony of the event is awful, but it is not cruel, rather it is the supreme touch of that pathos which seems the crowning motive of the book.

W.D. HOWELLS.

* * * * *

THE SHADOW OF THE CATHEDRAL

CHAPTER I

The dawn was just rising when Gabriel Luna arrived in front of the Cathedral, but in the narrow street of Toledo it was still night. The silvery morning light that had scarcely begun to touch the eaves and roofs, spread out more freely in the little Piazza del Ayuntamiento, bringing out of the shadows the ugly front of the Archbishop's Palace, and the towers of the municipal buildings capped with black slate, a sombre erection of the time of Charles V.

Gabriel walked for some time up and down the deserted square, wrapping himself up to his eyes in the muffler of his cloak, while at intervals his hollow cough shook him painfully. Without daring to stop walking on account of the bitter cold, he looked at the great doorway called "del Perdon," the only part of the church able to present a really imposing aspect. He recalled other famous cathedrals, isolated, occupying commanding situations, showing themselves freely in the full pride of their beauty, and he compared them with this Cathedral of Toledo, the mother-church of Spain, smothered by the swarm

7

of poverty-stricken buildings that surrounded it, clinging closely to its walls, permitting it to display none of its exterior beauties, beyond what could be seen from the narrow streets that closed it in on every side. Gabriel, who was acquainted with its interior magnificence, thought of the deceptive oriental houses, outwardly squalid and miserable, but inwardly rich in alabasters and traceries. Jews and Moors had not lived in Toledo for centuries in vain, their aversion to outward show seemed to have influenced the building of the Cathedral, now suffocated by the miserable hovels, pushed and piled up against it, as though seeking its protection.

The little Piazza del Ayuntamiento was the only open space that allowed the Christian monument to display any of its grandeur; under this little patch of open sky the early morning light showed the three immense Gothic arches of its principal front, the hugely massive bell tower, with its salient angles, ornamented by the cap of the Alcuzon, a sort of black tiara, with three crowns, almost lost in the grey mist of the wintry dawn.

Gabriel looked affectionately at the closed and silent fane, where his family lived, and where he himself had spent the happiest days of his life. How many years had passed since he had last seen it! And now he waited anxiously for the opening of its doorways.

He had arrived in Toledo by train the previous night from Madrid. Before shutting himself up in his miserable little room in the Posada del Sangre (the ancient Messon del Sevillano, inhabited by Cervantes) he had felt a feverish desire to revisit the Cathedral, and had spent nearly an hour walking round it, listening to the barking of the Cathedral watch-dog, who growled suspiciously, hearing the sound of footsteps in the surrounding streets. He had been unable to sleep; the fact of returning to his native town after so many years of misery and adventures had taken from him all desire to rest, and, while it was still night, he again stole out to await near the Cathedral the moment that it should be opened.

To while away the time he paced up and down the front, admiring again the beauties of the porch, and noting its defects aloud, as though he wished to call the stone benches of the Piazza and its wretched little trees as witnesses to his criticisms.

An iron grating surmounted by urns of the seventeenth century ran in front of the porch, enclosing a wide, flagged space, where in former times the sumptuous processions of the Chapter had assembled, and where the multitude could admire the grotesque giants on high days and festivals.

The first storey of the façade was broken in the centre by the great Puerta del Perdon, an enormous and very deeply-recessed Gothic arch, which narrowed as it receded by the gradations of its mouldings, adorned by statues of apostles, under open-worked canopies, and by shields emblazoned with lions and castles. On the pillar dividing the doorway stood Jesus in kingly crown and mantle, thin and drawn out, with the look of emaciation and misery that the imagination of the Middle Ages conceived necessary for the expression of Divine sublimity. In the tympanum a relievo represented the Virgin surrounded by angels, robed in the habit of St. Ildefonso, a pious legend repeated in various parts of the building as though it were one of its chief glories.

On one side was the doorway called "de la Torre," on the other side that called "de los Escribanos," for by it entered in former days the guardians of public religion to take the oath to fulfil the duties of their office. Both were enriched with stone statues on the jambs, and by wreaths of little figures, foliage, and emblems that unrolled themselves among the mouldings till they met at the summit of the arch.

Above these three doorways with their exuberant Gothic rose the second storey of Greco-Romano and almost modern construction, causing Gabriel the same annoyance as would a discordant trumpet interrupting a symphony. Jesus and the twelve apostles, all life size, seated at the table, each under his own canopied niche, could be seen above the central porch, shut in by the two tower-like buttresses which divided the front into three parts. Beyond, two rows of arcades of inferior design, belonging to the Italian palace, extended as far as those under which Gabriel had so often played as a child when living in the house of the bell-ringer.

The riches of the Church, thought Luna, were a misfortune for art; in a poorer church the uniformity of the ancient front would have been preserved. But, then, the Archbishop of Toledo had eleven millions of yearly revenue, and the Chapter as many more; they did not know what to do with their money, so started works and made reconstructions, and the decadent art produced monstrosities like that one of the Last Supper.

Above, again, rose the third storey, two great arches that lighted the large rose of the central nave. The whole was crowned by a balustrade of open-worked stone following the sinuosities of the frontage, between the two salient masses that guarded it, the tower and the Musarabé chapel.

Gabriel ceased his contemplation, seeing that he was no longer alone in front of the church. It was nearly daylight, and several women with bowed heads, their mantillas falling over their eyes, were passing in front of the iron grating. The crutches of a lame man rang out on the fine tiles of the pavement, and, out beyond the tower, under the great arch of communication between the archbishop's palace and the Cathedral, the beggars were gathering in order to take up their accustomed positions at the cloister door. The faithful and "God's creatures" knew one another; every morning they were the first occupants of the church, and this daily meeting had established a kind of fraternity, and with much coughing and hoarseness they all lamented the cold of the morning and the lateness of the bell-ringer in coming down to open the doors.

A door opened beyond the archbishop's arch, that of the tower and the staircase leading to the dwellings in the upper cloister. A man crossed the street rattling a huge bunch of keys, and, followed by the usual morning assemblage, he proceeded to open the door of the lower cloister, narrow and pointed as an arrow-head. Gabriel recognised him, it was Mariano, the bell-ringer. To avoid being noticed he remained motionless in the *Piazza*, allowing those to pass first through the Puerta del Mollete, who seemed so anxious to hurry into the Metropolitan church, lest their usual places should be stolen from them and occupied by others.

At last he decided to follow them, and slowly descended the same steps leading down into the cloister, for the Cathedral, being built in a hollow, is much lower than the adjacent streets.

Everything appeared the same. There on the walls were the great frescoes of Bayan y Maella, representing the works and great deeds of Saint Eulogio, his preaching in the land of the Moors, and the cruelties of the infidels, who, with big turbans and enormous whiskers, were beating the saint. In the interior of the Mollete doorway was represented the horrible martyrdom of the Child de la Guardia; that legend born at the same time in so many Catholic towns during the heat of anti-Semitic hatred, the sacrifice of the Christian child, stolen from his home by Jews of grim countenance, who crucified him in order to tear out his heart and drink his blood.

The damp was rapidly effacing this romantic fresco, that filled the sides of the archway like the frontispiece of a book, causing it to scale off; but Gabriel could still see the horrible face of the judge standing at the foot of the cross, and the ferocious gesture of the

9

man, who with his knife in his mouth, was bending forward to tear out the heart of the little martyr; theatrical figures, but they had often disturbed his childish dreams.

The garden in the midst of the cloister showed even in midwinter its southern vegetation of tall laurels and cypresses, stretching their branches through the grating of the arches that, five on each side, surrounded the square, and rising to the capitals of the pillars. Gabriel looked a long time at the garden, which was higher than the cloister; his face was on a level with the ground on which his father had laboured so many years ago; at last he saw again that charming corner of verdure—the Jews' market converted into a garden by the canons centuries before. The remembrance of it had followed him everywhere—in the Bois de Boulogne, in Hyde Park; for him the garden of the Toledan Cathedral was the most beautiful of all gardens, for it was the first he had even known in his life.

The beggars seated on the doorsteps watched him curiously, without daring to stretch out their hands; they could not tell if this early morning visitor with the worn-out cloak, the shabby hat, and the old boots, was simply an inquisitive traveller, or whether he was one of their own order, choosing a position about the Cathedral from whence to beg alms.

Annoyed by this curiosity, Luna walked down the cloister, passing by the two doors that opened into the church. The one called del Presentacion is a lovely example of Plateresque art, chiselled like a jewel, and adorned with fanciful and happy trifles. Going on further, he came to the back of the staircase by which the archbishops descended from their palace to the church; a wall covered with Gothic interlacings, and large escutcheons, and almost on the level of the ground was the famous "stone of light," a thin slice of marble as clear as glass, which gave light to the staircase, and was the admiration of all the countryfolk who came to visit the cloister. Then came the door of Santa Catalina, black and gold, with richly-carved polychrome foliage, mixed with lions and castles, and on the jambs two statues of prophets.

Gabriel went on a few steps further as he saw that the wicket of the doorway was being opened from inside. It was the bell-ringer going his rounds and opening all the doors; first of all a dog came out, stretching his neck as though he was going to bark with hunger, then two men with their caps over their eyes, wrapped in brown cloaks; the bell-ringer held up the curtain to let them pass out.

"Well, good-day, Mariano," said one of them by way of farewell.

"Good-night to the caretakers of God.... May you sleep well."

Gabriel recognised the nocturnal guardians of the Cathedral; locked into the church since the previous night, they were now going to their homes to sleep.

The dog trotted off in the direction of the seminary to get his breakfast off the scraps left by the students, free till such time as the guardians came to look for him, to lock themselves in the church once more.

Luna walked down the steps of the doorway into the Cathedral. His feet had scarcely touched the pavement before he felt on his face the cold touch of the clammy air, like an underground vault. In the church it was still dark, but above the stained glass of the hundreds of different-sized windows glowed in the early dawn, looking like magic flowers opening with the first splendours of day. Below, among the enormous pillars that looked like a forest of stone, all was darkness, broken here and there by the uncertain red spots of the lamps burning in the different chapels, wavering in the shadows. The bats flew in and out round the columns, wishing to prolong their possession of the fane, till the first rays of the sun shone through the windows; they fluttered over the heads of the devotees, who, kneeling before the altars, were praying loudly, as pleased to be in the Cathedral at that early hour as though it were their own house. Others chattered with the acolytes and other servants of the church, who were coming in by the different doors, sleepy and stretching themselves like workmen coming to their work. In the twilight, figures in black cloaks glided by on their way to the sacristy, stopping to make genuflections before each image; and in the distance, invisible in the darkness, you could still divine the presence of the bell-ringer, like a restless hobgoblin, by the rattle of his bunch of keys and the creaking of the doors he opened on his round.

The Cathedral was awake. Echo repeated the banging of the doors from nave to nave; a large broom, making a saw-like noise, began to sweep in front of the sacristy; the church vibrated under the blows of certain acolytes engaged in removing the dust from the famous carved stalls in the choir; it seemed as though the Cathedral had awoke with its nerves irritated, and that the slightest touch produced complaints.

The men's footsteps resounded with a tremendous echo, as though the tombs of all the kings, archbishops and warriors hidden under the tiled floor were being disturbed.

The cold inside the church was even more intense than that outside; this, together with the damp of its soil traversed by underground water drains, and the leakage of subterranean and hidden tanks that stained the pavement, made the poor canons in the choir cough horribly, "shortening their lives," as they complainingly said.

The morning light began to spread through the naves, bringing out of the darkness the spotless whiteness of the Toledan Cathedral, the purity of its stone making it the lightest and most beautiful of temples. One could now see all the elegant and daring beauty of the eighty-eight pillars soaring audaciously into space, white as frozen snow, and the delicate ribs interlacing to carry the vaulting. In the upper storey the sun shone through the large stained-glass windows, making them look like fairy gardens.

Gabriel seated himself on the base of one of the pilasters between two columns; but he was soon obliged to rise and move on, the dampness of the stone, and the vault-like cold throughout the whole building penetrated to his very bones.

He strolled through the naves, attracting the attention of the devotees, who stopped in their prayers to watch him. A stranger at that early hour, which belonged specially to the familiars of the Cathedral, excited their curiosity.

The bell-ringer passed him several times, following him with uneasy glance, as though this unknown man, of poverty-stricken aspect, who wandered aimlessly about at an hour when the treasures of the church were, as a rule, not so strictly watched, inspired him with little confidence.

Another man met him near the high altar. Luna recognised him also: it was Eusebio, the sacristan of the chapel of the Sagrario, "Azul de la Virgen," as he was called by the Cathedral staff, on account of the celestial colour of the cloak he wore on festival days.

Six years had passed since Gabriel had last seen him, but he had not forgotten his greasy carcase, his surly face with its narrow, wrinkled forehead fringed with bristly hair, his bull neck that scarcely allowed him to breathe, and that made every breath like the blast of a bellows. All the servants of the Cathedral envied him his post, which was the most lucrative of all, to say nothing of the favour he enjoyed with the archbishop and the canons.

"Virgin's blue" considered the Cathedral as his own peculiar property, and he often came very near turning out those who inspired him with any antipathy.

He fixed his bold eyes on the vagabond he saw walking about the church, making an effort to raise his overhanging brows. Where had he seen this strange fellow before? Gabriel noted the effort he made to recall his memory, and turned his back to examine with pretended interest a coloured panel hanging on a pillar.

11

Flying from the curiosity excited by his presence in the fane, he went out into the cloister; there he felt more at his ease, quite alone. The beggars were chattering, seated on the doorsteps of the Mollete; many of the clergy passed through them, entering the church hurriedly by the door of the Presentacion; the beggars saluted them all by name, but without stretching out their hands. They knew them, they all belonged to the "household," and among friends one does not beg. They were there to fall on the strangers, and they waited patiently for the coming of the English; for, surely, all the strangers who came from Madrid by the early morning train could only be from England.

Gabriel waited near the door, knowing that those coming from the cloister must enter by it. He crossed the archbishop's arch, and, following the open staircase of the palace, descended into the street, re-entering the church by the Mollete door. Luna, who knew all the history of the Cathedral, remembered the origin of its name. At first it was called "of justice," because under it the Vicar-General of the Archbishopric gave audience. Later it was called "del Mollete," because every day after high mass the acolytes and vergers assembled there for the blessing of the half-pound loaves, or rolls of bread distributed to the poor. Six hundred bushels of wheat—as Luna remembered—were distributed yearly in this alms, but this was in the days when the yearly revenues of the Cathedral were more than eleven millions.

Gabriel felt annoyed by the curious glances of the clergy, and of the devout entering the church. They were people accustomed to seeing each other daily at the same hour, and they felt their curiosity excited by seeing a stranger breaking in on the monotony of their lives.

He drew back to the further end of the cloister, then some words from the beggars made him retrace his steps.

"Ah! here comes old 'Vara de palo.'"

"Good-day, Señor Esteban!"

A small man dressed in black, and shaved like a cleric, came down the steps.

"Esteban! Esteban!" cried Luna, placing himself between him and the door of the Presentacion.

"Wooden Staff" looked at him with his clear eyes like amber, the quiet eyes of a man used to spending long hours in the Cathedral, with never a rebellious thought arising to disturb his immovable beatitude. He stood doubting for some time, as though he could scarcely credit the remote resemblance in this thin, pale face, to another that lived in his memory, but at last, with a pained surprise, he became convinced of its identity.

"Gabriel! my brother! is it really you?"

And the rigidly set face of the Cathedral servant, which seemed to have acquired the immobility of its pillars and statues, relaxed with an affectionate smile.

"When did you come? Where have you been? What is your life? Why have you come?"

"Wooden Staff" expressed his surprise by incessant questions, never giving his brother time to answer.

Gabriel at length explained, that he had arrived the previous night, and that he had waited outside the church since early dawn in the hopes of seeing his brother.

"I have now come from Madrid, but before that I was in many places: in England, in France, in Belgium, who knows where besides. I have wandered from one town to another, always struggling against hunger and the cruelty of men. My footsteps have been dogged by poverty and the police. When I rest a little, worn out by this Wandering Jew's existence, Justice, inspired by fear, orders me to move on, and so once again I begin my march. I am a man to be feared, Esteban, even as you now see me, with my body ruined before old age, and the certainty before me of a speedy death. Again, yesterday in Madrid, they told me I should be sent once more to prison if I stayed there any longer, and so in the evening I took the train. Where shall I go? The world is wide; but for me and other rebels it is very small, and narrows till it does not leave a hand's breadth of ground for our feet. In all the world nothing was left me but you, and this peaceful silent corner where you live so happily, and so, I came to seek you. If you turn me out, nothing will be left me but to die in prison, or in a hospital, if indeed they would take me in when they know my name."

And Gabriel, spent with his words, coughed painfully, a hollow cavernous cough that seemed to tear his chest. He expressed himself vehemently, moving his arms freely, with the gestures of a man used to speaking in public, burning with the zeal of his cause.

"Ah! brother, brother!" said Esteban, with an accent of mild reproof, "what has it profited you reading so many books and newspapers? What is the use of trying to disturb and upset things that are all right; and if they are all wrong, is there no other means of righting them possible? If you had followed your own path quietly, you would have been a beneficiary of the Cathedral, and, who knows, you might have had a seat in the choir among the canons, for the honour and profit of the family! But you were always wrong-headed, although you were the cleverest of us all. Cursed talent that leads to such misery! What I have suffered, brother, trying to hear about your affairs! What bitterness have I not gone through since you last came here! I thought you were contented and happy in the printing office in Barcelona, receiving a salary that was a fortune compared to what we earn here. I was disturbed at reading your name so often in the papers, at those meetings, where the division of everything is advocated, the death of religion and of the family, and I do not know what follies besides. The 'companion' Luna said this, or the 'companion' Luna has done the other, and I tried to hide from the people of the 'household' that this 'companion' could be you, guessing that such madness must turn out ill—furiously ill—and after—after came the affairs of the bombs."

"I had nothing to do with that," said Gabriel sadly. "I am only a theorist; I condemned the action as premature and inefficacious."

"I know it, Gabriel. I always thought you innocent. You so good, so gentle, who since you were a little one always astonished us by your kindness; you who seemed like a saint, as our poor mother used to say! You kill, and so treacherously, by means of such infernal artifices! Holy Jesus!"

And the "Wooden Staff" was silent, overcome by the recollection of those attempts that had overwhelmed his brother.

"But what is certain is," he continued after a little, "that you fell into the trap spread by the Government after those affairs. What I suffered for a while! Now and again I heard firing in the castle ditch beyond there, and I searched anxiously in the papers for the names of those executed, always fearing to find yours. There were rumours current of horrible tortures inflicted on those taken to make them confess the truth, and I thought of you, so frail, so delicate, and I feared that some day you would be found dead in a dungeon. And I suffered even more from my anxiety that no one here should know of your situation; you a Luna! a son of Señor Esteban, the old gardener of the Primate, with whom all the canons and even the archbishop talked. You mixed up with those infernal scoundrels who wish to destroy the world. For this reason when Eusebio the 'Virgin's Blue,' asked me if you could possibly be the Luna of whom he read in the papers, I replied that my brother was in America, that I heard from him now and again, but that he was occupied with a big business—you see what pain! Fearing from one moment to another that they would kill you, unable to speak, unable to complain, fearful of telling my distress even to my family. How often have I prayed in there! Accustomed as we of the 'household' are to associate daily with God and the saints, we may be a little hard and

13

narrow-minded, but misfortune softens the heart, and I addressed myself to Her who can do everything, to our patroness the Virgin of the Sagrario, begging her to remember you, who used to kneel at her shrine as a little child when you were preparing to enter the seminary."

Gabriel smiled gently as though admiring the simplicity of his brother.

"Do not laugh, I pray you—your smile wounds me. The Divine Lady did all she could for you. Months afterwards I learnt that you and others had been put on board ship with orders never to return to Spain, and, up to the present time, never a letter or a scrap of news, good or ill. I thought you had died, Gabriel, in those distant lands, and more than once I have prayed for your poor soul, that I am sure wanted it."

The "companion" showed in his eyes his gratitude for these words.

"Thanks, Esteban. I admire your faith, but I did not come out of that dark adventure as well as you imagine. It would have been far better to have died. The aureole of a martyr is worth more than to enter a dungeon a man and come out of it a limp rag. I am very ill, Esteban, my sentence is irrevocable. I have no stomach left, my lungs are gone, and this body that you see is like a dislocated machine that can hardly move, creaking in every joint, as though all the bits intended to fall apart. The Virgin who saved me at your recommendation might really have interceded a little more in my favour, softening my jailors. Those wretches think to save the world by giving free rein to those wild beast instincts that slumber in us all, relics of a far-away past. Since then, at liberty, life has been more painful than death. On my return to Spain, pressed by poverty and persecution, my life has been a hell. I dare stop in no place where men congregate; they hunt me like dogs, forcing me to live out of the towns, driving me to the mountains, into the deserts, where no human beings live. It appears I am still a man to be feared, more to be feared than those desperadoes who throw bombs, because I can speak, because I carry in me an irresistible strength which forces me to preach the Truth if I find myself in the presence of miserable and trodden-down wretches—but all this is coming to an end. You may be easy, brother, I am a dead man; my mission is drawing to a close, but others will come after me, and again others. The furrow is open and the seed is in its bowels— 'GERMINAL!' as a friend of my exile shouted as he saw the last rays of the setting sun from the scaffold of the gibbet. I am dying, and I think I have the right to rest for a few months. I wish to enjoy for the first time in my life the sweets of silence, of absolute quiet, of incognito; to be no one, for no one to know me; to inspire neither sympathy nor fear. I should wish to be as a statue on the doorway, as a pillar in the Cathedral, immovable, over whose surface centuries have glided without leaving the slightest trace or emotion. To wait for death as a body that eats or breathes, but cannot think or suffer, nor feel enthusiasm; this to me would be happiness, brother. I do not know where to go; men are waiting for me out beyond these doors to drive me on again. Will you let me stay with you?"

For all answer the "Wooden Staff" laid his hand affectionately on Gabriel's arm.

"Let us come upstairs, madman—you shall not die, I will nurse you; what you want is care and quiet. We will cure that hot head, which seems like that of Don Quixote. Do you remember when you were a child reading us his history in the long evenings? Go along, dreamer, what does it signify to you if the world is better or worse regulated? As we found it, so it has always been. What does signify is that we should live like Christians, with the certainty that the other life will be a better one, as it will be the work of God and not of man. Go up—let us go up."

And taking hold of the vagabond affectionately, they passed out of the cloister through the beggars, who had followed the interview with curious eyes, without, however, being able to hear a single word. They crossed the street and entered the staircase of the tower. The steps were of red brick, worn and broken; the whitewashed walls were covered on all sides with grotesque drawings and various inscriptions, scrawled by those who had ascended the tower, attracted by the fame of the big bell.

Gabriel went up slowly, gasping, and stopping at every step.

"I am ill, Esteban, very ill; these bellows let out the wind in every part."

Then, as though repenting his forgetfulness, he suddenly asked:

"And Pepa, your wife? I hope she is all right."

The brows of the Cathedral servant contracted, and his eyes became bright as though full of tears.

"She died," he said with laconic sadness.

Gabriel stopped suddenly, clinging to the handrail, struck with surprise; then, after a short silence, he went on, wishing to console his brother.

"But, Sagrario, my niece, she must have grown a beauty. The last time I saw her she looked like a queen, with her crown of auburn hair and her smiling face, with its golden bloom, like a ripe apricot. Did she marry the cadet, or is she still with you?"

The "Wooden Staff" appeared even more sad, and he looked grimly at his brother.

"She also died," he said drily.

"Sagrario also dead!" exclaimed Gabriel astounded.

"She is dead to me, which is the same thing. Brother, by all you love best in the world, do not speak to me of her."

Gabriel understood that he had opened some deep wound by his inquiries, and so said no more, beginning once more his ascent. During his absence a terrible event had happened in his brother's life—one of those events that break up a family and separate for ever those that survive.

They crossed the gallery covered by the archbishop's archway and entered the upper cloister called "the Claverias": four arcades of equal length to those of the lower cloister, but quite bare of decoration, and with a poverty-stricken aspect. The pavement was chipped and broken, the four sides had a balustrade running round between the flat pillars that supported the old beams of the roof. It had been a provisional work three hundred years ago, and had always remained in the same state. All along the whitewashed walls, the doors and windows belonging to the "habitacions" of the Cathedral servants opened without order or symmetry. These were transmitted with the office from father to son. The cloister, with its low arcade, looked like a street having houses on one side only; opposite was the flat colonnade with its balustrade, against which the pointed branches of the cypresses in the garden rested. Above the roof of the cloister could be seen the windows of another row of "habitacions," for nearly all the dwellings in the Claverias had two stories.

It was the population of a whole town that lived above the Cathedral, on a level with its roofs; and when night fell, and the staircase of the tower was locked, it remained quite isolated from the city. This semi-ecclesiastical tribe was born and died in the very heart of Toledo without ever going down into the streets, clinging with traditional instinct to the carved mountain of stone, whose arches served it as a refuge. They lived saturated with the scent of incense, breathing the peculiar smell of mould and old iron belonging to ancient buildings, and with no more horizon than the arches of the bell tower, whose height soared into the small patch of blue sky visible from the cloister.

15

The "companion" Luna thought he was returning with one step to the days of his childhood. Little children like the Gabriel of former days were playing about the four galleries, and sitting in that part of the cloister bathed by the first rays of the sun. Women, who reminded of his mother, were shaking the bedclothes out over the garden, or sweeping the red bricks opposite their dwellings; everything seemed the same. Time had left it quite alone, evidently thinking there was nothing there that he could possibly age. The "companion" could now see two sketches of lay brothers that he had drawn with charcoal when he was eight years old; had it not been for the children one might have thought that life had been suspended in that corner of the Cathedral, as though this aerial population could neither be born nor die.

The "Wooden Staff," frowning and gloomy since the last words were spoken, tried to give some explanation to his brother.

"I live in our same old house. They left it to me out of respect to the memory of my father. I am grateful to the clergy of the Chapter, taking into consideration that I am nothing but a sad old 'Wooden Staff.' Since my misfortune happened I have had an old woman to keep house, and Don Luis, the Chapel-master, lives with me. You will come to know him, a young priest of great talent, but quite hidden here: one of God's souls, whom they think crazy in the Cathedral, but who lives like an angel."

They entered into the house of the Lunas, which was one of the best in the Claverias. By the door two rows of flower vases in the shape of a clock-case fastened to the walls were filled with hanging plants; inside, in the sitting room, Gabriel found everything the same as during his father's lifetime. The white walls that with years had become like ivory, were still decorated with the old engravings of saints, the chairs of mahogany, bright with constant rubbing, looked like new, in spite of their curves, which showed them to belong to a previous century, and their seats almost ready to drop through. Through a half-open door he could see into the kitchen, where his brother had gone to give some orders to a timid-looking old woman. In one corner of the room, half hidden, was a sewing machine. It was the permanent remembrance the "little one" had left behind her after that catastrophe which had filled her father with such gloomy sadness. Through a back window of the room Gabriel could see the inner court, which made this "habitacion" one of the most charming in the Claverias, the open expanse of sky, and the upper rooms on all four sides, supported by rows of slender pillars, that made the courtyard look like a little cloister.

Esteban came back and rejoined his brother.

"You must say what you would like for breakfast. It would soon be ready; ask, man, ask for what you want, for though I am poor I shall take little credit to myself unless I can make you pick up a little and lose that look of a resuscitated corpse."

Gabriel smiled sadly.

"It is useless your troubling; my stomach is quite gone; a little milk is enough for it, and I am thankful if it retains it."

Esteban ordered the old woman to go into the town in search of the milk, and he had hardly seated himself by his brother's side when the door giving into the cloister opened, and the head of a young man appeared.

"Good-day, uncle!" he exclaimed.

His face was unhealthy and currish, the eyes were malicious, and above his ears were combed two large tufts of glossy hair.

"Come in, vagabond, come in," said the "Wooden Staff."

And he added, turning to his brother:

16

"Do you know who this is? No? It is the son of our poor brother, whom God has taken to his glory. He lives in the upper dwellings of the cloister with his mother, who washes the linen of the choir, and of the señores canons; and it is a delight to see how she crimps the surplices. Thomas, lad, bow to the gentleman; it is your uncle Gabriel, who has just arrived from America, and from Paris, and I don't know from where else besides! From very far off countries, very far off."

The young man saluted Gabriel, though he seemed rather scared by the sad and suffering face of their relative, whom he had heard his mother speak of as a mysterious and romantic being.

"Here, as you see him," proceeded Esteban, speaking to his brother, and pointing to his nephew, "he is the worst lot in the Cathedral. The Señor Obrero would more than once have turned him out into the street, were it not for respect to the memory of his father and grandfather, and also to the name he bears, for everybody knows the Lunas are as ancient in the Cathedral as the stones in its walls. No escapade enters his head but he hastens to carry it out, and he swears like a pagan even in full sacristy, under the very noses of the beneficiaries. Don't dare to deny it! Grumbler!"

And he shook his first at the lad, half severely, half smiling, as though in the bottom of his heart he felt some pride in his nephew's scrapes, who received his reprimand with grimaces that made his face twitch like that of a monkey, while his eyes retained their fixed and insolent stare.

"It is a real shame," continued the uncle, "that you should comb your hair in that fashion, like the Merry Andrews that come to Toledo from the Court on great festivals. In the good old times of the Cathedral they would have shaved your head for you. But in these days of alienation, of universal licence and misfortunes, our holy church is as poor as a rat, and poverty does not give the señores canons much inclination to examine details. It is a grievous pity to see how everything is going down. What desolation, Gabriel! If you could only see it! The Cathedral is as beautiful as ever, but we do not now see the former beauty of the Lord's worship. The Chapel-master says the same thing, and he is indignant to see that on great festivals only about half-a-dozen musicians take their place in the middle of the choir. The young people who live in the Claverias have not our great love for the mother-church; they complain of the shortness of their salaries without considering that it is the temporalities that support religion. If this goes on I should not be surprised to see this popinjay and other rascals like him playing at 'Rayuelo' in the crossways in front of the choir. May God forgive me!"

And the simple "Wooden Staff" made a gesture as though scandalised at his own words. He went on:

"This young fellow you see here is not satisfied with his position in life, and yet, though he is only a youth, he occupies the place his poor father could only attain to after thirty years' service. He aspires to be a toreador, and often on a Sunday he dares to take part in the bull-fight in the bull-ring of Toledo. His mother came down, dishevelled like a Magdalen, to tell me all about it, and I, thinking that as his father was dead I ought to act in his place, I watched for our gentleman as he returned tricked out smartly from the bull-ring, and I thrashed him up the tower staircase to his rooms with the same wooden staff that I use in the Cathedral, and he can tell you if I have not a heavy hand when I am angry. Virgin of the Sagrario! A Luna of the Holy Metropolitan Church lowering himself to be a bull-fighter! The canons did laugh, and even the Lord Cardinal himself, as I have been told, when they heard about the affair! A witty beneficiary has since nicknamed him

17

the 'Tato,' and so they all call him now in the Cathedral. So you see, brother, how much respect this rascal pays to his family."

The "Silenciario" attempted to annihilate the "Tato" with his glance, but this latter only smiled without paying much attention, either to his uncle's words or looks.

"You would hardly believe, Gabriel," he continued, "that this creature often wants a bit of bread, and it is for this reason he commits all these follies. In spite of his wrong-headedness, since the age of twenty he has occupied the position of 'Perrero' in the holy church, he has obtained what in better times only those could obtain who had served well and striven hard for years. He gets his six reals a day, and as he can go freely about the church he can show the curiosities to strangers; and so with the salary and the tips he gets, he is much better off than I am. The foreigners who visit the Cathedral, excommunicated people who look upon us as strange monkeys, and who think that anything interesting of ours is only worthy of a laugh, take a fancy to him. The English ask him if he is a toreador, and he—what does he want better than that! When he sees they pay him according as he pleases them, he brings out his pack of lies, for, unfortunately, no one has any check on the deceit, and he tells them about all the great bull-fights in which he has taken part in Toledo, and all about the bulls he has killed; and these blockheads from England make a note of it in their albums, and even some coarse hand may make a sketch of this imposter's head; all he cares for is that they should believe all his lies and give him a peseta on leaving. It matters very little to him, if when these heretics return to their own country they spread the report that in Toledo, in the Holy Metropolitan Church of all Spain, the Cathedral servants are bull-fighters, and assist in the ceremonies of worship between the bull runs. The sum total is, that he earns more than I do, but in spite of this he considers his employment beneath him. And such beautiful duties, too. To walk in the great processions before everyone, close to the Primate's great banner, with a staff covered with red velvet to support him should he chance to fall, and wearing a robe of scarlet brocade like a cardinal. Our Chapel-master, who knows a great deal about such things, says that when he wears that robe he looks like a certain Diente, or some name of the sort, who lived hundreds of years ago in Italy, and went down into hell, and afterwards described his journey in poetry."

Sounds of footsteps were heard on the narrow circular staircase in the thickness of the wall that led from the sitting-room to the storey above.

"It is Don Luis," said the "Wooden Staff," "he is going to say his mass in the chapel of the Sagrario, and afterwards to the choir."

Gabriel rose from his sofa to salute the priest. He was feeble and small of stature, but the thing about him that struck you at first sight was the disproportion between his shrunken body and his immense head. The forehead, round and prominent, seemed to crush with its weight the dark and irregular features, much pitted by smallpox. He was very ugly, but still the expression of his blue eyes, the brilliancy of his white and regular teeth, and the ingenuous smile, almost childlike, that played on his lips, gave his face that sympathetic expression which showed him to be one of those simple souls wrapped up in their artistic fancies.

"And so this gentleman is the brother of whom you have spoken to me so often," said he, hearing the introduction made by Esteban.

He held out his hand in a friendly way to Gabriel. They both looked very sickly, but their bodily infirmities seemed to be a bond of attraction.

"As the señor has studied in the seminary," said the Chapel-master, "he will know something about music."

"It is the only thing that I remember of all those studies."

"But having travelled so much all over the world, you must have heard a great deal of good music."

"That is so. Music is to me the most pleasing of all the arts. I do not know much about it, but I feel it."

"Very well, very well, we shall be good friends. You must tell me all sorts of things; how I envy you having travelled so much."

He spoke like a restless child, without sitting down. Although the "Silenciario" offered him a chair at each of his flirtings round the room, he wandered from side to side in his shabby cloak, his hat in his hand—a poor worn-out hat with not a trace of pile left, knocked in, with a layer of grease on its flaps, miserable and old, like the cassock and the shoes. But in spite of this poverty the Chapel-master had a certain refinement about him. His hair, rather too long for his ecclesiastical dress, curled round his temples, and the dignified way in which he folded his cloak round his body reminded one of the cloak of a tenor at the opera. He had a sort of easy grace that betrayed the artist who, under the priestly robes, was longing to get rid of them, leaving them at his feet like a winding sheet.

Some deep notes from the bell, like distant thunder, floated into the room through the cloister.

"Uncle, they are calling us to the choir," said the "Tato." "We ought to have been in the Cathedral before now; it is nearly eight o'clock."

"It is true, lad. I am glad you were here to remind me; let us be going."

Then he added, speaking to the musical priest:

"Don Luis, your mass is at eight o'clock. You can talk with Gabriel later on; now we must fulfil our obligations, for those who are late will, as you say, be turned out, even though our office hardly gives us enough to eat."

The Chapel-master assented sadly with a movement of his head, and went out, following the two Cathedral servants. He seemed to go unwillingly, as though forced to a task that was to him both irksome and painful. He hummed absently while giving his hand to Gabriel, who thought he recognised a fragment of Beethoven's Seventh Symphony in the low and uneven tones that came from the lips of the young priest.

Now that he was alone Luna stretched himself on the sofa, giving himself up to the fatigue he felt from his long wait before the Cathedral. His brother's old servant placed a little pitcher of milk by his side, and filling a cup, Gabriel drank, endeavouring to overcome the repugnance of his weak stomach, which almost refused to retain the liquid. His body, fatigued by his restless night and the long morning wait, at last assimilated the nourishment, and a soft, dreamy languor spread over him that he had not felt for a long time. He soon fell asleep, remaining for more than an hour motionless on the sofa, and though his breathing was disturbed, and his chest racked by his hollow cough, they were unable to wake him from his slumber.

When he did awake, it was suddenly, with a nervous start that shook him from head to foot, making him bound from the sofa as though a spring had been touched. It was the wariness produced by his ever present danger, that had become habitual to him; the habit of restlessness formed in dark dungeons, expecting hourly to see the door open, to be beaten like a dog, or led off between a double file of muskets to the square of execution; the habit of living perpetually watched, of feeling in every country the espionage of the police around him, the habit of being awoke in the middle of the night in his wretched room in some inn by the order to leave at once; the unrest of the ancient Asheverus, who, as soon as he could enjoy a moment's rest, heard the eternal cry—"Go on. Go on."

He did not try to sleep again, he preferred the present reality, the silence of the Cathedral which was to him as a gentle caress, the noble calm of the temple, that immense pile of worked stone, which seemed to press on him, enveloping him, hiding for ever his weakness and his persecutions.

He went out into the cloister, and, resting his elbows on the balustrade, looked down into the garden.

The Claverias seemed quite deserted. The children who had enlivened them in the early morning had gone to school, the women were inside their houses preparing their mid-day meal, there seemed to be no one in the cloister except himself; the sunlight bathed all one side, and the shadow of the pillars cut obliquely the great golden spaces flooding the pavement. The majestic silence, the holy calm of the Cathedral overpowered the agitator like a gentle narcotic. The seven centuries surrounding those stones seemed to him like so many veils hiding him from the rest of the world. In one of the dwellings of the Claverias you could hear the incessant tap, tap, of a hammer; it was that of a shoemaker whom Gabriel had seen through the window-panes, bending over his bench. In the square of sky framed by the roofs some pigeons were flying, lazily moving their wings, soaring in the vault of intense blue; some flew down into the cloister, and, perching on the balustrade, broke the religious silence with their gentle cooing; now and again the heavy door-curtains of the church were lifted, and a breath of air charged with incense floated over the garden of the Claverias, together with the deep notes of the organ, and the sound of voices chanting Latin words and solemnly prolonging the cadences.

Gabriel looked at the garden surrounded by its arcades of white stone, with its rough buttresses of dark granite, in the chinks of which the rain had left an efflorescence of fungus, like little tufts of black velvet. The sun struck on one angle of the garden, leaving the rest in cool green shade, a conventual twilight. The bell-tower hid one portion of the sky, displaying on its reddish sides, ornamented with Gothic tracery and salient buttresses, the fillets of black marble with heads of mysterious personages, and the shields with the arms of the different archbishops who had assisted at its building; above, near the pinnacles of white stone, were seen the bells behind enormous gratings; from below they looked like three bronze birds in a cage of iron.

Three deep strokes from a bell, echoing round the Cathedral, announced that the High Mass had arrived at its most solemn moment, the mountain of stone seemed to tremble with the vibration, which was transmitted through the naves and galleries, to the arcades and down to the lowest foundations.

Again there was silence, which seemed even deeper after the bronze thunders; the cooing of the pigeons could again be heard, and, down in the garden, the twittering of the birds, warmed by the sun's rays that began to gild its cool twilight.

Gabriel felt himself deeply moved; the sweet silence, the absolute calm, the feeling almost of non-existence overpowered him; and beyond those walls was the world, but here it could not be seen, it could not be felt; it remained respectful but indifferent before that monument of the past, that splendid sepulchre, in whose interior nothing excited its curiosity. Who would ever imagine he was there? That growth of seven centuries, built by vanished greatness for a dying faith, should be his last refuge. In the full tide of unbelief the church should be his sanctuary, as it had been in former days to those great criminals of the Middle Ages, who, from the height of the cloister mocked at justice, detained at the doors like the beggars. Here should be consummated in silence and calm the slow decay of his body, here he would die with the serene satisfaction of having died to the world long before. At last he realised his hope of ending his days in a corner of the sleepy Spanish Cathedral, the only hope that had sustained him as he wandered on foot along the highways of Europe, hiding himself from the civil guards and the police, spending his nights in ditches, huddled up, his head on his knees, fearing every moment to die of cold.

He clung to the Cathedral as a shipwrecked and drowning man clings to the spar of a sinking ship; this had been his hope, and he was beginning to realise it. The church would receive him, like an old and infirm mother, unable to smile, but who could still stretch out her arms.

"At last! At last!" murmured Luna.

And he smiled, thinking of the world of sorrows and persecutions that he was leaving behind him, as though he were going to some remote place, situated in another planet, from which he would never return; the Cathedral would shelter him for ever.

In the profound stillness of the cloister, that the sound of the street could not reach, the "companion" Luna thought he heard far off, very far off, the shrill sound of a trumpet and the muffled roll of drums, then he remembered the Alcazar of Toledo, dominating the Cathedral from its height, intimidating it with the enormous mass of its towers; they were the drums and trumpets of the Military Academy.

These sounds were painful to Gabriel; the world had faded from his sight, and when he thought himself so very far from it, he could still feel its presence only a little way beyond the roof of the temple.

CHAPTER II

Since the times of the second Cardinal de Bourbon Senior Esteban Luna had been gardener of the Cathedral, by the right that seemed firmly established in his family. Who was the first Luna that entered the service of the Holy Metropolitan Church? As the gardener asked himself this question he smiled complacently, raising his eyes to heaven, as though he would inquire of the immensity of space. The Lunas were as ancient as the foundations of the church; a great many generations had been born in the abode in the upper cloister, and even before the illustrious Cisneros built the Claverias the Lunas had lived in houses adjacent, as though they could not exist out of the shadow of the Primacy. To no one did the Cathedral belong with better right than to them. Canons, beneficiaries, archbishops passed; they gained the appointment, died, and others came in their places. It was a constant procession of new faces, of masters who came from every corner of Spain to take their seats in the choir, to die a few years afterwards, leaving the vacancies to be filled again by other newcomers; but the Lunas always remained at their post, as though the ancient family were another column of the many that supported the temple. It might happen that the archbishop who to-day was called Don Bernardo, might next year be called Don Caspar, or again another Don Fernando. But what seemed utterly impossible was that the Cathedral could exist without Lunas in the garden, in the sacristy, or in the crossways of the choir, accustomed as it had been for centuries to their services.

The gardener spoke with pride of his descent, of his noble and unfortunate relative the constable Don Alvaro, buried like a king in his chapel behind the high altar; of the Pope Benedict XIII., proud and obstinate like all the rest of his family; of Don Pedro de Luna, fifth of his name to occupy the archiepiscopal throne of Toledo, and of other relatives not less distinguished.

"We are all from the same stem," he said with pride. "We all came to the conquest of Toledo with the good King Alfonso VI. The only difference has been, that some Lunas took a fancy to go and fight the Moors, and they became lords, and conquered castles, whereas my ancestors remained in the service of the Cathedral, like the good Christians they were."

With the satisfaction of a duke who enumerates his ancestors, the Señor Esteban carried back the line of the Lunas till it became misty and was lost in the fifteenth century. His father had known Don Francisco III. Lorenzana, a magnificent and prodigal prince of the church, who spent the abundant revenues of the archbishopric in building palaces and editing books, like a great lord of the Renaissance. He had known also the first Cardinal Bourbon, Don Luis II., and used to narrate the romantic life of this Infante. Brother of the King Carlos III., the custom that dedicated some of the younger branches to the church had made him a cardinal at nine years old. But that good lord, whose portrait hung in the Chapter House, with white hair, red lips and blue eyes, felt more inclination to the joys of this world than to the grandeurs of the church, and he abandoned the archbishopric to marry a lady of modest birth, quarrelling for ever with the king, who sent him into exile. And the old Luna, leaping from ancestor to ancestor through the long centuries, remembered the Archduke Alberto, who resigned the Toledan mitre to become Governor of the Low Countries, and the magnificent Cardinal Tavera, protector of the arts, all excellent princes, who had treated his family affectionately, recognising their secular adhesion to the Holy Metropolitan Church.

The days of his youth were bad ones for the Señor Esteban; it was the time of the war of Independence. The French occupied Toledo, entering into the Cathedral like pagans, rattling their swords and prying into every corner at full High Mass. The jewels were concealed, the canons and beneficiaries, who were now called *prebendaries*, were living dispersed over the Peninsula. Some had taken refuge in places that were still Spanish, others were hidden in the towns, making vows for the speedy return of "the desired." It was pitiful to hear the choir with its few voices; only the very timid, who were bound to their seats and could not live away from them, had remained, and had recognised the usurping king. The second Cardinal de Bourbon, the gentle and insignificant Don Luis Maria, was in Cadiz, the only one of the family remaining in Spain, and the Cortes had laid their hands on him to give a certain dynastic appearance to their revolutionary authority.

When the war was over and the poor cardinal returned to his seat, the Señor Esteban was moved to pity to see his sad and childlike face, with the small round head, and insignificant appearance; he returned discouraged and disheartened, after receiving his nephew Ferdinand VII. in Madrid. All his colleagues in the regency were either in prison or in exile, and that he did not suffer a like fate was solely due to his mitre and to his name. The unfortunate prelate thought he had done good service in maintaining the interests of his family during the war, and now he found himself accused of being Liberal, an enemy to religion and the throne, without being able to imagine how he had conspired against them. The poor Cardinal de Bourbon languished sadly in his palace, devoting his revenues to works in the Cathedral, till he died in 1823 at the beginning of the reaction, leaving his place to Inguanzo, the tribune of absolutism, a prelate with iron-grey whiskers, who had made his career as deputy in the Cortes at Cadiz, attacking as deputy every sort of reform, and advocating a return to the times of the Austrians as the surest means of saving his country.

The good gardener saluted with equal cordiality the Bourbon Cardinal, hated by the kings, as the prelate with the whiskers, who made all the diocese tremble with his bitter and harassing temper, and his arrogance as a revolutionary Absolutist. For him, whoever occupied the throne of Toledo was a perfect man, whose acts no one should dare to discuss, and he turned a deaf ear to the murmurs of the canons and beneficiaries, who, smoking their cigarettes in the arbour of his garden, spoke of the genialities of this Señor de Inguanzo, and were indignant at the Government of Ferdinand VII. not being sufficiently firm, through fear of the foreigners, to re-establish the wholesome tribunal of the Inquisition.

The only thing that troubled the gardener was to watch the decadence of his beloved Cathedral. The revenues of the archbishop and of the Chapter had been greatly wasted during the war. What had occurred was what happens after a great flood, when the waters begin to subside and carry everything away with them, leaving the land bare and uninhabited. The Primacy lost many of its rights, the tenants made themselves masters, taking advantage of the disorders of the State; the towns refused to pay their feudal services, as though the necessity of defending themselves and helping in the war had freed them for ever from vassalage; further, the turbulent Cortes had decreed the abolition of all lordships, and had very much curtailed the enormous revenues of the Cathedral, acquired in the centuries when the archbishops of Toledo put on their casques, and went out to fight the Moors with double-handed swords.

Even so, a considerable fortune remained to the church of the Primacy, and it maintained its splendour as if nothing had happened, but the Señor Esteban scented danger from the depths of his garden, hearing from the canons of the Liberal conspiracies, the executions by shooting and hanging, and the exiling, to which the king Señor Don Fernando appealed, in order to repress the audacity of the "Negros," the enemies of the Monarchy and of religion.

"They have tasted the sweets," said he, "and they will return—see if they do not return, and take what is left! During the war they took the first bite, taking from the Cathedral more than half that was hers, and now they will come and take the rest; they will try and catch hold of the handle of the fryingpan."

The gardener was angry at the possibility of such a thing happening. Ay! and was it for this that so many lord archbishops of Toledo fought against the Moors? Conquering towns, assaulting castles and annexing pasture lands, which all came to be the property of the Cathedral, contributing to the great splendour of God's worship! And was everything to fall into the dirty hands of the enemies of anything that was holy? Everything that so many faithful souls had willed to them on their deathbeds, queens and magnates, and simple country gentlemen, who left the best part of their fortunes to the Holy Metropolitan Church, in the hope of saving their souls! What would happen to the six hundred souls, big and little, clerics and seculars, dignitaries and simple servants who lived from the revenues of the Cathedral?.... And was this called liberty? To rob what did not belong to them, leaving in poverty innumerable families who were now supported by the "great pot" of the Chapter?

When the sad forebodings of the gardener began to be realised, and Mendizabal decreed the dismemberment, the Señor Esteban thought he would have died of rage. But the Cardinal Inguanzo did better. Placed in his seat by the Liberals as his predecessor had been by the Absolutists, he thought it best to die in order to take no part in these attempts against the sacred revenues of the Church.

The Señor Luna, who was only a humble gardener, and who therefore could not imitate the illustrious Cardinal, went on living. But every day he felt more and more sorrowful, knowing that for shamefully low prices, many of the Moderates, who still came to High Mass, were stealthily acquiring to-day a house, to-morrow a farm, another day pasture lands, properties all belonging to the Primacy, but which had lately been put on the list of what was called national property.

Robbers! this slow subversion and sale, that rent in pieces the revenues of the Cathedral, caused the Señor Esteban as much indignation as though the bailiffs had entered his house in the Claverias to remove the family furniture, each piece of which embalmed the memory of some ancestor.

There were times in which he thought of abandoning his garden, and going to Maestrazgo, or to the northern provinces, in search of some of the loyal defenders of the rights of Charles V. and of the return to the old times. He was then forty years of age, strong and active, and though his temperament was pacific and he had never touched a musket, he felt himself fired by the example of certain timid and pious students, who had fled from the seminary, and were now, so it was said, fighting in Catalonia behind the red cloak of Don Ramon Cabrera.

But the gardener, in order not to be alone in his big "habitacion" in the Claverias, had married three years previously the daughter of the sacristan, and he had now one son; besides, he could not tear himself away from the church, he was another square block in the mountain of stone, he moved and spoke as a man, but he felt a certainty that he should perish at once if he left his garden. Besides, the Cathedral would lose one of the most important props if a Luna were wanting in its service, and he felt terrified at the bare thought of living out of it. How could he wander over the mountains fighting, and firing shots, when years had passed without his treading any other profane soil beyond the little bit of street between the staircase of the Claverias and the Puerta del Mollete?

And so he went on cultivating his garden, feeling the melancholy satisfaction that he was at least sheltered from all the wicked revolutionaries under the shadow of that colossus of stone, which inspired awe and respect from its majestic age. They might curtail the revenues of the temple, but they would be powerless against the Christian faith of those who lived under its protection.

The garden, deaf and insensible to the revolutionary tempests that broke over the church, continued to unfold its sombre beauty between the arcades, the laurels grew till they reached the balustrade of the upper cloister, and the cypresses seemed as though they aspired to touch the roofs; the creepers twined themselves among the iron railings, making thick lattices of verdure, and the ivy mantled the wall of the central arbour, which was surmounted by a cap of black slate with a rusty iron cross. After the evening choir the clergy would come and sit in here and read, by the soft green light that filtered through the foliage, the news from the Carlist Camp, and discuss enthusiastically the great exploits of Cabrera, while above, the swallows quite indifferent to human presence, circled and screamed in the clear blue sky. The Señor Esteban would watch, standing silently, this bat-like evening club, which was kept quietly hidden from those belonging to the National Militia of Toledo.

When the war terminated, the last illusions of the gardener vanished, he fell into the silence of despair and wished to know of nothing outside the Cathedral. God had abandoned the good and faithful, and the traitors and evil-doers were triumphant; his only consolation was the stronghold of the temple, which had lived through so many centuries of turmoil, and could still defy its enemies for so many more.

He only wished to be the gardener, to die in the upper cloister like his forefathers, and to leave fresh Lunas to perpetuate the family services in the Cathedral. His eldest son, Tomas, was now twelve years old, and able to help him in the care of the garden. After an interval of many years a second son had been born, Esteban, who, almost before he could walk, would kneel before the images in the "habitacion," crying for his mother to carry him down into the church to see the saints.

Poverty entered into the Cathedral, reducing the number of canons and prebendaries; at the death of any of the old servants, their places were suppressed, and a great many carpenters, masons, and glaziers who previously had lived there as workmen specially attached to the Primacy, and were continually working at its repairs, were dismissed. If from time to time certain repairs were indispensable, workmen were called in from outside, by the day; many of the "habitacions" in the Claverias were unoccupied, and the silence of the grave reigned where previously the population of a small town had gathered and crowded. The Government of Madrid (and you should have seen the expression of contempt with which the old gardener emphasised those words) was in treaty with the Holy Father to arrange something called the Concordat. The number of canons was limited as though the Holy Metropolitan was a college, they were to be paid by the Government the same as the servants, and for the maintenance of worship in this most famous Cathedral of all Spain—which, when it formerly collected its tithe, scarcely knew where to lock up such riches—a monthly pension of twelve hundred pesetas was now granted.

"One thousand two hundred pesetas, Tomas!" said he to his son, a silent boy, who took very little interest in anything but his garden. "One thousand two hundred pesetas, when I can remember the Cathedral having more than six millions of revenue! Bad times are in store for us, and were I anyone else I would bring you up to an office, or something outside the church; but the Lunas cannot desert the cause of God, like so many traitors who have betrayed it. Here we were born, here we must die, to the very last one of the family." And furious with the clergy, who seemed to put a good face on the Concordat and their salaries, thankful to have come out of the revolutionary tumults even as well as they had done, he isolated himself in his garden, locking the door in the iron railing, and shrinking from the assemblies of former times!

His little floral world did not change, its sombre verdure was like the twilight that had enveloped the gardener's soul. It had not the brilliant gaiety, overflowing with colours and scents of a garden in the open, bathed in full sunlight, but it had the shady and melancholy beauty of a conventual garden between four walls, with no more light than what came through the eaves and the arcades, and no other birds but those flying above, who looked with wonder at this little paradise at the bottom of a well. The vegetation was the same as that of the Greek landscapes, and of the idylls of the Greek poets—laurels, cypress and roses, but the arches that surrounded it, with their alleys paved with great slabs of granite in whose interstices wreaths of grass grew, the cross of its central arbour, the mouldy smell of the old iron railings, and the damp of the stone buttresses coloured a soft green by the rain, gave the garden an atmosphere of reverend age and a character of its own.

The trees waved in the wind like censers, the flowers, pale and languid with an anaemic beauty, smelt of incense, as though the air wafted through the doors of the Cathedral had changed their natural perfumes.

The rain, trickling from the gargoyles and gutters of the roofs, was collected in two large and deep stone tanks; sometimes the gardener's pail would disturb their green covering, letting one perceive for an instant the blue-blackness of their depths, but as soon as the circles disappeared, the vegetation once more drew together and covered them over afresh, without a movement, without a ripple, quiet and dead as the temple itself in the stillness of the evening.

At the feast of Corpus, and that of the Virgin of the Sagrario in the middle of August, the townspeople brought their pitchers into the garden, and the Señor Esteban allowed them to be filled from these two cisterns. It was an ancient custom and one much appreciated by the old Toledans, who thought much of the fresh water of the Cathedral, condemned as they were during the rest of the year to drink the red and muddy liquid of the Tagus. At other times people came into the garden to give little presents to Señor Esteban, the devout entrusted him with palms for their images, or bought little bunches of flowers, believing them to be better than those they could buy at the farms, because they came from the Metropolitan Church, and the old women begged branches of laurel for flavouring and for household medicines. These incomings, and the two pesetas that the Chapter had assigned to the gardener after the final dismemberment, helped the Señor Esteban and his family to get on. When he was getting well on in years his third son Gabriel was born, a child who from his fourth year attracted the attention of all the women in the Claverias; his mother affirmed with a blind faith that he was a living image of the Child Jesus that the Virgin of the Sagrario held in her arms. Her sister Tomasa, who was married to the "Virgin's Blue," and was the mother of a numerous family which occupied nearly the half of the upper cloister, talked a great deal about the intelligence of her little nephew, when he could hardly speak, and about the infantile unction with which he gazed at the images.

"He looks like a saint," she said to her friends. "You should see how seriously he says his prayers.... Gabrielillo will become somebody; who knows if we may not see him a bishop! Acolytes that I knew when my father had charge of the sacristy now wear the mitre, and possibly some day we may have one of them in Toledo."

The chorus of caresses and praises surrounded the first years of the child like a cloud of incense; the family only lived for him, the Señor Esteban, a father in the good old Latin style who loved his sons, but was severe and stern with them in order that they might grow up honourable, felt in the presence of the child a return of his own youth; he played with him, and lent himself smilingly to all his little caprices; his mother abandoned her household duties to please him, and his brother hung on his babbling words. The eldest, Tomas, the silent youth who had taken the place of his father in the care of the garden, and who even in the depths of winter went barefooted over the flower-beds and rough stones of the alleys, came up often bringing handfuls of sweet-scented herbs, so that his little brother might play with them. Esteban, the second, who was now thirteen and who enjoyed a certain notoriety among the other acolytes on account of his scrupulous care in assisting at the mass, delighted Gabriel with his red cassock and his pleated tunic, and brought him taper ends and little coloured prints, abstracted from the breviary of some canon.

Now and then he carried him in his arms to the store-room of the giants, an immense room between the buttresses and the arches of the nave, vaulted with stone. Here were the heroes of the ancient feasts and holidays. The Cid with a huge sword, and four set pieces representing as many parts of the world: huge figures with dusty and tattered clothes and broken faces, which had once rejoiced the streets of Toledo, and were now rotting under the roofs of its Cathedral. In one corner reposed the Tarasca, a frightful monster of cardboard, which terrified Gabriel when it opened its jaws, while on its wrinkled back sat smiling, idiotically, a dishevelled and indecent doll, whom the religious feeling of former ages had baptised with the name of Anne Boleyn.

When Gabriel went to school all were astonished at his progress. The youngsters of the upper cloister who were such a trial to "Silver Stick," the priest charged with maintaining good order among the tribe established in the roofs of the Cathedral, looked upon the little Gabriel as a prodigy. When he could scarcely walk he could read easily, and at seven he began to recite his Latin, mastering it quickly, as though he had never spoken anything else in his life, and at ten he could argue with the clergy who frequented the gardens, and who delighted in putting before him questions and difficulties.

The Señor Esteban, growing daily more bent and feeble, smiled delightedly before his last work; he was going to be the glory of his house! His name was Luna, and therefore he could aspire to anything without fear, because even Popes had come from that family.

The canons would take the boy into the sacristy after choir, and question him as to his studies. One of the clergy belonging to the archbishop's household presented him to the cardinal, who, after hearing him, gave him a handful of sugared almonds and the promise of a scholarship, so that he could continue his studies at the seminary gratuitously.

26

The Lunas and all their relations more or less distant, who were really nearly the whole population of the upper cloister, were rejoiced at this promise; what else could Gabriel be but a priest? For these people, attached to the church from the day of their birth, like excrescences of its stones, who considered the archbishops of Toledo as the most powerful beings in the world after the Pope, the only profession worthy of a man of talent was the Church.

Gabriel went to the Seminary, and to all the family the Claverias seemed quite deserted. The long, pleasant evenings in the house of the Lunas came to an end, at which the bell-ringer, the vergers, the sacristans and other church servants had been used to assemble, and listen to the clear and well modulated voice of Gabriel, who read like an angel—sometimes the lives of the saints, at other times Catholic newspapers that came from Madrid, or chapters from a Don Quixote with pages of vellum and antiquated writing—a venerable copy which had been handed down in the family for generations.

Gabriel's life in the Seminary was the ordinary and monotonous life of a hard-working student: triumphs in theological controversies, prizes in heaps, and the satisfaction of being held up to his companions as a model.

Sometimes one of the canons who lectured in the seminary would come into the garden:—

"The lad is getting on very well, Esteban; he is first in everything, and besides, is as steady and pious as a saint. He will be the comfort of your old age."

The gardener, always growing older and thinner, shook his head. He should only be able to see the end of his son's career from the heavens, should it please God to call him there. He would die before his son's triumph; but this did not sadden him, for the family would remain to enjoy the victory and to give thanks to God for His goodness.

Humanities, theology, canons, everything, the young man mastered with an ease which surprised his masters, and they compared him to the Fathers of the Church, who had attracted attention by their precocity. He would very soon finish his studies, and they all predicted that his Eminence would give him a professorship in the seminary, even before he sang his first mass. His thirst for learning was insatiable, and it seemed as though the library really belonged to him. Some evenings he would go into the Cathedral to pursue his musical studies, and talk with the Chapel-master and the organist, and at other times in the hall of sacred oratory he would astound the professors and the Alumni by the fervour and conviction with which he delivered his sermons.

"He is called to the pulpit," they said in the Cathedral garden. "He has all the fire of the apostles; he will become a Saint Bernard or a Bossuet. Who can tell how far this youth will go, or where he will end?"

One of the studies which most delighted Gabriel was that of the history of the Cathedral, and of the ecclesiastical princes who had ruled it. All the inherent love of the Lunas for the giantess who was their eternal mother surged up in him, but he did not love it blindly as all his belongings did. He wished to know the why and the wherefore of things, comparing in his books the vague old stories that he had heard from his father, that seemed more akin to legends than to historical facts.

The first thing that claimed his attention was the chronology of the archbishops of Toledo—a long line of famous men, saints, warriors, writers, princes, each with his number after his name, like the kings of the different dynasties. At certain times they had been the real kings of Spain. The Gothic kings in their courts were little more than decorative figureheads that were raised or deposed according to the exigencies of the moment. The nation was a theocratic republic, and its true head was the Archbishop of Toledo.

Gabriel grouped the long line of famous prelates by characters. First of all the saints, the apostles in the heroic age of Christianity, bishops as poor as their own people, barefooted, fugitives from the Roman persecution, and bowing their heads at last to the executioner, firm in the hope of gaining fresh strength to the doctrine for which they sacrificed their lives—Saint Eugenio, Melancio, Pelagio, Patruno and other names that shone in the past scarcely breaking through the mists of legend. Then came the archbishops of the Gothic era; those kingly prelates who exercised that superiority over the conquering kings by which the spiritual power succeeded in dominating the barbarian conquerors. Miracles accompanied them to confound the Arians, and celestial prodigies were at their orders to terrify and crush those rude men of war. The Archbishop Montano, who lived with his wife, and was indignant at the consequent murmurs, placed red-hot coals in his sacred vestments the while he said mass, and did not burn, demonstrating by this miracle the purity of his life. Saint Ildefonso, not content with only writing books against heretics, induced Santa Leocadia to appear to him, leaving in his hands a piece of her mantle, and he enjoyed the further honour of this same Virgin descending from heaven to present him with a chasuble embroidered by her own hands. Sigiberto, many years after, had the audacity to vest himself in this chasuble, and was in consequence deposed, excommunicated and exiled for his temerity.

The only books that were produced in those times were written by the prelates of Toledo. They compiled the laws, they anointed the heads of the monarchs with the holy oil, they set up Wamba as king, they conspired against the life of Egica, and the councils assembled in the basilica of Santa Leocadia were political assemblies in which the mitre was on the throne and the crown of the king at the feet of the prelate.

At the coming of the Saracen invasion the series of persecuted prelates begins again. They did not now fear for their lives as during the time of Roman intolerance; for Mussulmen as a rule do not martyr, and furthermore, they respect the beliefs of the conquered.

All the churches in Toledo remained in the hands of the Christian Muzarabés with the exception of the Cathedral, which was converted into the principal mosque.

The Catholic bishops were respected by the Moors, as were also the Hebrew rabbis; but the Church was poor, and the continual wars between the Saracens and the Christians, together with the reprisals which set a seal on the barbarities of the reconquest, made the continuance and life of worship extremely difficult.

Having arrived at this point Gabriel read the obscure names of Cixila, Elipando and Wistremiro. Saint Eulogio termed this last "the torch of the Holy Spirit, and the light of Spain"; but history is silent as to his deeds, and Saint Eulogio was martyred and killed by the Moors in Cordova on account of his excessive religious zeal. Benito, a Frenchman who succeeded to the chair, not to be behind his predecessors, made the Virgin send him down another chasuble to a church in his own country before he came to Toledo.

After these, came the interesting chronology of the warrior archbishops, warriors of coat-of-mail and two-edged sword, the conquerors who, leaving the choir to the meek and humble, mounted their war-horses and thought they were not serving God unless during the year they added sundry towns and pasture lands to the goods of the Church. They arrived in the eleventh century, with Alfonso VI., to the conquest of Toledo. The first were French monks from the famous Abbey of Cluny, sent by the Abbot Hugo to the convent of Sahagun, and they were the first to use the "don" as a sign of lordship. To the pious tolerance of the preceding bishops, accustomed to friendly intercourse with Arabs and Jews in the full liberty of the Muzarabé worship, succeeded the ferocious intolerance of the Christian conqueror. The Archbishop Don Bernardo was scarcely seated in the chair before he took advantage of the absence of Alfonso VI. to violate all his promises. The principal mosque had remained in the hands of the Moors by a solemn compact with the king, who, like all the monarchs of the reconquest, was tolerant in matters of religion. The archbishop, using his powerful influence over the mind of the queen, made her the accomplice of his plans, and one night, followed by clergy and workmen, he knocked down the doors of the mosque, cleansed it and purified it, and next morning when the Saracens came to pray towards the rising sun, they found it changed into a Catholic cathedral. The conquered, trusting in the word given by the conqueror, protested, scandalised, and that they did not rise was solely due to the influence of the Alfaqui Abu-Walid, who trusted that the king would fulfil his promises. In three days Alfonso VI. arrived in Toledo from the further end of Castille, ready to murder the archbishop and even his own wife for their share in this villainy that had compromised his word as a cavalier, but his fury was so great that even the Moors were moved, and the Alfaqui went out to meet him, begging him to condone the deed as it was accomplished, as the injured parties would agree to it, and in the name of the conquered he relieved him from keeping his word, because the possession of a building was not a sufficient reason for breaking the peace.

Gabriel admired as he read the prudence and moderation of the good Moor Abu-Walid; but with his enthusiasm as a seminarist he admired still more those proud, intolerant and warlike prelates, who trampled laws and people under foot for the greater glory of God.

The Archbishop Martin was Captain-General against the Moors in Andalusia, conquering towns, and he accompanied Alfonso VIII. to the battle of Alarcos. The famous prelate Don Rodrigo wrote the chronicle of Spain, filling it with miracles for the greater prosperity of the Church, and he practically made history, passing more time on his war-horse than on his throne in the choir. At the battle de las Navas he set so fine an example, throwing himself into the thick of the fight, that the king gave him twenty lordships as well as that of Talavera de la Reina. Afterwards, in the king's absence, he drove the Moors out of Quesada and Cazorla, taking possession of vast territories, which passed under his sway, with the name of the Adelantamiento. Don Sancho, son of Don Jaime of Aragon, and brother to the Queen of Castille, thought more of his title of "Chief Leader" than of his mitre of Toledo, and on the advance of the Moors went out to meet them in the martial field. He fought wherever the fighting was fiercest, and was finally killed by the Moslems, who cut off his hands and placed his head on a spear.

Don Gil de Albornoz, the famous cardinal, went to Italy, flying from Don Pedro the Cruel, and, like a great captain, reconquered all the territory of the Popes, who had taken refuge in Avignon. Don Gutierre III. went with Don Juan II. to fight against the Moors. Don Alfonso de Acuna fought in the civil war during the reign of Enrique IV.; and as a fitting end to this series of political and conquering prelates, rich and powerful as true princes, there arose the Cardinal Mendoza, who fought at the battle of Toro, and at the conquest of Granada, afterwards governing that kingdom; and Jimenez de Cisneros, who, finding no Moors left in the Peninsula to fight, crossed the sea and went to Oran, waving his cross and turning it into a weapon of war.

The seminarist admired these men, magnified by the mists of ancient history and the praises of the Church. For him they were the greatest men in the world after the Popes, and, indeed, often far superior to them. He was astonished that the Spaniards of the present times were so blind that they did not entrust their direction and government to the archbishops of Toledo, who in former centuries had performed such heroic deeds. The glory and advancement of the country was so intimately connected with their history, their dynasty was quite as great as that of the kings, and on more than one occasion they had saved these latter by their counsels and energy.

After these eagles came the birds of prey; after the prelates with their iron morions and their coats-of-mail came the rich and luxurious prelates, who cared for no other combats but those of the law courts, and were in perpetual litigation with towns, guilds, and private individuals in order to retain the possessions and the vast fortune accumulated by their predecessors.

Those who were generous like Tavera built palaces, and encouraged artists like El Greco, Berruguete and others, creating a Renaissance in Toledo, an echo from Italy. Those who were miserly, like Quiroga, reduced the expenses of the pompous church, to turn themselves into money-lenders to the kings, giving millions of ducats to those Austrian monarchs on whose dominions the sun never set, but who, nevertheless, found themselves obliged to beg almost as soon as their galleons returned from their voyages to America.

The Cathedral was the work of these priestly ecclesiastics; each one had done something in it which revealed his character. The rougher and more warlike its framework, that mountain of stone and wood which formed its skeleton; those who were more cultivated, elevated to the See in times of greater refinement, contributed the minutely-worked iron railings, the doors of lace-like stonework, the pictures, and the jewels which made its sacristy a veritable treasure house. The gestation of the giantess had lasted for three centuries; it seemed like those enormous prehistoric animals who slept so long in their mother's womb before seeing the light.

When its walls and pilasters first rose above the soil Gothic art was in its first epoch, and during the two and a half centuries that its building lasted architecture made great strides. Gabriel could follow this slow transformation with his mind's eye as he studied the building, discovering the various signs of its evolution.

The magnificent church was like a giantess whose feet were shod with rough shoes, but whose head was covered with the loveliest plumes. The bases of the pillars were rough and devoid of ornament, the shafts of the columns rose with severe simplicity, crowned by plain capitals at the base of the arches, on which the Gothic thistle had not yet attained the exuberant branching of a later florid period; but the vaulting which was finished perhaps two centuries after the first beginning, and the windows with their multi-coloured ogives, displayed the magnificence of an art at its culminating point.

At the two extreme ends of the transepts Gabriel found the proof of the immense progress made during the two centuries in which the Cathedral had been rising from the ground. The Puerta del Reloj, called also de la Feria, with its rude sculptures of archaic rigidity, and the tympanum, covered with small scenes from the creation, was a great contrast to the doorway at the opposite end of the crossway, that of Los Leones, or by its other name, de la Alegria, built nearly two hundred years afterwards, elegant and majestic as the entrance to a palace, showing already the fleshly audacities of the Renaissance, endeavouring to thrust themselves into the severity of Christian architecture, a siren fastened to the door by her curling tail serving as an example.

The Cathedral, built entirely of a milky white stone from the quarries close to Toledo, rose in one single elevation from the base of the pillars to the vaulting, with no triforium to cut its arcades and to weaken and load the naves with superimposed arches. Gabriel saw in this a petrified symbol of prayer, rising direct to Heaven, without assistance or support. The smooth, soft stone was used throughout the building, harder stone being used for the vaultings, and on the exterior the buttresses and pinnacles, as well as the flying buttresses like small bridges between them, were of the hardest granite, which from age had taken a golden colour, and which protected and supported the airy delicacy of the interior. The two sorts of stone made a great contrast in the appearance of the Cathedral, dark and reddish outside, white and delicate inside.

The seminarist found examples of every sort of architecture that had flourished in the Peninsula. The primitive Gothic was found in the earliest doorways, the florid in those del Perdon and de los Leones, and the Arab architecture showed its graceful horseshoe arches in the triforium running round the whole abside of the choir, which was the work of Cisneros, who, though he burnt the Moslem books, introduced their style of architecture into the heart of the Christian temple. The plateresque style showed its fanciful grace in the door of the cloister, and even the chirruguesque showed at its best in the famous lanthorn of Tome, which broke the vaulting behind the high altar in order to give light to the abside.

In the evenings of the vacation Gabriel would leave the seminary, and wander about the Cathedral till the hour at which its doors were closed. He delighted in walking through the naves and behind the high altar, the darkest and most silent spot in the whole church. Here slept a great part of the history of Spain. Behind the locked gates of the chapel of the kings, guarded by the stone heralds on pedestals, lay the kings of Castille in their tombs, their effigies crowned, in golden armour, praying, with their swords by their sides. He would stop before the chapel of Santiago, admiring through the railings of its three pointed arches the legendary saint, dressed as a pilgrim, holding his sword on high, and tramping on Mahomedans with his war-horse. Great shells and red shields with a silver moon adorned the white walls, rising up to the vaulting, and this chapel his father, the gardener, regarded as his own peculiar property. It was that of the Lunas, and though some people laughed at the relationship, there lay his illustrious progenitors, Don Alvaro and his wife, on their monumental tombs. That of Doña Juana Pimental had at its four corners the figures of four kneeling friars in yellow marble, who watched over the noble lady extended on the upper part of the monument. That of the unhappy constable of Castille was surrounded by four knights of Santiago, wrapped in the mantle of their Order, seeming to keep guard over their grand master, who lay buried without his head in the stone sarcophagus, bordered with Gothic mouldings. Gabriel remembered what he had heard his father relate about the recumbent statue of Don Alvaro. In former times the statue had been of bronze, and when mass was said in the chapel, at the elevation of the Host, the statue, by means of secret springs, would rise and remain kneeling till the end of the ceremony. Some said that the Catholic queen caused the disappearance of this theatrical statue, believing that it disturbed the prayers of the faithful; others said that some soldiers, enemies of the constable, on a day of disturbance, had broken in pieces the jointed statue. On the exterior of the church the chapel of the Lunas raised its battlemented towers, forming an isolated fortress inside the Cathedral.

In spite of his family considering this chapel as their own, the seminarist felt himself more attracted by that of Saint Ildefonso close by, which contained the tomb of the Cardinal Albornoz. Of all the great past in the Cathedral, that which excited his greatest admiration was the romantic figure of this warlike prelate; lover of letters, Spanish by birth, and Italian by his conquests. He slept in a splendid marble tomb, shining and polished by age, and of a soft fawn colour; the invisible hand of time had treated the face of the recumbent effigy rather roughly, flattening the nose, and giving the warlike cardinal an expression of almost Mongolian ferocity. Four lions guarded the remains of the prelate. Everything in him was extraordinary and adventurous even to his death. His body was brought back from Italy to Spain with prayers and hymns, carried on the shoulders of the entire population, who went out to meet it in order to gain the indulgences granted by the Pope. This return journey to his own country after his death

31

lasted several months, as the good cardinal only went by short journeys from church to church, preceded by a picture of Christ, which now adorns his chapel, and spreading among the multitude the sweet scent of his embalming.

For Don Gil de Albornoz nothing seemed impossible; he was the sword of the Apostle returned to earth in order to enforce faith. Flying from Don Pedro the Cruel, he had taken refuge in Avignon, where lived exiles even more illustrious than himself. There were the Popes driven out of Rome by a people who, in their mediaeval nightmare, tried to restore at the bidding of Rienzi the ancient republic of the Consuls. Don Gil was not a man to live long in the pleasant little Provençal court; like a good archbishop of Toledo, he wore the coat-of-mail underneath his tunic, and as there were no Moors to fight he wished to strike at heretics instead. He went to Italy as the champion of the Church; all the adventurers of Europe and the bandits of the country formed his army. He killed and burnt in the country, entered and sacked the towns, all in the name of the Sovereign Pontiff, so that before long the exile of Avignon was again able to return and occupy his throne in Rome. The Spanish cardinal after all these campaigns, which gave half Italy to the Papacy, was as rich as any king, and he founded the celebrated Spanish college in Bologna. The Pope, well aware of his robberies and rapacity, asked him to give some sort of accounts. The proud Don Gil presented him with a cart laden with keys and bolts.

"These," said he proudly, "belong to the towns and castles I have gained for the Papacy. These are my accounts."

The irresistible glamour that a powerful warrior throws over a man physically feeble was strongly felt by Gabriel, and it was augmented by the thought that so much bravery and haughtiness had been joined in a servant of the Church. Why could not men like this arise now, in these impious times, to give fresh strength to Catholicism?

In his strolls through the Cathedral Gabriel greatly admired the screen before the high altar, a wonderful work of Villalpando, with its foliage of old gold, and its black bars with silvery spots like tin. These spots made the beggars and guides in the church declare that all the screen was made of silver, but that the canons had had it painted black so that it might not be plundered by Napoleon's soldiers.

Behind it shone the majestic decorations of the high altar, splendid with soft old gilding, and a whole host of figures under carved canopies representing various scenes from the Passion. Behind the altar and the screen the gilding seemed to spring spontaneously from the white walls, marking with brilliant lights the divisions between the stalls. Beneath highly-decorated pointed arches were the tombs of the most ancient kings of Castille, and that of the Cardinal Mendoza.

Under the arches of the triforium an orchestra of Gothic angels with stiff dalmatics and folded wings sang lauds, playing lutes and flutes, and in the central parts of the pillars the statues of holy bishops were interspersed with those of historical and legendary personages.

On one side the good Alfaqui Abu-Walid, immortalised in a Christian church for his tolerant spirit, on the opposite side the mysterious leader of Las Navas who, after showing the Christians the way to victory, suddenly disappeared like a divine envoy—a statue of exceeding ugliness with a haggard face covered by a rough hood. At either end of the screen stood as evidences of the past opulence of the church two beautiful pulpits of rich marbles and chiselled bronze.

Gabriel cast a glance at the choir, admiring the beautiful stalls belonging to the canons, and he thought enthusiastically that perhaps some day he might succeed in gaining one to the great pride of his family. In his wanderings about the church he would often stop before the immense fresco of Saint Christopher, a picture as bad as it was huge—a figure occupying all one division of the wall from the pavement to the cornice, and which by its

32

size seemed to be the only fitting inhabitant of the church. The cadets would come in the evenings to look at it; that colossus of pink flesh, bearing the child on its shoulders, advancing its angular legs carefully through the waters, leaning on a palm tree that looked like a broom, was for them by far the most noticeable thing in the church. The light-hearted young men delighted in measuring its ankles with their swords and afterwards calculating how many swords high the blessed giant could be. It was the readiest application that they could make of those mathematical calculations with which they were so much worried in the academy. The apprentice of the church was irritated at the impudence with which these dressed up popinjays, the apprentices of war, sauntered about the church.

Many mornings he would go to the Muzarabé Chapel, following attentively the ancient ritual, intoned by the priests especially devoted to it. On the walls were represented in brilliant colours scenes from the conquest of Oran by the great Cisneros. As Gabriel listened to the monotonous singing of the Muzarabe priests he remembered the quarrels during the time of Alfonso VI. between the Roman liturgy and that of Toledo—the foreign worship and the national one. The believers, to end the eternal disputes, appealed to the "Judgment of God." The king named the Roman champion, and the Toledans confided the defence of their Gothic rite to the sword of Juan Ruiz, a nobleman from the borders of Pisuerga. The champion of the Gothic breviary remained triumphant in the fight, demonstrating its superiority with magnificent sword thrusts, but, in spite of the will of God having been manifested in this warlike way, the Roman rite by slow degrees became master of the situation, till at last the Muzarabé ritual was relegated to this small chapel as a curious relic of the past.

Sometimes in the evenings, when the services were ended and the Cathedral was locked up, Gabriel would go up to the abode of the bell-ringer, stopping on the gallery above the door del Perdon. Mariano, the bell-ringer's son, a youth of the same age as the seminarist, and attached to him by the respect and admiration his talents inspired, would act as guide in their excursions to the upper regions of the church; they would possess themselves of the key of the vaultings and explore that mysterious locality to which only a few workmen ascended from time to time.

The Cathedral was ugly and commonplace seen from above. In the very early days the stone vaultings had remained uncovered, with no other concealment beyond the light-looking carved balustrade, but the rain had begun to damage them, threatening their destruction, and so the Chapter had covered the Cathedral with a roof of brown tiles, which gave the Church the appearance of a huge warehouse or a great barn. The pinnacles of the buttresses seemed ashamed to appear above this ugly covering, the flying buttresses became lost and disappeared among the bare-looking buildings, built on to the Cathedral, and the little staircase turrets became hidden behind this clumsy mass of roofing.

The two youths climbing along the cornices, green and slippery from the rain, would mount to quite the upper parts of the building. Their feet would become entangled in the plants that a luxuriant nature allowed to grow amid the joints of the stones, flocks of birds would fly away at their approach; all the sculptures seemed to serve as resting-places for their nests, and every hollow in the stone where the rain-water collected was a miniature lake where the birds came to drink; sometimes a large black bird would settle on one of the pinnacles like an unexpected finial; it was a raven who settled there to plume his wings, and it would remain there sunning itself for hours; to the people who saw it from below it appeared about the size of a fly.

These vaultings caused Gabriel a strange impression; no one could guess the existence of such a place in the upper regions of the building. He would walk through the forest of

33

worm-eaten posts which supported the roof, through narrow passages between the cupolas of the vaulting that arose from the flooring like white and dusty tumours; sometimes there would be a shaft through which he could see down into the Cathedral, the depth of which made him giddy. These shafts were like narrow well-mouths at the bottom of which could be seen people walking like ants on the tile flooring of the church. Through these shafts were lowered the ropes of the great chandeliers, and the golden chains that supported the figure of Christ above the railing of the high altar. Enormous capstans showed through the twilight their cogged and rusty wheels, their levers and ropes like forgotten instruments of torture. This was the hidden machinery belonging to the great religious festivals; by these artifices the magnificent canopy of the holy week was raised and fastened.

As the sun's rays shone in between the wooden posts the dust of ages that lay like a thick mantel on the roof of the vaulting would rise and dance in them for a few seconds, and the huge old spiders' webs would wave like fans in the wind, while the footsteps of the intruders would occasion wild and precipitous scrambles of rats from all the dark corners. In the furthest and darkest corners roosted those black birds who by night flew down into the church through the shafts in the vaulting, and the eyes of the owls glowed with phosphorescent brilliancy, while the bats flew sleepily about sweeping the faces of the lads with their wings.

The bell-ringer's son would examine the deposits dropped in the dust, and would enumerate all the different birds who took refuge in the summit of the mountains of stone: this belonged to the hooting owl, and that to the red owl, and this again to the raven, and he spoke with respect of a certain nest of eagles that his father had seen as a young man, fierce birds who had endeavoured to tear out his eyes, and who had so thoroughly frightened him that he had been obliged to borrow the gun belonging to the night watchers on each occasion that his duties took him to the roof.

Gabriel loved that strange world, harbouring above the Cathedral with its silence and its imposing solitude. It was a wilderness of wood, inhabited by strange creatures who lived unnoticed and forgotten under the roof-tree of the church. Truly the good God had a house for the faithful down below, and an immense garret above for the creatures of the air.

The savage solitude of the higher regions was a great contrast to the wealth of the chapel of the Ochava, full of relics in golden vessels and caskets of enamel and precious marbles, to the quantities of pearls and emeralds in the magnificent treasury, heaped up as though they had been peas, and to the elegant luxury of the wardrobe, full of rare and costly stuffs and vestments exquisitely embroidered with every colour of the rainbow.

Gabriel was just eighteen when he lost his father. The old gardener died quietly, happy in seeing all his family in the service of the Cathedral and the good old tradition of the Lunas continued without interruption. Thomas, the eldest son, remained in the garden, Esteban, after serving many years as acolyte and assistant to the sacristans, was Silenciario, and had been given the Wooden Staff and seven reals a day, the height of all his ambition; and as far as regarded the youngest, the good Señor Esteban had the firm conviction that he had begotten a Father of the Church, for whom a place in heaven was especially reserved at the right hand of God Omnipotent.

Gabriel had acquired in the seminary that ecclesiastic sternness that turns the priest into a warrior more intent on the interest of the Church than on the concerns of his family. For this reason he did not feel the death of his father very greatly; besides, much greater misfortunes soon occurred to preoccupy the young seminarist.

CHAPTER III

There was great excitement both in the Cathedral and in the seminary, everyone discussing from morning till night the news from Madrid, for these were the days of the September revolution. The traditional and healthy Spain, the Spain of the great historical tradition had fallen. The Cortes Constituyentes were a volcano, a breath from the infernal regions, to those gentlemen of the black cassock who crowded round the unfolded newspaper, and, if they found comfort and satisfaction in a speech of Maesterola's they would suffer the agonies of death at the revolutionary harangues, which dealt such terrible blows at the olden days. The clergy had turned their eyes towards Don Carlos, who was beginning the war in the northern provinces; the king of the Vascongados mountains would be able to remedy everything when he came down into the plains of Castille. But years passed by, Amadeus had come and gone, they had even proclaimed a republic! And yet the cause of God did not seem to advance much, and Heaven seemed deaf. A republican deputy proclaimed a war against God, challenging Him to silence him; and so impiety stalked along immune and triumphant, and its eloquence flowed abroad like a poisonous spring.

Gabriel lived in a state of bellicose excitement—he forgot his books, he disregarded his future, he never thought now of singing his mass. What would happen to his career now that the Church was in peril, and that the sleepy poetry of past ages, that had enveloped him from his cradle like a perfumed cloud of old incense and dried roses, was on the point of vanishing?

Often some of the pupils disappeared from the seminary, and the professors would reply to the inquiries of the curious with a sly wink.

"They have gone out—with the good sort. They could not see quietly what was happening—'child's play,' 'follies.'"

But nevertheless such follies made them smile with paternal satisfaction.

He thought to be himself among those who fled, as the world seemed to be coming to an end. In certain towns the revolutionary mob had invaded and profaned the churches; as yet they had not murdered any of the ministers of God as in other revolutions, but still the priests were unable to go about the streets in their cassocks for fear of being hooted and insulted. The remembrance of the archbishops of Toledo, those brave ecclesiastical princes, implacable warriors against the infidels, fired his warlike feelings. As yet he had never been away from Toledo, away from the shadow of its Cathedral; Spain seemed to him as vast as all the rest of the world put together, and he began to feel the ardent desire of seeing something new, of seeing closer all the wonderful things he had read about in his books, stirring within him.

One day he kissed his mother's hand, without feeling any very great emotion towards the trembling and nearly blind old woman, for the seminary had for him more tender memories than the house of his fathers, smoked his last cigar with his brothers in the garden without revealing his intentions to them, and that night he fled from Toledo with a scapulary of the Heart of Jesus sewed into his waistcoat, and a beautiful silk scarf in his wallet, one of those worked by white hands in the convents of the city. The son of the bell-ringer went with him. They joined one of the insignificant bands who were devastating Murcia, but they soon went on to Valencia and Catalonia, anxious to perform greater exploits for the cause of God than merely stealing mules and extorting contributions from the rich.

Gabriel felt an intense delight in this wandering life, with its continual alarms owing to the proximity of the troops.

He had been made an officer at once, on account of his education, and because of the letters of recommendation that certain of the prebends of the Metropolitan Church had given him; letters lamenting greatly that a youth of so much theological promise should go and risk his life like a simple sacristan.

Luna enjoyed the free and lawless life of war with the zest of a collegian out of bounds; but he could not hide the feeling of painful disillusion that the sight of those armies of the Faith caused him. He had expected to find something akin to the ancient crusading expeditions: soldiers who fought for an ideal, who bent the knee before beginning the fight, so that God might be on their side, and who at night, after a hard-fought field, slept the pure sleep of an ascetic; instead of which he found an armed mob, mutinous to their leaders, incapable of that fanaticism which rushes blindfold to death, anxious only that the war might last as long as possible, so that they might continue the life of lawless wandering at the expense of the country, which they considered the best life possible; people who at the sight of wine, women or plunder would disband themselves, hungering, turning against their leaders.

It was the ancient life of the horde, surging up through civilisation, the atavic custom of stealing the stranger's bread and women by force of arms, the ancient Celtiberic love of factions and internal strife, that only caught hold of a political pretext in order to revive.

Gabriel, with very rare exceptions, found none in those badly-armed and worse-clothed bands who fought with a fixed idea; they were adventurers who wished for war for the sake of war; visionaries anxious for fortune; country lads from the fields, who in their passive ignorance had joined the factions, just as they would have stayed at home if they had had better counsels; simple souls who firmly believed that in the towns they were burning and destroying God's ministers, and who had thrown themselves into the fray so that society should not lapse into barbarism.

The common danger, the misery of the interminable marches to deceive the enemy, the scarcity suffered in the barren fields and on the rough hilltops on which they took refuge, made them all equals, enthusiasts, sceptics or rustics. They all felt the same desire to compensate themselves for their privations, to appease the ravenous beast they felt inside, awakened and irritated by a life of such sudden changes; as much by the wild abundance and plundering of a sack as by the distress endured in the long marches over interminable plains without ever seeing the slightest sign of life. On entering a town they would shout, "Long live religion," but on the slightest provocation they would do this, that and the other in the name of God and all the saints, not omitting in their filthy oaths to swear by everything most sacred in that same religion.

Gabriel, who soon became accustomed to this wandering life, ceased to feel shocked. The former scruples of the seminarist vanished, smothered under the crust of the fighting man, which became hardened with war.

The romantic figure of Doña Blanca, the king's sister-in-law passed before him, like a person in a novel; in her romantic energy this princess wished to emulate the deeds of the heroines of La Vendeé, and mounted on a small white horse, her pistol in her belt, and the white scarf tied over her floating tresses, she put herself at the head of these armed bands, who revived in the centre of the Peninsula the strife of almost prehistoric times. The flutter of the dark riding-habit of this heroine served as a standard to the battalions of Zouaves, to the troop of French, German, and Italian adventurers, the scum of all the wars on the globe, who found it pleasanter to follow a woman anxious for fame than to enlist themselves into the foreign legion of Algeria.

The assault of Cuenca, the sole victory of the campaign, made a deep impression on Gabriel's memory; the troops of men wearing the scarf, after they had knocked down the ramparts as weak as mud walls, rushed like overflowing streams through the streets. The firing from the windows could not stop them; they rushed in pale, with discoloured lips and eyes brilliant with homicidal mania, the danger overcome, and the knowledge that they were at length masters of the place drove them mad; the doors of the houses fell under their blows, terrified men rushed out to be pierced with bayonets in the streets, and in the houses you could see women struggling in the arms of the assailants, striking them in the face with one hand, while with the other they struggled to retain their clothes.

Gabriel saw how the roughest of the mountaineers destroyed in the Institute all the apparatus of the Cabinet of Physical Science, breaking it in pieces. They were furious with these inventions of the evil one, with which they thought the unbelievers communicated with the Government of Madrid, and they smashed on the ground with the butt ends of their muskets, and trampled with their feet, all the gilt wheels of the apparatus, and all the discs and batteries of electricity.

The seminarist was delighted at all this destruction; he also hated, but it was with a calm, reflective hate bred in the seminary, all positive and material sciences, for the sum total of his reasoning was that they came perilously near to the negation of God; those sons of the mountains in their blessed ignorance, had without knowing it done a great deed. Ah! if only the whole nation would imitate them! In former times there were none of these ridiculous inventions of science, and Spain was far happier. To live a holy life, the learning of the priests and the ignorance of the people was sufficient, for both together produced a blessed tranquillity; what did they want more? For so the country had existed for centuries, all through the most glorious period of its existence.

The war came to an end, the closely pursued rebels passed through the centre of Catalonia and were finally driven over the frontier, where they were compelled to give up their arms to the French custom-house officers. Many availed themselves of the amnesty, anxious to return to their own homes. Mariano, the bell-ringer, was one of these. He did not wish to live in a foreign land; besides, during his absence his father had died, and it was extremely probable that he might succeed to the charge of the Cathedral tower if he laid due stress on the merits of his family, his three years' campaigning for the sake of religion, and a wound he had received in his leg; he would really be able to compare himself with the martyrs for Christianity.

Gabriel preferred emigration. "He was an officer and therefore could not take the oath of allegiance to a usurping dynasty." This declaration he made with all the pride learnt in this caricature of an army, which emphasised all the ceremonies of ancient warfare, and who, ragged and shoeless as they were, with their swords by their sides, never failed to transmit orders to each other as "high-born officer." But the real reason which prevented Luna from returning to Toledo was that he wished to follow the course of events, to see new countries and different customs. To return to the Cathedral would mean to remain there for ever, to renounce everything in life, and he, who during the war had tasted of worldly delights, had no desire to turn his back on them quite so soon; also he was not yet of age, so he had plenty of time before him in which to finish his studies; the priesthood was a sure retreat, but one to which he was in no hurry to return just at present; besides, his mother was dead, and his brother's letters told him of no alteration in the sleepy life of the upper cloister, beyond that the gardener was married and that the "Wooden Staff" was courting a girl in the Claverias, it being against all the good traditions of these people to ally themselves with anyone outside the Cathedral.

Luna lived for more than a year in the emigrants' cantonments; his classical education and the sympathy aroused by his youth smoothed his path to a certain extent; he talked Latin with the French abbés, who were delighted to hear about the war from the young theologian, and at the same time they taught him the language of the country. These friends procured for him Spanish lessons among the upper middle classes who were friendly to the Church. In these days of penury he was saved by his friendship with an old legitimist Countess, who invited him to spend several days in her country house, introducing the warlike seminarist to all the grave and pious friends at her assemblies as though he had been a crusader newly returned from Palestine.

Gabriel's great desire was to go to Paris; his life in France had radically changed his ideas, he really felt as though he had fallen into a new planet. Accustomed to the monotonous life in the seminary, and to the nomadic existence during that mountainous and inglorious war, he was astonished at the material progress, the refinement of civilisation, the culture and the well-being of the people in France. He remembered now with shame his Spanish ignorance, all that Castilian phantasmagoria, fed by lying literature, that had made him believe that Spain was the first country in the world, and its people the noblest and bravest, and that all the other nations were a sort of wretched mob, created by God to be victims of heresy, and to receive overwhelming punishment each time that they ventured to interfere with this privileged country, which, though it eats little and drinks less, has yet produced the holiest saints and the greatest captains of Christendom.

When Gabriel could express himself fluently in French and had contrived to save a few francs for his journey, he went to Paris. A friendly abbé had procured him employment as corrector of proofs in a religious library close to Saint Sulpice. In this priestly quarter of Paris, with its hostels for the clergy and for religious families, as gloomy as convents, with its shops full of pious images, which flood the globe with varnished and smiling saints, was accomplished the great transformation of Gabriel.

This quarter of Saint Sulpice with its streets almost Spanish in their silence and peacefulness, with the sisters in black veils gliding by the walls of the seminary, drawn by the sound of the bells, was for the Spanish seminarist what the road to Damascus had been for the Apostle. The French Catholicism, cultivated, reasoning and respectful to human progress, bewildered Gabriel, whose fierce Spanish bigotry had taught him to despise all profane science. There was only one true learning in the world, and that was theology. The other sciences were only toys, only fit to amuse the eternal infancy of humanity. To know God and to meditate on the greatness of His power, this was the only serious study to which men could devote themselves; machinery, the discoveries of the positive sciences, in fact everything which did not treat of divinity and the future life, was only a bagatelle for the amusement of fools and people of no faith.

The former seminarist, who from his earliest childhood had despised all human progress, was stupefied when he perceived how earnestly all French Catholicism spoke of it. In correcting the proofs of so many religious works he could not but notice the profound respect which this despised science inspired in the good French priests, men of such far superior culture to that of the canons down there. And moreover he noticed a certain humble shrinking in the representatives of religion when they came face to face with science—a desire to please, not to be censorious, to help on with their sympathy any conciliatory solutions, so that dogma should not fall to the ground, finding no place in the rapid march of events that was hurrying humanity into the future with the whirl of its new discoveries. Entire books were written by eminent priests with the view of adjusting and bringing into line the revelations of the holy books and the discoveries of modern science, even at the risk of doing some violence to the former. The ancient and venerable Church that Gabriel had seen in his own country, immovable in its antiquated majesty, unwilling to move a single fold of its mantle for fear of losing some of the dust of ages, was stirring in France, endeavouring to renew itself, throwing on one side the ancient garments of tradition, like old rags that would turn it into ridicule, and stretching out its hands with almost despairing strength to catch hold of the modern achievements of science; the great enemy of yesterday, whose appearance had been ushered in with bonfires and shameful abjurations was triumphant to-day.

What had that fatal apple of Paradise contained, that after six thousand years of malediction that same Church had begun to venerate it, striving to make it forget its ancient persecutions? Why was religion, firm as a rock throughout the centuries, which had defied persecutions, schisms and wars, beginning to dissolve before the discoveries of a few men, and entering into that wild current which sought for the cause and explanation of everything? If it had the secular support of faith, why should it seek the assistance of reason to maintain its traditions and to justify its dogmas?

Gabriel felt the same fever of curiosity which had obliged him as a child to bend his back over the old volumes, bound in parchment, in the library of the seminary; he wished to be acquainted with the mysterious perfume of that hated science which had so disturbed God's priests, and had made them indirectly deny the beliefs of nineteen centuries. He wished to know why the sacred books were being dislocated and tortured in order to explain by geological periods the creation which God had accomplished in six days. What danger did they hope to avoid by making the divinity appear before science in order to explain its acts and fit them into the decisions of the latter? Whence came the instinctive fear of the religious authors of roundly affirming miracles? attempting instead to justify them by intricate and tentative reasonings, without daring to adduce as the decisive proof the incomprehensibility of supernatural prodigies.

For the time being Gabriel abandoned the tranquil atmosphere of the religious library. His reputation as a humanist had reached the ears of an editor living near the Sorbonne, so, without leaving the left bank of the Seine, he moved into the Latin quarter to undertake the correction of proofs in Latin and Greek. He earned in this way twelve francs a day—far more than those canons of Toledo, who formerly had appeared to him as great dukes. He lived in a small inn for students near to the School of Medicine, and his vehement discussions at night with his fellow-lodgers over the smoke of their pipes taught him as much as the books of that hated science. Those students who lent him books, or who told him of those he should search for in his free hours in the library on the hill of Saint Genevieve, laughed like pagans at the exalted ideas of the former seminarist.

For two years young Luna did little else but read; now and again he accompanied his friends in some escapade, throwing himself into the free and joyous life of the Quartier, wearing out the elbows of his sleeves on the tables of the beershops. The Mimi of Murger often passed before him, but less melancholy than the creation of the poet, and the ex-seminarist found his Sunday evening idylls in the woods surrounding Paris. But Gabriel was not of an amorous temperament; curiosity and the thirst for knowledge mastered him, and after these escapades from which he returned fresher, and with his brain keener, he threw himself with greater ardour into his studies.

History, true history, whose cold clearness contrasted so strongly with that intricate morass of miracles in the chronicles that he had read in his childhood, beat down the greater part of his beliefs. Catholicism was no longer for him the only religion, neither could he any longer divide the history of humanity into two periods, that before and that after the appearance in Judea of a handful of obscure men, who, spreading themselves over the world, preached a cosmopolitan morality drawn from the maxims of Orientals, and from the teachings of Greek philosophy.

Religions were for him human inventions, subject to the conditions of existence belonging to all organisms, its generous infancy capable of blind sacrifices, its self-contained and masterful manhood, in which the early sweetness was changed by the authoritative imposition of its power, and its inevitable age, with a long agony, in which the sick man, guessing his speedy end, clings to life with all the energy of desperation.

39

His faith in Catholicism as the only religion disappeared completely; losing his belief in dogmas he lost also, by inevitable logic, that belief in the monarchy which had driven him to fight in the mountains, and he understood clearly now the history of his country without prejudices of race. The foreign historians showed him the sad fate of Spain, arrested in the most critical period of her development, when she was emerging young and strong during the most fertile period of the Middle Ages, by the fanaticism of priests and inquisitors, and the folly of some of her kings, who, with utterly inadequate means, wished to revive the empire of the Caesars, draining the country for this mad enterprise. Those people who had broken with the Papacy, turning their backs for ever on Rome, were far happier and more prosperous than that Spain, which slept like a beggar at the door of the Church.

At this period of his intellectual development Gabriel had an ideal, and often of an evening he would leave his work to go and listen to him for an hour at the College of France: this was Ernest Renan; Gabriel admired him for a double reason, for his talent and for his history. The great man had also passed through a seminary, and even now had a priestly look as though he had suffered deeply from the pressure of the ecclesiastical yoke; he was a rebel, and Gabriel felt as though he belonged to his own family. "Truly the hammers to destroy the temple are forged within the temple," and the law fatal to all religions was being accomplished, when faith vanishes, and the multitude no longer feel the fervour of early days.

Gabriel was astonished to hear how the teacher could penetrate the intellectual development of the Hebrew people, which had served as the basis of Christianity, as he heard him demolish bit by bit the immense altarpiece, before which humanity had knelt for over nineteen centuries. The Spanish seminarist revolted against his old faith with all the impetuosity of his vehement temperament. How could he have believed all that and have considered it the height of human wisdom! Certainly Christianity had exercised a beneficial influence at one period of the infancy of humanity, it had filled men's lives in the Middle Ages when there was little to think of beyond religion, and, in a land desolated by strife, there was no other refuge for intellectual thought but the cathedral in the towns and the monastery in the country. "The fairs—the assemblies for business and pleasure," said the master, "were religious feasts; the scenic representations were mysteries, the journeys were pilgrimages and the wars crusades." After this the ways of life divided—religious life took one way and human life the other. Art placed nature above the ideal, and men thought more of earth than of heaven. Reason was born, and every advance that it made was one step backward for faith, and at last the time arrived when the clear-sighted, those who were anxious about the future, began to ask themselves what the new belief was likely to be which would replace the moribund religion. Luna had no doubts on the point—it was science, and science alone, which could fill the vacuum caused by that religion now dead for ever.

Influenced by the Hellenism of his master, which he assimilated easily, being accustomed to daily intercourse with the Greek authors, he dreamed that the humanity of the future would be an immense Athens, an artistic and learned democracy governed by great thinkers, with no strifes but those of the mind, with no ambition but that of cultivating the intellect, of gentle manners, and devoted to the joys of the mind and the culture of reason.

Of all his old beliefs, Gabriel only retained that of a creative God from a certain superstitious scruple. His ideas were rather disconcerted by astronomy, which he had taken up with an almost childish eagerness, attracted by the charm of the marvellous. That infinite space in which in olden days legions of angels had manoeuvred, and which had served the Virgin as a pathway in her terrestrial descents, he suddenly found to be peopled with thousands of millions of worlds, and the more powerful men's instruments became the more numerous they seemed to be, the distances being infinitely prolonged to immensities that were inconceivable. Bodies were attracted to one another travelling in space at the rate of millions of miles a minute, and all this cloud of worlds revolved without ever passing twice over the same spot in this immensity of silence, in which fresh stars, and again others and others, were continually being discovered as the instruments of observation became more perfect.

This God of Gabriel's having lost the corporeal form given to Him by religion, and as divulged in the history of the creation, lost at once all His attributes, and being magnified to fill the infinite and being absorbed into it, became so impalpable and subtle to the intellect as to appear a phantasm.

Nothing remained to Gabriel of all his ancient beliefs. His mind was like a bare field over which the whirlwind had passed, for his last belief, which had remained standing like a monolith in the midst of ruins, the belief in the history of creation, had now fallen.

But it was impossible to the former seminarist to remain inactive with his cargo of new ideas. He felt obliged to believe in something, to devote to the defence of some ideal all the faith in his character, to make some use of that fervour of proselytising which had been so much admired in the class of eloquence in the seminary, and so revolutionary sociology took possession of him. First of all it was Proudhon with his audacious writings, and afterwards the work was completed by some "militantes" who were working in the same printing office as himself—old soldiers of the Commune, who had lately returned from their exile in the prisons of Oceania, and were renewing their campaign against social organisation with an ardour increased tenfold by their painful sufferings and their desire of vengeance. With them he went to the anarchist meetings; there he heard Reclus and Prince Kropotkine, and the words of the since deceased Miquel Bakronhine came to him as the gospel of a Saint Paul of the future.

Gabriel had met with his new religion, and he gave himself over to it entirely, dreaming of the regeneration of humanity through its stomach. Believing in a future life, misfortunes gave the false consolation of happiness after death; but all religion was a lie, there was no other life but that of the present, and Luna rose in anger against the social injustice that condemned millions of beings to poverty and misery for the happiness of a few privileged thousands. Authority, which was the fount of all evil, was to him the greatest enemy; it must be destroyed, but men must be created who were capable of living without masters, priests or soldiers. The natural gentleness of his character, and the horror of violence with which his three years' campaigning had filled him, caused him rather to draw back from his new companions, who, dreaming of hecatombs from dynamite and the dagger to reform the world, obliged him to accept these new doctrines through fear. No; he believed in the strength of the "idea," and in the innocent evolution of humanity; he had only to work like the first apostles of Christianity certain of the future, but without hurrying, to see his ideas realised; he had only to fix his eyes on the day's work, without thinking of the long years and centuries before it would bear its fruit.

The ardour of his proselytising made him leave Paris at the end of five years. He was anxious to see the world, to study for himself all these social miseries, so as to judge what forces these disinherited could command for their great transformation. Besides, he began to find himself incommoded by the vigilance of the French police, on account of his intimacy with the Russian students of the Quartier Latin—young men with cold eyes and limp and dishevelled hair who were endeavouring to implant in Paris the vengeances of Nihilism. In London he came to know a young Englishwoman of weak health, but burning like himself with all the ardour of revolutionary propaganda, who would walk from morning till night in the lanes and surroundings of workshops and laboratories, distributing pamphlets and printed leaflets that she kept in a band-box that was always hanging on her arm. In a short time Lucy became Gabriel's companion; they loved each other without excitement, with a cold and quiet passion, more from community of ideas than anything else, for the love of revolutionists, dominated with the thought of rebellion against everything existing, has not much room for any other feeling.

Luna and his companion went to Holland and thence to Belgium, settling afterwards in Germany, always travelling from group to group of "companions," taking up different work with that facility of adaptation which seems universal among revolutionaries, who wander over the world penniless, enduring every sort of privation, but finding always in their difficulties some brotherly hand to raise them and set them again on the path.

After eight years of this life Gabriel's friend died of consumption. They were then in Italy, and Luna, finding himself alone, understood for the first time how much support the gentle companion of his life had given him. In his sorrow for the loss of Lucy he forgot for a while his revolutionary enthusiasm, lamenting only the void left in his life. He had not loved her as most men love, but she was his companion, his sister, they were alike in their pleasures and their sorrows, and their common poverty had welded them into one will. Moreover, Gabriel felt himself aged before his time by this life of soul-stirring adventures and painful privations. He had been imprisoned in many places in Europe, being suspected of complicity with the terrorists, he had often been beaten by the police, and he began to find a difficulty in travelling about the Continent, as his photograph figured with that of several other "companions" in the central police offices of the principal nations. He was a vagabond and dangerous dog, who would end by being kicked out of every place.

Gabriel could not live alone; he was accustomed to see those kind blue eyes near him, and to hear the caressing voice with its bird-like inflexions which had so much encouraged him in times of trial and difficulty, and he could not endure the solitude in a strange land after Lucy's death. A great longing for his native land awoke in him, he wished to return to Spain, to that land he had so often ridiculed, and which now in spite of its backwardness seemed to him so attractive. He thought of his brothers, fixed like plants to the stones of the Cathedral, never interesting themselves with what took place in the world, never seeking for news of him, as though they had entirely forgotten him.

With a sudden impulse, as though he were afraid of dying away from his native land, he returned to Spain. In Barcelona some of the "companions" had obtained for him the management of a printing press, but before taking up his post he wished to spend a few days in Toledo. He returned an old man, though he was barely forty, speaking four or five languages, and poorer than when he had left it. He found that his brother the gardener had died, and that the widow and her son had taken refuge in a garret in the Claverias, where she supported herself by washing the canon's linen. Esteban, the "Wooden Staff," received him with the same admiration he had felt for him while in the seminary. He talked a great deal about his travels, gathering together all the people in the upper cloister, so that they should listen to this man who had travelled all over the world, just as though he were going about his own house. In their inquiries they painfully entangled geography, as they could only comprehend two divisions in it, the countries of heretics, and the countries of Christians.

Gabriel pitied the great poverty of these people, and admired the humbleness of these Cathedral servants, content to live and die in the same place, without any curiosity as to what was taking place outside the walls. The church seemed to him a huge derelict. It was like the petrified skeleton of one of those immense and powerful animals of former days, that had been dead for ages, its body decayed, its soul evaporated, and nothing left but this framework, like to the shells found by geologists in prehistoric strata by whose structure they can guess at the soft parts of the vanished being. Seeing the ceremonies of worship which in former days had so moved him, he felt roused to protest, a longing to shout to the priests and acolytes to stop, and withdraw, as their times were passed, and faith was dead, and it was only from routine and the fear of outside opinion that people now frequented these places, which formerly religious fervour had filled from morning till night.

On his arrival in Barcelona Gabriel's life was a whirlwind of proselytising, of struggles, and of persecutions. The "companions" respected him, seeing in him the friend of all the great propagandists of "the idea," and one who might himself rank among the most famous revolutionists. No meeting could be held without the "companion" Luna; that natural eloquence which had caused such wonder on his entry into the seminary, bubbled up and spread like an intoxicating gas in these revolutionary assemblies, firing that ragged, hungry, and miserable crowd, making them tremble with emotion at the description of future societies set forth by the apostle, that celestial city of the dreamers of all ages, without property, without vices, without inequalities, where work would become a pleasure, and where there would be no other worship but that of science and art. Some of his hearers, the darker spirits, would smile with a compassionate gesture, listening to his maledictions against authority, and his hymns to the sweetness and triumph to be won by passive resistance. He was an idealist, one to whom they must listen because he had served the cause well; they who were the strong men, the fighters, knew well enough how to crush in silence that cursed society if it should show itself deaf to the voice of Truth.

When they exploded bombs in the streets the "companion" Luna was the first to be surprised at the catastrophe, he was also the first to be taken to prison on account of the popularity of his name. Oh! those two years passed in the castle of Montjuich! They had ploughed a deep furrow in Gabriel's memory, a deep wound that could not heal, that made him tremble at the slightest remembrance, disturbing his calm, and making him hot and cold with terror.

The madness of fear had taken possession of society, and all laws and regard to humanity, were trampled under foot to defend it. The justice of former ages, with its violent procedure was resuscitated in full civilisation. The judge was distrusted as being too cultured and scrupulous, and a free hand was given to the petty officers of justice, ordering them to introduce afresh all the old instruments of torture.

In the darkness of the night Gabriel saw his Moorish dungeon lighted up; some men in uniform seized him and dragged him down the staircase to a room where others were waiting with huge cudgels. A young man with a soft voice, in the uniform of a lieutenant, and with the lazy manners of a Creole, questioned him as to the various attempts that had occurred months before down in the town. Gabriel knew nothing, had seen nothing. But all the same these men were your companions; but he, having fixed his eyes on high, contemplating his visions of the future, had never realised that all around him this violence was surging and germinating. His reiterated negative rendered the men furious; the soft voice of the Creole became harsh with anger, and with menaces and blasphemies they all threw themselves upon him, and the cruel hunt of the man round and round the dungeon began, the cudgels falling on his body, beat his head or his legs indifferently, pursuing him into corners, following him as with a desperate bound he reached the opposite wall, opening the way with his bent head, his back resounding like an empty box beneath the blows. Now and then the desperation of pain inflamed the victim, the lamb turned into a wild beast, and before falling to the ground, cowering like a child before superior numbers, he would throw himself on the executioners, tearing them, and trying to bite them. Gabriel kept a button from the lieutenant's uniform which had remained in his fingers after one of these revolts of his weakness.

Afterwards, his tormentors, wearied by the inutility of their violence, left him forgotten in the dungeon. A loaf of bread and some bits of dry salt cod were his only food. Thirst, an infernal thirst, racked his bowels, contracted his throat, and burnt his mouth. At first he called piteously under the door for water, but afterwards he would beg no more, knowing beforehand what the answer would be. It was a calculated torture; they promised him as much water as he wished, after he should have disclosed the names of the guilty, confessing things of which he had no knowledge. Hunger strove in him against thirst, but fearing this latter most, he would throw this salted food into a corner as though it were poison. He was delirious with the delirium of a shipwrecked man tormented with visions of fresh water in the midst of the salt waves. In his nightmare he saw clear and murmuring brooks, great rivers; and seeking freshness for his mouth he would pass his tongue over the filthy walls, finding a certain alleviation in the lime of the whitewash.

The privations and the incarceration disturbed his mind with horrible ravings; often Gabriel was surprised at finding himself on all fours, growling and barking opposite the door without knowing how or why.

His tormentors seemed to forget him; they had other prisoners to look after. The jailors gave him water, but whole months passed without anyone entering his cell. Some nights he would hear vaguely and far off through the greasy walls wailing and sobs in the adjacent dungeons. One morning he was awoke by sounds as of thunder, in spite of a tiny ray of sunlight filtering through his loophole; hearing the jailors in the corridors near, he understood the mystery. They had been shooting some of the prisoners.

Luna received as a happiness this hope of death; he would renounce with pleasure that shadow of a life in a small stone box, tormented by physical pain and the fear of men's ferocity. His stomach, weakened by all these privations, refused for many days, with horrible nausea, to receive the bitter bread and the coppery mess. His want of exercise, the want of air, and the bad and scanty nourishment had made him fall into a mortal anaemia; he coughed continually, suffering great oppression on his chest. The knowledge he had acquired of the human body in his thirst for knowing everything did not admit of his being mistaken; he would die as poor Lucy had died.

After a year and a half of imprisonment he appeared before a council of war, mixed up with a mob of old men, women, and even quite young people, all weakened and broken by imprisonment, with their skin white and thick as chewed paper, and that dazed look in their eyes that comes from solitary confinement. Gabriel hoped he would be executed. When the fiscal came to the name of Luna on the long list he stopped an instant, shooting a ferocious glance at him—this man was among the theorists. It appeared from the declarations of witnesses that he took no direct part in the deeds of violence, and that in his speeches he had always deprecated them; still it must be remembered that he was one of the principal propagandists of anarchism, and that he had delivered speeches in all the workmen's societies frequented by the authors of the attempts.

An elderly captain bent towards another member of the council, speaking in his ear, but Gabriel caught his words:

"It is on these gentlemen who make speeches that we must lay our hand, so that they may be warned not to lecture any more on Tolstoi or Ibsen, or any of those foreign worthies who advocate throwing bombs."

Gabriel spent many months of solitary confinement in his prison. From words now and then dropped by his jailors he could guess at the fluctuations of his fate. Sometimes he would gather that he and all his companions in misfortune were to be sent to the jail in Africa, or again they would hint at his immediate liberation, or would prophesy that they were all to be shot en masse. When at the end of two years he left this gloomy castle, it was to be embarked with all his companions for exile. He was only the shadow of a man; his weakness made his walk as uncertain and tremulous as that of a child, but he forgot his own misery in trying to assist those of his companions who were even weaker than himself, and who bore the cruel scars of the torments they had endured.

The return to liberty recalled all his former gentleness and the philosophic pity with which he surrounded all men, pitying and pardoning their faults. On landing in England the more violent of his companions spoke of future vengeance on their persecutors, while Gabriel asked pardon for them, as blind instruments employed by society in a moment of terror, thinking they had saved it by their barbarity.

The climate of London aggravated Gabriel's illness, and in about two years he was obliged to move to the Continent, although England with its absolute liberty was the only land where he could have lived quietly and ignored.

His existence was a cruel one, always a fugitive through the different countries of Europe, driven from one place to another by the vigilance of the police, thrown into prison, or expelled on the slightest suspicion. It was a return to the ancient persecution of the gipsies, the constant hunting of independent people, leading vagabond lives, of the Middle Ages. His illness and his desire for rest and peace made him return to Spain. Time had produced a certain amount of tolerance towards the exiles, and in Spain everything is soon forgotten, and though the authorities are harder and less scrupulous than in other countries, still they interfere less on account of their improvidence and the carelessness natural to the race.

Sick and without any work by which he could earn his living, precluded from seeking work among the printers, as his name was encircled by a halo which terrified the masters, Gabriel fell into such extreme poverty that the little help and succour his companions could afford were unable to relieve it, and he travelled from end to end of the Peninsula begging from his fellows and hiding from the police.

His spirit was broken, he was conquered, and he had no longer strength to continue the struggle. Nothing remained for him but to die, but merciful death came slowly to his call. He thought of his brother, the only affection remaining to him in the world; he remembered the quiet family in the Claverias, of which he had caught a glimpse on his last visit to the Cathedral, and he turned to seek them as his last hope.

On his return to Toledo, he found the happy family dissolved; misfortune had come even to that silent and stagnant corner.

But the Cathedral, insensible to all human vicissitudes was there, the same as ever, and to it he clung, hiding himself in its recesses, hoping to die there in peace, with no other hope but to be forgotten; dying before his proper time, tasting the bitter happiness of annihilation, leaving behind him at the door, like an animal who sheds its skin, all that rebellion which had drawn upon him the hatred of society.

His happiness was not to think, not to speak, to mould himself to that dead world; he would be among the living statues peopling the upper cloister, one more automaton; he would imitate those beings who seemed to have absorbed into themselves something of the austerity of the granite buttresses, he would inhale like a healing balsam the scent of the rusty iron railings and the incense that spread through the church, the ancient perfume of the past centuries.

CHAPTER IV

On leaving the cloister in the mornings soon after daybreak, the first person Gabriel would see was Don Antolin, the "Silver Stick." This priest exercised an authority like that of Governor of the Cathedral, for all the lay servants were under his orders, and all the repairs of little importance were done under his supervision.

Down below, in the church, he watched the sacristans and the acolytes, careful that the canons and beneficiaries should have no cause of complaint in the services. Upstairs, in the cloister, he watched over the good behaviour and cleanliness of the families, being by the grace of the cardinal archbishop a sort of magistrate over that little town.

He occupied the best "habitacion" in the Claverias. At the great ceremonies he walked in front of the Chapter in his pluvial, carrying a silver stick nearly as tall as himself, making the tiles of the pavement re-echo with its blows. During High Mass and the choir in the evening he walked about the naves to check any irreverence on the part of the congregation or any inattention on that of the staff. At eight o'clock at night in the winter, and at nine in summer, he locked the door of the staircase leading to the upper cloister, putting the key in his pocket, and so all the people in the cloister remained quite isolated from the town. If now and again anyone was taken ill in the night, it was necessary to wake Don Antolin who, plunging his hand into the depths of his cassock, would produce his key, and deign to restore communication with the outer world.

He was about seventy years of age, small and wizened; age had scarcely tinged his shaven crown with grey, his forehead was broad and square, and rose straight beneath the silk cap he wore in winter. His features were rather drawn out, without a single wrinkle, and devoid of any expression that showed emotion, the jaw-bone narrow and sharp, and the eyes as inexpressive and motionless as the rest of the face, but with a cold, penetrating glance that was extremely disconcerting.

Gabriel had known him from his childhood; he was, to use his own expression, like a private soldier of the church, who by reason of his years and services had attained the rank of sergeant, but who could rise no further. When Luna first entered the seminary Don Antolin had just been ordained priest, and since then had passed his life in the sacristy of the Primacy where he had begun as acolyte.

On account of his absolute and irrational faith and his unbending adhesion to the Church, the professors in the seminary had pushed him on in his career, in spite of his ignorance; he was a son of the soil, having been born in a village in the mountains round Toledo. The Holy Metropolitan Church was to him the second house of God in the world, only ranking after Saint Peter's in Rome, and all ecclesiastical learning was to him like rays emanating from the Divine wisdom, which blinded him, and were to be adored with the profound respect of ignorance.

He had that blessed and entire want of education so appreciated by the Church in former years. Gabriel felt sure that if Silver Stick had been born in the flourishing times of Catholicism he would have become a saint on dedicating himself to the spiritual life, or he would have played an excellent part in the Inquisition on the arrival of that militant society. Having come into the world at the wrong time, when faith was weakened and the Church could no longer impose its laws by violence, the good Don Antolin had remained hidden in the lower administration of the Cathedral, assisting the Canon Obrero in the division and assignment of the money that the State allowed to the Primacy, giving long thought over the spending of each handful of farthings, endeavouring that the holy house, like the ruined families, should keep up its good outward appearance without revealing the poverty inside.

He had been promised several times a chaplaincy of nuns, but he was one of those faithful to the Cathedral, one of those quite in love with the great establishment. He was proud of the confidence that the Lord Archbishop placed in him, and of the frank friendliness with which the canons and beneficiaries spoke to him, and of his administrative conferences with the Obrero and the Treasurer. For this reason he could not repress a gesture of contemptuous superiority when having donned his pluvial, and clutching his silver stick, he advanced and spoke to any strange clergy from the neighbouring villages who visited the Primacy.

His faults were purely ecclesiastic; he saved in secret, with that cold, determined avarice so usual at all times in people attached to the Church. His greasy skull cap had been discarded as too old by its former owner, one of the canons; his cassock of a greenish black and his shoes had also belonged to some one of the beneficiaries; in the Claverias they all whispered of the monies hoarded by Don Antolin, and of his savings that were devoted to usury—loans that never went beyond two or three duros to the poorer servants of the church ground down by poverty, and which he recovered with interest at the beginning of every month when they were paid by the Canon Obrero. In him avarice and usury were joined to the most implicit honesty in regard to the interests of the church; he would punish relentlessly the smallest pilfering in the sacristy, and he made up his accounts for the Chapter with a minuteness that annoyed the Obrero. To every one his own, the church was poor and it would be a sin worthy of hell to deprive her of a single farthing; he, as a good servant of God was poor also, and he thought he was doing no wrong in drawing a certain profit from the money he had gathered together by dint of bargaining, and by many painful privations in the midst of his poverty.

His niece, Mariquita, lived with him, an ugly woman with masculine features and a fresh colour, who had come from the mountains to look after her uncle, of whose riches and power in the Primacy all his relations and friends in the village talked a great deal. She rode roughshod over all the other women in the Claverias, taking undue advantage of Don Antolin's supreme authority. The more timid formed round her a circle of adulation, endeavouring to evoke her protection by cleaning her house and cooking for her, while Mariquita, dressed in the habit, and with her hair most carefully combed—the only luxury allowed by her uncle—loitered about the cloister hoping to meet there some cadet, or that some of the foreigners visiting the tower or the hall of the giants would take notice of her. She made sheep's eyes at every man; and she, so hard and imperious to all the women, would smile sweetly on all the bachelors living in the Claverias. The "Tato" was a great friend of hers; he would come and visit her when her uncle was absent in order to air his graces as apprentice to a Torrero. Gabriel, with his delicate looks, his mysterious self-containment, and the confused story of all his great travels about the world interested her not less; she would even speak with marked deference to the "Wooden Staff," as he was both a man and a widower, and, as the "Perrero" wickedly said, the very sight of a pair of trousers nearly drove the poor woman mad in that establishment where the greater part of the men wore petticoats.

Don Antolin had known Gabriel since his childhood, and spoke to him in the second person. The ignorant priest still retained the remembrance of Luna's great triumphs obtained in the seminary, and though he saw him so poor and ailing, taking refuge in the Cathedral almost on charity, his "tuteo" of superiority was not free from admiration. Gabriel, on his side, feared Silver Stick, knowing his intolerant fanaticism. For this reason he confined himself to listening to him, careful in their conversation that not a single word should slip in which could betray his past. He would be the first to demand his expulsion from the Cathedral, where he wished to live unknown and silent.

On meeting each other in the cloister, the two men began with the same questions every morning:

"How is your health to-day?"

Gabriel showed himself an optimist. He knew that his illness had no remedy; still, that quiet life free from all emotions, and his brother's care, feeding him at all hours, like a bird and almost by force, had arrested the decay of his health. The course of the illness was slower—death was meeting with obstacles.

"I am better, Don Antolin. And yesterday, what sort of a day had you?"

Silver Stick plunged his dirty and horny hands into the recesses of his cassock, and produced three greasy little ticket-books, one red, one green and the third white. He turned over the leaves, considering the counterfoils of those he had torn out; he took the most respectful care of these little books, as though they were far more important than the big music books in the choir.

"A very slack day, Gabriel! Being in the winter, so few people travel. Our best time is in the spring, when they say the English come in by Gibraltar. They go first to the fair in Seville, and afterwards they come to have a look at our Cathedral. Besides, in milder weather the people come from Madrid, and although they grumble, the flies crowd to see the giants and the big bell, then I have to hurry with the tickets; one day, Gabriel, I took eighty duros. I remember it was at the last 'Corpus'; Mariquita had to sew up the pockets of my cassock, for they tore with the weight of so many pesetas; it was a blessing from the Lord."

He looked sadly at the little books, as though regretting that many days passed in winter when he only tore out one or two leaves. This plan of selling entrance tickets to see the treasures and curiosities of the Cathedral filled all his thoughts. It was the salvation of the church, the modern proceeding to help it on, and he felt proud of fulfilling this function, which made him one of the most important persons in the life of the temple.

"You see these green tickets?" said he to Gabriel. "These are the dearest, they cost two pesetas each. With these you can see everything that is most important—the treasury, the chapel of the Virgin, and the Ochavo with its relics which are unique in the world. The other cathedrals are dirt compared with ours, and their relics lies, many of them invented on account of the envy that our Holy Metropolitan Church inspired. You see these red ones? These only cost six reals, and with them you can visit the sacristies, the wardrobe, the chapels of Don Alvaro de Luna and of Cardinal Albornoz, and the Chapter-house, with its two rows of portraits of the archbishops which are wonders. Who would not scrape their purse to see such prodigies?"

Afterwards he added, showing the last ticket book with contempt:

"These white ones are only worth two reals. They are to see the giants and the bells. We sell a great many of those to the lower class who come to the Cathedral on feast days. Could you believe it, but many of the Protestants and Jews call this a robbery? The other day three soldiers came from the Academy with some country folks to see the giants, and they made quite a scandalous scene because we would not let them in for an old song. As if we were asking their charity! Many of them commit all sorts of nuisances about the Cathedral, just as if they were heretics, to say nothing of their drawing all sorts of abominable things and writing obscene words on the walls of the staircase. What shocking times, eh, Gabriel? What shocking times!"

Luna smiled silently, and Silver Stick, encouraged by what seemed to him acquiescence, went on with pride:

"And about these tickets, I invented them—that is to say, I am not really their inventor, but their introduction into this house is owing to me. You have travelled so much, and must have seen in those foreign countries that everything is shown on payment. The Lord Cardinal before this one, who is now in blessed glory (and he raised his hand to his skull cap) had also travelled a great deal—he was quite a 'modern,' and had he lived would have ended by putting electric light in the naves of the Cathedral. I heard him on one occasion speak of what was done in the museums and other interesting places in Rome and other towns; unrestricted entrance at all hours—on payment, an immense convenience to the public, who required to get no tickets beforehand to visit these things. So one day when the Obrero and I were biting our nails, seeing that this miserable thousand and odd pesetas (God forgive me!) that this unhappy State allows us, could not possibly suffice for our monthly expenses, I propounded my idea. Now, could you believe that some of the gentlemen in the Chapter opposed it? Some of the young canons spoke of the sellers in the Temple, you know who they were—certain Jews who drove the Lord out with scourges in their hand, for I know not what misdemeanours. The older ones said the Cathedral had always had its treasures open to all for centuries, and so it ought to go on. All the gentlemen were quite right, but you cannot do anything with a stupid canon, and at last the defunct cardinal, who is now in the enjoyment of God (another tug at his cap) interfered, and the Chapter were obliged, though with much grumbling, to accept the reform, and they ended by praising it. In all bitter there is a sweet! Do you know how much money I handed to the Lord Cardinal last year? More than three thousand duros, nearly as much as this sinful State allows us, and this without prejudice to anybody. The public pays, they admire and they go; in any case they are only birds of passage who come once, and when they go they do not return. And what are four wretched pesetas, when for that money you can see one of the most glorious churches in Christendom, the cradle of Spanish Catholicism, the Cathedral of Toledo!"

The two men were walking in the cloister on the side warmed by the sun at that early hour, the cleric had put away his ticket books, and his eyes were fixed on Gabriel, who thought that to smile in his enigmatic way, which Don Antolin accepted as assent, quite met the situation, and it encouraged him to continue his confidences.

"Ay, Gabriel! You cannot think that my heavy duties can be fulfilled without hard work; the Cardinal trusts me, the Chapter distinguish me with their regard, and the Obrero has no other hope but in my assistance. Thanks to these tickets we can carry the Cathedral along, and keep up its ancient appearance of grandeur, so that the public will come and admire. But we are poorer than rats, and we must be thankful that even some crumbs are left us from the past. If the wind or the hail break some of our glass in the naves, we can still lay our hands on some of the stores left by the Obreros of former days. Ay, señor! And to think there was a time when the Chapter maintained at its own expense inside the church, cutters and painters of glass, plumbers, and I know not what beside, so that any great works could be undertaken without seeking any help outside the house! If one of the tombs gets broken, even now we have quantities of borderings carved with saints and flowers that are wonderful to see. But what will happen when all these are finished? When the last pane of glass in the stores has been broken, and the last fragments of carving in the Obreria used up? We shall have to put cheap white panes in the windows to prevent the rain and wind coming in. The Cathedral will look like an inn—may God forgive me the comparison—and the priests of the Primacy will praise God dressed like the chaplain of a hermitage."

And Don Antolin laughed sarcastically, as though this future that he was anticipating was an absurd contradiction of the eternal laws.

"You will easily believe," he went on, "that they do not waste anything, and that they make money out of every possible thing. The garden that was for so many years in your family is now leased out by the Chapter, since your brother's death; twenty duros a year your Aunt Tomasa pays for her son to cultivate it, and this only because, as you know, the old woman is such a great friend of His Eminence, as they have known each other since they were children. I go about like a water carrier, all round the church and the cloisters, watching that no one plays tricks, for there are a lot of young light-hearted people, whom you cannot trust. One minute I am in the Ochavo, watching that your nephew the 'Tato' has sold the tickets to the foreigners (for he is quite capable of letting them in gratis if they tip him on leaving), and the next I am up in the cloister looking after that shoemaker who repairs the giants; they cannot deceive me, no one escapes me without paying; but, ay! it is a long while since I have sung mass. You can see me at mid-day when the Cathedral is closed reading my hours hurriedly in the cloisters, watching the clock in order to go down the moment the church is opened, when the strangers begin to come to see the treasury. This is not the life of a good Catholic, and if God does not lay it to my account that I am doing it all for the glory of His house, I fear that I shall lose my soul."

The two men walked up and down some time in silence, but Don Antolin could not hold his tongue for long when the subject was the economic life of the Primacy.

"And to think, Gabriel," he continued, "that having been what we were in former times, we should have come to this! You and most of those alive have no idea how rich this house used to be—as rich as a king, and often far richer. From a child no one has known as you have the history of our glorious archbishops, but of the fortune they amassed for God, you know nothing. Of course these temporalities do not interest learned people like you. Have you any idea what donations the kings and great lords gave in their lifetime to our Cathedral, or the legacies they left her on their deathbeds? You have a great deal to learn! I know all about it, I have searched in the Obreria, in the archives, in the library; everyone does what interests them, and I and the Señor Obrero have often raged at the indigence of the house, but I console myself by thinking of what we had, long before any of us were born. We were very rich, Gabriel—very, very rich. The archbishops of Toledo could have placed one or two crowns on their mitre, I dare not say three, for I think of the Supreme Pontiff. First of all, there is the Deed of Gift to the Cathedral, made by the King Alfonso VI., by reason of his having conquered Toledo. It was made a hermitage, after the election of the Bishop Don Bernardo, and I have seen it in the archives with my own sinful eyes, a parchment with Gothic letters, and at the head is written, 'The privileges of this Holy Church.' The good king gave to the Cathedral nine towns—if I wished I could tell you their names—several mills, and vineyards innumerable, houses and shops in the town, and he ends by saying with all the munificence of a Christian cavalier, 'This, therefore, in such a way I give, and I grant to this church and to you, Bernard, Archbishop, in free and perfect gift, that neither by homicide, nor any other calumny, shall it ever be forfeited. Amen.' Afterwards, Don Alfonso VII. gave us eight towns on the other side of the Guadalquiver, several ovens, two castles, the salt works of Belinchon, and a tenth of all the money coined in Toledo, for the vestments of the prebendaries. The VIII. of the name showered on the Cathedral a perfect rain of gifts, towns, villages, and mills. Illescas is ours, and a great part of Esquivias, as also the mortgage on Talavera. Afterwards came the fighting prelate, Don Rodrigo, who took much land from the Moors, and the Cathedral possesses one principality, the Adelantamiento de Cazorla, with towns like Baza, Niebla, and Alcaraz. And besides the kings there is a great deal to be said about the nobles, great princes who showed their generosity to the Holy Metropolitan Church. Don Lope de Haro, Lord of Vizcaya, not content with paying the cost of the building from the Puerta de los Escribanos as far as the choir, gave us the town of Alcubilete, with its mills and fisheries, and he also left a legacy so that in the choir when complines are sung, that lamp called the Preciosa should be lighted, which is placed by the great bronze eagle belonging to the big missal. Don Alfonso Tello de Meneses gave us four towns on the banks of the Guadiana, granted us tithes and bridge tolls, and I know not what riches besides. We have been very powerful, Gabriel; the territory of this diocese is larger than a principality. The Cathedral had property on the earth, in the air, and in the sea! Our dominions extended throughout the whole nation from end to end; there was not a single province in which we did not hold possessions. Everything contributed to the glory of the Lord, and to the comfort and welfare of His ministers; everything paid to the Cathedral: bread when it was baked in the ovens, the casting of the net, wheat as it passed through the mill, money as it came from the Mint, the traveller as he went on his way; the country people who then paid no taxes

50

or contributions served their king and saved their own souls, giving the best sheaf in every ten, so that the granaries of the Holy Metropolitan Church were quite insufficient to contain such abundance. What times were those, Gabriel! There was faith, Gabriel, and faith is the chief thing in life—without faith there is no virtue nor decency—nor nothing."

He stopped for a moment, quite out of breath with talking. The priest was so saturated with the atmosphere of the Cathedral, that in himself he seemed to unite all the various scents of the church; his cassock had collected the mouldy smell of the old stones and the rusty iron railings, and his mouth seemed to breathe of the gutters and the gargoyles, and the rank damp of the garrets.

With the rapid enumeration of all the past wealth Don Antolin warmed, even to indignation.

"And having been so rich, now we find ourselves in extreme poverty. And I, my son, a priest of the Lord, am obliged to go hither and thither with those tickets so that we may all live, just as though I were a seller of entrance tickets to a bull-fight, and the Lord's house were a theatre, having to endure all those foreign heretics, who come in without blessing themselves, and who look at everything through opera-glasses. And I have to smile at them because they pay us and provide us with some dessert for our poor stew! Carape! Jesus have mercy on me! I was going to say a sacrilege."

Don Antolin continued his angry complaints till, in passing the front of his house, Mariquita of the scowling and ugly countenance appeared at the door.

"Uncle, enough of walking. Your chocolate is getting cold."

But before the priest disappeared into his house, she went on, smiling amiably at Luna:

"Will you have some, Don Gabriel?"

And with her bold eyes, like a hungry wolf, she invited Luna to enter. She liked the masterful ways of the man, she said, and the ease which his former intercourse with the world had given him, and, moreover, for her woman's imagination Gabriel's mysterious past possessed a great attraction; his proud silence, the vague reports of his adventures, and the smile, as much compassionate as disdainful, with which he listened to the people of the upper cloister.

The insinuating Mariquita withdrew, and Gabriel continued his walk through the cloister, after finishing the little jar of milk that his brother brought him up every morning.

At eight o'clock, Don Luis, the Chapel-master, came out, his cloak wrapped as usual theatrically round him, and his big hat well tilted back, like a glory, round his enormous head; he was humming absently, restless with perpetual nervous movements; he inquired anxiously if the bell had yet rung for the choir, frightened by the threats of a fine in case he were late. Gabriel felt himself very much attracted by this poor priestly musician, who lived so despised in the furthest corner of the church, thinking far more of music than of dogma.

In the evenings Gabriel would often go up to the little room inhabited by the Chapel-master, on the tipper floor of the Lunas' house; the room contained all the priest's fortune—a little iron bed, which had belonged formerly to the seminarist, two plaster busts of Beethoven and Mozart, and an enormous pile of bundles of music, bound scores, loose sheets of ruled paper, so big and so piled up and disorderly that every now and then a pile would slip down, covering the floor of the little room with white sheets to its furthest corner.

"That is how all his money goes," said the Wooden Staff with an air of good-natured reproof, "he will never have a farthing. As soon as he gets his pay he orders more music from Madrid. It would be far better for Don Luis if he were to buy himself a new hat, even if it were a cheap one, so that the gentlemen of the choir should not laugh at the covering he has on his head."

In the winter evenings, after the choir, the musician and Gabriel took refuge in this little room. The canons, wishing to avoid the cold winds and the rain, took their daily walk in the galleries of the upper cloister, not wishing to forego this exercise to which their methodical existence had accustomed them. The rain would beat on the window of the little room, and in the dull grey twilight the musician would turn over his portfolios, or letting his hands wander over the harmonium, he would talk the while with Gabriel, who was seated on the bed.

The musician would grow excited, speaking of his love of art. In the midst of some peroration he would become suddenly silent, and bending over the instrument its melodies would fill the room, and floating down the staircase would reach the ears of the walkers in the cloister like a distant echo. Suddenly he would cease playing and resume his chattering, as though afraid that with his absent-mindedness his ideas would evaporate.

The silent Luna was the only listener he had met with in the Cathedral; the first who would listen to him for long hours without ridiculing him or thinking him crazy, and who often showed by his short interruptions and questions the pleasure with which he listened.

The end of the evening's conversation was always the same—the greatness of Beethoven, the idol of the poor musician.

"I have loved him all my life," said the Chapel-master, "I was educated by a Jeronomite friar, an old man driven from his convent who, after leaving it, had wandered over the world as a professor of the violoncello. The Jeronomites were the great musicians of the Church. You did not know this, neither should I have known it if this holy man had not taken me under his protection soon after I was born, and been to me a real father. It appears that in olden days each order devoted itself to some special thing. One, I think the Benedictines, copied and annotated old books; others made sweet liqueurs for the ladies, others were wonderfully clever in training cage birds, and the Jeronomites studied music for seven years, each one playing the instrument of his choice, and to these we owe that there has been preserved in the Spanish churches a little, but very little, good musical taste. And from what my little father told me, what wonderful orchestras these Jeronomites must have had in their convents! For the ladies it was a great delight to go on Sunday evenings to the parlour, where they met the good fathers, each one a master of his own particular instrument. These were the only concerts in those days, and with their pittance assured, and no anxiety as to housing or clothing themselves, and with the love of art as their only duty, you may imagine, Gabriel, what musicians they could become. For this reason, when the friars were expelled from their convents the Jeronomites were not the worst off. There was no need to beg masses in the churches or to live on the charity of devout families; they were able to earn their bread by an art conscientiously studied, and consequently they soon got places as organists and Chapel-masters; the Chapters really fought for them. Some were more venturesome, and, anxious to see more of that musical world which had seemed to them while in their convents a vision of Paradise, entered the orchestras of theatres, many travelling even to Italy, transforming themselves so entirely that even their own former prior could not have recognised them. One of these was my little father. What a man! He was a good Christian, but he had thrown himself so thoroughly into music that he retained very little of the former friar. When he was told that probably the convents would be re-established, he shrugged his shoulders with indifference, a new sonata interested him much more. He sometimes said things that have always lived in my memory. I remember one day when I was a child he took me to a meeting of musical friends in Madrid, who played, for their own pleasure only, the famous 'Seventh Symphony.' Do you know it? It is the freshest and most graceful of all Beethoven's works. I remember my little father leaving the room quite wrapped up in himself, with his head bent, dragging me along, for I could hardly keep up with his long footsteps, and when we got home he looked at me fixedly, as though I had been a grown-up person. 'Listen, Luis,' he said, 'and remember this well. There is only one Lord in the world, Our Lord Jesus Christ, and there are two lesser lords, Galileo and Beethoven.'"

The musician looked lovingly at the plaster bust which faced the room from one corner, with its leonine brows and the diffident eyes of a deaf person.

"I do not know much about Galileo," continued Don Luis. "I know that he was a very wise man, and a scientific genius. I am only a musician and I know very little about other things, but I adore Beethoven, and I think my little father did the same—he is a god; the most extraordinary man the world has ever produced. Don't you think so, Gabriel?"

His nerves were quivering with his excitement, and getting up, he walked rapidly up and down the room, trampling on all the loose sheets of music.

"Ay! how I envy you, Gabriel, having travelled so much, and having heard so many good things! The other night I could not sleep for thinking of all you had told me about your life in Paris—those beautiful Sunday afternoons when you would go to the Lamoureax concerts, or sometimes to Colonnas, giving yourself a surfeit of sublimity! And here am I, shut up, my only hope being perhaps to conduct a Mass of Rossini's at one of the great festivals! My only comfort is to read music, instructing myself thoroughly in those great works that so many fools in the towns can listen to half asleep and bored. Here I have, in this pile, the nine symphonies of the great man—his innumerable sonatas, his masses, and together with him, Haydn, Mozart, Mendelssohn, in fact all the great writers. I have even Wagner. I read them, and I play what is possible on the harmonium. But—it is just as if you were to describe the drawing and colours of a picture to a blind man, buried in this cloister. I know, blindly, that there are most beautiful things in this world—for those who can hear them."

The Chapel-master kept from the previous year the remembrance of a great happiness, and he spoke of it enthusiastically. He had been chosen by the Cardinal Archbishop to go to Madrid, to be one of a board of examiners for organists.

"That was the best time I ever had in my life, Gabriel. One evening I listened to Wagner, dressed in the clothes of a friend of mine, a violinist, who plays here in Toledo at the great festivals. I heard the Walkyria in the pit of the Real Theatre, another night I went to a concert; but the greatest night of all was the one on which I heard the Ninth Symphony of that ugly old fellow, of that deaf, bad-tempered genius who is listening to us."

And with one bound the musician rushed to the bust, kissing it with childish humility, just as a child would caress a stern and domineering father.

"You know the Ninth Symphony; true, Gabriel? And what did you feel as you listened to it? When I listen to music strange things happen to me. I close my eyes and I see unknown countries and strange faces, and whenever I hear the same works the same visions are repeated. If I speak about this with any of the people down below they say I am mad, but I know that you feel as I do, and I am not afraid that you will laugh at me. There are musical passages that make me see the sea, blue and boundless, with silvery waves, and this, though I have never seen the ocean; other works bring before me woods and castles, or groups of shepherds with white flocks; with Schubert I always see two lovers sighing at the foot of a linden tree, and certain French composers bring before my mind's eye beautiful women walking among beds of roses, dressed in violet, always violet. And you, Gabriel, do not you see these things?"

The anarchist assented—yes, music awoke in him also a world of fantastic visions, far more beautiful than reality.

"I remember," went on the priest, "what the Ninth Symphony made me see. I see it still if I only hum some of its passages. Oh! that graceful Scherzo with its strange tremolos! I thought, hearing it, that God and his court of saints had left the heavens to take a walk, leaving the little angels masters of the house, full liberty! Universal gambols! The heavenly children, without any restraint, sported from cloud to cloud, amusing themselves by scattering on the earth the garlands of flowers that the saints had left behind them; one let loose the rain and made it fall on the earth; another seized the key of the thunder and touched it, fearful peals which frightened all the revellers and made them fly. But they returned again to continue their graceful play, beginning afresh their noisy games that the thunder had disturbed. And the Adagio! What do you say about that? Do you know anything softer, more loving or so divinely peaceful? Human beings will never speak like this again, however much progress they make. Hearing it, I thought of those fresco-painted ceilings with mythological figures—gods and goddesses with pink flesh and flowing curves, Apollo and Venus reclining on a mountain of pink and gold clouds, like a lovely dawn."

"Chaplain, what has come to you?" said Gabriel; "this is not very Christian."

"No, but it is artistic," said the musician simply. "I do not trouble myself much about religion, I believe what I was taught, and I have never taken the trouble to inquire any further. Music alone occupies me, of which someone has said 'that it will be the religion of the future,' the purest manifestation of the ideal. Everything that is beautiful delights me, and I believe in it as a work of God. 'I believe in God and in Beethoven,' as his pupil said—and besides, how much religion the grandeur of music contains! Do you know the last quartet that Beethoven wrote? He felt he was dying, and he wrote on the edge of the score this terrible question: 'Must it be?' and lower down he added, 'Yes, it must be, it must be.' It was necessary to die, even for such a genius to leave life, while he still carried in his mind such glorious things, to pay the tribute of human renovation; and then he wrote that lament, that farewell to life, whose greatness cannot be equalled by any song, or by any words of religion."

The musician sat down to the harmonium, and for a long while played that last lament of the genius, his sorrowful complaint on crossing the threshold, not despairing and trembling through fear of the unknown, but with a brave melancholy, sinking into the eternal shadow, confident that nothing could obscure his genius.

These evenings of artistic communion in that corner of the sleepy Cathedral drew the two men together with an ever increasing affection. The musician talked, turning over his scores, or playing his harmonium; the revolutionist listened silently, only interrupting his friend by his painful cough. They were evenings of sweet sadness that these two men spent together, one dreaming of leaving the stone prison of the Cathedral to see the world, the other returning from life wounded and breathless, content with the obscure repose of the beautiful church, and guarding with prudent silence the secret of his past. Art shone for them like the rays of the sun in the grey and monotonous atmosphere of the Cathedral.

When they met in the early mornings in the cloister the conversation between the two friends generally ran on the same lines.

"This evening, eh?" the Chapel-master would say mysteriously. "I have some fresh music, we shall enjoy something new that I have been sent to-day, and besides, I wrote a little thing last night."

The anarchist nodded affirmatively, quite ready to serve as entertainment for this pariah of art, who saw in him his only audience, and who took so much kindly trouble to interest him.

While the services lasted Gabriel would walk alone in the cloisters; all the men were in the Cathedral, except the shoemaker, who was mending the giants. Tired of the chattering of the women who stood at the doors of the Claverias, he would go up to the dwelling of the bell-ringer, his old companion in arms, or he would go down into the garden by the remarkable staircase del Tenorio when it was open, or by the archbishop's archway crossing the street.

He delighted in passing an hour under the trees; he found in the garden as many memories of his family as in the "habitacion" upstairs. Besides, he was tired of always finding his walks bounded by stone walls, which reminded him of his prison, and he wanted the movement of the vegetation caressed by the breeze to foster the illusion that he was living in complete liberty in the open country.

In the arbour, where he had formerly so often seen his father, infirm and crippled with age, directing his eldest son, who received all his orders impassively, he would now meet his Aunt Tomasa, knitting her stockings, and watching with vigilant eyes the work of a boy whom she had taken into her service.

Gabriel's aunt was by far the most important person in the Claverias; her word was worth quite as much as Don Antolin's, the Silver Stick was afraid of her, bending before the powerful protection that they all guessed stood behind the poor old woman. In the days when her father, Gabriel's maternal grandfather, was sacristan in the Cathedral the functions of acolyte were exercised by a small boy, nephew of one of the beneficiaries of the Cathedral, who ended by paying for his education in the seminary. This little acolyte of half a century before was now a prince of the church, and the Cardinal Archbishop of Toledo. Old Tomasa and he had known each other as children, fighting over trifles in the upper cloister, or playing tricks on the beggars who sat at the Puerta del Mollete. The imposing Don Sebastian, whose look alone made the Chapter and all the clergy in the diocese tremble, became happy, fraternal and confidential, when now and then in the evenings he saw Tomasa. She was the only living reminder of his childhood in the Cathedral. The old woman would kiss his ring with great reverence, but very soon she would lapse into talking to him as one of her own family, often very nearly speaking to him in the second person. The cardinal, always surrounded by fear and adulation, often felt the necessity of the old woman's careless and frank conversation. The people belonging to the Cathedral declared that the Señora Tomasa was the only person who dared to tell the cardinal home-truths face to face, and the neighbours in the Claverias felt their pride flattered when they saw the prince of the church sweeping down the stone steps in his brilliant scarlet robes to sit in the arbour and gossip for a good hour with the old woman, while his attendants remained respectfully standing at the gate of the iron railings.

Tomasa was not puffed up with this honour; to her this ecclesiastical prince was only the friend of her childhood, who had had a certain amount of good luck; and in the end, he was only Don Sebastian, without going any further into ceremonies and formulas of respect. But her family knew how to take advantage of this friendship, especially her son-in-law, "Virgin's Blue," a hypocrite, as the old woman declared, who would make money out of the very cobwebs of the Cathedral; an insatiable locust who, profiting by the friendship of the cardinal and his mother-in-law, went on continually obtaining fresh privileges, without the priests and sacristans daring to make the slightest protest, seeing him so well protected.

Gabriel much enjoyed his aunt's talk. She was the only person born in the cloister who seemed to have freed herself from the soporific influence of the church. She loved the

55

Cathedral, as being her ancient roof-tree, but she did not retain much respect for the saints in the chapels, nor for the human dignitaries who sat in the choir. She laughed with the happiness of a healthy and placid old woman, her seventy years being, as she said, quite free from any evil done to her neighbour. Her language was free and easy, like that of a woman who has seen much, and does not believe in human majesty or irreproachable virtues; but the bed-rock of her character was its tolerance, her compassion for all faults, but she Was indignant with those who attempted to hide them.

"They are all men, Gabriel," she would say to her nephew, speaking of the clergy of the Cathedral. "Don Sebastian is only a man; all sinners who have much to answer for before God. They cannot be anything else, and so I forgive them. But believe me, nephew, I often feel inclined to laugh when I see the people kneeling before them. I believe in the Virgin of the Sagrario, and a little in God; but in these gentlemen! If you only knew them as I do! But, when all is said and done, we must all live, and the evil is not in having faults, but in attempting to hide them; playing a farce with the shamelessness of my son-in-law who, here as you see him, is as proud as a castle, beats his breast, kisses the ground like the Beatas, and yet he is anxious for my death, thinking I have something laid away in my chest; he filches what he can from the Virgin's poor-box, steals the wax tapers, and plays tricks with what is paid for masses, and yet he would be in the street if it were not for me, who always think of my poor sick daughter and my poor little grandchildren."

When Gabriel went down to see her in the garden, she always received him with the same salutation:

"Hola, you ghost! but to-day you are looking better, you are being patched up. I believe your brother will pull you through with all his care."

And then followed a comparison between her healthy and vigorous old age and his ruined youth, which was fighting so tenaciously against death.

"Here you see my seventy years, and never an illness in all my life. Summer and winter I never hear four o'clock strike in bed, and all my teeth are as sound as in the days when Don Sebastian came in his red dress as server in the church and wanted to steal half my breakfast. You Lunas have always been delicate; your father, long before he was my age, could barely walk, and was always complaining of rheum and of the damp in this garden. Here am I in it constantly, and I feel just the same as when I am upstairs in the Claverias. We, the Villalpandos, are made of iron; for, of course, we are descended from that famous Villalpando who made the screen of the high altar, the custodia, and an innumerable quantity of other things. He really must have been a giant, to judge by the ease with which he twisted and moulded every sort of metal."

Gabriel's ill-health awoke in her the deepest compassion, but all the same not quite free from malicious suggestions.

"How much you must have amused yourself about the world, eh, nephew? But that war was your perdition; without it you would now have had your stall in the choir, and who knows if you might not have come to be another Don Sebastian. The truth is, that from his childhood no one spoke half as much about him in the seminary as they did of you, and he certainly was no prodigy of learning. But you saw the world, and you took a fancy to those countries where they say the ladies are very pretty, and wear hats as large as parasols. You are a monster of ugliness now, but you were very smart, though I, who am your aunt, say so. And now you have come back so lean and suffering! You must have lived very fast; who knows what you have done in the world—sly boots! And your poor mother, who thought you would be a saint! God have mercy on us! Don't deny it; you have done no good and I hate lies. You did right to enjoy yourself and to take advantage

56

of every opportunity, but the misfortune is that you should have returned as you are, for it is pitiful to see you, but I have known a great many like you. I don't know what evil spirit possesses people belonging to the church, but once they throw themselves into life, they don't know where to stop, and they burn the candle at both ends till there is next to nothing left; many of them, like you, have passed through the seminary."

One morning Gabriel asked a question of his aunt that he had been long thinking about, but that he had never before dared to put into words. He wanted to know all about his niece, Sagrario, and what had happened in his brother's house.

"You who are so kind, aunt, you will tell me; everyone seems afraid to speak about it; even my nephew the Tato, who is such a chatterer and skins everyone in the Claverias, is silent when I ask him. What happened, aunt?"

The old woman's face grew very sad.

"A great misfortune, my son, such as was never known before in the upper cloister. The madness of the world came into the Cathedral, and made a nest in the most honoured, most ancient, and most respectable house in the Claverias. We are all good people, though we have never seen as much of the world as can be seen from a skylight, and live here as though wrapped in cotton wool, but you Lunas have always been the best among the best, to say nothing of us Villalpandos, who come close behind. Ay! if your mother could raise her head! If your father were alive! But I lay all the blame on your brother, as being weak and a simpleton, having that cursed blindness of all fathers, who ignore the danger in the hope of marrying their daughters well."

"Well, but how was it, aunt? What passed between my niece and the cadet?"

"What happens frequently in the world, but what has never happened here before. A thousand times I said to my brother, 'See, Esteban, this young gentleman is not for your daughter'—very sympathetic, very lively, and wearing the uniform of the Academy like no one else, leader of a group of the wildest cadets in all their escapades about the town, besides a son of a great family—wealthy people who did not allow him to come to Toledo with his purse empty. And she—the poor Sagrario, crazy with love, flattered by her cadet, as proud as possible when she walked on Sundays through the Zocodover and the Miradero between her mother and that handsome young lover, that all the girls in the place envied her. The beauty of your niece was the talk of all Toledo; the girls in the college for noble ladies, nicknamed her the 'sacristana' of the Cathedral; but the poor girl lived only for her cadet, and she seemed to devour him with her beautiful blue eyes. That idiot, your brother, let him come to the house, proud of the honour that was being done to the family. You know, Gabriel, the eternal blindness of those middle-class Toledans, who encourage with pride the courtship of one of their girls by a cadet, though they are perfectly well aware that it is most rare that one of these courtships should end in marriage. There is no woman here with the slightest pretence to a pretty face who has escaped without her mouthful of love for one of those red pantaloons. Even I remember when I was a girl how I would smooth my hair and pull out my dress when I heard the rattle of a sword on the flags of the cloister. It is a blindness that descends from mothers to daughters, and the worst is, that those cursed ones have all their cousins and their lovers in their own country, and to them they return as soon as they leave the Academy."

"That is true, aunt, but what happened to my niece?"

"When the young man passed out a lieutenant, his family decided he ought to return to Madrid. The farewells were like a scene at the theatre. I believe that even your brother and that simpleton his wife, who is now in glory, wept as though the lover were theirs. The young people sat for hours with clasped hands, gazing into each other's eyes, as though they would devour each other. He was the calmest; he promised to come every Sunday and to write every day, and at first he did so, but before long many weeks passed

57

without his coming, and the postman came up less often to the Claverias, and at last did not come at all—it was ended, the young lieutenant found other amusements in Madrid. Your poor niece was like one demented; the colour in her face faded, she was no longer like the beautiful ripe apricot, with the soft skin that made you long to bite it. She wept like a Magdalen in every corner—and one day the foolish girl fled—and up to now—"

"But where was she? Did no one search for her?"

"Your brother seemed quite dazed. Poor Esteban! several nights we found him half dressed in the upper cloister, as stiff as a post, gazing up at the heavens with eyes that looked like glass. He became furious if any of us spoke of searching for the child; the scandal was past remedy, and he did not wish to aggravate it by her return, bringing back a lost one to the Holy Metropolitan Church, and to the honoured house of the Lunas. For more than a year everyone in the Claverias seemed crushed by this blow; it seemed as though we were all in mourning. You see, that such a thing should occur in the Cathedral where the years pass by in blessed peace without any of us saying one word louder than the other! And then I remembered you. It seemed impossible that from these Lunas, so quiet and steady, should have sprung a girl with sufficient pluck to run away to Madrid, where she had never been before, to join a man, without fear of God or of her own people. To whom could I liken the unhappy child? To her uncle, to Gabriel who passed for a saint, but who, nevertheless, after fighting like a wolf, wandered all over the world just like a gipsy."

Gabriel made no protest at the conception his aunt had formed of his past.

"And after her flight? What did you know about the child?"

"At first a good deal, but latterly not a word. The two were living in Madrid together, peacefully and quietly, away from the world, as though they were man and wife. This lasted for a good while, and I, hearing about it, began to wonder if I had not been mistaken, and that the man we had blamed so much had repented and would end by marrying Sagrario. But at the end of the year everything was ended; he grew tired, and the family intervened, in order that the escapade should not cut short the career they had marked out for the young man. They even sought the aid of the police, to frighten the child, so that she should not molest the young officer in the first angry transports of her desertion. Afterwards—nothing certain is known. Now and again those who have gone to Madrid told me a little; some of them had seen her, but it would have been far better if they had not seen her. It is a disgrace, Gabriel; a dishonour for your family which is mine. This unhappy girl is the worst of the worst. I heard that she had been very ill, and I believe that she is so still. Just imagine, what a life! And for five years! What will have happened to the unfortunate girl! And to think that she is my sister's daughter!"

The Señora Tomasa spoke with deep feeling.

"Afterwards, Gabriel, you know what happened here; your poor sister-in-law died, we hardly knew why, it was only a matter of a few days; possibly she may have died of the shame, as she died saying that the fault was entirely hers. It broke one's heart to see the state your brother was in after all this. Esteban has never been good for much, and now after this affair of his daughter he seemed to become quite imbecile. Ay, nephew! I also have felt it greatly, even though you see me so happy, and so satisfied with life, every now and then the remembrance of that unhappy girl strikes me here, in my head, and I eat badly and sleep worse, thinking that a girl who, after all, is of our own blood, is wandering lost over the world, a plaything for men, without anyone sheltering her, as though she were all alone, as though she had no family."

The Señora Tomasa wiped her eye with the point of her forefinger, her voice shook and the tears fell over her wrinkled old cheeks.

"Aunt, you are very kind," said Gabriel, "but you ought to have searched more for this poor girl; you ought to have recovered her, to have saved her, to have brought her back here. We must be merciful to the weakness of others, especially when that other is one of our own flesh."

"Ay, son! Who do you say it to? A thousand times I have thought this, but I was afraid of your brother. He is like a bit of dough, but he turns into a wild beast if you speak to him of his daughter. Even if we found her and brought her here he would not receive her; he would be as angry as if you were proposing some sacrilege to him. He could not calmly bear her presence in the house which was that of your forefathers. Besides, though he does not say so, he fears the scandal among the neighbours in the Claverias who know what had happened. This is the easiest part to arrange, as they would be very careful not to open their mouths when I am among them. But your brother frightens me, and I do not dare."

"I will help you," said Gabriel firmly. "Let us seek for the child, and once we have found her I will undertake to manage Esteban."

"It will be most difficult to find her. For a long time we have heard nothing. Doubtless those who do see her are careful to say nothing for fear of paining us. But I will try and find out—we will see, Gabriel—we will think about her."

"And the canons? and the cardinal? Will they not oppose the return of the poor girl to the Claverias?"

"Bah! The thing happened some time ago, and few of them will remember it; besides, we might place the girl in a convent, where she would be looked after and quiet, and cause scandal to no one."

"No, not that, aunt. It is a cruel remedy. We have no right to try and save this poor girl at the cost of her liberty."

"You are right," said the old woman, after a few moments' reflection. "I don't care much for these nuns myself. Where would she be more likely to follow a good example than in the heart of her own family? We will bring her back to this house if she repents and wishes for peace. And I will scratch out the eyes of the first woman in the Claverias who dares to say anything against her. My son-in-law will probably pretend to be scandalised, but I will settle him. It would be much better if he did not wink at the walks that Juanito, that cadet nephew of Don Sebastian's, takes in the cloister whenever my granddaughter stands at the door. The crackbrained fellow dreams of nothing less than becoming related to the cardinal, and seeing his daughter a general's wife; he might remember poor Sagrario. And as far as regards Don Sebastian, you may be quite easy, Gabriel. He will say nothing but that we ought to bring the child back—and what should he say? People ought to be charitable one to another, and none more than they; for after all, Gabriel, believe me—they are only men, nothing but men!"

CHAPTER V

The people of the Primacy always received with obstinate silence the slightest allusion to the reigning prelate. It was a traditional custom in the Claverias, and Gabriel remembered to have noticed the same in his childhood.

If they spoke of the preceding archbishop, these people, so used to grumbling, like all those who live in solitude, would loose their tongues and comment on his history and his defects. There was nothing to fear from a dead prelate, and besides, it was an indirect praise to the living archbishop and his favourites to speak ill of the defunct. But if during the conversation the name of His reigning Eminence arose, they were all silent, raising their hands to their caps to salute, as though the prince of the church were able to see them from the neighbouring palace.

Gabriel, listening to his companions of the upper cloister, remembered the funeral judgment of the Egyptians. In the Primacy no one dared to speak the truth about the prelates, or to discuss their faults till death had taken possession of them.

The most that they dared to do was to comment on the disagreements among the canons, to compare their lists of those who saluted one another in the choir, or who glared at one another between versicle and antiphon like mad dogs ready to fly at one another, or to speak with wonder about a certain polemic discussed by the Doctoral and the Obrero in the Catholic papers in Madrid, which had lasted for three years, as to whether the deluge was partial or universal; answering each other's articles with an interval of four months.

A group of friends had collected round Gabriel. They sought him, feeling the necessity of his presence, experiencing that attraction exercised by those who are born to be leaders of men even though they remain silent. In the evenings they would meet in the dwelling of the bell-ringer, or when it was fine weather they would go out into the gallery above the Puerta del Perdon. In the mornings the assembly would be in the house of the shoemaker who mended the giants, a yellow little man, who suffered from continual pains in his head, which obliged him to wear sundry coloured handkerchiefs tied round his head in the fashion of a turban.

He was the poorest in all the Claverias; he had no appointment, and mended the giants without any remuneration in the hopes of succeeding to the first vacant place, feeling very grateful to those gentlemen of the Chapter who gave him his house rent free, on account of his wife being the daughter of a former old servant of the church. The smell of the paste and of the damp floor infected his house with the rank atmosphere of poverty. A hopeless fecundity aggravated this poverty; his sad, placid wife with her big yellow eyes appeared every year with a new baby tugging at her flabby breast, and several children crept along the cloister walls, dull and inert with hunger, with enormous heads and thin necks, always sickly, though none of them managed to die; afflicted by all the pains of anaemia, by boils that arose and vanished on their faces, and watery eruptions covering their hands. The shoemaker worked for the shops in the town, without, however, earning much money. From the rising of the sun one could hear the sound of his hammer in the cloister. This sole evidence of profane work attracted all the unoccupied to the miserable and evil-smelling dwelling. Mariano, the Tato, and a verger who also lived in the cloister, were those who most frequently met Gabriel, seated on the shoemaker's ragged and broken chairs, so low that one could touch the floor of red and dusty bricks with one's hands.

Often the bell-ringer would run to his tower to ring the usual bells, but his vacant place would be immediately occupied by an old organ-blower, or some of the servants from the sacristy, all attracted by what they heard of these meetings of the lower servants of the Primacy. The object of the assembly was to listen to Gabriel. The revolutionary wished to keep silence, and listened absently to their grumblings at the daily round of worship; but his friends longed to hear about those countries in which he had travelled, with all the curiosity of people who lived confined and isolated; listening to his descriptions of the beauties of Paris and the grandeur of London they would open their eyes like children listening to a fairy tale.

The shoemaker with his head bent, never ceasing his work, listened attentively to the recital of such marvels; when Gabriel was silent they all agreed on one point, those cities must be far more beautiful than Madrid; and just think how beautiful Madrid was! Even the shoemaker's wife, standing in the corner forgetful of her sickly children, would listen to Luna with wonder, her face enlivened by a feeble smile, which showed the woman through the animal resigned to misery, when Luna described the luxury of the women in foreign parts.

All these servants of the church felt their narrowed and dulled minds stirred by these descriptions of a distant world that they were never likely to see; the splendours of modern civilisation touched them much more nearly than the beauties of heaven as described in the sermons, and in the pungent and dusty atmosphere of the dirty little house they would see unrolled before their mind's eye beautiful and fantastic cities, and they would ask questions in all innocence as to the food and habits of those distant people, as though they believed them beings of a different species.

Towards evening, at the hour of the choir, when the shoemaker was working alone, Gabriel, tired of the monotonous silence of the cloister, would go down into the church.

His brother, in a woollen cloak with a white neck band, and a staff as long as an ancient alguacil's, stood as sentry in the crossways, to prevent the inquisitive passing between the choir and the high altar.

Two tablets of old gold with Gothic letters, hung on to one of the pilasters, set forth that anyone talking in a loud voice or making signs in the church would be excommunicated; but this menace of former centuries failed to impress the few people who came to vespers and gossiped behind one of the pillars with some of the church servants. The evening light, filtering through the stained glass, threw on the pavement great patches of colour, and the priests as they walked over this carpet of light would appear green or red according to the colours flashed from the windows.

In the choir the canons sang for themselves only in the emptiness of the church; the shutting of the iron gates of the screen, opened to admit some late-coming priest, echoed like explosions throughout the building, and above the choir the organ joined in at times between the plain song, but it sounded lazily, timidly, as though from necessity, and seemed to lament its feebleness in the gathering twilight.

Gabriel had not completed the round of the Cathedral before he was joined by his nephew, the Perrero, who left his conversation with the servers and acolytes, and with the errand boy belonging to the Secretary of the Chapter, whose fixed seat was at the door of the Chapter-house. Luna was always very much diverted by the pranks of the Tato, and the confidence and carelessness with which he moved about the temple, as though having been born in it deprived him of all feeling of respect The entry of a dog into the nave caused great excitement.

"Uncle," said he to Luna, "you shall see how I can open my cloak."

Seizing the two ends of his garment he advanced towards the dog with the contortions and bounds of a wrestler; the animal, knowing this of old, endeavoured to escape through the nearest door, but the Tato, cutting off his retreat, drove him into the nave, and, pretending to pursue him, drove him from chapel to chapel, finally rounding him up where he could give him some good sound whacks. The dismal howlings disturbed the singing of the canons, and the Tato laughed more than ever to see behind the iron railing of the choir, the angry gesture of the good Esteban threatening him with his wooden staff.

"Uncle," said the depraved Perrero one evening, "you, who think you know the Cathedral so well, have you ever seen the lively things in it?"

The wink of his eye, and the gesture accompanying the words showed that the things might very well be more than lively.

"I am always very much interested," he went on, "with the jokes the ancients allowed themselves. Come along, uncle, it will amuse you for a little; you, like all those who think they know the Cathedral, will have passed many times by these things without noticing them."

61

Going along the outside of the choir, the Tato led Gabriel to the front opposite the door del Perdon. Under the great medallion, which serves as a back to the Mount Tabor, the work of Berruguete, opens the little chapel of the Virgin of the Star. "Look well at that image, uncle. Is there another like it in all the world? She is a courtezan, a siren who would drive men mad if she only fluttered her eyelids."

For Gabriel this was no new discovery; from his childhood he had known that beautiful and sensual figure, with its worldly smile, its rounded outlines, and its eyes with their expression of wanton gaiety as though she were just going to dance.

The child in her arms was also laughing and placing his hand on the bosom of the beautiful woman, as though he intended to tear the covering from her breast. The image of painted stone, stuffed and gilt, wore a blue mantle strewn with stars, from whence its name.

"Even you, who have read so much, uncle, may possibly not know the history of this chapel, which is far more ancient than the Cathedral. The woolstaplers, carders, and weavers of Toledo had their patroness here long before the church was built, and they only gave up their right to the ground on the condition that they should be entire masters of the chapel, and do in it whatever they pleased and in all this piece of the Cathedral as far as those nearest pillars. Oh! the trouble this wrought! On the days they held their feasts to the Virgin they never paid any heed to the canons in the choir, and they greatly disturbed all the offices with 'rabeles,' lutes and disorderly songs. If the canons begged them to be silent, they replied that it was they in the choir who ought to keep silence, considering that they were in their own chapel, which was far more ancient than the Cathedral. Did you know this, uncle?"

"Yes, I remember it now. The Archbishop Valero Loza brought a suit against them at the beginning of the eighteenth century; you can see his tomb at the foot of the altar. He lost his suit, and died from disappointment. He desired to be buried in that place, so that the insolent wool merchants should trample on him in death, even as they had vanquished him in his lifetime. The haughtiness of these ecclesiastical princes drove them to the proudest humility. But is this all you wished to show me?"

"You shall see better things than this. Let us say good-bye to the Virgin. But do look at her! What a face! What alluring eyes! The beautiful woman! I spend hours looking at her; she is my sweetheart. Oh! the many nights I have dreamt of her."

They walked on a little towards the great doorway of the Cathedral, so as to obtain a better view of the exterior face of the choir. Above the three hollows or chapels that pierce it runs a frieze of ancient relievos, the work of some obscure mediaeval artist. Gabriel recognised these coarse sculptures as being contemporaneous with the Puerta del Reloj, and by far the most ancient work in the Cathedral.

"Look you, in the first medallion Adam and Eve are as naked as worms; but the Lord drives them out of Paradise, and they are obliged to dress themselves to appear in the world; and see what they do directly they get their clothes. But look at the fifth medallion on our right hand; the old gossip who cut that had a lively turn of mind."

Gabriel looked for the first time attentively at these forgotten sculptures. They were carved with all the naturalistic simplicity of the Middle Ages, with all the directness with which the artists represented their profane conceptions, with the desire to perpetuate the triumph of the flesh in some ignored corner of the mystical buildings, in order to testify that human life was not dead.

The Tato was delighted at the surprise on his uncle's face.

"Eh! what do you think of that? I discovered it wandering about the church. The canons sing every day on the other side of this wall without ever suspecting what gay doings they have over their heads. And the stained glass, uncle, look at it well. At first so many colours blind one and the forms are indistinct; besides, the lead cuts the figures and it is difficult to make out anything, but I know them to my fingers' ends. They are stories, things of their own times, that these glass-workers painted; the intrigues have been forgotten, and no one has disentangled them."

He pointed to the windows of the second nave, through which the evening light was shining with a ruddy glow.

"Look up there," went on the Perrero. "A gallant in a red cape and sword mounts by a rope ladder; at the window a nun is waiting for him. It seems something like the Don Juan Tenorio that they represent at All Saints'. Further on, you see those two in bed, and people knocking at the door. They must be the same pair of birds with the family surprising them. Then in the next window—look well at it—lovers, with scarcely any clothes beyond bare skin. These things belong to the days when people had no shame, when they went with their heads covered and the rest of their flesh bare."

Gabriel smiled at the whimsical ideas with which ancient art inspired the Perrero.

"But in the choir, uncle, there is also something to see. Let us go there; the service is over and the canons are coming out."

Luna felt overpowered by admiration as he always did on entering the choir. Those magnificent stalls, the work on one side of Philip of Burgundy, and on the other side of Berruguete, bewildered him with their profusion of marbles, jaspers, gildings, statues and medallions. It was the genius of Michael Angelo reviving in the Toledan Cathedral.

The Perrero examined the lower stalls, ferreting out among the Gothic relievos the discoveries enjoyed by his unwholesome curiosity. This first row of stalls, almost on a level with the ground, were occupied by the inferior clergy, and were anterior by half a century to the upper stalls; but in those fifty years art had made a great stride, from the hard and rigid Gothic to the flowing lines and good taste of the Renaissance. They had been carved by Maestre Rodrigo at the time when Christian Spain, roused to enthusiasm, was helping the Catholic kings with all its strength to complete the reconquest. On the backs of the stalls, and on the entablature of the frieze fifty-four carved pictures represented the principal incidents of the conquest of Granada.

The Tato did not look at these carvings of walnut or oak, with troops of horsemen and companies of soldiers scaling the walls of Moorish towns. What interested him most were the arms of the stalls, the handrails of the steps leading to the upper seats, and the salients dividing the stalls which served to rest the head, all covered with animals, grotesque beings, dogs, monkeys, big birds, friars, and little birds, all in difficult postures, some beautiful, some obscene. Hogs and frogs wound themselves up together in inextricable tangles, monkeys with ignoble gestures were mixed up with interlaced birds in never ending variety—it was a world of caricatures of voluptuousness, of monkey-like actions and satirical suggestions, in which appeared carnal passion with the most grotesque animal grimaces.

"Look here, uncle. Is not this capital—it is far the best."

And the Tato showed Gabriel the little chubby figure of a preaching friar with enormous donkey's ears.

When they came out of the choir Gabriel spied the Chapel-master close to the fresco of Saint Christopher. He had just emerged from a little door close to the giant, which led by a circular staircase to the musical archives. He was carrying under his arm a big book with dusty pages which he showed to Gabriel.

"I am taking it upstairs. You shall hear something out of it; it is worth the trouble."

63

And turning his eyes from the book to the little door close by he exclaimed:

"Ay! these archives, Gabriel, how it pains one! Each time I visit them I come out sadder. The vandals have been at work there; nearly all the music books have pages torn out, pieces cut out wherever there was an illuminated letter, a vignette or anything pretty. The señor canons do not care for music, neither do they understand it, and they are incapable of devoting a few pesetas so that it might be heard on festival days. It is quite enough for them to walk in procession to some piece of Rossini's; and as far as regards the organ, all they care about is that it must play slowly, very slowly. The slower it plays, the more religious they think it, even though the organist may be playing a Habanera."

He continued looking at the little door with melancholy eyes as though he were ready to weep over the decay of music.

"In there, Gabriel, are many beautiful works, that ought not to be forgotten as long as art lives in the world. In profane music we have not been great, but believe me that Spain has been far otherwise with religious authors. That is, provided that profane music and religious music really exist, which I doubt; for me there is only—music—and I think he will be a clever man who draws the line where one ends and where the other begins. Behind this wall of Saint Christopher's, the works of all the great Spanish musicians sleep, mutilated and covered with dust. Perhaps it is better they do sleep, when you hear what is sung in this choir! Here you will find Christobal Morales, who three hundred years ago was Chapel-master here, and began the reform of music twenty years before Palestrina. In Rome he shares the glory with the famous master; his portrait is in the Vatican, and his lamentations, his motets, and his Magnificat rest here, forgotten for centuries. And Victoria? Do you know him? Another of the same period; his jealous contemporaries called him 'Palestrina's monkey' taking all his works to be imitations, in consequence of his long sojourn in Rome; but, believe me, instead of being plagiarisms from the Italian, they are far superior. Here also is Rivera, a Toledan master who no one remembers, but in the archives there is a whole volume of his masses, and Romero de Avila, who more than anyone had studied the Muzarabé chants, and Ramos de Pareja, not the least musician of the fifteenth century, who wrote in Bologna his book 'De Musica Tractatus,' and destroyed the ancient system of Guido de Arezzo, discovering the tonality of sound; and the Monk Urena, who added the note 'si' to the scale, and Javier Garcia, who in the last century reformed music, leading it towards Italy (God forgive him!), a beaten track from which we have not yet emerged; and Nebra, the great organist of Carlos III., who, a century before Wagner was born, used musical discords. When he wrote the Requiem for the funeral of Dona Barbara di Braganza, foreseeing the surprise and difficulties that the musicians and singers would meet with in the innovations in his score, he wrote on the margin, 'This is to give notice that there are no mistakes in the score.' His Litany became so celebrated that it was forbidden to copy it, under pain of excommunication; but I think to-day the persons who remember it would be the excommunicated. Believe me, Gabriel, these archives are a pantheon of great men, but a pantheon, unluckily, from which no one emerges."

Then he added, lowering his voice:

"The Church has never been a great lover of music. To feel and understand it you must be born a musician, and you know well enough that these gentlemen who are paid to sing in the choir know nothing about music. When I see you, Gabriel, smiling at religious things, I guess by your manner how much you conceal, and I am sure you are right. I was interested to know the history of music in the Church. I have followed step by step the long Calvary of this unhappy art, carrying the cross of worship uphill through the long centuries. You have heard people often talk of religious music, as if it were a thing apart, believed in by the Church; but it is all a lie, for religious music does not exist."

64

The Perrero had moved off when he heard that the Chapel-master, whose loquacity was indefatigable when he spoke of his art, had started on the theme of music. He had formed his own opinion of Don Luis and told it to everyone in the upper cloister. He was a simpleton who only knew how to play melancholy ditties on his harmonium, without ever thinking of enlivening the poor people in the Claverias by playing something to which they could dance, as the niece of Silver Stick had asked him.

The priest and Gabriel walked slowly through the silent naves talking the while; the only people to be seen were a group of the household at the door of the sacristy, and two women kneeling before the railing of the high altar praying aloud. The early twilight of the winter evenings was beginning to darken the Cathedral, and the first bats were coming down from the vaulting and fluttering through the columns.

"Ecclesiastical music," said the artist, "is a real anarchy; but in the Church everything is anarchy. I believe there is a great deal to be said for the unity of the Catholic worship throughout the world. When Christianity began to form itself into a religion it did not invent even a single bad melody; it borrowed its hymns and the manner of singing them from the Jews, a primitive and barbarous music that would shock our ears if we heard it now. Out of Palestine, and where there were no Jews, the earliest Christian poets—Saint Ambrose, Prudencio and others—adopted their new hymns and psalms to the popular songs that were then in vogue in the Roman world, or possibly to Greek music. It seems as though that word 'Greek music' ought to mean a great deal; is it not so, Gabriel? The Greeks were so great in their poetry and in the plastic arts that anything that bears their name would seem to be surrounded by an atmosphere of undying beauty. But it is not so: the march of the arts has not been parallel in human life; when sculpture had its Phidias, and had reached its climax, painting had hardly passed that rudimentary stage that we see in Pompeii, and music was only a childish babbling. Writing could not perpetuate music, for there seemed as many musical styles as there were peoples, and everything was left to the judgment of the executant. You could not fix on parchment what mouths and instruments played, and so progress was impossible. For this reason, though there was a Renaissance for sculpture, for painting, for architecture, at the revival of the arts after the Middle Ages, music was found in the same elementary stage in which it was at the break-up of the ancient world."

Gabriel nodded his head assenting to the words of the Chapel-master.

"This was the first Christian music," continued Don Luis. "Confided to tradition and transmitted orally, the religious songs soon became disfigured and corrupt. In every church they sang in a different way, and religious music became a hotch-potch. The mystics leaned to rigid unity, and in the sixth century Saint Gregory published his 'Antifonario,' a collection of all liturgic melodies, purifying them according to his ideas. They were a mixture of two elements: the Greek, rather oriental and florid, very much like the present debased style; and the grave and rough Roman. The notes were expressed by letters, the Phrygian and Lydian styles followed, and so the intricacies of Greek music continued though much altered, with fioriture, rests, and breathing pauses. The collection became lost, and many who think a return to the old style would be best, much regret it. To judge by the fragments that remain, if such music was now executed it would have very little that was religious about it, as we understand religion in art to-day; it would more resemble the songs of the Moors, or the Chinese, or those of some schismatic Greeks who still use the ancient liturgies. The harp was the principal instrument in the churches till the organ appeared in the tenth century, a rough and barbarous instrument that had to be played with blows, and was supplied with wind from inflated skins. Guido di Arezzo made a musical rule on the basis of Gregory's collection, and this was sufficient for the invention of the pentagramma to be assigned to the Benedictine. They continued to use the letters of Boccio and Saint Gregory as notes, but they placed them on lines of three different colours. The imbroglio continued; to learn music badly took twelve years, and then they could not manage that singers from different towns could read from the same score. Saint Bernard, dry and austere as his times, ridiculed this music as not being solemn enough; he was a man antagonistic to all art; he would have liked to see the churches dismantled and without any architectural adornments; and the slower the music was, the better it seemed to him. He was the father of plain song, and he maintained that the more drawn out the music was, the more religious it became. But in the thirteenth century Christians found this chant most wearisome. The cathedrals in those days were the point of attraction: the theatre, the centre of all life. People went to the church to pray to God and to amuse themselves, forgetting for the moment all the wars and the violence and confusion outside. Once again popular music came into the churches, and you could hear intoned in the cathedrals all the songs most in vogue, and which were often obscene. The people took part in the religious music, singing in different tones, each one as seemed best to him, and these were the first beginnings of concerted singing. In those days religion was joyful, popular—democratic as you would say, Gabriel; there was no Inquisition, nor suspicion of heresy to embitter the soul with fanaticism and fear. All the coarse wind and stringed instruments that the artisans had in the towns, or the labourers in the fields, came into the churches, and the organ was accompanied by violas, violins, bagpipes, flutes, guitars and lutes. The plain song was the established liturgy almost throughout Europe; but the people disliked it, and interspersed it with songs, and at the great festivals, religious hymns were sung, adapted to the popular melodies then in fashion, such as 'The song of the armed man,' 'Morencia, give me a kiss,' 'I know not what confuses me,' 'Weep for me, lady,' 'Bad luck to him who married you,' and others in the same style. And Rome, you will ask, and the Church? What did it say about such disorders? The Church lived without artistic perception: it never had any. What are the boundaries between religious and profane music? From the sixteenth to the seventeenth century all critics have asked themselves this question, but the Church let them talk, accepting everything without remark. Now and again Rome made itself heard by a Papal bull, to which no one paid any attention, because the Pontiff was incapable of saying this is religious art, and the other is profane. Palestrina was entrusted with the task of reforming church music; the Pope showed himself disposed not to leave anything but plain song, and to suppress even that if necessary. The mass of Papa Marcelo and other melodies was the result of this, but things did not advance much. It was necessary in order that music should be purified inside the Church that the great secular musical movement should begin with the Italian Monteverde, with the Frenchman Rameau, and with the Germans Sebastian Bach and Handel; what splendid times, Gabriel! And just think what genius followed: Gluck, Haydn, Mozart, Mehül, Boieldieu, and, above all, our good friend Beethoven."

The Chapel-master was silent for a little as though the name of his idol imposed on him a religious silence. Presently he continued.

"All this avalanche of art passed over the Church, and she, according to her habit, appropriated everything that was most to her taste; in any country the Catholic religion adopted the music most in accordance with its traditions—in Spain we have been saturated with the Italian style since the days of Palestrina, and German or French music never came to us. We were first of all fuguists and contrapuntists; but after the 'Stabat Mater' of Rossini we felt the attraction of theatrical melody so strongly that we have never wished to taste a fresh dish. Religious music in Spain has run parallel with Italian opera, a thing of which the canons are ignorant; they would be furious if at the mass you played them anything by Beethoven, which they would consider profane, but they listen with mystic unction to fragments which have gone the round of all the theatres in Italy.

And about the plain song, you will ask? The plain song had its nest in this Primacy. It was preserved here for centuries and purified; all the best was collected in Toledo, and from the books in this Cathedral have gone forth the chorales of all the churches in Spain and America. Poor plain song! it has long been dead. You see for yourself, Gabriel, who comes to the Cathedral at the hour of the choir? No one, absolutely no one. The matins are recited, and all the offices are intoned in the midst of perfect solitude. The people who still believe know nothing of the liturgy; they do not prize it and have forgotten all about it; they are only attracted by the novenas, the triduos and retreats, all that is termed tolerated and extra-liturgic worship. The Jesuits, with their cunning, guessed that they must give their services a theatrical attraction, and for this reason their churches—gilt, carpeted, and decked with flowers like dressing-rooms—are always full, whereas the old cathedrals are as empty as tombs. They have not proclaimed the necessity for this reform aloud, but they have put it into practice by abolishing the singing in Latin, and substituting all sorts of romances and songs. In the churches, with the exception of the Tantum-ergo, nothing is sung in Latin, sermons and hymns are in the language of the country, just as in a Protestant church. For the mass of devout people, who believe without thinking, religions only differ in their exterior forms. It would be impossible to consign such a multitude to the bonfires, or that half Europe should again be in the clutches of the thirty years' war, or that the Popes should launch excommunication after excommunication, only to find in the end that the only difference between a Catholic or an evangelical church is a few images and a few wax tapers, but that the worship in both is the same. But we must go, Gabriel; they are going to lock up."

The bell-ringer was hurrying through the naves, shaking his bunch of keys and startling the bats which were becoming more and more numerous. The two devout women had disappeared; no one remained in the Cathedral save Gabriel and the Chapel-master. From the farther end of the nave were coming the night watchmen, to take up their charge till the following morning, preceded by the dog.

The two friends went out into the cloister, guided through the dusk by the rich glow from the stained glass windows; outside, the last rays of the sun were touching both the garden and the cloister of the Claverias with crimson.

"I repeat," continued the musical priest, looking back at the door from which they had come out, "that in there they do not love music and they do not understand it. The Church has only rendered one service to music, and that without wishing it: they have been obliged to have instrumentalists and vocalists for the services, and that made them support the chapels and choir-schools that have served for musical education in default of schools. We who represent art in the cathedrals are as much despised as were the minstrels in the old chapels, players of the clarion and bassoon. For the canons, all that sleeps in the musical archives is so much Greek, and we, the artistic priests, form a race apart, and are only just a step above the sacristans. The Chapel-master, the organist, the tenor, contralto, and the bass form the chapel. We are clergy like the canons, we become beneficiaries by appointment, we have studied religious science as they have, and, moreover, we are musicians; but in spite of this we receive less than half the salary of a canon, and to remind us constantly of our inferior position we have to sit in the lower stalls. We, the only ones in the choir who know anything about music, have to occupy the lowest places. The precentor is by right the chief of the singers, and the precentor is a canon named by Rome without competition, probably not knowing a note of the pentagramma. Oh! the anarchy, friend Gabriel! Oh! the contempt of the Church for music which has always been its slave and never its daughter! In many convents of nuns the organist and the singers are despised and called sergeants. There seems money for everything in the Church: the revenues of the building are ample for everything except for music. The canons look upon us as fools masking in ecclesiastical robes. When the feast of Corpus or that of the Virgin of the Sagrario comes round, and I dream of a fine mass worthy of the Cathedral, the Canon Obrero attacks me and begs for something Italian and simple, an affair of half-a-dozen musicians that I must pick up in the town, and then I have to conduct a few bungling musicians, raging to hear how the miserable orchestra sounds under these vaults, which were built for something grander. In the end, friend Luna, it is dead, quite dead."

The complaint of the Chapel-master did not surprise Gabriel. Everyone in the Cathedral complained of the miserable and sordid way in which the services were conducted. Some, like the Silver Stick, declared that it was due to the impiety of the age, others, like the musician, made that same religion responsible, but they did not dare to say so aloud. Respect to the Church and to the higher powers, instilled since their childhood, kept the population of the Cathedral silent. The greater part of the servitors of the Church were living morally in the sixteenth century, in an atmosphere of servility and superstitious fear of their superiors, feeling the injustice of their position, but without daring to give form, even in their thoughts, to their vague notions of protest.

Only at night, in the silence of the upper cloister, in the privacy of those families who were born and died among the stones of the Cathedral, did they dare to repeat the murmurs of the Church, the interminable tangle of tattle which grew over the monotonous ecclesiastical existence, the complaints of the canons against His Eminence, and what the cardinal said about the Chapter, an underground war which was reproduced at every archiepiscopal elevation, intrigues and heart-burnings of celibates, embittered by ambition and favouritism, primitive hatreds that reminded one of the time when the clergy elected their own prelates and ruled over them, instead of groaning as now under the iron rule of the archbishop's will.

Everyone in the cloister knew of these quarrels, and the remarks that the canons allowed themselves to make in the sacristy reached their ears; but these humble servitors kept silence when these murmurs were repeated in their presence, fearing to be reported by their neighbour, who possibly might covet their post. It was the terror of the Inquisition still alive amidst this little stagnant world.

The Perrero was the only one who seemed to have no fear, and who spoke openly about the Chapter and the cardinal. What did it matter to him! Possibly he may have wished to be turned out of "that den" to give himself up to his favourite pursuit, going to the bull-ring without any objections from the household. Moreover, he delighted in speaking evil of the gentlemen of the Chapter, who had given him more than one cuff when he was an acolyte.

He gave nicknames to all the canons, and pointing them out one by one to Gabriel, related the most intimate secrets of their lives. He knew the houses where each prebendary passed the evening after the choir time, and the names of all the ladies and nuns who crimped their surplices, and could tell of the fierce and deadly rivalries between these admirers of the Chapter, endeavouring to vanquish each other by the exquisite way in which they washed and ironed the canonical batiste. As the choir were coming out he pointed out the precentor, an obese prebendary with his face covered with red spots.

"Look at him, uncle," he said to Gabriel, "that rash on his face is a record of the past. He was a great gallant, never fixing himself long anywhere. The other evening he said to a chaplain of the chapel of the kings, 'Those captain professors at the Academy think that in point of women they cull the best in Toledo, but where is the Church! The seculars must lower their flag!'"

He laughed as he pointed out a group of young priests, carefully shaved, with their cheeks blue and shining, dressed in silk mantles that diffused a strong scent of musk as they moved. These were the dandies of the Chapter, the young canons, who often made journeys to Madrid to confess their patronesses—ancient marchionesses who, by dint of influence, had gained for them a seat in the choir. At the Puerta del Mollete they stopped a few moments to arrange the folds of their cloaks before they went into the street.

"They are going out to court the ladies," said the Tato. "Brrrum! make way for Don Juan Tenorio!"

When they had watched all the canons come out, the Perrero spoke to his uncle about the cardinal.

"In these days he is given over to the fiends. No one in the palace can manage him; his internal complaint nearly drives him mad."

"But is it true he is so very ill?" asked Gabriel.

"Everyone says so; ask your Aunt Tomasa. They say they are such great friends because she makes a lotion that calms him like an angel's hand. In the morning when he wakes in a bad temper all the palace trembles, and very soon all the diocese. He is a good man, but when the mad dog bites him everyone must fly. I have seen him on pontifical days wearing his mitre, looking at us with such eyes, as though he were ready to seize his crozier and belabour us all with it, from what the aunt says—if he did not drink!"

"Then the complaints of the Chapter are true."

"He does not get drunk. No, señor, give the devil his due, but a glass now, and another presently, and a third if a friend comes to see him, must obfuscate him. It is a habit he brought with him from Andalusia, where he was bishop before coming here. But nothing common, a fine and refreshing drink, only to keep up his strength, nothing more. And the wine is first class, uncle; I know it from one of his household. He gives as much as fifty duros the arroba! They keep him the best in all la Mancha, a vintage from the time of the French, a syrup that warms the stomach and tempers it as though it were an organ. From what the Aunt Tomasa says, the doctors patch him up, and then he does his best to get ill again with this glorious wine."

The Tato, in the midst of his cynical mockery, still showed a regard for the prelate.

"Do not believe, uncle, that he is a nonentity. Apart from his bad temper he is really a strong man, even as you see him here, with his small white and shining head like a baby's, that seems even smaller above his immense corporation; but it carries something in it! He has spoken a great deal in Madrid, and all the newspapers took as much notice of him as though he were Guerra. His wisdom finds a remedy for everything. If they speak of the poverty and misery in the world, he sings the old song: bread for the poor, charity from the rich, and much Christian doctrine for everyone; that men ought not to quarrel because I have more than you, and there ought to be patience and decency in the world, for that is what is wanting. What nonsense, eh, uncle? You laugh at it? But His Eminence's recipe rather pleases me, especially that about the bread; but the cursed Catechism is in fault as we have all learnt from our childhood."

The Perrero grew quite excited speaking about his prince:

"And as a man? A masterful man; no hypocrisy about him, nor hiding his head. Everyone knows he was a soldier in his younger days. The Aunt Tomasa remembers seeing him in the cloister with his helmet with horse-hair crest, his sergeant's epaulets, and his rattling broad sword. He is not afraid of anything, is not easily scandalised, and does not make a fuss about things. Last year a Portuguese lady arrived here, who nearly drove all the cadets out of their senses with her silk stockings and her big hats. You know Juanito, and you are aware that he is the son of a nephew of His Eminence who died some years ago. Well, the youngster paraded up and down the Zocodover in his uniform with the Portuguese lady on his arm to arouse the jealousy of his companions in the Academy. One day the young woman presented herself at the palace, and the servants, seeing her so beautifully dressed, made no difficulty about letting her in, thinking she was some lady from Madrid. His Eminence received her with a paternal smile, and listened to her without winking. A friend of mine, one of the pages who was present, told me about it. She came to complain to the cardinal that his nephew, the cadet, had entertained her for two days without giving her a farthing. His Eminence smiled modestly: 'Lady, the Church is poor, but I do not wish that for this misfortune the good name of the family should suffer. Take this and it will be remedied,' and he handed her two duros. The Portuguese, encouraged by her good reception, began to bawl and complain, thinking she would terrify Don Sebastian by making a scandal. But you should have seen the fury of His Eminence as he shouted to the page, 'Boy, call the police'; and the look on his face was such that the Portuguese lady vanished as quickly as she could, leaving the two pieces of silver on the table."

Gabriel laughed, listening to the story.

"He is a strong man, believe me, uncle. I like him because he holds the Chapter in his fist. He is not like his predecessor, who was like a sop in milk, who only knew how to pray, and trembled before the last-made canon. He is quite capable of going down into the choir one evening and turning them all out with blows from his crozier. It is more than two months since he has been down into the Cathedral, neither has he seen the canons. The last time they sent a deputation to the palace everybody trembled. They went to propose I know not what reform to the Primate, and they began by saying, 'My lord, the Chapter thinks—.' Don Sebastian, turned into a basilisk, interrupted them, 'The Chapter cannot think anything; the Chapter has not common sense,' and he turned his back, leaving them petrified. Afterwards, he began shouting, and thumping the furniture with his fists, saying he would fill all the vacancies in the Cathedral with the dregs of the clergy, that he would fill the Chapter with drunkards, with impostors, etc. 'I will harass the Chapter,' he shouted, 'I will dirty it; I will teach them to talk less of me; I will cover them, yes, sir, I will cover them with....' And you may guess, uncle, with what His Eminence wished to cover the canons. And the poor man was right. Why should those in the choir interfere with this way or that way that Don Sebastian lives, or if he has those bonds or others? Does not he let them live as they choose? Does he ever say a word to them about their scandalous visits, although all Toledo knows of them?"

"And what do the canons say about the cardinal?"

"They say Juanito is his grandson, and that his father, who died, and who passed as nephew of His Eminence, was really his son by a certain lady when he was bishop in Andalusia. But this does not seem to irritate Don Sebastian much; but what does irritate him and makes him behave like a fiend is when they speak of Doña Visitacion."

"And who is that lady?"

"Come, that is good! You do not know Doña Visitacion? When no one inside the Cathedral or out of it can speak of anybody else? She is the niece of Don Sebastian, who lives with him in the palace. It is she who rules everything, and Don Sebastian, who is so terrible with everyone else, becomes like an angel when he sees her. He rages and screams and bites the days when he is ill, but if Doña Visita appears, he controls himself at once; he suffers in silence, moans like a child, and it is sufficient for her to say a soft word, or give him a caress for His Eminence to slobber with delight. He loves her dearly."

"But what is she?" asked Gabriel with interest.

"Clearly she is what you think. What else could she be? She was from her childhood in the college for noble ladies, and as soon as the cardinal came to Toledo he took her out, and brought her to the palace. What a blind infatuation is Don Sebastian's! And the thing is, the object is hardly worth it—a very thin, pale little girl, with large eyes and a soft skin; that is all. They say she sings, and plays the piano, and reads and knows a great many things that they teach in that wealthy college, and by God's grace can keep His Eminence in order. She comes sometimes into the Cathedral by the arch, dressed as a beatita with the habit and mantilla, accompanied by a very ugly servant."

"She cannot be what you think, youngster."

"Go on; all the Chapter affirm it, and even the most steady canons thoroughly believe it. Even those who are friends and favourites of His Eminence, and carry him tales about all the grumbling against him, do not deny it with any warmth. And Don Sebastian gets angry, and is furious each time any murmurs about this reach his ears. If they told him the choir intended to give a dance he would be less irritated than when he hears them wag their tongues about Doña Visita."

The Perrero was silent for a few moments as though he were doubtful about saying something serious.

"The lady is very good and kind. They all love her in the palace because she speaks so gently. Besides, she makes use of the great power she has over the cardinal to prevent the violence of His Eminence, who very often, when he is racked with excessive pain, would throw cups and plates at the heads of his servants. Why should they interfere with her? Does she do them any harm? Let everyone do as he likes in his own house, and he who does evil, let God punish him."

He scratched his head as though he were once more doubtful.

"And as to what Doña Visita is to the Cardinal," he added, "I have no doubt whatever. I have facts to go on, uncle, and I know how they live. One of the servants has often seen them kissing—that is to say, not the two kissing. No, she does the kissing, and Don Sebastian receives her kittenish ways with the smile of an angel. The poor man is so old!"

And the Tato ended his confidences with various indecent remarks.

All this grumbling against the cardinal, that came from the sacristy up to the cloister, annoyed Gabriel's brother greatly. The "Wooden Staff," who was a staunch private soldier of the Church, could not bear to hear with equanimity those attacks on his superiors; in his opinion they were all calumnies. The canons had spoken of all the preceding archbishops precisely as they now spoke of Don Sebastian, but this did not in the least prevent their all being called saints after their deaths. When he discovered the Tato repeating in the Claverias all the gossip from down below, he threatened him with all his authority as head of the house.

Esteban was also very much concerned at the state of his brother's health. He was pleased at the very prudent behaviour of the latter, who conformed with silent respect to all the customs of the Cathedral, never permitting a word to escape him that could reveal his past; he felt beyond measure proud of the atmosphere of admiration that surrounded his brother, and the attention with which the simple inhabitants of the cloister listened to the account of his travels, but the state of his health was a continual anxiety, the certainty that death had laid its hand upon him, and that it was solely the care with which he was surrounded that retarded the fatal moment.

There were days in which the Silenciario smiled with pleasure, seeing Gabriel a better colour, and hearing less frequently his painful cough.

"You are going on well, brother," he would say joyfully.

"Yes," replied Gabriel, "but do not have any illusions. *That* will come at its own hour, it has me in its grasp. It is only you who are holding it back, but one day it will be stronger than you."

The certainty that death would at last be victorious made Esteban redouble his efforts. He thought that frequent nourishment was the only remedy, and he scarcely ever approached Gabriel without something in his hands.

"Eat this. Drink what I bring you."

He struggled valiantly with that broken constitution, with that stomach disordered by poverty, with those lacerated lungs and with that heart subject to constant disturbance of its functions, with that human machine dislocated by a life of suffering and trials.

The constant watching over the sick man had upset Esteban's economic life; his miserable wages and the poor assistance the Chapel-master could give were insufficient even for that extra mouth, which consumed more than all the others in the household put together. At the end of the month Esteban was obliged to invoke the aid of Silver Stick to enable him to get along the last few days, entering thus into the humble and miserable flock bound by the priest's usury. Sometimes the Chapel-master, waking for an instant to reality, would give him a few pesetas, sacrificing the joy of obtaining a fresh score.

Gabriel guessed the privations that his brother underwent, and was anxious to contribute to the expenses of the little household. But what work could he obtain in his concealment in the Cathedral? He wished for some post in the service of the church, in order to receive at the beginning of every month a few pesetas from the hands of Silver Stick; but all the posts were occupied, death alone could cause a vacancy, and there were many eager ones watching for the opportunity to urge their family claims.

The impossibility of being useful to his brother, of helping to make his sacrifices less expensive, weighed heavily on Gabriel, and disturbed the otherwise placid monotony of his life. He inquired of Esteban as to what he could possibly do, not to remain inactive, but his brother always answered with his kindly expression: "Take care of yourself, only take care of yourself; you have no other duty but to look after your own health, I am here to do all the rest."

When Holy Week came round Gabriel found an opportunity of getting a few days' work. They were going to put up in the Cathedral the famous "Monument" between the choir and the Puerta del Perdon. It was a heavy and complicated erection, of a sumptuous and rococo style, which had cost the second Cardinal de Bourbon a fortune at the beginning of last century. A real forest of woodwork formed the basis of the monument; the riches of the cardinal had created a prodigality of solidity and sumptuousness, and several days were required to fit together the Holy Catafalque, and not a few workmen.

Gabriel interviewed Don Antolin asking for a place on the works. The wages were seven reals a day, which he would be able to give his brother for two weeks; and he, who had been used in former days to have his work so lavishly paid, accepted this small daily wage as a piece of unexpected good fortune.

The "Wooden Staff" was indignant. Gabriel was ill and ought not to risk his poor health in the fatigues of this work. What was he going to do, coughing and suffocating every moment? How was he going to undertake the heavy work of carrying the framework and fixing it together? The invalid tranquillised him. He knew what those works were in the church; everything was done with parsimony, but without much regard to time. The workmen in the service of the church worked with that calm laziness, and that slow prudence which characterised every act of religion. Besides, Silver Stick, knowing his condition, would reserve the least heavy work for him; he could fix screws and bolts, place the candelabra in line on the steps, and arrange the tapestry; he trusted him as a man of good taste who had seen much in his travels.

Gabriel worked for two weeks on the monument. This time of relative activity seemed to give him a certain amount of relief. He moved about, intent on giving orders to his fellow-workers; he went from the church to the top of the Claverias, where the monument was stored, and seeing himself covered with dust, and with his limbs fatigued by the constant coming and going, he deluded himself into thinking he was strong again.

During these two weeks he never went to the shoemaker's house, and so lost sight of his various friends. The bell-ringer and his friends were lost in astonishment. A man of so much learning, to work like one of themselves in order to help his brother!

The Señora Tomasa stopped him one morning by the iron railing of the garden.

"I have news, Gabriel. I think I know where our child is. I won't say any more; but be ready to help me. The day when you least expect it you may see her in the Cathedral."

The erection of the monument was finished. All that part of the church between the choir and the door del Perdon was occupied by this showy and ponderous fabric. According to their traditional custom all the Toledans gathered to admire—the steps covered with rows of burning lights, the Roman legionaries in alabaster leaning on their lances, and the rich curtain with its innumerable folds that hung from the vaulting down to the platform of the monument.

On the evening of Holy Thursday Gabriel stood considering what was in some sense his work, surrounded by a group of worshippers. The Cathedral shone with its immaculate whiteness, in spite of the black veils that covered both statues and altars. The clouds of colour from the lovely rose windows relieved the funereal aspect of the religious ceremony, while from the choir a tenor voice intoned the lamentations of the oriental prophet.

Gabriel felt someone pulling his jacket, and turning, saw the gardener's widow.

"Come, nephew, we have got her here; she is waiting for you in the cloister."

Coming out, the Señora Tomasa pointed to a woman sitting crouched on the stone coping of the garden, wrapped in an old cloak, and with the headkerchief drawn down over her eyes.

Gabriel would never have recognised her. He remembered the pretty smiling face of former years, and he looked almost with horror at the tarnished youth, haggard with prominent cheek-bones, of the face before him. The eyes deep sunk in the sockets without eyebrows or eyelashes, with the pupils still beautiful, but dulled with a glassy opacity. Everything about her revealed poverty and desolation; the dress was a summer one, and from under it showed her split boots much too large for her feet.

"Salute him, child," said the old woman. "It is your Uncle Gabriel, one of God's angels, in spite of his misfortunes, and you owe it to him that we searched for you."

The gardener's widow pushed Sagrario towards her Uncle, but the young woman lowered her head, moved her shoulders and drew back, as though she could not endure the presence of a member of her family; she covered her face with her wretched cloak to hide her tears.

"Aunt, let us go home," said Gabriel, "it is not good for the child to be here."

At the cloister staircase they made the young woman pass on in front; she went up with her head bent and without looking, as though her feet trod those broken steps instinctively.

"We arrived from Madrid this morning," said the gardener's widow as they went up. "I kept her at an inn till it was time to bring her to the Cathedral in the evening. It is the best time, for Esteban is in the choir, and you will have time to settle things here. I spent three days there. Ay, Gabriel, my son, what things I have seen, what hells there are for poor women! and we call ourselves Christians, but I think we are fiends! Mercifully I had friends at court—some old bell-ringers who had been in the Cathedral and who remembered the gardener's widow. I wanted everything, even money, to get this unhappy girl out of the devil's clutches."

73

The upper cloister was quite deserted. On arriving at the door of the Lunas the girl seemed to wake up, and drew quickly back with a look of terror, as though inside the "habitation" some great danger was awaiting her.

"Go in, woman, go in," said the aunt; "it is your home. You had to come back some time or other."

And she pushed her till she was through the door. Once inside the sitting-room her tears ceased; she looked round with astonishment, no doubt surprised at finding herself there. Her eyes examined everything with a sort of stupefaction, as though marvelling that everything should be in the same place as five years before, and with an exactitude that made her doubt if such a long time had really elapsed. Nothing seemed changed in that little world under the shadow of the Cathedral. She only, who had left it in the bloom of her youth, now returned aged and broken.

There was a long silence between the three people.

"Your room, Sagrario," said Gabriel at last gently, "is the same as when you left it. Go in and do not come out till I call you. Be calm and do not cry; trust me. You do not know me well, but the aunt will have told you that I am interested in your fate. Your father will soon be coming; hide yourself and be silent. I repeat it again, do not come out till I call you."

When the old woman and her nephew were alone they could hear the girl's suffocating sobs that burst out on seeing her old room. Afterwards they heard a sound as though she were throwing herself on the bed, and the violence of her grief seemed to become more and more uncontrolled.

"Poor child!" said the old woman, who was very nearly crying also, "she is good, and she has repented of her sins; if only her father had sought her out when that rascal deserted her, what shame and misery it would have spared her. And her health? I really think she is worse than you are, Gabriel. Oh, those men! with their honour which is nothing more than lies! What is honourable is to be charitable and compassionate to others, and to harm no one. I said this the other day when I was shocked at the shamelessness of my son-in-law, who was furious at my going to Madrid to find the child. He spoke of the honour of the family, and that if Sagrario returned no decent people could live in the Cathedral, and that he could not allow his daughter to stand at the door; and he such a thief that he steals the Virgin's wax every day, and deceives the devout who pay him for masses that are never said; that is why his skin shines so and he is so fat. With so much honour."

After a short silence the old woman looked undecidedly at Gabriel.

"Well, shall we begin the struggle? Shall I call Esteban?"

"Yes, call him, he will be in the Cathedral. And you, shall you dare to be present at the interview?"

"No, son, manage it yourself. You know Esteban, and you know me. I should either begin to cry, or I should turn and rend him for his obstinacy. You will manage better by yourself, for this God has given you those talents that you have used so badly."

The old woman went away, and Gabriel remained alone for more than half an hour, looking out of a window into the deserted cloister. The yearly commemoration of the death of God spread in the priestly tribe on the roofs, an atmosphere of sadness even more marked than that inside the church. All the women and children of the Claverias were down below admiring the monument, the "habitacions" seemed quite deserted. As he sat Gabriel saw his brother pass by the window, and in another moment he appeared at the door.

"What do you want, Gabriel? What has happened to you? The aunt frightened me with her summons. Are you worse?"

"Sit down, Esteban. I am well, calm yourself."

The "Wooden Staff" looked with surprise at Gabriel; his strange seriousness alarmed him and the prolonged silence in which he appeared to be arranging his thoughts without knowing where to begin.

"Speak, man! Do make a beginning; you alarm me."

"Brother," said Gabriel gravely, "you know very well that I have respected the mystery in your life that I found on my return here. You said to me, 'My daughter is dead,' and you never showed any wish to speak of her, and you can say if I have ever touched your old wound by the slightest allusion."

"Well, and what then? When are you going to stop?" said Esteban, becoming very gloomy; "why do you speak to me on a day so holy of things that cause me so much pain?"

"Esteban, we shall never understand each other if you hold on to your prejudices. Do not make that gesture, but listen to me calmly; do not act like an automaton, pulled by the same wires that moved our grandfathers and our ancestors. Be a man, and act according to your own thoughts. You and I have different beliefs. Setting aside religion which I know is a consolation to you, you know that I am silent as to mine, so as not to render my life here impossible. But apart from this, you believe that the family is a work of God, an institution of supernatural origin. I believe it to be a human institution based on the necessities of the species. You condemn for ever anyone who betrays the laws of the family, or who deserts his banner, you sentence him to death and oblivion. I pity his weakness and forgive. We understand honour from a different point of view. You believe in the Castillian honour—that traditional and barbarous honour, more cruel and dismal even than dishonour; a theatrical honour, whose impulses are never founded on human feeling, but on the fear of what others will say, the desire to appear greater and more dignified in the eyes of others than to your own conscience. For the adulterous wife, death; for the murderer, revenge; for the fugitive daughter, contempt and forgetfulness; this is your gospel. I have another standard; for the wife who forgets her duties, contempt and oblivion; for that fragment of our own flesh who flies from us, love, support, gentleness, even endeavouring to compass her return to us. Esteban, we are separated by our beliefs, the gulf of centuries lies between us, but you are my brother, we love each other, and I only desire your good. I bear the same name of which you are so proud, and I loved our poor parents as much as you could love them, and in the name of all these I tell you that this situation must come to an end; you must not live insensible and frozen in what you call your dignity, without the remembrance of your daughter wandering about the world, troubling you. You, who are so kind, who have sheltered me in the most difficult crisis of my life, how can you sleep, how can you eat, without your life being embittered by the remembrance of your lost daughter? What do you know about her now? May she not be dying of hunger while you eat? May she not be lying in a hospital while you are living in the home of your fathers?"

Esteban's brow contracted, and he wore his gloomiest look as he listened to his brother.

"It is useless for you to strive, Gabriel, nothing can come of it. Have I denied you anything? Am I not ready to do anything for my brother? But do not speak to me of that; she has caused me much pain, she has broken my life, how I did not die, I know not. Have you thought well that for centuries the family of the Lunas have been the mirror of the Cathedral, respected by even the archbishops, and now, suddenly to find oneself among the lowest, exposed to the ridicule of all and looked upon with compassion by the veriest little acolyte! What I have suffered! The times I have wept with rage alone in this home, hearing what they were saying behind my back. And then," he added quietly as though grief were paralysing his voice, "there was that unhappy martyr who died of shame; my poor wife who left the world so as not to see my grief and the contempt of others! And do you wish me to forget all this? For the rest, Gabriel, I cannot express what I feel as well as you do. But honour—is honour. It is to live in my house without fear of being shamed, to sleep at night without fearing to see in the darkness our father's eyes, asking why I allow a lost woman to live under the same roof that the Lunas won for themselves by centuries of service to the house of God; it is to avoid people mocking at our family. Let them say, 'Those Lunas! how unfortunate they are,' but they shall never say the Lunas are a family wanting in shame. By our love, brother, leave me; do not speak to me of this. Those evil doctrines have poisoned your mind; not only have you ceased to believe in God, but you have ceased to believe in honour."

"And what is all this?" said Gabriel, warming. "You yourself do not know. 'Honour is honour.' Well, I say, children are children. You, man of prejudices, you do not wait to consider that those beings are the continuation of our own existence. Your religion makes you think children are a fruit from God, nevertheless you think yourself better and more perfect when you reject and curse those gifts of Heaven if they cause you any trouble. No, Esteban, the love of children and pity for their faults ought to come before all prejudices. This eternal life of the soul, that lying promise of religion, is only true through our children. The soul dies with the body; it is no more than a manifestation of our own thoughts, and thought is a cerebral function, but children perpetuate our own being throughout the generations and the centuries; it is they who make us immortal, and that preserve and transmit something of our personality, even as we have inherited something from our ancestors. He who forgets those beings who are his own creation is more worthy of execration than he who leaves life by suicide. The disappointments of life, the laws and customs invented by men, what are they before the instinctive affection we feel for beings that have proceeded from ourselves, and who perpetuate the infinite variety of our habits and thoughts? I abhor those wretches who, in order not to disturb the commonplace peace of matrimony, abandon the children they have outside the house. Paternity is the most noble of all animal functions, but the animals have more courage and dignity than man in fulfilling it. No animal of the higher sort abandons or disowns its cub, and yet there are many men who turn their backs on their children for fear of what people will say. If I, having a son, were enamoured of the most beautiful woman in the world, and she required me to forget that son, I would stifle my passion sooner than abandon the little one. If my son sinned against every human law, and was sent to prison, even there would I follow him, defying the execration of the world, sooner than deny that he is my work. We are united for ever to the creatures to whom we give life, it is a compromise of solidarity that we make with the species when we work for its continuance. He who breaks the chain and flies is a coward."

"You will not convince me, Gabriel," screamed Esteban. "I will not!—I will not!"

"I repeat it is cowardly on your part. This honour that weighs so heavily on you is a cruel and antiquated honour that settles all the conflicts of life by shedding blood. Why do you not seek the man who stole your daughter? Why do you not kill him like a father in an old play? Is it because you are a fearful man and have not learnt the art of murder, and that arms are his profession? If you had taken lawless vengeance, relying only on what you think your right, his powerful family would have retaliated on you; but you have not revenged yourself through an instinct of self-preservation, through fear of prison and all the punishments invented by society; you have been afraid in spite of your anger, and this fear you indulge at the expense of cruelty to the weaker creature. Your anger only falls on your daughter. Come, Esteban, this is not worthy of a man."

The "Wooden Staff" shook his head obstinately.

"You will not convince me, I do not wish to hear you. That woman shall not return here; did she not leave me? Let her follow her own path."

"She left you from impulses of that instinct which all healthy beings possess. That instinct for the preservation of the species, which poetry beautifies and which it calls 'Love.' If she had left you after receiving the blessing of a man before an altar, you would have been delighted, and would have received her with open arms whenever she came to see you. She left you to be deceived, to fall into misery and shame, and, seeing her so unhappy, does she not deserve more pity at your hands than if you saw her living happily? Reflect, Esteban, on the way in which your poor daughter fell. What had you taught her to enable her to defend herself from the evil in the world? How was she armed to preserve intact what you call honour? You and your wife had set her the example of the respect due to wealth and high birth by allowing that young man to come to your house, thinking it an honour that a gentleman should have fallen in love with your daughter. When the inevitable results of social inequality came about she could not give him up; she had one of those noble natures that rise in revolt against the prejudices of the world, even at the risk of suffering all the bitterness of their rebellion, and she fell vanquished. Whom can you blame? Her ignorance, her life of isolation from the world, or yourselves who never taught her better, and who, blinded by ambition, let her wander to the edge of the precipice? Blame her less than anybody. Unhappy girl! She has paid with interest her noble defiance of social prejudices. She has been vanquished in the social fight—a corpse that has to be buried; and you, her father, ought to be the one to fulfil that work of mercy."

Esteban, with his head bent, continued to make gestures of refusal.

"Brother," said Gabriel solemnly; "if you hold tenaciously to your refusal I have only one thing more to say. If your daughter does not return here, I must go. Everyone has his scruples; you fear the gossip of the people; I fear myself and what my thoughts can throw in my face in my solitary moments. Since I have been your guest I have thought constantly of your daughter, and ever since I have known what happened in this house I have proposed to myself that the unhappy victim should return here. You will not let her return? Well then, I must go. I should be a thief if I ate your bread while a creature who is flesh of your flesh suffers hunger, or if I should be nursed in my illness while she, who is possibly worse than I am, has no friendly hand to comfort her. If she does not return, I am not your brother, but an intruder, usurping the share of affection and comfort that ought to fall to her. Brother, everyone has his own code of morality; yours is taught by the priests, mine I have made for myself, and though it is less apparent, it may very likely be more strict. In the name of my morality I say to you, Esteban, my brother, either your daughter returns here or I go away. I must return to the world to be persecuted like a wild beast, to the hospital, to the prison, to die like a dog in the ditch by the roadside. I do not know what will become of me, but one thing is certain, it is that I shall go to-morrow, or even to-day, so as not to enjoy a moment more what is not mine. I, who consider the appropriation of the goods of the world by a privileged minority as an iniquitous robbery, cannot enjoy knowingly the comforts that belong by natural right to another unhappy being. I can only enjoy them sharing them with her."

Esteban had risen to his feet with a gesture of despair.

"Are you mad, Gabriel? Do you wish to leave me? And you say it so calmly? Your presence here is the only joy of my life after so many misfortunes. I am accustomed to see you. I must care for you, you are my whole family; before I had no interest, I lived without hope. Now I have one, to see you strong and well, and can you say so carelessly that you will leave me? No, you shall not go—only this was wanting to me—after the daughter, the brother; kill me once for all!—Lord God, take me to Thyself!"

77

And the simple servant of the Church raised his hands in supplication while his eyes filled with tears.

"Be calm, Esteban. Let us speak like men, without exclamations and tears. Look at me, I am calm, but do not think for that it is less certain that I shall go to-day if you do not grant me what I pray."

"But—and she? Where is she that you plead so earnestly for her?" said Esteban. "Have you seen her and spoken to her? Is she in Toledo? Have you with the insolence of your unbelief even brought her into the Cathedral?"

Gabriel, seeing him tearful and broken by his threat of leaving, thought the decisive moment had arrived, and opening the door of Sagrario's room he called:

"Come out, child, ask your father's pardon."

He looked astounded, then he fixed his eyes on Gabriel as though he could not guess who that woman was. What joke had his brother prepared?

With a brutal impulse he tore the woman's hands from her face, looking at her earnestly; even so he did not recognise her. In the midst of a painful silence he stood a long while looking at her. Little by little, in that face so altered by illness, he began to trace the well-known features. In the tearful eyes devoid of eyelashes something reminded him of the blue eyes of the lost daughter. The discoloured lips, surrounded by deep lines, quivered painfully, murmuring always the same word:

"Pardon! pardon!"

At the sight of such a wreck the father felt his courage fail; his eyes expressed an immense, an overwhelming sadness.

He retreated backwards to the door of the "habitacion," followed by the young woman, dragging herself on her knees and stretching out her hands.

"Brother, it is well," he said despairingly; "you are stronger than I am, let your will be accomplished. Let her remain, as you wish it, but do not let me see her!—remain, both of you. It is I that will go."

CHAPTER VI

The sewing machine clicked from early morning till night in the house of the Lunas. This and the hammering of the shoemaker were the only sounds of work that disturbed the holy silence of the upper cloister.

When Gabriel left his bed at sunrise, after a night of painful coughing, he would find Sagrario already in the entrance room preparing her machine for the day's work. From the day following that of her return to the Cathedral she had devoted herself to work with sullen silence as a means of returning unnoticed to the Claverias, trusting that the people would forgive her past. The gardener's widow procured her work, and so the sound of the stitching was continually heard in the old "habitacion," accompanied very often by melodies from the Chapel-master's harmonium.

The "Wooden Staff" moved about his house like a shadow. He remained continually in the Cathedral or in the lower cloister, only coming up to the "habitacion" when it was absolutely necessary. He ate his meals with his head bent, in order not to look at his daughter, who was seated opposite to him at the other end of the table, ready to burst into tears at the sight of her father before her. A painful silence oppressed the family. Don Luis being so absent-minded, seemed the only one not to perceive the situation, and chatted gaily with Gabriel about his hopes and his musical enthusiasms. Everything seemed to him quite natural; nothing disturbed him, and the return of Sagrario to the family hearth had not caused him the slightest surprise.

When dinner was over Esteban fled, not to return to the house till night-time; after supper he locked himself into his own room, leaving his brother and his daughter in possession of the entrance sitting-room. The machine began to work again, and Don Luis fingered his harmonium till nine o'clock, when Silver Stick locked the tower staircase, rattling his bunch of keys with a noise that equalled a curfew. Gabriel felt indignant at his brother's obstinacy.

"You will kill the child; what you are doing is unworthy of a father."

"I cannot help it, brother; it is impossible for me to look at her. It is sufficient for me to tolerate such things in the house. Ay! if you could only tell how the people's looks wound me!"

In reality the scandal produced by the return of Sagrario to the Claverias had been much less than he had feared. She seemed so ill and so weary that none of the women felt any animosity against her, and the energetic protection of her Aunt Tomasa imposed respect. Besides, those simple women of instinctive passions could not now feel towards her that hostile envy that her beauty and the cadet's courtship had formerly inspired. Even Mariquita, Silver Stick's niece, found a certain salve to her vanity in protecting with disdainful tolerance that unhappy girl who in former days had attracted the attention of every man who visited the upper cloister.

Curiosity only disturbed the calm of the Claverias for about a week. Little by little the women ceased to stand about the Luna's door to watch Sagrario bending over her machine, and the girl quietly continued her sad and hard-working life. Gabriel seldom left the "habitacion." He spent whole days by the young woman's side, endeavouring by his presence to atone for the hostile aloofness of her father. It pained him that she should find herself so despised and solitary in her own house. Every now and then the Aunt Tomasa came to see them, enlivening them with the optimism of her happy old age. She was pleased with her niece's conduct; to work hard so as not to be a drag on her obstinate old father, and to help towards the maintenance of the house, was clearly what was required; but all the same there was no reason she should kill herself with work—calm and good humour, this bad time would lead to a better; she was there to get things straight with that fiend-possessed Gabriel, and she made the gloomy "habitacion" ring with her healthy laugh and lively words.

At other times Gabriel's friends would invade the house, abandoning the assemblies at the shoemaker's. They could not bear Luna's absence, they wanted to hear him, to consult him, and even the shoemaker when his work was not urgent would leave his bench and, smelling of paste, with his apron tucked into his belt and his head rolled up in striped handkerchiefs, would come and sit by Sagrario's machine.

The young woman fixed her sad eyes with admiration on her uncle. She had always from her childhood heard her parents speak with respect of that extraordinary relative who was travelling in foreign countries; she vaguely remembered him as a shadow crossing her love dream when he had spent a few days in the Cathedral before establishing himself in Barcelona, astonishing them all by the accounts of his travels and his foreign customs. Now she returned to find him aged, as sickly as herself, but influencing all who surrounded him by the mysterious power of his words, that were like heavenly music to those poor narrow-minded souls.

In the midst of her sadness Sagrario had no other pleasure but to listen to her uncle; she felt the same as did those simple men who left their work to seek Luna in their anxiety to hear fresh things from his lips. Gabriel was the modern world that for so many years had rolled on far from the Cathedral, never touching it, but which had at last entered in to stir and awaken a handful of men who were still living in the sixteenth century.

The appearance of Sagrario had brought about a change in Luna's life; he became more communicative, and he lost a great deal of the reserve he had imposed upon himself when he took refuge in the stony lap of the church. He no longer forced himself to keep silence and to hide his thoughts; the presence of a woman seemed to enliven him and wake once more his propagandist fervour. His companions saw a new Gabriel—more loquacious and more disposed to communicate to them the "new things," that were already upheaving the traditional course of their thoughts, and that even now had on many nights disturbed their sleep.

They talked, discussed and consulted Luna, so that he could clear their confused ideas, and above the voices of the men sounded the continual click, click of the sewing machine, always busy, like an echo of the universal work surging in the world, while the calm of the Infinite spread itself through the precincts of the church.

All those men, accustomed to the slow, regular, quiet duties of the church, with long periods of rest, admired the nervous activity of Sagrario.

"You will kill yourself, child," said the old organ-blower. "I know very well what it is like, I have done something of the same sort; I blow and blow at those bellows, and when it is a mass with much music, such as Don Luis loves, I end by cursing the organ and him who invented it, for indeed it nearly breaks my arms."

"Work!" said the bell-ringer with emphasis. "Work is a punishment from God! You all know its origin. It was the eternal penalty imposed on our first parents by the Lord when He drove them out of Paradise. It is a chain that we must drag on for ever."

"No, señor," replied the shoemaker. "As I have read in the newspapers, work is the greatest of all the virtues, not a punishment; laziness is the mother of vice, and work is a virtue. Is it not so, Don Gabriel?"

The shoemaker looked at the master, watching for his words as a thirsty man looks for water.

"Work," said Gabriel, "is neither a punishment nor a virtue; it is a hard law to which we have to submit for self-preservation and for the welfare of the species. Without work life could not exist."

And with the same fervid enunciation with which he had in former times swayed the multitude at those meetings of protest against society, he explained to this half-dozen men and the quiet sewer, who stopped her machine to listen, the greatness of universal work, which every day laboured on the earth, to subdue it and force it to yield sustenance for man.

It was a struggle the whole twenty-four hours against the blind forces of Nature. The army of work extended over the whole globe, exploring the continents, leaping to the islands, sailing the seas, and descending to the bowels of the earth. How many were its soldiers? No one could count them—millions and millions. At daybreak no one was absent from the roll-call; the casualties were replaced, the gaps that poverty and misfortune opened in the ranks were filled up immediately. As soon as the sun rose the factory chimney began to smoke, the hammer broke the stone, the file bit the metal, the plough furrowed the earth, the ovens were lighted, the pump worked its piston, the hatchet sounded in the wood, the locomotive moved amidst clouds of vapour, the cranes groaned on the wharves, the steamers cut the waters, and the little barks danced on the waves dragging their nets. None were absent from work's review. All hurried on, driven by the fear of hunger, defying danger, not knowing if they would live till night, or if the sun rising over their heads would be the last in their lives. And that daily concentration of human energies began with the first light of day in all parts of the world, wherever men had assembled and built towns and constituted societies, or even in the deserts to be reclaimed by their energies.

The stonemason breaks the stone with his hammer, and at every breath is poisoned by inhaling the invisible particles. The miner descends to the hell of modern times with no other guide than the glimmer from his lamp, to wrest from the strata of the earliest ages relics of the earth's infancy, those carbonised trees that gave shade to prehistoric animals. Far from the sun and far from life, he defies death, just as the mason, poised on a slight scaffolding despises giddiness, watched only by the birds, surprised to see a creature without wings perched on such a dizzy height.

The workman in the factory, changed by a fatal and mistaken progress into a slave of machinery, lives fastened to it like another wheel, a spring of human flesh, struggling with his physical weariness against the iron muscles that never tire; brutalised daily by the deafening cadence of pistons and wheels to give us the innumerable products of industry rendered necessary by the life of civilisation.

And these millions and millions of men who support the existence of society, who fight for it against the blind and cruel forces of Nature, who every morning return to the struggle, seeing in this monotonous and continual sacrifice the sole aim of their existence, form the immense family of wage-earners, living on the surplus of a privileged minority, contenting themselves to subsist on the smallest part of what these reject, submitting to a wretched remuneration, always the lowest, without hope of saving or of emancipation.

"It is this egotistical minority," said Gabriel, having arrived at this point, "who have falsified truth, endeavouring to persuade the majority of workers that work is a virtue, and that the only mission of man on earth is to work till he perishes. This code, invented, by the great capitalists, misquotes science, declaring that people can only live healthily who devote themselves to work, and that all inaction is fatal, but is silent as to what science adds—that excessive work destroys men with far greater rapidity than if they were living in idleness. They say that work is a painful necessity for the preservation of life, but they do not say it is a virtue, because repose and sweet inaction are far more grateful to men and to all animals than exertion and fatigue. The fable of Paradise, the story of the Biblical God imposing the sweat of labour as a punishment in order to earn subsistence, shows that in all times the natural temperament of man considered rest as the pleasantest condition, and that work must be considered as an evil indispensable to life, but all the same an evil. Ruled by the instinct of preservation, man ought only to work just as much as is necessary for food. But as the immense majority do not work for themselves alone, but for the profits of a minority of employers, these require that a man should work as much as he is able, even if he dies from his over-exertion, and in this way they become rich, hoarding the surplus from production. Their contention is that a man should work more than is required for himself, that he should produce more than is required for his own necessities. In this surplus lies their wealth, and to obtain it they have invented a monstrous and inhuman morality, that by means of religion and even of philosophy, glorifies work, saying that work is the greatest of all virtues and idleness the source of all vices. And this makes me ask, if idleness is a vice in the poor, how is it that among the rich it is counted as a sign of distinction and even of elevation of mind? And if work is the greatest of all virtues, how is it that capitalists endeavour to amass wealth in order to free themselves and their descendants from the practice of so great a virtue? Why is it that this society which exalts work with every sort of poetical conception relegates the worker to the lowest rank? Why do they receive with greater enthusiasm a soldier who has fought, more or less, than an aged workman who has spent seventy years working without any one praising him or being grateful to him for so much virtue?"

81

The servants of the Cathedral nodded their heads, assenting to what fell from the master; they looked up to him as simple people always look up to those who come down to them as apostles of a new idea.

The continual friction with Gabriel had caused to germinate in their minds, stunted by the traditional atmosphere, a growth of ideas, like the microscopic mosses the winter rains had formed on the granite buttresses of the church. Hitherto they had lived resigned to the life that surrounded them, moving like somnambulists on the undecided boundary which separates soul from instinct, but the unexpected presence of that fugitive from social battles was the impulse that launched them into full thought, walking tentatively and with no other light than that of their master.

"You," went on Gabriel, "do not suffer from the slavery of work like those who live among modern factories. The Church does not require great exertions from you, and the service of God does not destroy you from over-fatigue, though it kills you with hunger. There exists a monstrous inequality between the salaries of those down below who sit in the choir and sing and what you earn, who lend to worship all the strength of your arms. You will not die of fatigue, it is true; many a workman in the towns would laugh at the lightness of your duties; but you languish from poverty. I see in this cloister the same anaemic children that I saw in workmen's slums, I see what you eat and what you are paid. The Church pays its servants as in the days of faith; she believes that we still live in the times when whole towns would throw themselves into the work with the hope of gaining heaven, and would help to raise cathedrals without any more positive recompense than the workman's stew and the blessing of the bishop; and all this while, you, beings of flesh who require nourishment, deceive your stomachs and those of your wives and children with potatoes and bread, while down below those wooden images are covered with pearls and gold in senseless profusion, and without its ever occurring to you to ask yourselves why the idols who have no wants should be so rich, while you are unable to satisfy your own and live in misery."

The listeners looked at each other in astonishment, as though these words were an illuminating flash. They were doubtful for a moment as though frightened, and then the faith of conviction illuminated their faces.

"It is true," said the bell-ringer in a gloomy tone.

"It is true," repeated the shoemaker, throwing into his words all the bitterness of his grinding life of poverty, with a constantly increasing family, and with no other help but his inadequate work.

Sagrario remained silent. She did not understand many of her uncle's sayings, but she received them all as gospel coming from him, and they sounded in her ears like delicious music.

Gabriel's reputation spread among the humble inhabitants of the church, and all the servants of the Primacy gossiped about his wisdom. The clergy took notice of him, and more than once on rainy evenings the canon librarian, taking his walk in the cloisters, tried to make Gabriel talk; but the fugitive, with a remnant of prudence, showed himself towards the cassocks, as they themselves said, coldly courteous and reserved, fearing that they would expel him if they became acquainted with his views.

Only one priest of all those he saw in the upper cloister had inspired him with any confidence. This was a young man of wretched appearance, with worn-out clothes, a chaplain of one of the innumerable convents of nuns in Toledo. He received seven duros a month, which were all his means of supporting himself and his old mother, a common peasant woman, who had denied herself bread in order to give an education to her son.

"You see, Gabriel," said the priest. "You see how it is—such a great sacrifice to earn less than a common labourer earns in my village. Why did they ordain me with so much ceremony? Was it for this I sang mass in the midst of so much pomp, as though in wedding the Church I were uniting myself to wealth?"

His poverty made him the slave of Don Antolin, and in the last third of the month he came almost every day to the cloister, trying to soften Silver Stick with his prayers and induce him to lend a few pesetas. He even flattered Mariquita, who could not show herself shy with him, in spite of his cassock.

"He has a very good appearance," she said to the women of the Claverias with the enthusiasm inspired by every man. "I like to see him by the side of Don Gabriel and to hear them talk as they walk in the cloister. They look like two great noblemen. His mother called him Martin, no doubt because he resembled the Saint Martin by that painter they call El Greco, that hangs in some parish church, but I forget which."

To cajole Don Antolin was a far more arduous task, and the poor little curate suffered much in his endeavours to propitiate the miser, who was irritated if his miserable loans were not repaid at the proper time. Silver Stick with his love of authority was delighted to hold a priest and an equal under his thumb, so that those in the Claverias should see that he did not order about the small fry only. Don Martin was for him only a servant in a cassock, and he made him come up to the cloister nearly every evening on various pretexts. His delight Was to keep him whole hours standing in front of his door, obliged to listen and to pay attention to all his words.

Gabriel felt pity for the moral dependency in which the poor young man lived, and he would often leave his niece, going out into the cloister to join them. His other friends were not long in discovering him; first of all the bell-ringer, then the organ-blower, and presently the verger, the Perrero, and the shoemaker would join the group, of which Silver Stick was the nucleus. Don Antolin was delighted to see himself surrounded by so many people, never imagining that Gabriel was the attraction, thinking always it was his authority that inspired fear and respect.

Recognising equality with no one but Luna, to him only he addressed his conversation, as though the others had no other duty but to listen to him in silence; if anyone spoke to him he pretended not to hear, but continued addressing Gabriel. Mariquita, huddled up in a shawl, followed them with her eyes from the door, sharing her uncle's pride in seeing himself surrounded by such a group, who accompanied him in his stroll up and down the cloister; the proximity of so many men seemed to turn her head.

"Uncle! Don Gabriel!" she called in a coaxing voice. "Won't you come in; you will be more comfortable inside the house, because, even though it is sunny, it is very cold."

But the uncle paid no attention to her words, and continued his walk on the side of the cloister bathed by the sun, talking pompously on his favourite theme, the present poverty of the Cathedral and its greatness In former times.

"These cloisters in which we are," he said; "do you believe that they were built to serve as a refuge to the humble secular people who now live in them? No, señor, although the Church was generous, she would not have built these 'habitaciones,' with their inner courtyards and their colonnades for Wooden Staffs and vergers, etc. This cloister, which was to have been as large and beautiful as the one below, was begun by the great Cardinal Cisneros" (Don Antolin raised his hand to his cap) "so that the canons should live in them subject to conventual regulations; but the canons in those days were very rich, and, being great lords, would not consent to live shut up here; they all protested, and the cardinal, who was very quick-tempered, wished to keep them in leading strings, but one of them started to Rome with their complaints, sent by his comrades. Cisneros, being governor of the kingdom, placed guards at all the ports, and the emissary was arrested as he was going to embark at Valencia. The end of it all was that after a long suit the gentlemen of the Chapter came off victorious, and lived out of the Primacy, and the

Claverias remained unfinished with this low roof and this balustrade, both provisional. But even as it is kings have lived in this cloister; that great monarch, Philip II., spent several days here. What glorious times! when the kings, who had palaces at their command, preferred living in these rooms, so as to be inside the Cathedral and nearer to God. Such kings, such people. For this reason Spain was greater then than ever. We were masters of the world. We had power and money, and we lived happily on earth in the certainty of reaching heaven after death."

"That is true," said the bell-ringer; "those were the good times, and for their return we fought in the mountains. Ay! if only Don Carlos had been victorious! if only there had not been traitors amongst us! Is it not true, Gabriel? You who fought in the war as I did, you can say if I am not right."

"Hold your tongue, Mariano," said Gabriel, smiling sadly. "You do not know what you are saying. You fought and shed your blood for a cause that even now you do not understand. You went to the war as blindly as I did. Do not look so sullen; it is no use contradicting. Well then, let us see, what did you wish for when you went out to fight for Don Carlos?"

"I? First of all that every man should come by his own. Did not the crown belong to his family? Well, let it be given to him."

"And is this all?" asked Luna with displeasure.

"That was the least of it. What I wanted, and do want, is that the nation should have a good master, an upright lord, and a good Catholic, who without restraints of laws or Cortes, should govern us all with bread in one hand and a stick in the other. For the robber, garrote him! for the honoured, 'you are my friend!' A king who will not allow the rich to crush the poor, and who will not allow any one to die of hunger who wishes to work. Come, I think I am explaining myself clearly."

"And all this, do you believe that it existed at any time, or that your king would be able to restore it? Those centuries that you describe as those of greatness and well-being were really the worst in our history; they were the cause of Spanish decadence, and the beginning of all our ills."

"Stop there, Gabrielillo," said Silver Stick. "You know a great deal, and have travelled and read much more than I have, but we cannot swallow that. I am very much interested in the question, and I will not allow you to take advantage of the ignorance of Mariano and these others. How can you say that those times were evil, and that the fault is theirs of what is happening to us now? The true culprit is liberalism, the unbelief of the age, which has let the devil loose in our house. Spain, when it does not trust its kings and has no faith in Catholicism, is like a lame man who drops his crutches and falls to the ground. We are nothing without the throne and the altar, and the proof of this is everything that has happened to us since we had revolutions. We have lost our islands, we count for nothing among the other countries. The Spaniards who are the bravest men in the world, have been defeated, there is not a peseta anywhere, and all those gentlemen who harangue in Madrid vote fresh taxes and we are always involved in difficulties. When was this ever seen in former times? When?"

"Worse and more shameful things were seen," said Luna.

"You are mad, youngster! Those travels have corrupted you, till I believe you are hardly a Spaniard! Look you, that he denies what everybody knows, what is taught in all the schools! And the Catholic kings; were they nothing? You need no books to know that. Go into the choir, and you will see on the lower stalls all the battles that those religious kings gained over the Moors with the help of God. They conquered Granada and drove out the infidels who had held it seven centuries in barbarism. Afterwards came the discovery of America. Who could accomplish that? No one but ourselves; and that good queen who pawned her jewels so that Columbus should accomplish his voyage. You cannot deny all this, it seems to me. And the Emperor Charles V.! What have you to say about him? Do you know any more extraordinary man! He fought all the kings of Europe, and half the world was his, 'the sun never set on his dominions,' we Spaniards were masters of the world; you cannot either deny this. And still we have said nothing of Don Philip II., a king so wise and so astute that he made all the monarchs of Europe dance at his pleasure, as though he were pulling them with a string. Everything was for the greater glory of Spain and the splendour of religion. Of his victories and greatness we have said nothing; if his father was victorious at Pavia, he overturned his enemies at St. Quintin. And what do you say about Lepanto? Down in the sacristy we preserve the banners of the ship that Don Juan of Austria commanded. You have seen them; one of them represents Jesus crucified, and they are so long, so very long, that when they were fastened to the triforium, the ends had to be turned up so that they should not trail on the ground. So, was Lepanto nothing? Come, Gabriel, you really must be mad to deny certain things. If someone had to conquer the Moors lest they should possess themselves of all Europe and endanger the Christian faith, who did it? The Spaniards. When the Turks threatened to become masters of the seas, who went out to meet them? Spain and her Don Juan. And who went to discover a new world but the ships of Spain; and who sailed round the world but another Spaniard, Magallanes; and for everything great it has always been us, always us, in those days of religion and prosperity. And what can we say about learning? Those centuries produced Spain's most famous men—great poets and most eminent theologians; no one has equalled them since. And to show that religion is the source of all greatness, the most illustrious writers have worn the religious habit. I guess what will be your argument, that after such glorious kings came others less distinguished, and so the decadence commenced. I know something about that also. I have heard the librarian of the Cathedral and other people of great learning say this. But this really means nothing. These are the designs of God, by which He puts His people to the proof, just as He does with individuals, bringing them down to low estate, to raise them again to great honour, so that they may continue in the right way. But we will not speak of this; if there has been a decadence we do not want to know anything about it. We want the glorious past, the brilliant times of the Catholic kings, of Don Carlos and the two Philips, and it is on them that we fix our eyes when we talk of Spain returning to her good old times."

"But those centuries, Don Antolin," said Gabriel calmly, "were those of Spanish decadence; in them was begun our ruin. I am not surprised at your anger; you repeat what you have been taught. There are people here of the highest education who are not less irritated if you touch what they call their golden age. The fault is in the education that is given in this country. All history is a lie, and to know it so misrepresented it would be far better not to know it at all. In the schools the past of the country is taught from the point of view of a savage, who appreciates a thing because it shines and not because of its worth or utility. Spain was great, and was on the high road to become the first nation in the world, by solid and positive merits that the hazards of war or policy could not have destroyed; but that was before the centuries that you praise, before the times of the foreign kings: in the Middle Ages which held great hopes, which have vanished since the consolidation of national unity. Our Middle Ages produced a cultivated, industrious and civilised people like none other in the world; they had in them the materials for the building of a great nation; but foreign architects came in who hastily ran up this edifice; those first few years of existence that astound you with the splendour of novelty, and among whose ruins we are still groping."

Gabriel forgot all his prudence in the ardour of discussion. He felt no fear of Silver Stick, with his manner of an inquisitor incapable of reasoning. He wished to convince him; he felt all the fervour, all the irresistible impulse of his proselytising days, without trying in any way to disguise his feelings from consideration of the atmosphere surrounding him. Don Antolin listened to him in astonishment, fixing on him his cold glance. The others listened, feeling confusedly the marvel that such ideas should be enunciated in the cloister of a cathedral. Don Martin, the chaplain of the nuns, who stood behind his miserly protector, showed in his eyes the eager sympathy with which he heard Luna's words.

He described the Hispano-Roman people over whom the Gothic invasion swept, without, however, causing a gap, because before long the conquerors had succumbed to the lower Latin degeneration, remaining without strength, spending themselves in theological struggles and dynastic intrigues like those of Byzantium. The regeneration of Spain did not come from the north with the hordes of barbarians, but from the south with the invading Arabs. At first they were few, but they were sufficient to conquer Roderick and his corrupt courtiers. The instinct of the Christian nationality revolting against the invaders, and the gathering together of the whole soul of Spain on the rocky heights of Covadonga to fall once more upon their conquerors, was all a lie. The Spain of those days gratefully welcomed the people from Africa and submitted without resistance. A squadron of Arab horsemen was sufficient to make a town open its gates. It was a civilising expedition more than a conquest, and a continual current of immigration was established over the Straits. Over them came that young and vigorous culture, of such rapid and astonishing growth, which seemed to conquer though it was scarcely born: that civilisation created by the religious enthusiasm of the Prophet, who had assimilated all that was best in Judaism and in Byzantine civilisation, carrying along with it also the great Indian traditions, fragments from Persia and much from mysterious China. It was the Orient entering into Europe, not as the Assyrian monarchs into Greece, which repelled them seeing her liberties in danger, but the exact opposite, into Spain, the slave of theological kings and warlike bishops, which received the invaders with open arms. In two years they became masters of what it took seven centuries to dispossess them. It was not an invasion contested by arms, but a youthful civilisation that threw out roots in every part. The principle of religious liberty which cements all great nationalities came in with them, and in the conquered towns they accepted the Church of the Christians and the synagogues of the Jews. The Mosque did not fear the temples it found in the country, it respected them, placing itself among them without jealousy or desire of domination. From the eighth to the fifteenth century the most elevated and opulent civilisation of the Middle Ages in Europe was formed and flourished. While the people of the north were decimating each other in religious wars, and living in tribal barbarity, the population of Spain rose to thirty millions, gathering to herself all races and all beliefs in infinite variety, like the modern American people. Christians and Mussulmans, pure Arabs, Syrians, Egyptians, Jews of Spanish extraction, and Jews from the East all lived peaceably together, hence the various crossings and mixtures of Muzarabes, Mudejares, Muladies and Hebrews. In this prolific amalgamation of peoples and races all the habits, ideas, and discoveries known up to then in the world met; all the arts, sciences, industries, inventions and culture of the old civilisations budded out into fresh discoveries of creative energy. Silk, cotton, coffee, oranges, lemons, pomegranates, sugar, came with them from the East, as also carpets, silk tissues, gauzes, damascene work and gunpowder. With them also came the decimal numeration algebra, alchemy, chemistry, medicine, cosmology and rhymed poetry. The Greek philosophers, who were nearly vanishing into oblivion, saved themselves by following the footsteps of the Arab conquerors. Aristotle reigned in the university of Cordoba. That spirit of chivalry arose among the Spanish Arabs, which has since been appropriated by the warriors of the north, as though it were a special quality belonging to Christian people. While in the barbarous Europe of the Franks, the Anglo-Normans, and the Germans, the people lived in hovels, and the kings

86

and barons in rocky castles blackened by the smoke of their fires, devoured by vermin, dressed in coarse serge, and fed like prehistoric man, the Spanish Arabs were raising their fantastic Alcazars, and, with the refinement of ancient Rome, they met at their baths to converse on all literary and scientific questions. If any monk from the north felt the hunger of learning, he came to the Arab universities or the Jewish synagogues of Spain, and the kings of Europe thought they would be cured of their infirmities if, by dint of golden bribes, they could procure a Spanish physician.

When little by little the aboriginal element separated itself from the invaders and small Christian nationalities arose, the Arabs and the old Spaniards (if indeed after the constant mingling of blood there was any difference between the two races) fought chivalrously without exterminating each other after the battles, mutually respecting one another, with long intervals of peace, as though they wished to retard the moment of final separation, and often joining in various enterprises.

A system of liberty ruled in most of the Christian States. The Cortes arose much earlier than in the other western countries of Europe, and the Spanish people governed and regulated their expenses themselves, seeing only in their king a military chief. The municipalities were little republics with their own elected magistrates. The town militia realised the ideal of a democratic army. The Church at one with the people lived peacefully with the other religions in the country; an intelligent bourgeoisie created large industries in the interior, and fitted out the first navy of the times at their own cost, and Spanish products were more sought after than any other in all the ports of Europe. There were towns then as populous as any of the modern capitals; whole populations devoted themselves to weaving different kinds of stuffs, and everything was cultivated on the soil of the Peninsula.

The Catholic kings marked the apogee of national strength, but it was the beginning also of its decadence. Their reign was great because the flow of energy begun in the Middle Ages lasted till their times; but it was execrable, because their tortuous policy turned Spain from the right way, rousing in us religious fanaticism and the ambition of universal empire. Two or three centuries ahead of the rest of Europe, Spain was for the world of those days what England is for our own times. If we had followed the same policy of religious toleration, of fusion of races, of industrial and agricultural work in preference to military enterprises, where should we not be now?

Gabriel asked this question, interrupting his ardent description of the past.

"The Renaissance," continued Luna, "was more Spanish than Italian. In Italy the literature of antiquity, and Greco-Roman art revived, but the Renaissance was not entirely literary. The Renaissance represents the springing into life of a new and cultivated society, with arts and manufactures, armies and, scientific knowledge, etc. And who accomplished this but Spain, that Arab-Hebrew-Christian Spain of the Catholic kings? The Gran Capitan taught the world the art of modern warfare; Pedro Navarro was a wonderful engineer; the Spanish troops were the first to use firearms, and they created also the infantry, making war democratic, as it gave the people the superiority over the noble horsemen clad in armour; finally, it was Spain who discovered America."

"And does all this seem little to you?" interrupted Don Antolin. "Do you not exactly agree with what I said? We have never seen so much power and greatness united in Spain as in the times of those kings, who with reason some call the Catholics."

"I agree that it was a grand period of our history; the last that was really glorious, the last gleam that flashed before that Spain, who alone walked in the right way, was extinguished. But before their deaths the Catholic kings commenced the decadence by dismembering that strong and healthy Spain of the Arabs, the Christians and the Jews. You are right, Don Antolin, to say that those kings are not called the Catholics for nothing. Doña Isabel with her feminine fanaticism established the Inquisition, so science extinguished her lamp in the mosques and synagogues, and hid her books in Christian convents. Seeing that the hour for praying, instead of reading, had come, Spanish thought took refuge in darkness, trembling in cold and solitude, and ended by dying. What remained devoted itself to poetry, to comedies and theological tracts. Science became a pathway that led to the bonfire; and then came a fresh calamity, the expulsion of the Spanish Jews, so saturated with the spirit of this country, loving it so dearly, that even to-day, after four centuries, scattered on the shores of the Danube or the Bosphorus there are Spanish Jews who weep, like old Castillians, for their lost country:

'Perdimos la bella Sion;
Perdimos tambien España
Nido de consolacion.'

"That people who had given Maimonides to the science of the Middle Ages, and who were the mainstay of all the industries and commerce of Spain, left our country *en masse*. Spain, deceived by its extraordinary vitality was opening its own veins to satisfy the growing fanaticism, believing that it could survive this loss without danger. Afterwards came what a modern writer has called 'the foreign body,' interposing itself in our national life—those Austrians who came to reign and caused Spain to lose her distinctive character."

"Gabriel," interrupted the priest, "you are talking absurdities. The true Spain began with the emperor, and went on equally gloriously under Don Philip II. This is the pure and uncorrupted Spain that we ought to take as an example, and which we hope to restore."

"No. The pure and uncorrupted Spain, the Spanish Spain without foreign admixture, is that of the Arabs, Moors and Jews, that of religious tolerance, that of industrial and agricultural wealth, and of free municipalities; that which perished under the Catholic kings. What came after was a Teutonic and a Flemish Spain turned into a German colony, serving as a mercenary under foreign standards, ruining itself in undertakings in which it had no interest, shedding blood and gold for the ambition of the so-called Holy Roman Empire. I can understand the enchantment that the emperor exercised over the bigoted and ignorant people who worshipped the past. A great man that Don Carlos! Brave in fight, astute in politics, jolly and hearty as one of the burgomasters of his own country; a great eater, a great drinker, and loving to catch the girls round the waist. But he had nothing Spanish about him. He only appreciated his mother's heritage for what he could wring out of it. Spain became a servant to Germany, ready to supply as many men as were required, and to furnish loans and taxes. All the exuberant life garnered in this country by Hispano-Arab culture was absorbed by the north in less than a hundred years. The free municipalities disappeared, their defenders went to the scaffold both in Castille and Valencia; the Spaniard abandoned his plough or his weaving to range the world with an arquebus on his shoulder, and the town militias were transformed into bands which fought all over Europe without knowing why. The flourishing towns became villages; churches were turned into convents; the popular and tolerant clergy were changed into friars who imitated with servile complacency the German fanaticism. The fields remained barren for want of hands to cultivate them, the poor dreamt of becoming rich from the sack of the enemy's towns and left their work; the industrious burghers abandoned commerce as only fit for heretics, and became nurseries of clerks and petty magistrates; and the armies of Spain as unbeaten and glorious as they were ragged, with no pay but pillage and in continual mutiny against their chiefs, flooded our country with a swarm of wretched vagabonds, from whence proceeded the bully, the beggar with his blunderbuss, the highwayman, the wandering hermits, the starving nobleman, and all those characters of which picturesque novels have availed themselves."

88

"But, the devil, Gabriel!" cried indignantly Silver Stick; "do you deny that Don Carlos, who built the Alcazar of Toledo, and Don Philip II., who lived in this very cloister, were two great kings?"

"I do not deny it; they were two extraordinary men, but they killed Spain for ever. They were two foreigners, two Germans; Philip II. clothed himself with a false Spaniardism to continue the German policy of his father. This masquerading caused us great harm, because there are many men now who think of him as the noblest representation of a Spaniard. The absurd inventions and lapses from truth to which those times give rise are enough to drive one mad. Many Catholics dream of canonising Philip II. for the cold cruelty with which he exterminated heretics, but such a king had really no Catholicism but his own; he was heir to the German Cæsarism, that eternal hammer of the Popes. Driven by pride, he was always sailing to the windward of schism and heresy; that he did not break with the Pontificate was solely that this latter feared that the Spanish soldiery, who had twice entered Rome, would remain there for ever, and that it would have to submit to all their extortions. The father and son robbed us with dissimulation of our nationality, and dissipated our life for their purely personal plans of reviving the Cæsarism of Charlemagne and forming the Catholic religion to their own imagination and taste. They nearly destroyed the ancient religious feeling of Spain, so cultivated and tolerant from its continual intercourse with Mahomedanism and Judaism; that Spanish Church, whose priests lived peacefully in the towns with the alfaqui and the rabbi, and who punished with moral penalties those who from excess of zeal disturbed the worship of the infidels. That religious intolerance which foreign historians consider a purely Spanish product was really imported by the German Caesars. It was the German friar who came with his devout brutality and his crazy theology, not tempered as in Spain by Semitic culture. With their intolerance and impracticability they provoked the revolution of the Reformation in the northern countries, and, driven out of them, they came here to plant afresh their ignorance and fanaticism. The ground was well prepared. When the free towns whose municipalities were republics fell, the people also languished; the foreign seed produced in a short time an immense forest, the forest of the Inquisition and the fanaticism which still exists; the modern woodmen cut and lop, but they soon fall off wearied; the arms of one man can do little against a trunk that has grown for centuries. Fire, nothing but fire, can exterminate that cursed vegetation."

Don Antolin opened his eyes in horror. He was not angry now, he seemed quite thunderstruck by Luna's words.

"Gabriel, my son!" he exclaimed; "you are 'greener' than I thought.
Just think where you are; remember what you are saying. We are in the
Holy Metropolitan Church of all the Spains."

But Luna was fairly launched by the renewal of his historical remembrances and he was not to be stopped, driven on as he was by his propagandist zeal. He was fired by the old oratorical fervour, and he spoke as at those meetings when he could scarcely continue his speech for the applause, and the protests and surging of the multitude obstructing the police.

The horror of the priest only seemed to excite him more.

"Philip II.," he continued, "was a foreigner, a German to the very bones. His grave taciturnity, his slow and penetrating mind, were not Spanish, they were Flemish. The impassibility with which he received the reverses which ruined the nation was that of a foreigner who was bound by no ties of affection to the country. 'It is better to reign over corpses than over heretics,' he said, and corpses the Spaniards really were, condemned not to think, but to lie in order to conceal their thoughts. All the ancient offices had disappeared. Outside the Church there was no future for any adventurous soul, except in America—which ceased to be of any use to the nation after it became converted into the

89

treasure chest of the king—or to be a soldier fighting in Europe for the rehabilitation of the Holy German Empire, for the subjection of the Pope to the Emperor or the extinction of the reformed religion, undertakings that in no way concerned Spain, but were all the same very blood-letting affairs, even for those who escaped with their lives. All the handicraftsmen disappeared, carried away to the armies, and the towns became filled with invalids and veterans, carrying their rusty swords, their only proof of personal valour. All the middle-class guilds were suppressed; there only remained nobles proud of being servants to the king and a populace who only asked for bread and entertainments, like the Romans, and contented themselves with the broth from the convents and the burning of heretics organised by the Inquisition.

"After this, ruin overwhelmed us; after the great Caesars, so fatal to Spain, came the little ones—Philip III., who gave the final blow by expelling the Moors; Philip IV., a degenerate with literary fancies, who wrote verses and courted nuns, and the miserable Charles II.

"Spain had never been so religious, Don Antolin," said Luna. "The Church was mistress of everything; the ecclesiastical tribunals judged even the king himself, but secular justice could not touch even the hem of a garment of the lowest sacristan, even though he committed the greatest crimes in the public streets. Only the Church could judge its own; as Barrioneuva relates in his memoirs, friars armed to the teeth wrested from the king's justice at the foot of the scaffold, in broad daylight in the midst of the Plaza Mayor in Madrid, one of their own brothers condemned for murder. The Inquisition, not satisfied with burning heretics, judged and punished gangs of cattle-lifters. Men of letters, terrified, took refuge in ornamental literature as the last refuge of thought, confining themselves to the production of witty novels or plays, in which a fantastic honour was exalted which only existed in poets' imagination, while the greatest corruption of morals reigned. The great Spanish genius ignored or feigned to ignore what the religious revolution beyond the frontiers was saying. Quevedo only, who was the most daring, ventured to say:

'With the Inquisition....
Hush! Silence!'

the sad epitaph of Spanish thought which preferred to perish as it could not speak the truth. In order to live quietly and support themselves in those days of ignorance, many poets sought the shadow of the Church and wore its vestments. Lope de Vega, Calderon, Tirsode Molina, Miradamerscua, Tarriga, Argensola, Gongora, Rioja, and others were priests, many of them after stormy lives. Montalban was a priest and employed in the Inquisition, and even the poor Cervantes, in his old age, had to take the habit of St. Francis. Spain had eleven thousand convents, more than a hundred thousand friars, and forty thousand nuns, and to these must be added seventy-eight thousand priests and the innumerable servitors and dependents of the Church, such as alguaciles, familiars, jailors, and notaries of the Inquisition, sacristans, stewards, buleros, convent door-porters, choristers, singers, lay brothers, novices—and I know not how many other people. In exchange, the nation from a population of thirty millions had shrunk to seven millions in less than two hundred years. The expulsion of Jews and Moors by religious intolerance, the continual foreign wars, the emigration to America in the hopes of growing rich without work, hunger, the lack of sanitation, and the abandonment of agriculture, had brought about this rapid depopulation. The revenues of Spain had fallen to fourteen million ducats, whereas the clerical revenue had risen to eight millions; the Church possessed more than half the national fortune! What times! Eh, Don Antolin?"

Silver Stick listened coldly, as though he had formed some definite idea about Luna, and therefore did not make much account of his words.

"However bad they were," he said slowly, "they could not be worse than they are at present. At all events no one robbed the Church. Everyone was contented in his poverty, thinking of heaven, which is the only truth, and the worship of God which corresponds to it. Is it that you possibly do not believe in God?"

Gabriel avoided an answer, and went on talking of those times.

"It was a period of barbarism and stagnation, and while Europe was developing and progressing the people who had been foremost in all civilisation were now left far behind. The kings, inspired by Spanish pride and the hereditary pretensions of the German Caesars, conceived the mad idea of mastering all Europe, with no more support than a nation of seven million of inhabitants, and a few companies of ill-paid and starving soldiers. The gold from America had gone to fill the Dutchmen's purses, and in this undertaking, worthy of Don Quixote, the nation received blow after blow. Spain became more and more Catholic, poorer and more barbarous. She aspired to conquer the whole world, yet in the interior she had whole provinces uninhabited; many of the old towns had disappeared, the roads were obliterated and no one in Spain knew for certain the geography of the country though few were ignorant of the situation of heaven and of purgatory. The farms of any fertility were not occupied by granges but by convents, and along the few highways bivouacked bands of robbers, who took refuge, when they found themselves pursued, in the monasteries, where they were welcomed for their piety, and for the many masses they ordered for their sinful souls.

"The ignorance was atrocious, the kings were advised even in warlike matters by priests. Charles II., when the Dutch troops offered to garrison the Spanish towns in Flanders, consulted with the clerics as on a case of conscience, because this might facilitate the diffusion of heresy, and he ended by preferring to let them fall into the hands of the French, who, although they were enemies, were at all events Catholics. In the university of Salamanca the poet Torres de Villarroel could not find a single work on geography, and when he spoke of mathematics, the pupils assured him it was a kind of sorcery, a devilish science that could only be understood by anointing oneself with an ointment used by witches. The theologians rejected the project of a canal to unite the Tagus and the Manzanares, saying that this would be a work against the will of God; but having laid this down—fiat—the two rivers joined themselves even though they had been separated from the beginning of the world. The doctors of Madrid begged Philip IV. to allow the refuse to remain in the streets 'because the air of the town being exceedingly keen, it would cause great ravages unless it were impregnated with the vapours from the filth,' and a century later, a famous theologian in Seville registered in a public document with those who were discussing with him, 'that we would far rather err with Saint Clement, Saint Basil and Saint Augustin, than agree with Descartes and Newton.'

"Philip II. had threatened with death and confiscation anyone who published foreign books or who circulated manuscripts, and his successors forbade any Spaniard to write on political subjects, so, finding no ways of expansion for thought, they devoted themselves to fine arts and poetry; painting and the theatre rose to a higher level than in any other country; they were the safety valves of the national genius; but this spring of art was only ephemeral, for in the midst of the seventeenth century a grotesque and debasing decadence overwhelmed everything.

"The poverty in those centuries was horrible; that same Philip II., though he was lord of the world, put up titles of nobility for sale for the sum of six thousand reals, noting on the margin of the decree 'that it was not necessary to inquire much into the quality and origin of the people.' In Madrid the people sacked the bakeries, fighting with their fists for the bread. The president of Castille travelled through the province with the executioner to wring the scanty harvest from the peasants. The collectors of taxes, finding nothing that they could collect in the towns, tore off the roofs of the houses, selling the woodwork and the tiles. The families fled to the mountains whenever they saw in the distance the king's representative, and so the towns remained deserted and fell into ruins. Hunger came in even to the royal palaces, and Charles II., Lord of Spain and of the Indies, was unable on several occasions to procure food for his servants. The ambassadors of England and Denmark were obliged to sally forth with their armed servants to seek for bread in the suburbs of Madrid.

"And amidst all this the innumerable convents, masters of more than half the country and the sole possessors of wealth, showed their charity by distributing soup to those who had strength to fetch it, and by founding asylums and hospitals, where the people died of misery though they were certain of reaching heaven. The ancient manufactures had all disappeared. Segovia, so famous for its cloth, that had employed over 40,000 persons in its manufacture, only held 15,000 inhabitants, and these had so completely forgotten the art of weaving wool that when Philip V. wished to re-establish the industry, he was obliged to import German weavers.

"And it was the same thing in Seville, in Valencia, and in Medina del Campo, so famous for their fairs and their manufactures," continued Gabriel. "Seville which in the fifteenth century had 16,000 silk weavers, at the end of the seventeenth could only produce 65. Though it is true in exchange its Cathedral clergy numbered 117 canons, and it had 78 convents, with more than 4,000 friars and 14,000 priests in the diocese. And Toledo? At the close of the fifteenth century it employed 50,000 artisans in its silk and wool weaving and in its factory of arms, to say nothing of curriers, silversmiths, glovers, and jewellers; at the end of the seventeenth century it had hardly 15,000 inhabitants. Everything was decayed, everything was ruined; twenty-five houses belonging to illustrious families had passed into the hands of the convents, and the only rich people in the town were the friars, the archbishop and the Cathedral. Spain was so exhausted at the end of the Austrian rule that she saw herself nearly divided among the different powers of Europe, like Poland, another Catholic country like ours. The quarrels among the kings were the only thing that saved her."

"If those times were so bad, Gabriel," said Silver Stick, "how was it the Spaniards showed such unanimity? How was it there were no 'pronunciamientos' and risings in these deplorable times?"

"What could they do? The despotism of the Caesars had imposed on the Spaniards a blind obedience to the kings as the representatives of God, and the clergy had educated them in this belief from the community of interests between the Church and the throne. Even the most illustrious poets corrupted the people, exalting servility to the monarchy in their plays. Calderon affirmed that the property and life of a citizen did not belong to himself but to the king. Besides, religion filled everything; it was the sole end of existence, and the Spaniards meditating always on heaven, ended by accustoming themselves to the miseries of earth. Do not doubt but the excess of religion was our ruin, and came very near exterminating us as a nation. Even now we are dragging along the consequences of this plague which lasted for centuries. To save this country from death what had to be done? The foreigners had to be called in, and the Bourbons came. See how low we had fallen that we had not even soldiers. In this land, even if we were wanting in other advantages, we could from the earliest days reckon on good warlike leaders; but look, in the war of succession we had to have English and French generals, and even officers, for there was not a Spaniard who could train a cannon or command a company; we had no one to serve us as a minister, and under Philip V. and Fernando VI. all the Government were foreigners, strangers called in to revive the lost manufactures, to reclaim the derelict lands, to repair the ancient irrigation channels, and to found colonies in the deserts inhabited by wild beasts and bandits. Spain, who had colonised half the world after her own fashion, was now re-discovered and colonised by Europeans. The

Spaniards seemed like poor Indians, guided by their Cacique the friar, with their rags covered with scapularies and miracle-working relics. Anti-clericalism was the only remedy against all this superstition and ruin, and this spirit came in with the foreign colonists. Philip V. wished to suppress the Inquisition and to end the naval war with the Mussulman nations which had lasted for a thousand years, depopulating the shores of the Mediterranean with the fear of the Barbary and Turkish pirates. But the natives resisted any reform coming from the colonists, and the first Bourbon had to desist, finding his crown in danger. Later on his immediate successors, having deeper roots in the country dared to continue his work. Carlos III. in his endeavour to civilise Spain laid a heavy hand on the Church, limiting its privileges and curtailing its revenues, being careful of earthly things and forgetful of the heavenly. The bishops protested, speaking in letters and pastorals 'of the persecutions of the poor Church, robbed of its goods, outraged in its ministers, and attacked in its immunities,' but the awakened country rejoiced in the only prosperous days it had known in modern times before the disestablishment. Europe was ruled by philosophic kings and Charles III. was one of them. The echo of the English revolution still vibrated through the world; the monarchs now wished to be loved and not feared, and in every country they struggled against the ignorance and brutality of the masses, bringing about progressive reforms by royal enactment and even by force. But the great evil of the monarchical system was its heredity, the power settled in one family, for the son of a clever man with good intentions might be an imbecile. After Charles III. came Charles IV., and as if this were not sufficient, in the year of his death the French revolution broke out, which made all the kings in Europe tremble, and the Bourbons of Spain quite lost their heads, which they were never able to recover. They went astray, wandering from the right way, throwing themselves once more into the arms of the Church as the only means of avoiding the revolutionary danger, and they have not yet returned, nor will they, to the right track. Jesuits, friars and bishops became once more the counsellors at the palace, as they still are, as in the times when Carlos II. concocted his military and political plans with a council of theologians. We have had false revolutions which have dethroned people, but not ideas. It is true we have advanced a little, but timidly, with halting footsteps and disorderly retreats, like one who advances fearfully, and suddenly, at the slightest noise, rushes back to the point of departure. The transformation has been more exterior than interior. The minds of the people are still in the seventeenth century; they still feel the fear and cowardice engendered by the inquisitorial bonfires. The Spaniards are slaves to their very marrow; their pride and their energies are all on the surface; they have not lived through three centuries of ecclesiastical servitude for nothing. They have made revolutions, they are capable of rebelling, but they will always stop short at the threshold of the Church, who was their mistress by force and remains so still, even though its power has vanished. There is no fear of them entering here. You may remain quite easy, Don Antolin, though in justice many accounts might be required of her from the past. Is it because they are as religious as formerly? You know that this is not the case, though they complain with reason of the way in which the ancient grandeur of the Church has been extinguished without popular aid."

"That is true," said Silver Stick; "there is no faith. No one is capable of making any sacrifice for the house of God. Only in the hour of death, when fear comes in, do some of them remember to assist us with their fortune."

"There is no faith, that is the truth. The Spaniard, after that religious fever that nearly killed him, lived in a state of perfect indifference, not from scientific reflection but from inability to think at all. They know they will go either to heaven or hell; they believe it because they have been taught so, but they let themselves be carried on by the stream of life, without the strength to choose either one place or the other. They accept the established, living in a sort of an intellectual somnambulism. If now and then thought awakening suggests some criticism it is smothered at once by fear; the Inquisition still lives among us though we have no longer the bonfires, but we are terribly afraid of 'what will be said.' A stationary and narrow-minded society is our modern holy office. He who raises his protest, rising above the general and common monotony, draws upon himself the stupid anger of scandalised man, and suffers punishment; if he is poor he is put to the proof of hunger, his means of life being cut away from him, and if he is independent he is burned in effigy, creating emptiness around him. Everyone must be correct and agree to what is established, and hence it arises, that, bound to one another by fear, never an original thought arises, there is no independent thought, and even the learned keep to themselves the conclusions they draw from their studies. As long as this goes on the task of the revolutionary is useless in this country; they may change the apparent nature of the soil, but when the pickaxe strikes they come at once on the stones of ages, solid and compact. The national character though it has lost its religious faith is unchanged. Faith is dead, but the corpse still remains with the appearance of life, occupying the same place and obstructing the pathway. The Church is poor and driven into a corner compared to what it was formerly, Don Antolin, but do not fear, its situation will not be aggravated, the tide has risen to its full height and will not overflow; as long as the people in this country are afraid to say what they think, as long as they are scandalised by a new idea, and tremble at what their neighbours will say, so long will they laugh at revolutions, for however much they break out, none of these will bring the water to your mouths."

Don Antolin laughed on hearing this.

"But Gabrielillo, man—you must be mad. All this reading and travelling has turned your head. At first I was indignant, thinking you were among those who wished for another revolution to take away the little that is left to us, proclaiming the republic and suppressing all ecclesiastical things, but I see that you go much beyond this, that you conform to nothing, and that everything seems to you the worst; and this rather pleases me, because I see you are not a terrible enemy to be feared as you fire from too far. It seems to me that your head is as much affected as your chest. But do all these revolutions we have had seem as nothing to you? Do you think the country is still as savage as you have described it in past years? But I," continued the priest ironically, "hear a great deal said about the progress of the country, and I know that we have railways, and that the long chimneys are arising in all the town suburbs, and many of the impious are delighted at this, comparing them to the church belfries."

"Bah!" exclaimed Gabriel indifferently. "There is a little of this progress; the revolutions have placed Spain in touch with other countries, the progressive current has caught this country and is carrying it along as the Asiatics and others are carried; no one can escape it nowadays. But we advance at very low water, inert and without strength; if we advance it is with the current, and not by our own energy, while other people stronger than we swim and swim, advancing at every stroke. How have we contributed to this progress? Where are our manifestations of modern life? The railways, few and bad, are the work of foreigners, and are their property; the grass grows between the rails, which shows that we still follow the holy calm of carts and wagons. The most important industries, metallurgy and mines, are all in the hands of foreigners or of Spaniards who are subject to them, living under their bountiful protection. Commerce languishes under an old-fashioned protection which enhances the price of all commodities, and so there is no capital forthcoming; money remains hidden in earthen jars in the fields as treasure, or in the towns is devoted to usury as in past times; the most daring venture to invest in public stock; Government continues the mismanagement, certain of always finding someone to lend, and pointing to this credit as a proof of the country's prosperity. There are in Spain two million hectares of uncultivated land, twenty-six millions of unirrigated arable land, and only one million irrigated. This cultivation of unirrigated land, which has come to be almost our only agriculture is a concession that Spanish indolence makes to hunger, a perpetual demonstration of the fanaticism that trusts in prayer or in the rain from heaven more than in human progress. The rivers rush to the sea through scorched-up provinces overflowing in winter, not to fertilise, but to carry away everything in the volume of the inundation; there is plenty of stone for churches and new convents, but none for dykes and reservoirs; they build belfries and cut down the trees that attract the rain. And do not tell me again, Don Antolin, that the Church is poor and in no ways in fault; the poor are yourselves, you of the old and traditional Church, you of the religion 'à la Española,' for in this as in everything else there are fashions, and the faithful follow the most recent; for here are the Jesuits, the most modern manifestation of Catholicism, the 'latest novelty,' with their Sacred Heart of Jesus and other French idolatries, building palaces and churches in all directions, diverting the money that formerly went to the Cathedrals, the only evidence of wealth in the country. But let us return to our progress. Worse even for agriculture than the drought is the ignorance and routine of the labourers, every new invention or scientific appliance repels them, thinking it evil. 'The old times were the good ones, our ancestors cultivated in this way and so ought we'; and so ignorance is turned into a sort of national glory, and we cannot hope for any remedy at present. In other countries the universities and high schools send out reformers, men fighting for progress; here the centres of learning only send out a proletariat of students who must live, besieging all the professions and public appointments, with the sole desire to open themselves a way to continuous employment. They study (if you can call it study) for a few years, not to learn, but to gain a diploma, a scrap of paper which authorises them to earn their bread. They learn anything that the professor teaches, without the slightest desire to inquire any further. The professors are for the greater part doctors or barristers practising their profession, who come between whiles and sit for an hour in their chairs, repeating like a phonograph what they have said for many previous years, and then they return to their sick or their lawsuits, without caring in the least what is being said or written in the world since they got their appointments. All Spanish culture is at second hand, purely on the surface, 'translated from the French,' and even this is only for the scanty minority who read, for the rest of those so-called intellectuals have no other library but the text-books they studied as children, and all they learn of the progress of human thought is from the newspapers. The parents who are desirous of securing as soon as possible the future of their sons who are seeking a career, send them to these centres of learning when they scarcely know how to speak; the man-student of other countries, in the full plenitude of his thinking powers, does not exist here. The universities are full of children, and in the different institutes you only see short trousers, and the Spaniard, before he shaves himself for the first time, is a licentiate and on the high road to become a doctor; the wet nurse will end by sitting by the professor. These children who receive the baptism of science at an age when in other countries they are playing with their toys, being confirmed in the title that proclaims their scientific acquirements, study no more; these are the intellectuals who are to direct and save us, and who to-morrow may be legislators and ministers. Come, my good man, it is enough to make one laugh!"

Gabriel did not laugh, but Silver Stick and the others applauded his words. Any criticism against the present times delighted the priest.

"This country is drained, Don Antolin, nothing remains standing. The number of towns which have vanished since our decadence commenced is incalculable. In other countries ruins are carefully preserved, as so many stone pages of their history; they are cleaned, preserved, supported and strengthened, and paths opened round them so that all can examine them. Here, where Roman, Byzantine and Arab art have passed, and also the

Mudejar, the Gothic and the Renaissance—in fact, all the styles of Europe—the ruins in the country are hidden and disfigured by herbage and creepers, and in the towns they are mutilated and disfigured by the vandalism of the people. They are constantly thinking of the past, and yet they despise its remains; what a country of dreams and desolation! Spain is no longer a country, it is an ill-arranged and dusty museum, full of old things that attract all the curious of Europe, but in which even the ruins are ruined."

The eyes of Don Martin, the young curate, fastened themselves on Gabriel. They seemed to speak to him and express the pleasure with which he heard his words. The other listeners, silent and with bowed heads, did not feel less the enchantment of those propositions which sounded so audaciously in the restful and rank atmosphere of the cloister. Don Antolin was the only one who laughed, finding Gabriel's ideas quite charming but absolutely crazy It was getting late and the sun had sunk below the roofs of the Cathedral. Silver Stick's niece called to them once again from the door of her house.

"We are coming, child," said the priest, "but I have one thing first to say to this gentleman."

And addressing himself to Luna, he continued:

"But, Hombre de Dios!—but I ought not to call you that as you are so turbulent—you think everything is out of joint. The Spanish Church, worn out as you say, has become very poor, and still you say this revolution is a very small affair. What do you wish for? What is it that you desire so that things might be settled? Tell us your secret quickly and let us go, for the cold is very sharp."

And he laughed again, looking at Gabriel with paternal pity as though he were a child.

"My remedy!" exclaimed Gabriel, taking no notice of the priest's gesture. "I have no remedy whatever, it is the progress of humanity that alone offers one. All the nations on earth have passed through the same evolutions; first of all they were ruled by the sword, then by faith, and now by science. We ourselves have been ruled by warriors and priests, but now we tarry at the gate of modern life, without the strength or wish to take science by the hand, who is the only guide we could have, hence our sad situation. Science is nowadays in everything—in agriculture, in all manufactures, in arts and crafts, in the culture and well-being of the people; it is even in war. Spain still lives far from the sun of science, at most she knows a pale reflection, cold and feeble, that comes to us from foreign countries. The failure of faith has left us without strength, like those creatures who, having suffered from a severe illness in their youth, remain anaemic for ever, without possible recuperation, condemned to premature old age."

"Bah! Science!" said Silver Stick, turning towards his house; "that is the eternal cry of all the enemies of religion. There is no better science than to love God and His works. Good evening."

"Very good evening, Don Antolin; but remember this, we have not yet done with faith and the sword; sometimes one directs us or the other drives us; but of science, never a word, unless Spain has changed in the last twenty-four hours."

CHAPTER VII

After this evening Gabriel avoided the meetings in the cloister, so as to have no more discussions with Silver Stick. He repented of his audacity, and when he was alone reflected on the danger to which he had exposed himself in expressing his views so freely. He felt terrified at the possibility of being expelled from the Cathedral to roam the world afresh; he reproached himself, throwing in his own teeth his folly in hurling himself against the prejudices of the past. What could he hope to effect by changing the thoughts of these poor people? What weight could the conversion of these few men, stuck like limpets to the stones of the past, have in the emancipation of humanity?

The Cathedral was to Gabriel like a gigantic tumour, which blistered the Spanish epidermis, like scars of its ancient infirmities. It was not a muscle capable of development, but an abscess which bided its time either to be extirpated, or to disappear of itself through the working of the germs it contained; he had chosen this ruin as his refuge and he ought to be silent, to be prudent so that his ingratitude should not be flung in his face.

Moreover, his brother Esteban, breaking the cold reserve into which he had retired since the arrival of his daughter, counselled prudence.

"His mind seems possessed by the demon, Esteban," said the priest, "and he explains his views with the most perfect calmness in this holy house, as though he were in one of those infernal clubs which exist in foreign countries. Where on earth has your brother been to learn such things? Never have I heard such frightful heresies. Tell him that I shall forget it all as I have known him since his childhood, and that I remember he was the pride of our seminary, but more especially because he is ill, and it would be inhuman to drive him out of the Cathedral; but he must not repeat this scandal. Silence! Let him keep all those atrocities in his own head, if it so pleases him to lose his soul; but in this holy house, and especially before its staff, not a word. Do you understand? not a word. The next thing will be that he will hold meetings in the Holy Metropolitan Church. Besides, your brother must remember that, after all, at this moment, he is eating the bread of the Church, as he lives on you, and is supported by you, and it is not right to speak in this way of the most excellent work of God, and try to point out all its defects."

This last consideration weighed the most with Gabriel, and it wounded his dignity. Don Antolin said rightly, he was no more than a parasite of the Cathedral, and having taken refuge in her lap, he owed her gratitude and silence. He would keep silence. Had he not decided when he took refuge there to live as one dead? He would live like an animated corpse, which in some religious orders is the supreme of human perfection. He would think like everyone else, or rather, he would try not to think at all, but would simply vegetate there till his last hour came, like the plants in the garden or the fungus on the buttresses of the cloister.

The Cathedral servants seated themselves round the sewing machine, hoping in vain that their master would come down, but content on the whole, though they did not see him, to be near him, to look at his empty seat, and to talk to the girl who expressed such ingenuous admiration for her uncle's conversation. The Chapel-master was delighted that Luna, his sole admirer, had returned to visit him; during his temporary eclipse the poor musician had suffered all the bitterness of solitude, despairing with almost infantile rage, as though an immense audience had turned its back on him. He caressed Gabriel as though he was the woman he loved, listening to his coughing, and recommending all sorts of fantastic remedies imagined by himself, uneasy at the progress of his malady and trembling at the idea that death might tear from him his only listener.

He told Gabriel of all the music he had studied during his absence. When the sick man coughed much, he would cease playing his harmonium, and begin long talks with his friend, always on the subject of his constant preoccupation, musical art.

"Gabriel," said the musician one evening; "you who are so keen an observer, and who knows so much, has it ever struck you that Spain is sad, and has not the sweet sentimentality of true poetry? She is not melancholy, she is sad, with a wild and savage silence. She either laughs in wild peals, or weeps moaning. She has not the gentle smile, the joyful brightness that distinguishes the man from the animal. If she laughs it is showing all her teeth; her inner meaning is always gloomy, with the obscurity of a cavern in which all passions rage like wild beasts seeking for an outlet."

"You say truly, Spain is sad," replied Luna. "She does not now go dressed in black, with the rosary hanging to the pommel of her sword as in former years. Still in her heart she is always dressed in mourning and her soul is gloomy and wild. For three hundred years the poor thing has endured the inquisitorial anguish of burning or being burnt, and she still feels the spasm of that life of terror. There is no joy here."

"There certainly is not, and you find this more in music than in any other phase of Spanish life. The Germans dance the gay and voluptuous waltz with a 'bock' in their hand, singing the *Gaudeamus igitur*, that students' hymn glorifying the material life free from care. The French sing amid rippling laughter, and dance with their free and elastic limbs, greeting with rapturous applause their fantastic and monkey-like movements. The English have turned their dance into gymnastics, with the energy of a healthy body delighting in its own strength. But all these people, when they feel the sweet sadness of poetry, sing Lieds, romances, ballads, something soft and flowing, that rests the soul and speaks to the imagination. Here even the popular dances have much that is priestly, recalling the priestly stiffness of the sacred dances, and the circling frenzy of the priestess, who ended by falling in front of the altar with foaming mouth and bloodshot eyes. And our songs? They are most beautiful, the products of many civilisations, but most sad, despairing, gloomy, revealing the soul of a sick and tainted people, who find their greatest pleasure in human bloodshed, or urging on dying horses in the enclosure of a circus. Spanish joy! Andalusian merriment! I cannot help laughing at it. One night in Madrid I assisted at an Andalusian fête, all that was most typical, most Spanish. We went to enjoy ourselves immensely. Wine and more wine! And accordingly the bottle went round, with ever frowning brows, gloomy faces, abrupt gestures. 'Ole! come along here! This is the joy of the world!' but the joy did not appear in any part. The men looked at one another with scowling brows, the women stamped their feet and clapped their hands with a stupid vacuity in their looks, as though the music had emptied their brains. The dancers swayed like erect serpents, with their mouths open, their looks hard, grave, proud, unapproachable, like dancers who were performing a sacred rite. Now and then above the monotonous and sleepy rhythm, a song, harsh and strident like a roar, like the scream of one who falls with his body run through. And the poetry? As dreary as a dungeon, sometimes very beautiful, but beautiful as might be the song of a prisoner behind his bars, dagger thrusts to the faithless wife, offences against the mother washed out in blood, complaints against the judge who sends to prison the caballeros of the broad-brimmed sombreros and sashes. The adieus of the culprit who watches in the chapel the light of his last morning dawn. A poetry of death and the scaffold that wrings the heart and robs it of all happiness; even the songs to the beauty of women contain blood and threats. And this is the music that delights the people in their hours of relaxation and that will go on 'enlivening' them probably for centuries. We are a gloomy people, Gabriel, we have it in our very marrow, we do not know how to sing unless we are threatening or weeping, and that song is the most beautiful which contains most sighs, most painful groans and gasps of agony."

"It is true, the Spanish people must necessarily be so. It believes with its eyes shut in its kings and priests as the representatives of God, and it moulds itself in their image and likeness. Its merriment is that of the friars—a coarse merriment of dirty jests, of greasy words and hoarse laughs. Our spicy novels are stories of the refectory composed in the hours of digestion, with the garments loosened, the hands crossed on the paunch, and the triple chin resting on the scapulary. Their laughter arises always from the same sources—

grotesque poverty, the troublesome hangers on, the tricks of hunger to rob a companion of his provision of begged scraps. The tricks to filch purses from the gaily-dressed ladies who flaunt in the churches, who serve as models to our poets of the golden age to depict a lying world devoid of honour. The woman enslaved behind iron bars and shutters, more dishonest and vicious than the modern woman with all her liberty. The Spanish sadness is the work of her kings, of those gloomy invalids who dreamt of conquering the whole world while their own people were dying of hunger. When they saw that their deeds did not correspond to their hopes, they became hypochondriacs and despairingly fanatical, believing their ruin to be a punishment from God, giving themselves over to a cruel devotion in order to appease the divinity. When Philip II. heard of the wreck of the *Invincible*, the death of so many thousand men, and the sorrow of half Spain, he never even winked an eyelid. 'I sent it to fight with men, not with the elements,' and he went on with his prayers in the Escorial. The imperturbable gloom and ferocity of the kings re-acted on the nation, and this is why for many centuries black was the favourite colour at the court of Spain. The sombre groves in the royal palaces, with their gloomy winter foliage, were and still are their favourite resorts; the roofs of their country palaces are black, with towers surmounted by weather-cocks, and dark cloisters like monasteries."

Shut into that small room with no other listener than the Chapel-master, Gabriel forgot the discretion he had imposed on himself with a view to the continuance of his quiet existence in the Cathedral. He could speak without fear in the presence of the musician, and he spoke warmly about the Spanish kings and of the gloom that from them had filtered through the country.

Melancholy was the punishment imposed by Nature on the despots of the Western decadence. When a king had any artistic predispositions, like Fernando VI., instead of tasting the joy of life he nearly died of weariness listening to the airs on the guitar feebly tinkled by Farinelli. As they were born with their minds closed to every inspiration of beauty or poetry, they spent their lives gun in hand in the woods near Madrid, shooting the deer and yawning with disgust at the fatigues of the chase, while the queens amused themselves at a distance hanging on to the arm of one of the bodyguard. They could not live with impunity for three centuries in close contact with the Inquisition, exercising power simply as papal delegates, under the direction of bishops, Jesuits, confessors, and monastic orders, who only left to the Spanish monarchy the appearance of power, turning it, in fact, into an oppressed theocratic republic. The gloom of Catholicism penetrated into their very bones, and while the fountains of Versailles were playing among their marble nymphs, and the courtiers of Louis XIV. were decked like butterflies in their multi-coloured garments, as shameless as pagans among the beautiful goddesses, the court of Spain, dressed in black, with a rosary hanging at its girdle, assisted at the burnings and, girt with the green scarf of the holy office, honoured itself by undertaking the duties of alguacil at the bonfires of heretics. While humanity, warmed by the soft breath of the Renaissance, was admiring the Apollos and adoring the Venus' discovered by the plough amid the ruins of mediaeval catastrophes, the type of supreme beauty for the Spanish monarchy was the criminal of Judea. The black and dusty Christs in the old cathedrals, with the livid mouth, the skeleton and distorted body, the feet bony, and dripping with blood, much blood,—that liquid so loved by the religious when doubt begins and faith weakens, and to impose dogma they place their hand on the sword.

"For this reason the Spanish monarchy has been steeped in gloom, transmitting its melancholy from one generation to another. If by any chance there appeared among them anyone happy and pleased with life, it was because in the blue blood of the maternal veins there was a plebeian drop, which pierced like the rays of the sun into a sick room."

Don Luis listened to Gabriel, receiving his words with affirmative gestures.

"Yes, we are a people governed by gloom," said the musician. "The sombre humour of those dark centuries lives in us still. I have often thought how difficult life must have been to an awakened spirit. The Inquisition listening to every word, and endeavouring to guess every thought. The conquest of heaven the sole ideal of life! And that conquest becoming daily more difficult! Money must be paid to the Church to save one's self, and poverty was the most perfect state; and again, besides the sacrifice of all comfort, prayers at all hours, the daily visits to the church, the life of confraternities, the disciplines in the vaults of the parish church, the voice of the brother of Mortal Sin interrupting sleep to remind one of the approach of Death; and added to this fanatical and weary life the uncertainty of salvation, the threat of falling into hell for the slightest fault, and the impossibility of ever thoroughly appeasing a sullen and revengeful God. And then again, the more tangible menace, the terror of the bonfire, engendering cowardice and debasing suspected men."

"In this way we can understand," said Gabriel, "the cynical confession of the Canon Llorente explaining why he became secretary to the Holy Office: 'They began to roast, and in order not to be roasted I took on me the part of roaster.' For intelligent men there was nothing else to be done. How could they resist and rebel? The king, master of all lives and property, was only the servant of bishops, friars, and familiars. The kings of Spain, except the first Bourbons, were nothing but servants of the Church; in no country has been seen as palpably as in this one the solidarity between Church and State. Religion succeeded in living without the kings, but the kings could not exist without religion. The fortunate warrior, the conqueror who founded a throne, had no need of a priest. The fame of his exploits and his sword were enough for him, but as death drew near he thought of his heirs, who would be unable to dispose of glory and fear to make themselves respected as he had done, and he drew near to the priest, taking God as a mysterious ally who would watch over the preservation of the throne. The founder of a dynasty reigned 'by the grace of strength' but his descendants reigned 'by the grace of God.' The king and the Church were everything for the Spanish people. Faith had made them slaves by a moral chain that no revolutions could break; its logic was indisputable—the belief in a personal God, who busied Himself with the most minute concerns of the world, and granted His grace to the king that he might reign, obliged them to obey under pain of going to hell. Those who were rich and well placed in the world grew fat, praising the Lord who created kings to save men the trouble of governing themselves; those who suffered consoled themselves by thinking that this life was but a passing trial, after which they would be sure to gain a little niche in heaven. Religion is the best of all auxiliaries to the kings; if it had not existed before the monarchs these last would have invented it. The proof is that in these times of doubt they are firmly anchored to Catholicism, which is the strongest prop of the throne. Logically the kings ought to say, 'I am king because I have the power, because I am supported by the army.' But no, señor, they prefer to continue the old farce and say, 'I, the king, by the grace of God.' The little tyrant cannot leave the lap of the greater despot; it is impossible to them to maintain themselves by themselves."

Gabriel was silent for some time; he was suffocating, his chest was heaving with the spasms of his hollow cough. The Chapel-master drew near alarmed.

"Do not be uneasy," said Luna, recovering himself; "it is so every day. I am ill and I ought not to talk so much, but these things excite me, and I feel irritated by the absurdities of the monarchy and religion, not only in this country, but all over the world. But, notwithstanding, I have felt real pity, profound commiseration for a being with royal blood. Can you believe it? I saw him quite close in one of my journeys through Europe. I do not know how the police who guarded his carriage did not drive me away, fearing a possible attempt, but what I felt was compassion for the kings who have come so late into a world that no longer believes in the divine right; and these last twigs, sprouting from the worm-eaten and rotten trunk of a dynasty, carry in their poor sap the decay of the rotten branches. It was a youth, as sick as I am, not by the chances of life, but weakly from his cradle, condemned before his birth to suffer from the malady that came to him with his life. Just imagine, Don Luis, if at this time for the preservation of my own interests I begot a son, would it not be a coldly premeditated attempt against the future?"

And the revolutionist described the young invalid: his thin body, artificially strengthened by hygiene and gymnastics, his eyes heavy and sunk deep in their sockets, the lower jaw hanging loose like that of a corpse, wanting the strength that keeps it fixed to the skull.

"Poor youth! Why was he born? What would be accomplished in his journey through the world? Why had Nature, who so often refuses fecundity to the strong, shown herself prodigal to the loveless union of a dying consumptive? What was the use to him of having carriages and horses, liveried servants to salute him, and ninnies to give him food; it would have been far better had he never appeared in the world but had remained in the limbo of those who are never born. Like the squire of Don Quixote, who finding himself at last in the plenty of Barataria, had by his side a doctor Recio to restrain his appetite, this poor creature could never enjoy with freedom the pleasures of the remains of life left to him."

"They pay him thousands of duros," added Gabriel, "for every minute of his life, but no amount of gold can procure him a drop of fresh blood to cure the hereditary poison in his veins. He is surrounded by beautiful women, but if he feels arising the happy tremors of youth, the sap of the spring of life, the predisposition of a family who have only been notable for the victories won in love's battles, he must remain cold and austere, under his mother's vigilant eye, who knows that carnal passion would rapidly end a life so weak and uncertain. And the end of all these sad and painful privations—inevitable death. Why was this poor creature born? Often the greatness of the earth is worse than a malediction, and reasons of State are the most cruel of all torments for an invalid, obliging him to feign a health he does not feel. To speak of the illness of the king is a crime, and the courtiers living under the shadow of the throne consider the slightest allusion to the king's health as a sacrilege, a crime worthy of punishment, as though he were not a human being subject like others to death."

"I do not care much for politics," said the Chapel-master; "kings and republics are all the same to me, I am a votary of art. I do not know what monarchy may be in the other countries that you have seen, but in Spain it seems quite played out. It is tolerated like so many relics of the past, but it inspires no enthusiasm and no one is inclined to sacrifice themselves for it, and I believe that even the people who live in its shadow, and whose interests are most bound up with those of the crown, have more devotion on their tongues than in their hearts."

"It is so, Don Luis," said Gabriel; "for nearly a century the monarchy has been dead in Spain; the last loved and popular king was Fernando VII. Since then the nation has asserted itself, becoming emancipated from the old traditions, but the kings have not progressed; on the contrary, they have gone back, withdrawing themselves daily more and more from the anticlerical and reforming tendencies of the first Bourbons. If in educating a prince nowadays his masters were to say, 'We will try and make a Carlos III. of him,' even the stones of the palace would be scandalised. The Austrians have revived like those parasitic plants which, having been torn up, reappear after a little while. If in the life of the kings they seek for examples in the past, they remember the Austrian Caesars, but it is complete oblivion of those first Bourbons who morally killed the Inquisition, expelled the Jesuits, and fostered the material progress of the country; they renounce the memory of those foreign ministers who came to civilise Spain. Jesuits, friars and clerics order and direct as in the best times of Charles II. To have had as minister a Count of Aranda, the friend of Voltaire, is a shame of the past and to be passed over in silence. Yes, Don Luis, you say well, the monarchy is dead. Between it and the country there is the same relation as between a corpse and a living man. The secular laziness, the resistance to all change, and the fear of the unknown that all stationary people feel, are the causes of the continuance of this institution, that has not like other countries the military outlet or the aggrandisement of its territory as a justification of its existence."

With this the conversation ended that evening in the Chapel-master's little room.

Gabriel found himself drawn afresh by the affection of his admirers in the Claverias. They coaxed him and followed him, lamenting his absence. They could not live without him, so declared the shoemaker. They had become accustomed to listen to him, they felt the desire of being enlightened, and they begged the master not to desert them.

"We meet in the tower now," said the bell-ringer; "Silver Stick looks on our meetings with an evil eye, and he has gone so far as to threaten the shoemaker to turn him out of the Claverias if the meetings continue to be held in his house. He will not interfere with me; he knows my character. Besides, if he rules in the upper cloister, I rule in my tower. I am quite capable, if he comes to disturb us with his spying, of throwing him down the stairs, the miserly devil!"

And he added with an affectionate expression, a great contrast to his usual rough and taciturn character:

"Come, Gabriel, we expect you in my house. When you are tired of keeping your niece and that crazy Don Luis company, come up for a little while. We cannot get on without your words. Don Martin has been quite enthusiastic since he heard you the other evening; he wants to see you; he says he would go from one end of Toledo to the other to hear you. He wishes me to let him know if you decide on rejoining your friends, because Don Antolin in speaking to him sets you down as a madman and a heretic who does not know what to be after. But he is an ignoramus who, after studying for his profession, can do no better than sell tickets and squeeze the poor."

Luna returned to the meetings in the bell-ringer's house. The greater part of the morning he sat by his niece, soothed by the tic-tac of the machine, which caused a gentle drowsiness, watching the cloth pass under the presser with little jumps, spreading the peculiar chemical scent of new stuffs.

He watched Sagrario always sad, devoting herself to her work with taciturn tenacity; when now and then she raised her head to regulate her cotton and met Gabriel's glance, a faint smile would pass over her face.

In the isolation in which the anger of her father had left them they felt obliged to draw together as though a common danger threatened them, and their bodily infirmities were a further bond of union. Gabriel pitied the fate of the poor young woman, seeing how hardly the world had treated her after her flight from the family hearth. Her long illness had changed her greatly and still caused her pain, her once beautiful teeth were no longer white and regular, and the lips were pallid and drawn; her hair had grown thin in places, but she contrived to conceal this with locks of the auburn hair, remains of her former beauty, which she dressed with great skill; but in spite of this her youth was beginning to assert itself, giving light to her eyes and charm to her smile.

Many nights Gabriel, tossing on his bed unable to sleep, coughing, and with his head and chest bathed in cold sweat, would hear in the room adjoining the suppressed moans of his niece, timid and smothered so that the rest of the household should not be disturbed.

"What was the matter with you last night?" asked Gabriel the following morning. "What were you moaning for?"

And Sagrario, after many denials, finally admitted her discomfort:

"My bones ache; directly I get to bed the pain begins and I feel as though my limbs were being torn asunder. And you, how are you? All night I heard you cough, and I thought you were suffocating."

And the two invalids stricken by life forgot their own aches and pains to sympathise with those of the other, establishing between their hearts a current of loving pity, attracted to each other not by the difference of sex, but by the fraternal sympathy aroused by each other's misfortunes.

Very often Sagrario would try to send her uncle away; it pained her to see him sitting close by her, doing nothing, coughing painfully, fixing his eyes upon her as though she were an object of adoration.

"Get up from here," the girl would say gaily—"it makes me nervous seeing you so very quiet keeping me company when what you want is life and movement. Go to your friends; they are expecting you in the bell-ringer's tower. They have been talking about me, thinking it is I who keep you in the house. Go out to walk, uncle! Go and speak of those things that stir you so much, and that those poor people listen to open-mouthed. Be careful as you go up the stairs; go slowly and stop often, so that the demon of the cough, may not get hold of you."

Gabriel spent the later hours of the morning in the bell-ringer's "habitacion." The walls of ancient whitewash were adorned by faded and yellow engravings, representing episodes in the Carlist war, remembrances of the mountain campaign which for long years had been the pride of Mariano, but of which now he never spoke.

Here Gabriel met all his admirers. Even the shoemaker worked at night in order not to deprive himself of this meeting. Don Martin, the curate, also came up, concealing himself carefully so that Silver Stick should not see him. It was a small community grouping itself round the sick apostle, with all the zeal inspired by the unknown.

Gabriel answered all these men's questions, that so often betrayed the simplicity of their minds. When a fit of coughing seized him, they all surrounded him with concern written on their faces. They would have wished even at the cost of their own lives to restore him to health. Luna, carried away by his enthusiasm, ended by narrating to them the story of his life and sufferings, and so the prestige of martyrdom came to increase the ardour of these people. The narrowed minds of these sedentary men, living tranquil and safe in the Cathedral, made them admire the adventures and torments of this fighter; for them he was a martyr to this new religion of the humble and oppressed, and besides, their innocence converted him into a victim of that social injustice which they daily hated more.

For them there was no other truth but Gabriel's words; the bell-ringer, although the roughest and most silent among them, was the most advanced in his conversion. His admiration for Gabriel which dated from their childhood, his dog-like fidelity, carried him on with leaps and bounds, making him accept at once even the most distant ideals.

"I am whatever you are, Gabriel," he said firmly. "Are you not an anarchist? I will be one also—indeed, I think I have always been one. Do you not preach that the poor should live and the rich should work; that everyone should possess what he earns, and that we should all help one another? Well, this is just what I thought when we wandered over the country with our guns and our scarf. And as far as religion is concerned, which formerly nearly drove us mad, I feel perfectly indifferent. I am convinced on hearing you that it is a sort of fable invented by clever people in order that we, the poor and unfortunate, should submit to the miseries of this world hoping for heaven; it is not badly imagined, for in the end those who die and do not find heaven will not return to complain."

One day Gabriel wished to go up where the bells were hung. It was now well on in spring; it was warm, and the intense blue of the sky seemed to attract him.

"I have not seen the 'big bell' since I was a child," he said. "Let us go up; I should like to see Toledo for the last time."

And accompanied by his admirers, indeed, almost carried by them, he went slowly up the narrow spiral staircase. Arrived at the top, the soft wind was murmuring through the great iron railings, the cages of the bells. From the centre of the vault hung the famous "Gorda," an immense bronze bell, with all one side split by a large crack; the clapper, which was the author of the mischief, lay below it, engraved and as thick as a column, and a smaller one now occupied the cavity. The roofs of the Cathedral, dark and ugly, lay at their feet, and in front on a hill rose the Alcazar, higher and larger than the church, as though keeping up the spirit of the emperor who built it, Caesar of Catholicism, champion of the faith, but who nevertheless strove to keep the Church at his feet.

The city spread out around the Cathedral, the houses disappearing in the crowd of towers, cupolas and absides. It was impossible to look on any side without meeting with chapels, churches, convents and ancient hospitals. Religion had absorbed the industrious Toledo of old, and still guarded the dead city beneath its hood of stone. From some of the belfries a red flag was floating, bearing a white chalice; this meant that some newly-ordained priest was singing his first mass.

"I have never been up here," said Don Martin, sitting by Gabriel's side on one of the rafters, "without seeing some of these flags; ecclesiastical recruiting never ceases, there are always visionaries to fill its ranks. Those who really have faith are the minority, the greater part enter because they see the Church still triumphant and seemingly commanding, and they think that in her ranks some tremendous career is waiting for them. Unlucky wights! I also was led to the altar with music and oratorical shouts, as though I were walking to a triumph. Incense spread its clouds before my eyes, all my family wept with emotion at seeing me nothing less than a minister of God. And the day following all this theatrical pomp, when the lights and the censers were extinguished and the church had recovered its ordinary aspect, began this miserable life of poverty and intrigue to earn one's bread—seven duros a month! To endure at all hours the complaints of those poor women, with their tempers embittered by seclusion, common as the lowest servants, who spend their lives gossiping in the parlour of what is passing in the towns, inventing scandals to please the canons, or the families who protect the house. And there are priests who envy me! hungering against me for this coveted chaplaincy of nuns! looking upon me as a flattering hanger-on of the archiepiscopal palace, not understanding how otherwise, being so young, I could have hooked out this preferment that allows me to live in Toledo on seven duros a month!"

Gabriel nodded his head, sympathising with the young priest's complaints.

"Yes, it is you who are deceived. The day for making great fortunes in the Church is past, and the poor youths who now wear the cassock and dream of a mitre make me think of those emigrants who go to distant countries famous through long centuries of plunder, and find them even more poverty-stricken than their own land."

"You are right, Gabriel. The day of the all-powerful Church is past; she has still in her udders milk enough for all, but there are few who can fasten on to them and fill themselves to repletion, while others groan with hunger. One could die of laughing when one hears of the equality and the democratic spirit of the Church. It is all a lie; in no other institution does so cruel a despotism reign. In early days Popes and bishops were elected by the faithful, and were deposed from power if they used it badly. The aristocracy of the Church exists still; it may be a canon upwards, or one who succeeds in crowning himself with a mitre; from them no account is required. Among the laity appointments are changed, ministers are turned out, soldiers are degraded—even kings are dethroned; but who exacts responsibility from Pope or bishops once they are anointed and in more or less frequent intercourse with the Holy Spirit? If you want Justice you are sent before

104

tribunals equally formed by the aristocrats of the Church; there is no power more absolute on earth, not even the Grand Turk, who in a measure is responsible through fear of revolts in his seraglio. Here, in the seraglio of the Church, we are all less than women. If it happens that a priest, weary of persecution, feeling the man once more rising beneath his cassock, deals a heavy blow at his tyrant, he is declared mad; the climax of hypocrisy! They try to demonstrate that in the Church one lives in the best of worlds, and it is only the lack of reason that causes any rebellion against its authority."

Don Martin was silent for a long while as though he were searching in his memory; at length he continued:

"You also laugh at the idea of the actual poverty of the Church in Spain. She is like the great ruined noblemen, who still have enough to live upon in idleness, but who think themselves miserably poor compared to their former wealth; the Church has the nostalgia of those former centuries when she possessed half the wealth of Spain. Poor she is if she thinks of those times, but if you compare her with the Catholicism of other modern nations you find that, as in former years, she is by far the most favoured and best paid establishment in the State. She absorbs forty-one millions of the revenue, which is enormous in a country which only devotes nine millions to schools and teaching, and one million to the relief of the poor. To maintain an intercourse with God costs a Spaniard five times as much as to learn to read. But this forty-one millions is a blind. My own poverty made me inquisitive, and I wished to know what the clergy in Spain really receive, and what comes to our hands, the rank and file. The demands and pensions of the Church are an intricate tangle, apart from the forty-one millions. There is not a single ministry in which the Church has not struck her roots; she is paid by the Ministers of State for foreign missions, which are no use to anyone, by the Ministers of War and Marine for military clergy, and by the Ministers of Public Instruction and Justice. She is paid to support the pomp of the Roman Pontiff, as we maintain his ambassador in Spain, which is as though I allowed myself the luxury of keeping servants, and laid on my neighbour the obligation of paying them. She is paid for the repairs to churches, for episcopal libraries, for the colonisation of Fernando Po, for unforeseen occurrences, and I do not know how many supplemental items besides! And you must take into account what the Spanish people pay the Church voluntarily apart from what the State gives. The Bull of the Holy Crusade produces two and a half million pesetas annually; besides this you must consider what the parochial clergy draw from their congregations, the annual gifts to the religious orders for their ministry and offices (and this is the fattest portion), and the ecclesiastical revenue from the Ayuntamientos and deputations. In short, this Church, which is continually speaking of its poverty, draws from the State and the country more than three hundred million pesetas annually—nearly double what the army costs; although they are always complaining in the sacristies of these modern times, saying that everything is devoured by the military, and that the fault of everything that has happened is theirs, as they threw themselves on to the side of that cursed liberty. Three hundred millions, Gabriel! I have calculated it carefully! And I, who form part of this great establishment, receive seven duros a month; the greater part of the vicars in Spain are paid less than an excise officer, and thousands of clergy live from hand to mouth, wandering from sacristy to sacristy trying to obtain a mass to put the stew on the fire; and if bands of clergy do not go into the highways to rob, it is only from fear of the civil guard, and because after a couple of days of hunger a third may come in which they may beg some scraps to eat; there is always a crumb to allay hunger, and no cassock ever falls in the street dying of want, but there are a great many clerics who spend their existence deceiving their stomachs, trying to imagine they nourish themselves, till some sudden illness comes which hurries them out of the world. Where, then, does all this money go? To the aristocracy of the Church, to the true sacerdotal caste; but we who are

105

in religion are people of the backstairs. What a terrible mistake, Gabriel! To renounce love and family affection, to fly all worldly pleasures, the theatre, concerts, the cafe; to be looked upon by people, even by those who think themselves religious, as a strange being, a sort of intermediate, neither a man nor a woman; to wear petticoats and to be dressed like a lugubrious doll; and in exchange for all these sacrifices to earn less than a man who breaks stones on the road. We live idly, certain that we shall never fall from over-work, but our poverty is greater than that of many workmen; we cannot acknowledge it, nor put ourselves in the way of begging alms, for the honour of our cloth. And besides, why should they keep us if we are of no practical use and cost the country so dear? When the religious domination came to an end in Spain it was only we, the lower ones, who suffered in consequence. The priest is poor, the temple is poor also; but the prince of the Church retains his thousands of duros yearly, and his great ecclesiastical state, and he sings his psalms tranquilly, certain that his pittance is in no danger. The revolution up to now has only prejudiced the lower clergy; the power of the Church is ended, it is gone; what we see is only its corpse, but an enormous corpse that will cost a great deal to remove, and whose preservation will swallow up a great deal of money."

"It is true the Church is defunct; what we fight are only its remains. The vulgar believe it still lives because they can see and touch it, forgetting that a religion counts centuries in its life as minutes, and that generation after generation pass between its death and burial. Centuries before the birth of Jesus Paganism had fallen. The Athenian poets mocked the gods of Olympus on the stage, and the philosophers despised it. All the same Christianity required many years of propaganda and the political support of the Caesars to bring it to an end, and even then it was not done with, for dogmas are like men who leave behind something of themselves in the family who succeed them. Religions do not disappear suddenly through a trapdoor; they are extinguished slowly, leaving some of their beliefs and their ceremonies to the religions that follow them. We have been born in one of those times of transition, we are present at the death of a whole world of beliefs. How long will the agony last? Who knows? Two centuries? Possibly less may be wanted to crystallise in humanity a fresh proof of its uncertainty and of its fear of the great mystery of nature, but death is certain, inevitable. But what religion has been eternal? The symptoms of dissolution are visible everywhere. Where is that faith that drove those warlike multitudes to the crusades? Where is that fervour which continued building cathedrals for a couple of hundred years with angelic patience to shelter a host under a mountain of stone? Who scourges themselves to-day, or tortures their flesh, or lives in the desert musing continually on death and hell? Three centuries of intolerance and of excessive clerical severity have made our nation the most indifferent to all religious matters. The ceremonies of worship are followed by routine, because they appeal to the imagination, but no one takes the trouble to understand the foundations of the beliefs they profess; they live as they please, certain that in their last hours it is sufficient to save their souls, to die surrounded by priests with a crucifix in their hands. In former days the pressure from clergy, friars, and inquisitors was so great that the machine of faith burst into a thousand pieces, and there is no one now who can fit the pieces together, which require the co-operation of all. And that was a piece of good luck, friend Don Martin; a century more of religious intolerance and we should have been like those Mussulmen in Africa, who live in barbarism on account of their excessive bigotry, after having been the civilising Arabs of Cordoba and Granada."

"Do you know," said the young curate, "why Catholicism has held up its appearances of power? It is because from ancient times, in all Latin countries, it has possessed itself of every avenue through which human life must pass."

"It is true, no religion has been so cautious as ours, or has ambushed itself better to entrap men. None has chosen with such certainty in the time of power the positions it can hold strongly in its decadence. It is impossible to move without stumbling against her. She knows of old that man as long as he is healthy, in the plenitude of his vital strength, is by instinct irreligious. When he lives comfortable the so-called eternal life concerns him very little. He only believes in God and fears Him in the hour of supreme cowardice, when death opens before him the bottomless pit of nothingness, and his pride as a rational animal revolts against the complete extinction of his being. He wishes his soul to be immortal, and so he accepts the religious phantasies of heaven and hell. The Church, fearing the irreligiousness of health, has occupied, as you say, all the avenues of life, so that no man shall accustom himself to live without her, appealing solely to her in the hour of death. The dead provide much money, they are her best asset; but she wishes equally to reign over the living. Nothing escapes her despotism and her spying. She insinuates herself into all human concerns from the greatest to the most insignificant, she interferes in both public and private life; she baptizes the child when it comes into the world, accompanies the child to school, monopolises love, declaring it shameful and abominable if it does not submit to her benediction, and divides the earth into two categories—the consecrated, for those who die in her bosom, and the dunghill in the open air for the heretic. The Church interferes in dress, laying down what is honest and Christian wear and what is scandalous frivolity. She interferes in the most intimate relations of domestic life, and even penetrates into the kitchen, turning Catholicism into a culinary art, ruling what ought to be eaten, what ought or ought not to be mixed, and anathematizing certain foods, which, being good enough the rest of the year, become the most horrible sacrilege if partaken on certain days. She accompanies a man from his birth, and does not leave him even after he is laid in the tomb; she keeps him chained by his soul, making it wander through space, passing from one place to another, ascending the pathway to heaven, according to the sacrifices imposed on themselves by his successors for the benefit of the Church. A greater or more complete despotism no tyrant could possibly imagine."

It was mid-day. The bell-ringer had disappeared; suddenly the rattle of chains and pulleys was heard and a dull thunder made the tower tremble; all the stones and metal and even the surrounding ether vibrated. The big "Gorda" had just rung, deafening the bystanders. A few moments afterwards, from the front of the Alcazar, came the sound of martial music, trumpets, and drums.

"Let us go," said Gabriel. "Really, Mariano might have warned us and spared us this surprise."

And he added, smiling ironically:

"It is always the same; it is the parasites who shine the most and make the most noise; they make up in noise what they lack in utility."

The festival of Corpus drew near without anything occurring to ruffle the quiet life of the Cathedral. Sometimes in the upper cloister they spoke of His Eminence's health. His serious quarrels with the Chapter had obliged him to keep his bed, and he had just had an attack which made them fear for his life.

"It is his heart," said the Tato—who was usually very well informed about things in the palace—"Doña Visita is weeping like a Magdalen and cursing the canons, seeing Don Sebastian so ill."

As Wooden Staff sat down to table with his family he began to speak of the decadence of the feast of Corpus, which had been so famous in Toledo in former times. In his desire to complain he forgot the bitter silence he had imposed on himself in his daughter's presence.

"You will hardly recognise our Corpus," he said to Gabriel. "Of all that we remember nothing remains but the famous tapestries that are hung outside the Cathedral. The giants are not drawn up before the Puerta del Perdon, and the procession is shorn of its glory."

The Chapel-master also complained bitterly.

"And the mass, Señor Esteban? Just think what a mass for such a solemn festivity! Four instruments from outside the house, and a Rossini mass of the lightest description so as not to cost much. It would have been far better for this to have played the organ alone."

According to an ancient custom, on the vesper before the feast, the band of the Academy of Infantry played in the evening before the Cathedral. All Toledo came to hear the serenade, which was an event in the monotonous life of the town, and from the province of Madrid many strangers came for the bull-fight on the following day.

Mariano, the bell-ringer, invited his friends to listen to the serenade from the Greco-Roman gallery on the principal front. At the hour when the lights were usually extinguished in the Claverias and Don Antolin locked the street door, Gabriel and his friends glided cautiously to the bell-ringer's "habitacion." Sagrario was also persuaded to come by her uncle, who in this way managed to tear her from her machine. She really must enjoy some little amusement; she ought to appear in the world now and then; she was killing herself with all that tiresome work.

They all sat in the gallery. The shoemaker had brought his wife, always with a small baby at her flabby breast. The Tato was talking delightedly to the organ-blower and the verger about the bull-fight on the following day, and Mariano stood by his adored comrade, while his wife, a woman as rough as himself, spoke with Sagrario.

The men were deploring the absence of Don Martin. Probably he had gone down below among the people who filled the square, doubtless dreading that he must be up before daybreak to say mass to the nuns.

The palace of the Ayuntamiento was decorated with strings of light, which were reflected on to the façade of the Cathedral, giving the stones a rosy flush as of fire.

Among the trees walked groups of girls with flowers and white blouses, like the first appearances of spring. The cadets followed them, their hands on the pommels of their swords, walking along with their pinched-in waists and their full pantaloons à la Turc. The archiepiscopal palace remained entirely closed. Above the rosy light in the piazza, spread the beautiful summer sky, clear and deep, spangled with innumerable brilliant stars.

When the music ceased, and the lights began to fade, the inhabitants of the Cathedral felt unwilling to leave their seats. They were very comfortable there, the night was warm, and they, accustomed to the confinement and the silence of the Claverias, felt the joy of freedom, sitting on that balcony with Toledo at their feet and the immensity of space above them.

Sagrario, who had never been out of the upper cloister since her return to the paternal roof, looked at the stars with delight.

"How many stars!" she murmured dreamily.

"There are more than usual to-night," said the bell-ringer. "The summer sky seems a field of stars in which the harvest increases with the fine weather."

Gabriel smiled at the simplicity of his companions. They all wondered at God, so foreseeing and so thoughtful, who had made the moon to give light to men by night, and the stars so that the darkness should not be complete.

"Well, then," inquired Gabriel, "why is there not a moon always if it was made to give us light?"

There was a long silence. They were all thinking over Gabriel's question. The bell-ringer, being most intimate with the master, ventured to put the question about which they were all thinking. "What were the heavens, and what was there beyond the blue?"

The square was now deserted and in darkness, there was no light but the gentle shimmering of the stars scattered in space like golden dust. From the immense vault there seemed to fall a religious calm, an overwhelming majesty that stirred the souls of those simple people. The infinite seemed to bewilder them with its vast grandeur.

"You," said Gabriel, "have your eyes closed to immensity, you cannot understand it. You have been taught a wretched and rudimentary origin of the world, imagined by a few ragged and ignorant Jews in a corner of Asia, which, having been written in a book, has been accepted down to our days. This personal God, like to ourselves in His shape and passions, is an artificer of gigantic capacity, who worked six days and made everything existing. On the first day He created light, and on the fourth the sun and stars; from whence then came that light if the sun had not then been created? Is there any distinction between one and the other? It seems impossible that such absurdities should have been credited for centuries."

The listeners nodded their heads in assent; the absurdity appeared to them palpable—as it always did when Gabriel spoke.

"If you wish to penetrate the heavens," continued Luna, "you must get rid of the human conception of distance. Man measures everything by his own stature, and he conceives dimensions by the distance his eyes can reach. This Cathedral seems to us enormous because underneath its naves we seem like ants; but, nevertheless, the Cathedral seen from far is only an insignificant wart; compared with the piece of land we call Spain it is less than a grain of sand, and on the face of the earth it is a mere atom—nothing. Our sight makes us consider thirty or forty yards a dizzy height. At this moment we think we are very high because we are near the roof of the Cathedral, but compared to the infinite this height is as small as when an ant balances on the top of a pebble not knowing how to come down. Our sight is short, and we who can only measure by yards, and apprehend short distances, must make an immense effort of imagination to realise infinity. Even then it escapes us and we speak of it very often as of a thing that has no meaning. How shall I make you understand the immensity of the world? You must not believe, as our ancestors did, that the earth is flat and stationary and that the heaven is a crystal dome on which God has fastened the stars like golden nails, and in which the sun and moon move to give us light, you must understand that the earth is round, and whirls round in space."

"Yes, we do know a little about that," said the bell-ringer doubtfully, "for we were taught so at school. But, really, do you think it moves?"

"Because in your littleness as human beings, because to our microscopic mole-like sight the immense mechanism of the world is lost, do not for a moment doubt it. The earth turns. Without moving from where you are, in twenty-four hours you will have made the complete circuit with the globe. Without moving our feet we rush along at the rate of four hundred leagues an hour, a velocity that the fastest trains cannot attain. You are astonished? We rush along without knowing it. Our planet does not only turn on itself, but at the same time it turns round the sun at the rate of nearly a hundred thousand miles an hour. Every second we cover thirty thousand miles. Men have never invented a cannon ball that could fly so quickly. You move through space fixed to a projectile which whirls with dizzy speed, and, deceived by your smallness, you think you are living immovable in a dead cathedral. And this velocity is as nothing compared with others. The sun round which we turn, flies and flies through space, carrying on by its attraction the earth and the other planets. It goes through immensity, dragging us along, travelling towards the unknown, without ever striking other bodies, finding always sufficient space to move in with a rapidity which makes one giddy; and this has gone on for thousands

109

and millions of centuries without either it or the earth who follows it in its flight ever passing twice over the same spot."

They all listened to Gabriel open-mouthed with astonishment, and their bright eyes seemed dazed and bewildered.

"It is enough to drive one mad," murmured the bell-ringer. "What then is man, Gabriel?"

"Nothing; even as this earth, which seems so large, and that we have peopled with religions, kingdoms and revelations from God, is nothing. Dreams of ants! even less! This same sun which seems so enormous compared to our globe is nothing more than an atom in immensity. What you call stars are other suns like ours, surrounded by planets like our earth, but which are invisible on account of their small size. How many are they? Man brings his optical instruments to perfection and is able to pierce further into the fields of heaven, discovering ever more and more. Those which are scarcely visible in the infinite appear much nearer when a new telescope is invented, and beyond them in the depths of space others and again others appear, and so on everlastingly. They are unaccountable. Some are worlds inhabited like ours; others were so, and revolve solitary in space, waiting for a fresh evolution of life; many are still forming; and yet all these worlds are no more than corpuscles of the luminous mist of the infinite. Space is peopled by fires that have burnt for millions, trillions and quadrillions of centuries, throwing out heat and light. The milky way is nothing but a cloud of stars that seem to us as one mass, but which in reality are so far apart that thousands of suns like ours with all their planets could revolve among them without ever coming into collision."

Gabriel remembered the travelling of sound and light. "Their velocity is insignificant compared with the distances in space. The sun, which is the nearest to us, is still so far that for a sound to go from us to it would take three millions of years. Poor human beings will never be able to travel with the rapidity of sound.

"These suns travel like ours towards the unknown with giddy flight, but they are so distant that three or four thousand years may pass without man being aware that they have moved more than a finger's breadth. The distances of infinity are maddening. The sun is a nebula of inflammatory gas, and the earth an imperceptible molecule of sand.

"The luminous ray of the Polar star requires half a century to reach our eyes; it might have disappeared forty-nine years ago, and still we should see it in space.

"And all these worlds are created, grow and die like human beings. In space there is no more rest than on earth. Some stars are extinguished, others vary, and others shine with all the power of their young life. The dead planets dissolved by fires furnish the material for new worlds; it is a perpetual renewal of forms, throughout millions and millions of centuries, that represent in their lives what the few dozen years to which we are limited, are in our own. And beyond all those incalculable distances there is space, and more space on every side, with fresh conglomerations of worlds without limit or end."

Gabriel spoke in the midst of solemn silence. The listeners closed their eyes as if such immensity stunned them. They followed in imagination Gabriel's description, but their narrowed minds wished to place a term to the infinite, and in their simplicity they imagined beyond these incalculable distances a vault of firm matter millions of leagues thick. Surely all that strange and fantastic work must have a limit. What was at the back of it? And the barrier created by their imagination fell suddenly; and again they flew through space, always infinite, with ever new worlds.

Gabriel spoke of them and of their life with absolute certainty. Spectral analysis showed the same composition in the stars as on the earth, consequently if life had arisen in our atom, most certainly it must exist in other celestial bodies, though probably in different forms; in many planets it had already ended, in many it was still to come; but surely all those millions of worlds had had, or would have, life.

Religions, wishing to explain the origin of the world, paled and trembled before the infinite. It was like the Cathedral tower, which covered with its bulk a great part of the heavens, hiding millions of worlds, but which was of insignificant size compared to the immensity it hid, less than an infinitesimal part of a molecule—nothing. It seemed very great because it was close to men, concealing immensity, but when men looked above it, getting a full grasp of the infinite, they laughed at its Lilliputian pride.

"Then," inquired timidly the old organ-blower, pointing to the Cathedral, "what is it they teach us in there?"

"Nothing," replied Gabriel.

"And what are we—men?" asked the Perrero.

"Nothing."

"And the governments, the laws, and the customs of society?" inquired the bell-ringer.

"Nothing. Nothing."

Sagrario fixed her eyes, grown larger by her earnest contemplation of the heavens, on her uncle.

"And God," she asked in a soft voice; "where is God?"

Gabriel stood up, leaning on the balustrade of the gallery; his figure stood out dark and clear against the starry space.

"We are God ourselves, and everything that surrounds us. It is life with its astonishing transformations, always apparently dying, yet always being infinitely renewed. It is this immensity that astounds us with its greatness, and that cannot be realised in our minds. It is matter that lives, animated by the force that dwells in it, with absolute unity, without separation or duality. Man is God, and the world is God also."

He was silent for a moment and then added with energy:

"But if you ask me for that personal God invented by religions, in the likeness of a man, who brought the world out of nothing, who directs our actions, who classifies souls according to their merits, and commissions Sons to descend into the world to redeem it, I say seek for Him in that immensity, see where He hides His littleness. But even if you were immortal you might spend millions of years passing from one star to another without ever finding the corner where He hides His deposed despotic majesty. This vindictive and capricious God arose in men's brains, and the brain is a human being's most recent organ, the last to develop itself. When man invented God the world had existed millions of years."

CHAPTER VIII

On the morning of Corpus the first person Gabriel saw on leaving the cloister was Don Antolin, who was looking over his tickets, placing them in line in front of him on the stone balustrade.

"This is a great day," said Luna, wishing to smooth down Silver Stick. "You are preparing for a great crowd; no doubt many strangers will come."

Don Antolin looked intently at Gabriel, evidently doubting his sincerity; but seeing that he was not laughing, he answered with a certain satisfaction.

"The feast is not beginning badly; there are a great many who wish to see our treasures. Ay, son! indeed we want it badly. You who rejoice in our troubles may be satisfied. We live in horrible straits. Our feast of Corpus is worth very little compared with former times; but all the same, what economies we have had to make in the Obreria, to provide the four ochavos that the extra festivity will cost!"

Don Antolin remained silent for some time, still looking intently at Luna, as though some extraordinary idea had just occurred to him. At first he frowned as though he were rejecting it, but little by little his face lit up with a malicious smile.

"By the way, Gabriel," he said in a honeyed tone which contained something very aggressive, "I remember at the time of the monument in Holy Week you spoke to me of your wish to earn some money for your brother. Now you have an opportunity. It will not be much; still it will be something. Would you care to be one of those who carry the platform of the Sacrament?"

Guessing the wish of the malicious priest to annoy him, Gabriel was on the point of answering haughtily, but suddenly he was tempted by the wish to foil Silver Stick by accepting his proposal; he wished to astound him by acceding to his absurd idea; besides, he thought that this would be a sacrifice worthy of the generosity with which his brother treated him. Even though he could not assist with much money, he could show his wish to work, and the scruples of his self-love vanished before the hope of carrying home a couple of pesetas.

"You do not care about it," said the priest in mocking accents, "you are too 'green,' and your dignity would suffer too much by carrying the Lord through the streets of Toledo."

"You are mistaken. As for wishing it, I do wish it, but you must remember it is very heavy work for an invalid."

"Do not let that trouble you," said Don Antolin resolutely; "you will be at least ten inside the car, and I have chosen all strong men; you would go to complete the number, and I should recommend you to accept in order to earn a little."

"Then we will clench the business, Don Antolin; you may reckon on me, I am always ready to earn a day's wage whenever it turns up."

His great wish to get out of the Cathedral had finally decided him, his wish once more to walk through the streets of Toledo, that he had not seen during his seclusion in the cloister, and without anyone being able to take notice of him. Besides, the ironical situation tickled him extremely, that he of all men with his round religious denials should be the one to pilot the God of Catholicism through the devout crowd.

This spectacle made him smile, possibly it was a symbol; certainly Wooden Staff would greatly rejoice, he would look upon it as a small triumph for religion, that obliged His enemies to carry Him on their shoulders. But he himself would look upon it in a different way; inside the eucharistic car he would represent the doubt and denials hidden in the heart of worship, splendid in its exterior pomp, but void of faith and ideals.

"Then we are agreed, Don Antolin. I will come down shortly into the Cathedral."

They parted, and Gabriel, after quietly digesting the milk his niece brought him, went down into the Cathedral without saying a word to anyone about the work he intended carrying out; he was afraid of his brother's objections.

In the lower cloister he again met Silver Stick, who was talking to the gardener's widow, showing her contemptuously a bunch of wheat ears tied with a red ribbon. He had found it in the holy water stoup by the Puerta del Alegria. Every year on the day of Corpus he had found the same offering in the same place; an unknown had thus dedicated to the Church the first wheat of the year.

"It must be a madman," said the priest. "What is the good of this? What does this bunch mean? If at least it had been a cart of sheaves as in the good old times of the tenths!"

And while he threw the ears with contempt into a flower border in the garden, Gabriel thought with delight of the atavic force which had resuscitated in a Catholic church, the pagan offering: the homage to the divinity of the firstfruits of the earth fertilised by the spring.

The choir was ended and the mass beginning when Gabriel entered the Cathedral, the lower servants were discussing at the door of the sacristy the great event of the day. His Eminence had not come down to the choir and would not assist at the procession. He said he was ill, but those of the household laughed at this excuse, remembering that the evening before he had walked as far as the Hermitage of the Virgin de la Vega. The truth was he would not meet his Chapter; he was furious with them, and showed his anger by refusing to preside over them in the choir.

Gabriel strolled through the naves. The congregation of the faithful was greater than on other days, but even so the Cathedral seemed deserted. In the crossways, kneeling between the choir and the high altar, were several nuns in starched linen bibs and pointed hoods, in charge of sundry groups of children dressed in black, with red or blue stripes according to the colleges to which they belonged; a few officials from the academy, fat and bald, listened to the mass standing, bending their heads over their cuirass. In this scattered assemblage, listening to the music, stood out the pupils from the school of noble ladies, some of them quite girls, others proud-looking young women in all the pride of their budding beauty, looking on with glowing eyes, all dressed in black silk, with mantillas of blonde mounted over high combs with bunches of roses—aristocratic ladies with "*manolesca*" grace, escaped from a picture by Goya.

Gabriel saw his nephew the Tato dressed in his scarlet robes like the noble Florentine, striking the pavement with his staff to scare the dogs. He was talking with a group of shepherds from the mountains, swarthy men twisted and gnarled as vine shoots, in brown jackets, leather sandals, and thonged leggings; women with red kerchiefs and greasy and mended garments that had descended through several generations. They had come down from their mountains to see the Corpus of Toledo, and they walked through the naves with wonder in their eyes, starting at the sound of their own footsteps, trembling each time the organ rolled, as though fearing to be turned out of that magic palace, which seemed to them like one in a fairy tale. The women pointed out with their fingers the coloured glass windows, the great rosettes on the porches, the gilded warriors on the clock of the Puerta de la Feria, the tubes of the organs, and finally remained open-mouthed in stupid wonder. The Perrero in his scarlet garments seemed like a prince to them, and overwhelmed with the respect they felt for him, they could not succeed in understanding what he said, but when the Tato threatened with his staff a mastiff following closely at his master's heels, those simple people decided to leave the church sooner than abandon the faithful companion of their wild mountain life.

Gabriel looked through the choir railings; both the upper and lower stalls were full. It was a great festival, and not only were all the canons and beneficiaries in their places, but all the priests of the chapel of the kings, and the prebends of the Muzarabé chapel—those two small churches who live quite apart with traditional autonomy inside the Cathedral of Toledo.

In the middle of the choir Luna saw his friend the Chapel-master in his crimped and pleated surplice, waving a small bâton. Around him were grouped about a dozen musicians and singers, whose voices and instruments were completely smothered each time the organ sounded from above, while the priest directed with a resigned look the music, which lost itself feeble and swamped in the solitude of the immense naves.

At the High Altar, on its square car, stood the famous Custodia, executed by the celebrated master Villalpando. A Gothic shrine, exquisitely worked and chiselled, bright with the shimmering of its gold in the light of the wax tapers, and of such delicate and airy work that the slightest motion made it shiver, shaking its finials like ears of corn.

Those invited to the procession were arriving in the Cathedral. The town dignitaries in black robes, professors from the academy in full dress with all their decorations, officers of the Civil Guard, whose quaint uniform reminded one of that of the soldiers of the early part of the century. Through the naves with affectedly skipping steps came the children, dressed as angels—angels à la Pompadour, with brocaded coat, red-heeled shoes, blonde lace frills, tin wings fastened to their shoulders, and mitres with plumes on their white wigs. The Primacy got out for this festivity all its traditional vestments. The gala uniform of all the church attendants belonged to the eighteenth century, the time of its greatest prosperity. The two men who were to guide the car had powdered hair, black coats, and knee breeches, like the priests of the last century. The vergers and Wooden Staffs wore starched ruffs and perukes, and though they had scarcely enough to eat, brocade and velvet covered all the people from the Claverias; even the acolytes wore gold embroidered dalmatics.

The High Altar was decorated by the "Tanta Monta" tapestries—those famous hangings of the Catholic kings, with emblems and shields, given by Cisneros to the Cathedral. The auxiliary bishop said mass, and his attendant deacons were perspiring under the traditional mantles and chasubles covered with beautiful raised embroidery in high and splendid relief, as stiff and uncomfortable as ancient armour.

The surroundings of the Cathedral were disturbed by the gathering for the procession; the doors of the sacristies slammed, opened and shut hurriedly by the various officials and people employed. In that quiet and monotonous life the annual occurrence of a procession which had to pass through many streets caused as much confusion and disturbance as an adventurous expedition to a distant country.

When the mass ended the organ began to play a noisy and disorderly march, rather like a savage dance, while the procession was being marshalled in order. Outside the Cathedral the bells were ringing, the band of the academy had ceased playing its quick march, and the officers' words of command and the rattle of the muskets could be heard as the cadets drew up in companies by the Puerta Llana.

Don Antolin, with his great silver staff and a pluvial of white brocade, went from one place to another collecting the employees of the Church; Gabriel saw him approaching, red-faced and perspiring.

"To your post; it is time."

And he led him to the High Altar by the Custodia. Gabriel and eight other men crept inside the scaffolding, raising the cloth with which its sides were covered. They were obliged to bend themselves inside the erection, and their duty was to push it, so that it should move along on its hidden wheels. Their only duty was to push it; outside, the two servants in black clothes and white wigs were in charge of the front and back shaft or tiller, which guided the eucharistic car through the tortuous streets. Gabriel was placed by his companions in the centre; he was to warn them when to stop and when to recommence their march. The monumental Custodia was mounted on a platform with a great counterpoise, and between it and the framework of the car was about a hand's breadth of space, through which Gabriel looked, thus transmitting the orders of the front pilot.

"Attention! March!" shouted Gabriel, obeying an outside signal.

And the sacred car began to move slowly down the inclined wooden plane that covered the steps of the High Altar. It was obliged to stop on passing the railings. All the people knelt, and Don Antolin and the Wooden Staffs having opened a way between them, the canons advanced in their ample red robes, the auxiliary bishop with his gilded mitre, and the other dignitaries in white linen mitres without ornament whatsoever. They all knelt around the Custodia. The organ was silent, and, accompanied by the hoarse blare of a trombone, they intoned a hymn in adoration of the Sacrament; the incense rose in blue clouds around the Custodia, veiling the brilliancy of its gold. When the hymn ceased the organ began to play again, and the car once more resumed its march. The Custodia trembled from base to summit, and the motion made a quantity of little bells hanging on to its Gothic adornments tinkle like a cascade of silver. Gabriel walked along holding on to one of the crossbeams, with his eyes fixed on the pilots, feeling on his legs the movements of those who pushed this scaffolding, so similar to the cars of Indian idols.

On coming out of the Cathedral by the Puerta Llana, the only door in the church on a level with the street, Gabriel could take in the whole procession at a glance. He could see the horses of the Civil Guards breaking the regularity of the march, the players of the city kettledrums dressed in red, and the crosses of the different parishes grouped without order round the enormous and extremely heavy banner of the Cathedral, like a huge sail covered with embroidered figures. Beyond, all the centre of the street was clear, flanked on either side by rows of clergy and soldiers carrying tapers, the deacons with their censers, assisted by the roccoco angels carrying the vessels for the Asiatic perfume, and the canons in their extremely valuable historical capes. Behind the sacrament were grouped the authorities, and the battalion of cadets brought up the rear, their muskets on their arms, their shaven heads bare, keeping step to the time of the march.

Gabriel breathed with delight the air of the public streets. He who had seen all the great capitals of Europe admired the streets of the ancient city after his long seclusion in the Cathedral. They seemed to him very populous, and he felt the surprise that great modern improvements must cause to those used to a retired and sedentary life.

The balconies were hung with ancient tapestries and shawls from Manilla; the streets were covered with awnings, and the pavement spread thickly with sand, so that the eucharistic car should glide easily over the pointed cobble stones.

Up the hills the Custodia advanced laboriously, the men inside the car sweating and gasping. Gabriel coughed, his spine aching with the enclosure in the movable prison, and the dignity of the march was disturbed by the words of command from the Canon Obrero, who, in scarlet robes with a staff in his hand, directed the procession, reproving the pilots and those who pushed the car inside for their jerky and irregular movements.

Apart from these discomforts, Gabriel was delighted with his extraordinary escapade through the town; he laughed, thinking what the crowd, kneeling in veneration, would have said had they known whose eyes were looking out at them from underneath the car. No doubt many of those officials escorting God, in their white trousers, red coats, with swords by their sides and cocked hats would have had news of his existence; they would surely have heard some one speak of him, and they probably kept his name in their memory as that of a social enemy. And this reprobate, rejected by all, concealed in a hole in the Cathedral like those adventurous birds who rested in its vaultings, was the man who was guiding the footsteps of God through this most religious city!

A little after mid-day the Custodia returned to the Cathedral, passing in front of the Puerta del Mollete. Gabriel saw the exterior walls hung with the famous tapestries. As soon as the farewell hymns were ended the canons despoiled themselves quickly of their vestments, rushing to the door on their dismissal without saluting. They were going to their dinners much later than usual, as this extraordinary day upset the even course of

115

their lives. The church, so noisy and illuminated in the morning, emptied itself rapidly, and silence and twilight once more reigned in it.

Esteban was furious when he saw Gabriel emerging from the eucharistic car.

"You will kill yourself, such work is not for you. What caprice could have seized you?"

Gabriel laughed. Yes, it was a caprice, but he did not repent of it. He had taken a turn through the town without being seen, and he could give his brother sufficient for two days' maintenance; he wished to work, not to be a heavy charge on him.

Wooden Staff was softened.

"You idiot, have I asked anything of you? Do I want anything else but that you should live quietly and get better?"

But, as though he wished to acknowledge this exertion on his brother's part by something which would please him, when he returned to the Claverias he dropped his usual sullen face, and spoke to his daughter during the meal.

Towards evening the Claverias were quite deserted. Don Antolin hurried down with his tickets, rejoicing in the knowledge that many strangers were waiting for him. The Tato and the bell-ringer had slipped furtively down the tower stairs, dressed in their best clothes; they were going to the bull-fight. Sagrario obliged to be idle in order to keep the feast day holy, had gone to the shoemaker's house, and while he was showing the giants to the servants and soldiers of the academy, and the peasants from the country, Luna's niece helped to mend the clothes for the poor woman crushed by poverty and the superabundance of children.

When the Chapel-master and the Wooden Staff went down to the choir, Gabriel went out into the cloister. He could only see there a cadet who was walking up and down, with his hand on the pommel of his sword, holding it horizontally like the fiery tizonas of former days. Luna recognised him by the full pantaloons and the wasplike waist, which made the Tato declare that this particular cadet wore stays—it was Juanito the cardinal's nephew. He often walked in the cloister, hoping for an opportunity to talk with Leocadia, the beautiful daughter of the Virgin's sacristan. From the parents he had nothing to fear, but the future warrior had a certain dread of Tomasa, as the old lady looked on these visits with an evil eye, and threatened to make them known to his uncle the Cardinal.

Gabriel had often spoken to the cadet, for when the youth met him in the cloister he always stopped to speak, endeavouring by the platitudes of his conversation to justify his presence in the Claverias; but Luna was surprised to meet him there on a festival afternoon.

"Are you not going to the bull-fight?" he inquired. "I thought everyone from the academy would be in the Plaza."

Juanito smiled, caressing his moustache; it was his favourite gesture, as it raised his arm, giving him the satisfaction of displaying the sleeve adorned with sergeant's stripes. He was not a common cadet, he had his stripes, and though this did not seem much to one who dreamed of being a general, still it was a step in the right direction. No; he did not go to bull-fights. In truth he was an *habitué* but he had sacrificed himself in order to talk for a whole afternoon with his sweetheart at the door of her house in the silence of the Claverias. The grandmother had gone down into the garden, and "Virgin's Blue" would not be long in going out and leaving the coast clear, as if the matter in no way concerned him. "The beautiful evening, friend Gabriel!" He had far more serious and important affairs than the new comers at the academy, who spent all their Sundays at the cafés, or walking up and down like fools—everyone at the academy, even the professors, envied him his sweetheart.

"And when is the wedding to be?" said Gabriel gaily.

Master Stripes looked most important as he replied: "There were many things to be done before—first of all to bring his uncle to consent, which might not be easy, and to follow the guiding of his good star to attain a certain rank; but he was intended for great things, so it was only a matter of a few years.

"I, friend Luna, am of the stuff of young generals; it is the good luck of the family. My uncle, when he was only an acolyte, was certain he would become a cardinal, and he succeeded. I shall rise much faster. Besides, you know that to be an archbishop of Toledo is not a small thing. My uncle has many friends in the palace, and commands in the ministry of war just as though he were a general. In point of fact he is far more a soldier than a cleric! And to prove it to you, there is the only thing he has ever written, a prayer to the Virgin for the soldiers to recite before they go into action."

"And you, Juanito, do you really feel any vocation for a military life?"

"A great deal—ever since I knew how to open books and read them I have wished to rival those great captains that I saw in the prints, erect on their horses, with swords in their hands, proud and handsome. Believe me, no one enters on this career without a vocation; many are entered in the seminaries against their will, but no one can make a soldier by force; anyone who comes to the academy has the longing in himself."

"And are all of them as sure of the result as you are?"

"Oh, yes; all," said the cardinal's nephew smiling, "except that the immense majority have not such probabilities of making a name. But, such as we are, there is not one amongst us who dreams of the possibility of vegetating as a captain in a reserve regiment, or of dying of old age as a commandant. We all of us see first of all youth glorified by the uniform, full of adventures (for you know all the women fight for us), by the joy of life, loved and respected everywhere, head and shoulders above our countrymen; and when old age approaches, and we begin to get fat and bald, the gold braid of a general, politics, and, who knows, possibly the portfolio of war! This is in everyone's thoughts. No one believes but that the future holds a bâton for him, and that he has only to unhook it and fasten it to his belt. I know for certain what is awaiting me, the rest dream and hope for it, and so we go on living."

Gabriel smiled as he listened to the cadet.

"You are all deceiving yourselves, like those poor youths who enter the seminaries, believing that a mitre awaits them or a fat benefice on the other side of the door. It is the influence and attraction still exercised by the great things that have been. Let us see—apart from the material result of the profession—why do you become soldiers?"

"For the sake of glory!" said the cadet pompously, remembering the harangues of the colonel director of the academy. "For our country, whose defence is entrusted to us! and for the honour of our flag!"

"Glory!" said Gabriel, ironically. "I know all about that. Very often, seeing you all so young and inexperienced, so full of vain hopes, I have reconstructed in my own mind what might be called the psychology of the cadet. I can guess all that you thought before entering the academy, and I foresee the bitter and crushing disillusion that awaits you on leaving it. The history of wars and the artistic trappings of the uniform have seduced your youth. Afterwards, warlike tales of an irresistible fascination—Bonaparte with his little band crossing the bridge at Arcola amid showers of bullets. And then our own generals, not to go further—Espartero at Luchana, O'Donnel in Africa, and, above all, Prim, that almost legendary leader, directing the battalion at Castillejos with his sword. 'I wish to be the same,' say these youths; 'where one man has arrived another may also succeed'; enthusiasm is taken for predestination, and each one thinks himself created by God on purpose to be a famous leader. In the meanwhile you live in Toledo, dreaming of glory, of hairbreadth enterprises, of gigantic battles and noisy triumphs. But when, with the two stars on your arm you go to a regiment, the first thing that comes to meet you at the barrack gate, even before you receive the salute of the sentry, is the ugly and disagreeable reality. He who dreams of covering himself with glory and becoming a great leader before he is thirty, thinking of nothing but strategic combinations and original fortifications, must occupy himself with the washing and decency of a lot of wild lads, who come in from the fields reeking with excessive health; try the rations, discuss drawers and shirts, calculate the lasting of ankle boots and hempen shoes, and he who never went near the kitchen at home, was most carefully looked after by his mother, and thought that everything was women's work except giving words of command and drawing soldiers up in line, now finds the first requirement in a regiment is to be cook, tailor, shoemaker, etc., very often receiving reprimands from his superiors if he prove lazy in those duties."

"That is true," said Juanito laughing; "but without these things there cannot be an army, and an army is necessary."

"We are not discussing if it is necessary or no. I only wish to point out that you (or perhaps not you, as you enter on a good footing, but certainly your companions) are self-deceivers, and are preparing without knowing it the shipwreck of your lives, precisely like those other youths who, poorer, or perhaps less energetic, crowd to enter the Church. The Church has come to an end as there is no longer faith; military glory has ended in Spain as there are no longer wars of conquest, and our character as strong fighting men has been lost for centuries. If we have a war, it is either civil or colonial—wars that might be called disasters—without glory and without profit, but in which men die as at Thermopyle or Austerlitz, as a man can only die once; but without the consolation of fame, or of public applause, without in fact that aureole that you call glory. You have all been born too late; you are the warriors of a people who must perforce live in peace; just as those seminarists will be the future priests in a country where there are no longer miracles nor faith, only routine and utter stagnation of thought."

"But if we have no foreign wars, if conquests have come to an end, we serve at least to defend the integrity of Spanish soil, to guard our own homes. Is it that you think," said the cadet nettled, "we are incapable of dying for our country?"

"I do not doubt it; that is the only thing Spaniards are capable of doing, to die most heroically, but in the end to die. Our history for the last two centuries has been nothing but a tale of heroic deaths—'Glorious defeat in such a place,' 'Heroic disaster in some other.' By sea and by land we have astonished the world, throwing ourselves blindly into danger, showing a good front, without flinching, with the stoicism of a Chinaman. But nations do not grow great from their contempt of death, but through their ability to preserve life. The Poles were the terror of the Turks, and some of the best soldiers in Europe, yet Poland has ceased to exist. If any great European power *could* invade us—you will remark I say *could*, for in these things the wish is not the same as the power, I know exactly what would happen; the Spaniards would know how to die, but you may be perfectly certain the invaders would not require more than two battles to sweep away entirely all our military preparations. And all this, which could be scattered in a couple of days, what sacrifices it costs the country!"

"Then," said the cadet ironically, "I presume we must suppress the army, and leave the nation undefended."

"As things are to-day there is no hope of that happening. As long as all Europe is armed and the smallest country has an army, Spain will have one also. It is not for her to set an example; and besides, the example would be of no use, it is as though one having a few thousand pesetas should endeavour to initiate the remedy to social injustice by sacrificing himself and giving them up."

118

After a long silence Gabriel spoke again very quietly, noticing the ironical and even aggressive manner of the cadet.

"No doubt you are pained by what I say; believe me I feel it, as I have no wish to wound the beliefs of anyone, least of all of those who have formed to themselves an ideal of life. But truth is truth. The social question does not trouble you. Is it not so? You know nothing about it, you have never thought about it for an instant and it is the same with all your, companions, but nevertheless, what you suffer in your prestige, in your love of country and of your standard, has no other cause but the social disorder at present rampant in the world. Wealth is everything, capital is lord of the world. Science directs humanity as the successor of faith, but the rich have possessed themselves of its discoveries, and have monopolised them to continue their tyranny. In the economic world they have made themselves masters of machinery and of all progress, using them as chains to enslave the workman, forcing an excess of production, but limiting his daily wage to what is strictly necessary. In the life of nations the same thing repeats itself—war to-day is nothing but an appliance of science, and the richest countries have acquired the greatest improvements in the art of extermination. They have crowds of recruits, thousands of enormous cannon, they can keep millions of men under arms, with every sort of modern improvement, without becoming bankrupt. But to poor countries, their only remaining course is to hold their tongues, or to rage uselessly, as the disinherited do against those in possession of their property. The most cowardly and sedentary people on the face of the globe may become invincible warriors if they have the money. The bravery of chivalry came to an end with the invention of powder, and the pride of race has faded for ever before the advent of trade. If the Cid came to life again he would be in jail, he would have become a highwayman, unable to adjust himself to the inequalities and injustice of modern life. If the Gran Capitan were now minister of war, he would probably be unable even with this military tax which oppresses the country to put his regiments in condition to undertake a fresh war in Italy. It is money, that cursed money! which has killed the finest part of soldiering—personal bravery, initiative, originality—just as it has crushed the workman, making his life a hell."

The cadet listened attentively to Gabriel, understanding for the first time that in great nations there is something more than the warlike sympathies of the monarch and the bravery of the army. He saw suddenly that wealth was the basis and mainspring of all military enterprise.

"Then," he said thoughtfully, "if foreign nations do not attack us it is not because they fear us."

"No; that we are permitted to live in peace is because these omnipotent powers with all their ambitions and jealousies preserve a certain equilibrium. They are like the great capitalists who, occupied with vast projects of speculation, neglect either from carelessness or contempt the small undertakings that lie at their door. Do you believe that Switzerland or Belgium or other small countries live in peace surrounded by great powers because they have an army? They would exist just the same if they had not a single soldier, and the military power of Spain is not greater than that of one of these small countries; the poverty of the country and the scanty population oblige us to be humble. In these days there are two kinds of armies those organised for conquest and those whose only use is to keep order at home, that are no more than police on a large scale, with guns and generals. That of Spain, however much it costs, and however much they increase it, comes under the latter classification."

"And if it is only this," said the cadet, "is it not something? We keep peace at home, and we watch over the tranquillity of our country."

"Yes, but that could be done by fewer people and for less money. Besides, how about glory? Will you youths, full of illusions, overflowing with aggressiveness and energy for

119

new undertakings, resign yourselves to this profession of watchmen and caretakers to a country? Your future will be as monotonous as that of a priest in his cathedral. Every day the same—to drill men to move this or that way, to play at dominoes or billiards in a cafe, to walk about in uniform or take a nap in the guard-room. There can be nothing for you beyond a small disturbance at the tax on provisions, a strike, a closing of shops to protest against the taxes, and then to fire on a mob armed with sticks and stones. If at any time in your life you are ordered to fire, you may be sure it will be on Spaniards. The Government do not wish for an army as they know it is useless for the exterior defence of the nation; besides, the national finances do not admit of its maintenance, and they are consequently satisfied with an embryonic organisation which is always insubordinate, distracted by incessant and contradictory reforms, copying foreign improvements as a poor girl copies the robes of a great lady. Believe me, there is nothing pleasant in living such a narrowed and monotonous life, with no other chance of glory but that of shooting a workman who protests or a people who complain."

"But, how about liberty? How about political progress?" inquired the cadet. "I have heard it said by a captain at the academy that if the Liberal party exists in Spain it is through the army."

"There is a great deal in that," said Gabriel. "It is indubitably the most important service the army has rendered to the State; without it, who knows where the civil wars would have ended in this country, so stationary and so timid about all reforms! I repeat it, I do not ignore this service, but, believe me, that civil wars between liberty and political absolutism will never be repeated, neither could the guerilla warfare of the Independence with any definite issue. The means of communication and military progress have put an end to mountain warfare. The Mauser, which is the arm of the day, requires well-provided parks of ammunition to follow it, cartridge magazines at its back, and all this is incompatible with party fighting."

"But you will admit that we are of some use, and that we render the nation good service."

"I admit it in the actual state of things, but I should admit it more fully if you were fewer. The greater part of the grant is spent, but all the same you live in poverty, decent and hidden, but poverty all the same. A lieutenant earns less than many operatives, but he must buy himself showy uniforms, be smart, and frequent when he wants amusement the same places as the rich. He can only see before him long years of waiting and of hidden poverty, borne with dignity, until some promotion provides him with a few duros more monthly. You all suffer dragging on this existence of slaves to the sword, the nation who pays grumbles at seeing you inactive, and forgets other superfluous expenses to fix its complaints solely on the military. Believe me, for a modern army, you are too few and badly organised; to keep the peace at home you are too many and too dear. The fault is not yours, your vocation has come too late, when fate has rendered Spain powerless for adventurous undertakings. If she revives she will have to follow a direction which will certainly not be that of the sword. For this reason I say that these youths stray from the right path when they seek for glory where their ancestors thought to find it."

The appearance of Silver Stick cut short the dialogue. He ran in, pale with excitement, gasping, rattling his bunch of keys.

"His Eminence is coming," he said, hurriedly. "He is already under the arch; he wishes to spend the evening in the garden; it is a whim! They say he is quite unmanageable to-day."

And he ran on to open the staircase del Tenorio, which put the Claverias in communication with the lower cloister.

The cadet was alarmed at the unexpected proximity of his uncle. He did not wish to meet him there, he feared the cardinal's temper, and fled towards the tower staircase on his way to the bull-fight, sacrificing his sweetheart sooner than meet with Don Sebastian.

Gabriel, who now found himself alone in the cloister, leant against a column and watched the progress of this terrible prince of the Church. He saw him come out of the doorway leading to the abode of the giants, followed by two servants. Luna was able to examine him well for the first time. He was enormous; but in spite of his age carried himself erectly; over his black cassock with the red borders hung his gold cross. He was leaning with a martial air on a staff of command, and the gold tassels of his hat fell on the pink skin of his fat neck, which was fringed with white hair. His small and penetrating eyes looked on all sides in the hopes of discovering some delinquency, something contravening the established rules, which would enable him to break out into shouts and menaces and so give vent to his ill humour and to the anger which furrowed his brows.

He disappeared by the staircase del Tenorio, preceded by Don Antolin, who, after opening the iron gates, had placed himself at his orders, shaking with fear. The silence and solitude of the Claverias were undisturbed, it seemed as though the people hidden in their houses remained absolutely still, guessing the danger that was passing.

Gabriel, leaning on the balustrade, watched the cardinal enter the lower cloister, walking round two sides till he came to the garden gate. A slight gesture from the prelate was sufficient to stop the two servants, and he walked on alone through the central avenue towards the summer-house where Tomasa was fast asleep between its leafy walls, her knitting in her hands.

The old woman awoke at the sound of footsteps, and seeing the prelate, gave a cry of surprise.

"Don Sebastian! You here!"

"I wished to visit you," said the cardinal with a benevolent smile, seating himself on a bench. "It must not be always you who come to seek me. I owe you many visits, and here I am."

Plunging one hand into the depths of his cassock, he drew forth a small gold case and lighted a cigarette. He stretched out his legs with the complacency of one who being always accustomed to wear the frowning brow of authority, finds himself for a few moments at liberty.

"But have you not been ill?" inquired the gardener's widow. "I had thought of coming round to the palace this afternoon to inquire after your health from Doña Visita."

"Hold your tongue, you fool; I have never felt better, especially since this morning. The slap I have given to *those* by not going into the choir to pray with them has put me in a splendid humour, and in order that they may thoroughly understand my meaning I have come to see you. I wish them all to know that I am quite well, and that what is said about my illness is untrue. I wish all in Toledo to understand that the archbishop will not see his canons, and that he does so from a sense of dignity, not from pride, as at the same time he can come down to see his old friend the gardener's widow."

And the terrible old man laughed like a child to think of the annoyance this visit would cause his Chapter.

"Do not believe, however, Tomasa," he continued, "that I have come to see you solely for this reason. I felt sad and worried in the palace this afternoon. Visitacion was busy with some friends from Madrid, and I had that heartache I sometimes feel when I think of the past. I felt that I must come and see you, more especially as it is always cool in the Cathedral garden, whereas outside it is as hot as an oven. Ah! Tomasa! how strong I see you! So slim and so active. You wear better than I do; you are not wrapped in fat like this sinner, and you have not the pains that disturb my nights. Your hair is still dark, your teeth are well preserved, and you do not need like this old cardinal to have a mechanism inside your mouth; but all the same, Tomasa, you are just as old as I am. We have very few years of life left to us, however much the Lord may wish to preserve us. What would I not give to return to those days when I ran up to your house in my red gown in search of your father, the sacristan, and stole your breakfast. Eh, Tomasa?"

The two old people, forgetting social differences, recalled the past with the friendly resignation of those advancing towards death. Everything was the same as in their childhood—the garden, the cloister; nothing about the Cathedral had changed.

His Eminence, closing his eyes, fancied himself once more the restless acolyte of fifty years before; the blue spirals from his cigarette seemed to carry his thoughts back through the interminable labyrinths of the past.

"Do you remember how your poor father used to laugh at me? 'This boy,' he would say in the sacristy, 'is a Sixtus V. What do you wish to be?' he would ask me, and I always gave the same answer, 'Archbishop of Toledo.' And the good sacristan would laugh again at the certainty with which I spoke of my hopes. Believe me, Tomasa, I thought much of him when I was consecrated bishop, regretting his death. I should have been delighted with his tears of joy seeing me with the mitre on my head. I have always loved you, you are an excellent family, and have often satisfied my hunger."

"Silence, señor, silence, and do not recall those things. I am the one who ought to be grateful for your kindness, so simple and genuine in spite of your rank, which comes next after the Pope. And the truth is," added the old woman with the pride of her frankness, "that no one is the loser. Friends like I am you can never have; like all the great ones of the earth, you are surrounded by flatterers and rascals. If you had remained a simple mass priest no one would have sought you out, but Tomasa would have always been your friend, always ready to do you a service. If I love you so much it is because you are kind and affable, but if you had put on pride like other archbishops, I should have kissed your ring and—'Good-bye.' The cardinal to his palace, the gardener's widow to her garden."

The prelate received the old woman's frankness smilingly.

"You will always be Don Sebastian to me," she continued. "When you told me not to call you Eminence or to use the same ceremonies as other people, I was as pleased as if I had been given the mantle of the Virgin del Sagrario. Such ceremonies would have stuck in my throat and made me ready to cry out, 'Let him have his fill of Eminence and Illustrious, but we have scratched each other thousands of times when we were little, and this big thief could never see a scrap of bread or an apricot in my hand without trying to snatch and devour it!' You may be thankful I spoke of you as 'usted' when you became a beneficiary of the Cathedral, for, after all, it would not do to 'thou' a priest as if he were an acolyte."

Silence fell on the two old people, their eyes wandered tenderly over the garden, as if each tree or arcade covered with foliage contained some memory.

"Do you know what I have just remembered," said Tomasa. "I remember that we saw each other just here many many years ago, at least forty-eight or fifty. I was with my poor elder sister who had just married Luna the gardener, and in the cloister wandering round me was he who afterwards became my husband. We saw a handsome sergeant come into the summer-house with a great jingle of spurs, a sword on his arm, and a helmet with a tail just like the Jews on the Monument. It was you, Don Sebastian, who had come to Toledo to visit your uncle the beneficiary, and who would not leave without visiting your friend Tomasita. How handsome and smart you were. I do not say it to flatter you, it is truth. You looked like being a rogue with the girls! And I still remember you said something to me about how pretty and fresh you thought me after so many years absence.

You don't mind my reminding you of this? Really? It was only a soldier's gallant jests. How many would say that now? When you left, I said to my brother-in-law, 'He has put on the uniform for good and all; it is useless his uncle, the beneficiary, thinking of making a priest of him.'"

"It was a youthful sally," said the cardinal smiling, remembering with pride the dashing sergeant of dragoons. "In Spain, there are only three professions worthy of a man—the sword, the Church and the toga. My blood was hot and I wanted to be a soldier, but unluckily I fell on times of peace, my promotion would have been very slow, and in order not to embitter my uncle's last years, I renewed my studies and turned to the Church. One can serve God or one's country as well in one place as another, but, believe me, very often in spite of the pomp of my cardinalate I think with envy of that soldier you saw. What happy times they were! Even now the sword draws me. When I see the cadets I would gladly exchange with some of them, giving them my crozier and cross. And possibly I might have done better than any of them! Ah! if only the great times of the reconquest could return when the prelates went out to fight the Moors! What a great Archbishop of Toledo I should have been!"

And Don Sebastian drew up his fat old body, and proudly stretched out his arms with all the remains of his former strength.

"You have always been a strong man," said the gardener's widow. "I say very often to some of the priests who speak of you and criticise you: 'You must not trifle with His Eminence, he is quite capable of going one day into the choir—some he likes and some he does not—and driving you all out at one fell swoop.'"

"I have more than once been tempted to do so," said the prelate firmly, his eyes flashing with energy, "but I have been prevented by the thought of my charge and my character as a peaceful priest. I am the shepherd of a Catholic flock, not a wolf who tears the sheep in his fierceness. But sometimes I can bear no more, and God forgive me! I have often been tempted to raise the shepherd's crook and chastise with blows that rebel flock who harbour in the Cathedral."

The prelate became excited, speaking of his quarrels with the Chapter; the placidity of mind produced by the quiet of the garden disappeared as he thought of his hostile subordinates. He felt obliged as at other times to confide his troubles to the gardener's widow with that instinctive kindly feeling which often causes highly-placed people to confide in humble friends.

"You cannot imagine, Tomasa, what those men make me suffer. I will subdue them because I am the master, because they owe me obedience by the rule of discipline without which there can be neither Church nor religion; but they oppose and disobey me. My orders are carried out with grumbling, and when I assert myself even the last ordained priest stands on what he calls his rights, lays complaints against me and appeals either to the Rota or to Rome. Let us see, am I the master or am I not? Ought the shepherd to argue with his sheep and consult how to guide them in the right way? They sicken and weary me with their complaints and questions. There is not half a man amongst them, they are all cowardly tale-bearers. In my presence they lower their eyes, smile and praise His Eminence, and as soon as I turn my back they are vipers trying to bite me, scorpion tongues which respect nothing. Ay, Tomasa, my daughter! pity me! when I think of all this it makes me quite ill."

The prelate turned pale, rising from his seat as though he felt a sudden spasm of pain.

"Do not worry yourself so much," said the old woman, "you are above them all, and you will overcome them."

"Clearly, I shall defeat them; if not, it would fill my cup, for it would be the first time I had been vanquished. These squabbles among comrades do not trouble me much after all, for I know in the end I shall see my detested enemies at my feet. But it is their tongues, Tomasa!—what they say about the beings I love most in the world, that is what wounds me, and is killing me."

He sat down again, coming quite close to the gardener's widow, so as to speak in a very low voice.

"You know my past better than anyone; I have such great confidence in you that I have told you everything. Besides, you are very quick, and if I had not told you, you would have guessed. You know what Visitacion is to me, and most certainly you are aware of what those wretches say about her. Do not play the fool; everyone inside and outside the Cathedral listens to these calumnies and believes them. You are the only one who does not credit them because you know the truth. But ay! the truth cannot be told, I cannot proclaim it, these robes forbid me."

And he seized a handful of his cassock with his clenched fingers as if he would rend it.

A long silence followed. Don Sebastian looked fixedly at the ground, clutching with his hands as though he were trying to grasp invisible enemies; every now and then he felt a stab of pain and sighed uneasily.

"Why do you think about these things?" said the gardener's widow; "they only make you ill, and you ought not to have disturbed yourself to come and see me, you would have done better to remain in the palace."

"No, you distract my mind from them, it is a great comfort to tell you of my troubles. Up there I feel in despair, and have to exert all my self-command to suppress my anger. I do not wish my servants to understand, for they are quite capable of laughing at me, neither do I wish poor Visitacion to know anything. I cannot dissimulate. I cannot feign happiness when I am so irritated! What a hell I suffer! I cannot say that I have been a man, and that I have been weak as the flesh of which I am made, that I have with me the fruit of my faults, and that I will not separate myself from them, though persecuted by calumny. Every man acts as he is able, and I wish to be good in spite of my faults. I might have separated from my children, I might have deserted them, as others have done to preserve their reputation as saints, but I am a man, and I am proud of them; I am a man with all his defects and all his virtues, neither greater nor less than the general run of humanity. The feeling of paternity is so deeply rooted in me that I would sooner lose my mitre than abandon my children. You remember when Juanito's father, who passed as my nephew, died, how deeply I felt it, I thought I should have died also. Such a fine, handsome man, and with such a brilliant future before him! I would have made him a magistrate, president of the supreme court, minister, anything I wished! And in twenty-four hours he was dead as though Heaven wished to punish me. It is true I have my grandson remaining, but this Juanito in no way resembles his father, and I confess it to you, I do not care much for him. I can only see in him the most distant reflection of my poor son. Of my past, of that time which was the happiest of my life, all I have left me is Visitacion. She is the living image of the poor dead one. I worship her! and this feeble ray of happiness these wretched people disturb with their calumnies. It is enough to make one kill them!"

Overcome by the happy recollection of the spring-time which had flowered during the first years of his episcopate, far away in an Andalusian diocese, he repeated once again to Tomasa the tale of his relations with a certain devout lady, who from her childhood had felt a horror of the world. Devotion had drawn them together, but life was not long in asserting her rights, opening herself a way by their almost mystical relations, and finally uniting them in a carnal embrace. They had lived faithful to each other in the secrecy of ecclesiastical life, loving each other with scrupulous prudence, so that no rumour of their relations had ever publicly transpired, until she died, leaving two children. Don Sebastian, a man of strong passions, was almost vehement in his paternal feelings—those two beings were the image of the poor dead woman, the remembrance of the only idyll which had softened a life wholly given over to ambition, and the calumnies circulated by his enemies, founded on the presence of his daughter in the archiepiscopal palace nearly drove him mad.

"They believe her to be my mistress!" he said angrily. "My poor Visitacion, so good, so affectionate, so gentle to all, changed to a courtesan by these wretches! A sweetheart that I have taken for my amusement from the college of Noble Ladies! As if I, old and infirm, were able to think of such things! Brutes! wretches! Crimes have been committed for less!"

"Let them say on. God is in heaven and sees us all."

"I know it, but this is not enough to quiet me. You have children, Tomasa, and you know what it is to love them. It is not only what is done against them that wounds us, but what is said. What days of suffering I endure! You know since my boyhood all my dreams have been to rise to where I am. I used to look at the throne in the choir and think how comfortable I should be in it—of the immense happiness of being a prince of the Church. Well, now I am on the throne. I have spent half a century removing the stones from my path, leaving my skin and even my flesh on the brambles of the hillside. I only know how I was able to rise from the black mass and obtain a bishopric! Afterwards—now I am an archbishop! now I am a cardinal! At last I can rise no higher! And what is it all? Happiness always floats before us like the cloud of light which guided the Israelites. We see it, we almost touch it, but it never lets itself be caught. I am more unhappy now than in the days when I struggled to rise, and thought myself the most unfortunate of men. I am no longer young; the height on which I stand draws all eyes to me and prevents me defending myself. Ay, Tomasa! pity me, for I am worthy of compassion! To be a father and to be obliged to hide it as a crime! To love my daughter with an affection which increases more and more as I draw nearer to death, and have to endure that people should imagine this pure affection to be something so repugnant!"

And the terrible glance of Don Sebastian, which terrified all the diocese, was clouded with tears.

"Moreover, I have other troubles," he went on, "but they are those of a far-seeing man who fears the future. When I die, all that I have will be my daughter's. Juanito inherits what belonged to his mother, who was rich; besides, he has his profession and the support of my friends. Visitacion will be very rich. You know my adversaries throw in my face what they call my avarice. Avaricious I am not, but foreseeing, and anxious for the well-being of those belonging to me. I have saved a great deal. I am not one of those who distribute bread at the gate of his palace, nor who seek popularity through almsgiving. I have pasture lands in Estremadura, many vineyards in La Mancha, houses, and above all State stock—much stock. As a good Spaniard I have wished to help the Government with my money, more especially as it bears interest. I do not quite know how much I possess, but certainly twenty millions of reals, and probably more, all saved by myself and increased by fortunate speculations. I cannot complain of fate, and the Lord has helped me. Everything is for my poor Visitacion. I should delight in seeing her married to a good man; but she will not leave me. She is drawn to the Church, and that is my fear. Do not be surprised, Tomasa; I, a prince of the Church, fear to see how she is attracted by devotion, and I do all I can to turn her from it. I respect a religious woman, but not one who is only happy in the Church. A woman ought to live; she ought to be happy as a mother. I have always looked badly on nuns."

"Let her be, señor," said the gardener's widow; "there is nothing strange in her love for the Church. Living as she does she could scarcely do otherwise."

"For the present time, I have no fear. I am by her side, and her being fond of the society of the nuns signifies very little to me. But I may die to-morrow, and just imagine what a splendid mouthful poor Visitacion and her millions would be, left alone, with this predilection to religious life, of which those cunning people would be sure to take advantage! I have seen a great deal. I belong to the class, and I am in the secret. There is no lack of religious orders who devote themselves to hunting heiresses for the greater glory of God, as they say. Besides, there are many foreign nuns with great flapping caps travelling about here, who are lynxes for that sort of work, and I am terrified lest they should pounce on my daughter. I belong to the ancient Catholicism, to that pure Spanish religion, free from all modern extravagances. It would be sad to have spent my life in saving, only to fatten the Jesuits or those sisters who cannot speak Castilian. I do not wish my money to share the fate of that of the sacristans in the proverb. For this reason, to the annoyance I feel at my struggles with this inimical Chapter, I must add the distress I feel at my daughter's feeble character. Probably she will be hunted; some rake will laugh at me and possess himself of my money."

Excited by his gloomy thoughts, he gave vent to an interjection both caustic and obscene, a memory of his soldiering days; in the presence of the gardener's widow there was no need to control himself, and the old woman was accustomed to this relief of his temper.

"Let us see," he said imperiously after a long silence. "You, who know me better than anyone, am I as bad as my enemies suppose? Do I deserve that the Lord should punish me for my faults? You are one of God's souls, simple and good, and you know more of all this by your instinct than all the doctors of theology."

"You bad, Don Sebastian? Holy Jesus! You are a man like all others, neither more nor less; but you are sincere, all of one piece, without deceit or hypocrisy."

"A man—you have said it. I am a man like the rest. We who attain a certain height are like the saints on the fronts of the churches: from below we cause admiration for our beauty, but viewed closely we cause horror from the ugliness of the stones corroded by time. However much we wish to sanctify ourselves, keeping ourselves apart, we are still nothing but men—creatures of flesh and blood like those who surround us.

"In the Church those who free themselves from human passion are most rare. And who knows if, even among those few privileged ones, some are not driven by the demon of vanity to increase the asceticism of their lives, thinking of the glory of being on an altar! The priest who succeeds in subduing his flesh falls into avarice, which is the ecclesiastical vice *par excellence*. I have never hoarded from vice; I have saved for my own, but never for myself."

The prelate was silent for a long while; but in his irresistible desire to confide in the simple old woman he went on.

"I am sure that God will not despise me when my hour comes. His infinite mercy is above all the littleness of life. What has been my fault? To have loved a woman, as my father loved my mother; to have had children as the apostles and saints had. And why not? Ecclesiastical celibacy is an invention of men, a detail of discipline agreed upon at the councils; but the flesh and its exigencies are anterior by many centuries; they date from Paradise. Whoever crosses this barrier, not from vice, but from irresistible passion, because he cannot conquer the impulse to create a family and to have a companion, fails indubitably towards the laws of the Church, but he does not disobey God. I fear the approach of death; many nights I doubt and tremble like a child. But I have served God in my own way. In former times I would have served Him with my sword, fighting against the heretics. Now I am His priest and do battle for Him whenever I see the impiety of the age curtailing anything of His glory. The Lord will forgive me, receiving me into His bosom. You, who are so good, Tomasa, and have the soul of an angel beneath your rough exterior, do you not think so?"

The gardener's widow smiled, and her words fell slowly on the silence of the dying evening.

"Tranquillise yourself, Don Sebastian. I have seen many saints in this house, and they have been worth much less than you. To ensure their salvation they would have abandoned their children. To maintain what they call purity of soul they would have renounced their family. Believe me, no saints enter here; they are men, nothing but men. You have nothing to repent of in following the impulse of your heart. God created us in His image and likeness, and also planted in us family love. All the rest, chastity, celibacy and other trifles, you invented for yourselves, to distinguish yourselves from the common herd of people. Be a man, Don Sebastian, and the more you show yourself such the better it will be for you, and the better the Lord will receive you in His glory."

CHAPTER IX

A few days after Corpus Don Antolin went one morning in search of Gabriel. Silver Stick smiled at Luna, speaking to him in a patronising way.

He had thought of him all night; it pained him to see him idle, walking about the cloister; it was the want of occupation that inspired him with such perverse ideas.

"Let us see," he continued, "would it suit you to come down with me every afternoon into the Cathedral, to show the Treasury and the other curiosities? A great many foreigners come who can scarcely make themselves understood when they question me; you will understand them, as you know French and English, and, your brother says, many other languages. The Cathedral would be a gainer, as it would show these strangers that we have an interpreter at our disposal; you would be doing us a favour and would lose nothing by it. It is always an amusement to see new faces; and about the recompense ..."

Don Antolin stopped here, scratching his head beneath his skull cap. He would see what he could screw out of the funds of the Obreria; if just at first nothing could be managed, as the revenues of the Primacy were meagre and at their lowest ebb, no doubt something could be given later on.

He looked anxiously for Gabriel's answer, who, however, was quite agreeable; when all was said and done he was a guest of the Cathedral and owed it something. And from that afternoon he went down at the hour of choir to show the foreigners all the treasures of the church.

There was no lack of travellers who showed Don Antolin's coloured tickets waiting for the time to see the jewels. Silver Stick could never see a stranger without imagining that he was a lord or a duke, and often felt very much surprised at the shabbiness of their clothing; according to his ideas only the great ones of the earth could give themselves the pleasure of travelling, and he opened wide his incredulous and scandalised eyes when Gabriel told him that many were shoemakers from London or shopkeepers from Paris, who during their holidays treated themselves to a trip through the ancient country of the Moors.

Five canons in their choir surplices advanced up the nave, each one holding a key in his hand; these were the guardians of the treasure. Each one opened the lock confided to his custody, the door swung heavily, and the chapel, with its antique treasures, was opened.

In large glass cases, like a museum, was displayed the ancient opulence of the Cathedral: statues of chiselled silver, large globes crowned by graceful little figures all of precious metal, ivory caskets of complicated work, custodias and viriles of gold, enormous gilt dishes, embossed with mythological subjects reviving the joy of paganism in that sordid and dusty corner of the Christian Church, and precious stones spread their varied colours over pectorals, mitres and mantles for the Virgin. There were diamonds so immense as to make one doubt their being genuine, emeralds the size of pebbles, amethysts, topaz, and pearls—very many pearls, strewn by the hundreds and thousands on the Virgin's garments. The foreigners were amazed at all this wealth and dazzled by the quantity, while Gabriel, who had become accustomed to see it daily, looked at it carelessly. The Treasury presented a deplorable spectacle of neglect: the riches had aged with the Cathedral, the diamonds did not flash, the gold seemed tarnished and dusty, the silver was blackened, the pearls were opaque and sick, the smoke from the wax tapers and the damp atmosphere of the church had sadly dulled everything.

"The Church," said Gabriel to himself, "ages everything she touches. The treasures lose their brilliancy in her hands, like jewels that fall into the power of usurers. The diamond becomes dulled in the bosom of the great miser, and the most beautiful picture becomes blackened on her altars."

After the visit to the Treasury came the exhibition of the Ochavo, the octagonal chapel of dark marbles, that pantheon of relics where the most repulsive human remains—skulls with their ghastly grin, mummified arms and worn-eaten vertebras—were shown in gold or silver shrines. The gross and credulous piety of former days displayed itself in the full tide of unbelief, so that even Don Antolin, so uncompromising when he spoke of the glories of his Cathedral, lowered his voice and hurried over his explanations as he showed a piece of the mantle worn by Santa Leocadia when she "appeared" to the Archbishop of Toledo, quite understanding the difficulty of explaining how an apparition could wear garments of stuff.

Gabriel translated faithfully Don Antolin's explanation, repeating it again and again with imperturbable gravity, while the canons who escorted the batch of strangers drew a few paces away with an absent look, to avoid questions.

One day a phlegmatic Englishman interrupted the interpreter.

"And have you not amongst all these things a feather from the wings of St. Michael?"

"No, señor, and it is a great pity," said Luna, equally seriously, "but you will probably find it in some other Cathedral; we cannot have everything here."

In the Chapter-house, a mixture of Arab and Gothic architecture, the foreigners were much interested by the double row of portraits of the Toledan archbishops hanging on the wall, with their mitres and golden croziers. Gabriel called their attention to the picture of Don Cerebruno, a mediaeval prelate, so called from his enormous head; but it was the wardrobe which more especially surprised the foreigners.

It was a room surrounded by large cupboards and shelves of old wood; above these the walls were covered with dusty and torn pictures, copies of Flemish paintings that the canons had relegated to this corner; round the room were placed in line the ancient armchairs of the church, some of Spanish workmanship, austere, with straight lines and ravelled coverings, others of Greek design with curved feet inlaid with ivory. The capes and chasubles were piled on the shelves, according to colours, with the collars outside the heap, so that people could examine the wonderful embroidery. A whole world of patterns appeared with every possible brilliancy of colour on a few inches of stuff. The astonishing art of the ancient embroiderers made the silk a series of vivid pictures; the collar and the narrow stripes on the front of a cape were large enough to reproduce all the scenes of the biblical creation and the passion of Jesus. Brocade and silk unrolled the magnificence of their textures. One cape was a garden of flame-coloured carnations, another was a bed of roses and other fantastic flowers with twisted stamens and metallic petals. The sacristans produced from the deep shelves, as though they were books, the splendid and famous frontals of the high altar. There were special ones for each festival; that for St. John's Day was brightly coloured with verbenas, purple bunches of grapes, and golden lambs that fat little angels were caressing with their chubby hands. The most ancient, of soft and rather faded colours, showed Persian gardens with blue waters in which fabulous reddish beasts were drinking.

The visitors were bewildered seeing all this vast collection of stuffs and embroideries unrolled piece after piece—all the past of a Cathedral which, having millions of revenue, employed for its embellishment armies of embroiderers, acquiring the richest textures of Valencia and Seville, reproducing in gold and colours all the episodes from the Holy books, and the torments of the martyrs, all the glorious legends of the Church, immortalised by the needle, before printing had been able to do so.

Gabriel returned every evening to the upper cloister, wearied out with walking the length and breadth of the Cathedral. During the first few days he was delighted with the novelty of seeing fresh faces, to hear the rustle of the visitors who, branching off from the great stream of travellers who inundated Europe, came as far as Toledo. But after a little while the people he saw every afternoon seemed to him just the same. There were the same questions, the same stiff and hard-featured Englishwomen, and the same o-o-o-h's of cold and conventional admiration, and the same identical way of turning their backs with rude pride when there was nothing else to be shown. Returning to the quiet of the upper cloister after the daily exhibition of the Treasury, Gabriel thought the poverty of the Claverias even more revolting and intolerable. The shoemaker seemed sadder and yellower in the rank atmosphere of his den, bending over his bench hammering the soles, his wife more feeble and ill, the miserable slave of maternity, weakened by hunger, and offering to her little son as his only hope of food those flaccid breasts in which there was nothing left but a drop of blood. The little child was dying! Sagrario, who had left her machine to spend the greater part of the day in the shoemaker's room said so in a low voice to her uncle. She did all the work of the house, while the poor mother, motionless in a chair, with the little one in her lap, looked at it with weeping eyes. When the baby woke from its stupor it would wearily raise its head from its little neck, which had become a mere thread; the mother to stifle its feeble moans would press it to her breast, but the child would turn away its mouth guessing the inutility of expending its strength on that rag of flesh from which it could only succeed in extracting the last drop.

Gabriel examined the child, noting its extreme emaciation and the spots that scrofula had spread over its straw-coloured skin. He shook his head incredulously when the neighbours who had gathered round the invalid each diagnosed some particular ailment, and recommended every imaginable sort of household remedy, from decoctions of rare herbs and stinking ointments to applications on the chest of miracle working prints, and tracing seven crosses on the navel with as many paternosters.

"It is hunger," said Luna to his niece, "nothing but hunger." And depriving himself of part of his own food, he sent to the shoemaker's house the milk that had been brought up for himself. But the child's stomach could not retain the liquid too substantial for its weakness, and threw it up as soon as swallowed. The Aunt Tomasa, with her energetic and enterprising character, brought a woman from outside the Cathedral to nourish the child, but after two days, and before the effects became visible, she came no more, as if she had felt disgusted at the miserable and corpse-like little body touching her. In vain the gardener's widow searched; it was not easy to find generous breasts who would give their milk for very little pay.

In the meanwhile the child was dying. All the women came in and out of the shoemaker's house, and even Don Antolin would stand at the door in the mornings.

"How is the little one? Just the same? It is all in God's hands."

And he would retire, doing the shoemaker the great charity of not speaking to him about the pesetas he owed him, on account of the sick child.

"Virgin's Blue" was annoyed by this incident, which upset the calm of the cloister, and disturbed the bliss of his digestion as a happy and well-fed servant of the Church. It was a shame that that shoemaker should be allowed to live in the Claverias with all that flock of wretched and scurvy children; one would die every month; all sorts of illness would lay hold on them. By what right were they in the Cathedral when they drew no wage from the Obreria? Such stinking excrescences ought to remain outside the Lord's house.

His mother-in-law was furious.

"Silence, you thief of the saints!" she cried. "Silence, or I will throw a dish at you! We are all sons of God, and if things were as they should be, all the poor ought to live in the Cathedral. Instead of saying such things it would be much better if you gave those unhappy people part of what you have stolen from the Virgin."

The sacristan shrugged his shoulders with contempt. If they had not enough to eat they should not have children. There he was himself with only one daughter—he did not think he had any right to more—and so thanks to Our Lady he was able to save a scrap for his old age.

Tomasa spoke of the shoemaker's child to the good gentlemen of the Chapter when they came into the garden for a few minutes after choir. They listened absently, putting their hands in their cassocks.

"It is all God's will! What poverty!"

And some gave her ten centimes, others a real, one or two even a peseta. The old woman went one day to the Archbishop's palace. Don Sebastian was engaged and unable to see her, but he sent her two pesetas by one of the servants.

"They don't mean badly," said the gardener's widow, giving her collection to the poor mother, "but each one lives for himself, and his neighbour may manage as he can. No one divides his cloak with another—take this, and see how you can get out of your trouble."

They fed a little better in the shoemaker's house; the miserable scrofulous children collected in the cloister profited most by the baby's illness; it was growing daily weaker, lying motionless for hours, with almost imperceptible breathing, on its mother's lap.

When the unhappy child died, all the people of the Claverias rushed to the home. Inside could be heard the mother's wailings, strident, interminable, like the bellowing of a wounded beast; outside the father wept silently, surrounded by his friends.

"It died just like a bird," he said with long pauses, his words broken by sobs. "His mother held him on her knees—I was working—'Antonio, Antonio!' she called, 'see, what is the matter with the child, it is moving its mouth and making grimaces?' I ran up quickly, its face was quite dusky—as if it had a veil over it. It opened its mouth, a couple of twitches with its eyes staring, and its neck fell over—just the same as a bird, just the same."

He wept, repeating constantly the resemblance between his son and those birds who die in winter from the cold.

The bell-ringer looked gloomily at Gabriel.

"You who know everything, is it true that it died of hunger?"

And the Tato with his scandalous impetuosity shouted loudly—

"There is no justice in the world! All this must be altered! Fancy a child dying of hunger in this house, where money runs like water, and where all those creatures are dressed in gold!"

When the little corpse was carried to the cemetery, the cloister seemed quite deserted; all its life was concentrated in the shoemaker's house, all the women surrounded the mother. Despair had rendered that sick and feeble woman furious. She no longer wept: her child's death had made her ferocious—she wished to bite or to dash her skull against the wall.

"Ay! my s-o-o-o-n! my Antonio!"

At night Sagrario and the other women remained in the house to look after her. In her desperation she wished to make some one responsible for her misfortune, and she fixed on those highest in the cloister. Don Antolin had not helped her with the smallest alms; his affected niece had scarcely been in to see the little one, nothing interested her but men.

"It is all Silver Stick's fault," wailed the poor mother—"he is a thief. He grinds our poverty with his usurer's snares. Never a farthing did he give for my son. And that Mariquita is just the same. Yes, señor, I do say so. She only thinks of decking herself out so that the cadets may see her."

"For mercy's sake, woman, they will hear you," begged some of the terrified women.

But others scouted this fear. "Let Don Antolin and his niece hear them! What did it matter? The Claverias were tired of the rapacity of the uncle, and the magnificent airs that ugly woman gave herself! Because they were poor they were not going to spend their lives trembling before that couple. God only knew what the uncle and niece did when they were alone in the house together!"

A breath of rebellion had passed over that sleepy world. It was the unconscious influence of Gabriel. What he had said to his friends had been passed on to all the men in the Claverias, getting even to the women. They were confused and garbled ideas, that very few could understand, but they cherished them like fresh pure air reviving their minds. They sounded in their ears like a pleasant echo from the outside world. It was sufficient for them to know that this quiet life of submission they had led up to now was not immutable—they had a right to something better—and that human beings ought to rebel against injustice and oppression.

Don Antolin, who knew well enough the crew confided to his care, was not long in perceiving this moral upturn. He felt hostility and rebellion on every side. The debtors answered him haughtily, alleging their poverty as a reason for no longer enduring his avarice; his imperious orders were tardily executed, and he had a clear perception that they were laughing behind his back as he walked through the cloister, and making threatening gestures. One day his legs trembled beneath him and his eyes were dimmed, hearing how the Perrero replied to one of his reprimands, having returned late to the Cathedral, and obliging him to descend and open the door after he had gone to bed. The Tato made him understand, with an insolent expression, that he had bought a knife, and that he intended its first fleshing to be in the bowels of some priest or other who ground down the poor.

His niece complained to Don Antolin, they paid no attention to her and flouted her, no woman now ever came to help her gratuitously in her household duties. They replied insolently that those who wanted servants must pay for them. What was her uncle thinking about? It was certainly time to assert his authority and to lay a heavy hand on these people.

131

She herself, so lively and energetic in her own house, was now obliged to retire snorting with rage or weeping, whenever she stationed herself at her door. All the women of the Claverias wished to revenge themselves for their former thraldom, standing already on the declivity of disrespect.

"Look at her!" screamed the shoemaker's wife to her neighbours, "always so dressed up, the ugly jade. She decks herself with the blood that vampire of an uncle sucks from the poor."

And from the iron gratings of the upper Claverias, giving on the roofs, there was generally a voice singing the ancient couplet, no doubt inspired by the Cathedral garden—

"Las amas de los curas y los laureles
Como nunca dan fruto siempre estan verdes."

It was this that ended the patience of Don Antolin; this insulting conjecture about himself and his niece that disturbed his miserly chastity. He visited the cardinal to complain of the inhabitants of the cloister, but His Eminence, who lived in a perpetual rage, grew furious listening to him and very nearly thrashed him. Why did he come to him with such tales? For what reason had he been given any authority? Was there nothing left of a man beneath his cassock? He who was wanting in the good discipline of the house—turn him out into the street at once! More energy, and be careful never to trouble him again with such insignificant tales, otherwise the person who would be turned into the street would be Silver Stick himself.

Don Antolin felt a little braver after this interview, although he swore mentally never again to visit that terrible prelate. He was determined to reassert his authority, by punishing the weakest, whom he considered as the origin of all these scandals. The shoemaker should be expelled from the Claverias, as he was there through no other right but that his wife had been born there. Mariquita, bewildered by her uncle's energy, must needs speak to some one about these intentions, and so the news circulated through the cloister.

Don Antolin did not dare to move a step further, terrified by the silent unanimity with which the whole population rose against him.

The Tato looked at him with mocking and threatening eyes, in which Silver Stick could plainly read "Remember the knife"; but what terrified Don Antolin more than anything was the silence of the bell-ringer, and the savage and hostile glance with which he responded to his words.

Even the good Wooden Staff, Esteban, protested in his own way, saying quietly to Don Antolin:

"Is it really true that you intend turning out the shoemaker? You will do wrong, very wrong, for after all he is very poor, and his wife was born in the cloister. These innovations always bring misfortune, Don Antolin."

So the priest, finding he had no support, and seeing hostility on every side, put off his energetic resolutions till the following day, even reproving his niece when she threw his weakness in his face.

The Canon Obrero, from whom he had implored help, did not care to disturb the blessed peace of his existence by mixing himself up in the quarrels of the smaller people. It was Silver Stick's own affair; he could punish or expel any one he thought fit without fear of anybody. But Don Antolin, dreading the responsibility that might accrue from energetic action, ended by delivering himself over to Gabriel and begging for his assistance. That man was the one who wielded the real authority in the upper cloister; all those who had listened to him followed his advice blindly.

"Help me, Gabrielillo," said the priest with an agonised expression. "If you cannot restore order, this will end badly; they even insult my poor niece, and some day I shall turn half the people of the Claverias out into the street, as I hold authority from His Eminence for everything. Ay, señor! I do not know what has happened here; surely the devil must have got loose in our upper cloister! How these people have changed to me!"

Luna guessed Don Antolin's thoughts and his allusions to the devil who had got loose in the cloister. That devil was himself. No doubt Silver Stick was right. Without intending it he had introduced discord into the Cathedral. He had sought calm and forgetfulness in that refuge, and the spirit of rebellion had followed him even into this concealment. He recalled his thoughts on the first day, when he was alone in the silent cloister; he wished to be another stone in the Cathedral, without thought, without feeling, to spend the rest of his life fixed to that ruin, with the embryonic life of the fungus on the buttress, but the spirit of the outside world had entered in with him.

Luna remembered how travellers in time of plague had crossed the sanitary cordon—they were well and happy, nothing betrayed the infection in their bodies; but the poisonous germs travelled in the folds of their clothes and in their hair, carrying death without knowing it, helping it to leap all barriers and obstacles, without being in the least aware of it. He was the same, but instead of spreading death, he spread tumultuous and rebellious life. The protest of the lower orders that had been surging throughout the world, for more than a century, had entered with him into this still remaining fragment of the sixteenth century. He had awakened those men, who had been like the sleepers in the legend, motionless in their cave for ages, while the centuries rolled on and the world was transformed.

The awakening of these people was sudden and violent, like that of a people in revolution. They were ashamed of the old errors that they had worshipped, and this made them receive as gospel everything that was new, without quailing before the consequences.

It was the faith of a people which, once it takes form, rushes onwards, accepting everything, justifying everything, the only requirement being its novelty, and casting aside contemptuously those traditional principles which it had just abandoned.

The cowardly submission of Silver Stick was the first victory of those more daring souls who formed Luna's surrounding. The avaricious and despotic priest lowered his eyes before them, smilingly anxious to make himself agreeable. This they owed to the master, for he was now the true ruler of the upper cloister. Don Antolin consulted him before making any arrangements, and his ugly niece smiled on Gabriel as the daughters of the conquered might smile on a triumphant hero.

They now no longer hid themselves in the bell-ringer's house for their meetings; they formed a circle in the cloister during the evenings, discussing the audacious doctrines taught by Luna, without now being intimidated by the religious atmosphere. They sat with the look of lords, surrounding their master, while in the opposite gallery walked Silver Stick like a black phantom, reading his book of hours, and casting now and then an uneasy glance on the group. Even his ancient vassal, the chaplain of the nuns, had dared to leave him to go and listen to Gabriel.

Don Antolin with the keenness of his ecclesiastical training, guessed the intensity of the evil produced by Luna. But for the moment his egoism was stronger than his reflection. Let them talk—what did it matter? It was only a little ebullition of pride in those people, nothing more. All words and wind in the head. Meanwhile they had better not ask for any more money! In exchange he had a very good auxiliary in Luna, who, sharing his authority, spared him many annoyances, and the Cathedral disposed of his services gratuitously as interpreter to the foreigners.

These already began to talk of the great intelligence and education of the Toledan sacristans, a praise Don Antolin received as though it were entirely deserved by himself.

Gabriel was far more alarmed than Don Antolin at the effect of his words; he bitterly repented having been led to speak of his past and of his ideals. He had sought for peace and silence, but he was still surrounded, though in a smaller degree, by the atmosphere of proselytism and blind enthusiasm, as in the days of his martyrdom. He had wished to efface himself and to disappear on entering the Cathedral, but fate mocked him, reviving the agitation in the midst of his concealment, to disturb the peace of that ruin. Society had forgotten him, but he unconsciously was agitating, and drawing to himself the attention of the outside world.

The enthusiasm of these neophytes was a danger, and his brother, the Wooden Staff, without understanding the full extent of the evil, warned him with his usual good sense.

"You are turning the heads of these poor men, with the things you tell them. Be careful; they are very well meaning, but they are very ignorant. And having been ignorant all their lives, it is dangerous to turn such men into sages at one blow. It is as if I, being accustomed to the homely stew, were taken to-day to His Eminence's table. I should gorge myself and drink too much; at night I should have a colic, and should probably hop the twig."

Gabriel acknowledged the truth of this prudent advice, but he could not draw back—he was driven on by the affection of his disciples and his own ardour as propagandist. It was a great delight to him to see the wonder in those virgin minds, entering tumultuously into the luminous palaces constructed by human thought during the last century.

The description of the future of humanity inflamed all Luna's ardour. He spoke of the happiness of men, after a revolutionary crisis which would change all the organisation of humanity with mystic rapture, like a Christian preacher describing heaven.

"Man ought to seek happiness solely in this world, for after death there only existed the infinite life of matter with its endless combinations, but the human being was effaced as entirely as a plant or an animal—he fell into oblivion when he sank into the tomb. Immortality of the soul was one of the illusions of human pride worked up by religions, who laid their foundations on this lie. It was only in this life that man could find heaven. Everyone embarked on immensity in the same ship, the earth. We were all comrades in our dangers and our struggles, and we ought to look upon one another as brothers seeking the common welfare. And what about the unequal distribution of goods, the division of classes, the ability to work, and, above all, the struggle for existence, that the philosophers and poets of the oppressing classes paint as an indispensable condition of progress? Communism is the holiest aspiration of humanity, the divine dream of man since he began to think in the first dawn of civilisation. Religions had endeavoured to establish it, but religion had been shipwrecked and was moribund, and only science could enforce it in the future. They must stop on the way they were going, as humanity was marching on the road to perdition, therefore it was necessary to return to the point of departure. The first man who had cultivated a portion of the earth and garnered the fruits of his toil, thought it was his for ever, and left it to his sons as their property; they engaged other men to cultivate it for them—so these men became robbers, appropriators of the universal heritage. It was the same with those who possessed themselves of the invention of human genius, machines, etc., for the benefit of a small majority, subjecting the rest of mankind to the law of hunger. No, everything was for everyone. The earth belonged to all human beings without exception, like the sun and the air; its products ought to be divided between everyone with due regard to their necessities. It was shameful that man, who only appeared for an instant on this planet—a minute, a second, for his life was no more than this in the life of immensity—should spend this mere breath of existence fighting with his kin, robbing them, excited by the fever of plunder, not even enjoying the majestic calm of a wild beast, which when it has eaten, rests, without ever thinking of doing harm from vanity or avarice. There ought to be neither rich nor poor— nothing but men. The only inevitable division must be that between brains more or less highly organised. But the wise, from the fact of being so, ought to show their greatness, sacrificing themselves for the more simple, without seeking to assist the greatness of their minds by material advantages; for in stomachs there were no categories or ranks. Everything that exists, even the smallest production that man considers his exclusive work, is the work of the past and present generations. By what right can anyone say 'This is mine, mine only'? Man is not consulted before he is formed if he wishes to burst forth into life. He is born—and from the fact of being born he has a right to well-being." Gabriel proclaimed his supreme formula, "Everything for everyone, and well-being for all."

His friends listened in profound silence. The right to well-being sank profoundly into their minds; it was the saying that most cruelly touched their poverty, taunted by the contrast of the wealth of the Church.

Don Martin, the young chaplain, was the only one who timidly raised any objections to the master's sayings. He wished to know if, when everything was for everyone, when man should have recognised his right to happiness, without laws or compulsion to force him to production—would he work? seeing that work was a necessity, and not a virtue, as those who employ labour say, to glorify it.

Gabriel loudly affirmed the necessity of work in the future. The man of the future would work without being forced to do so by his necessities; he would not be ruled by the body and its imperious requirements; his conscience would be inspired with the clear understanding of solidarity with his fellows and the certainty that if one abandoned social duties others would follow the example, thus rendering life in common impossible and so returning to the actual times of poverty and robbery.

"Why do not the few men of culture and sound conscience living at present kill and rob?" exclaimed Gabriel. "It is not through fear of the law and its representatives, for a clear intelligence, if it takes the trouble, can easily find ways of evading both; neither can it be through fear of eternal penalties and divine punishment, as such men do not believe in these inventions of the past. It is from that respect to his fellows which is felt by every elevated mind, from the consideration that all violence should be avoided, for if everyone gave themselves over to it, all social life must disappear. When this understanding, which now only belongs to a few, embraces all humanity, men will live ruled by their own consciences without laws or police, working from social duty, without requiring man to be the only spring of activity, and sweating without compassion to be the only way to ease."

Throughout all his revolutionary raptures Luna had no illusions as to the present. Humanity was at present an infected land, in which the best seeds rotted, or which at best produced only poisonous fruits; we must wait till the equalising revolution begun in the human conscience a century ago should be completed, after that it would be possible and easy to change the basis of society; he had a blind faith in the future. Man must progress in the same way as communities; these reckoned their evolutions by centuries, but man by millions of years. How could a man of to-day be compared to the biped animal of prehistoric times, though bearing visibly the traces of the animalism from which he had lately emerged? Living in fellowship with his ancestors the monkeys, the principal difference being the first babblings of speech, and the first trembling spark that began to burn in his brain.

From the ravenous beast of former days, suffering from all the cruel forces of nature and living in fraternal misery with the lower animals, the man of to-day was evolved, asserting his superiority to his ancestors, dominating all nature. From the men of to-day, in whom the passions of their former animalism are finding their equilibrium with the gradual unfolding of the mind, will arise that superior and perfect being indicated by philosophers, pure from all animal egoism, and endeavouring to change the actual cruel, restless, and uncertain life, into a period of happy and prosperous equality.

The animalism at present dominant in man exasperated Gabriel; it was the great stumbling-block to all his generous views of the future, and he explained to his astonished listeners the transformations of natural creatures and of the origin of man, and the wondrous poem of the evolution of nature from the original protoplasm to the infinite varieties of life. We still carry in us the marks of our origin. One could not help laughing at the God of the Jews, who had modelled a man from clay, like a sculptor. Unlucky artist! Science pointed out much carelessness and bungling in His work, without being able to justify such mistakes. The skin of our bodies did not serve us as a covering like the fur of an animal. How could we then believe it? Why were nipples given to human males, if they were of no use for milk giving? Why was the vertebral column at the back of the body as in quadrupeds, when it would have been more logical, in creating a man who stands on his feet, to place it in the centre of the body as a strong support, thus avoiding the curvatures and weakness of the spine that are now suffered by this disequilibrium in the support of its weight?

Gabriel enumerated the various inexplicable inconsistencies and incongruities found in the human body, presuming it to be of divine origin.

"I feel prouder," said he, "of my animal origin; to be a lineal descendant of inferior beings than to have emerged imperfect from the hand of a stupid God. I feel the same satisfaction that a nobleman feels in speaking of his ancestors when I think of our remote forefathers, those men-beasts, exposed like the animals to all the cruel severity of nature, who, little by little, through hundreds of centuries, have transformed themselves, triumphing in the unfolding of their minds, their brains, and their social instincts. Making clothes, edible foods, arms, tools and houses, neutralising the exterior influences of nature. What hero or discoverer in the four thousand years comprising our history can compare with those elementary men who have slowly evolved and maintained on the earth the existence of our species, exposed thousands of times to annihilation. The day on which our ancestors cared for the sick and wounded, instead of abandoning them as all animals had previously done; on which the first seed was planted, the first arrow shot, brought nature face to face with the greatest of her revolutions. Only one in the future will be able to equal it; if man in remote times was able to free his body, now he requires the great revolution to free his mind. The races who go furthest in their intellectual development will be the ultimate survivors; they will be masters of the earth, destroying all others. The least wise in those days will probably be far superior to the most cultivated intellects of the present times. Each individual will find his happiness in the happiness of his fellows, and no one will try to exercise compulsion on his neighbour. No laws or penalties will exist, and voluntary associations will supply through the influence of reason the present power of authority. This will be in the future—far, very far off. But what do centuries matter in the life of humanity! They are like seconds in our existence. On the day when man shall be transformed into this superior being, with the full development of all his intellectual faculties, now so embryonic, this earth will no longer be the vale of tears spoken of by religion, but the paradise dreamed of by the poets."

In spite of the enthusiasm with which Gabriel spoke, his hearers did not appear to share these illusions. They were silent, and their attitude was one of coldness before the immense distance of that future to which their master confided all his hopes of universal prosperity. They wished for it at once, with the eagerness of a child who is shown a dainty which is afterwards put out of its reach. The sacrifices, the slow work for the future, struck no chord in their minds. From Gabriel's explanations they only drew the fact that they were unhappy, but that they had the same right to happiness and comfort as those privileged few whom they had formerly respected in their ignorance. As a certain portion of human felicity belonged to them they wished to possess it at once, without delay or resistance, with all the fervour of one claiming what belongs to him. Luna remarked in this silence a certain rebellion, like those ironical gestures with which his companions in Barcelona had received his illusions about the future and his anathemas against violence of action.

These ardent neophytes outdistanced their teacher; they listened to him with respect, but they were obliged to isolate themselves from him in order to digest his teachings in their own fashion. Don Martin was the only one who followed him in his visionary excursions into the future. The bell-ringer, the organ-blower, the shoemaker and the Tato now went up nightly to the bell-ringer's house, without summoning the master, and there they gave vent to their hatred of everything existing, under the forgotten old prints, yellow and wrinkled, which pictured the inglorious episodes of the Carlist war.

This nocturnal reunion was a continual complaint against social injustice. They thought themselves even more unfortunate when they took an exact review of their situation. The shoemaker recalled with tearful eyes the little child who had died of hunger, and spoke of the misery of his offspring, so numerous as to render his work useless. The organ-blower spoke of his miserable old age, the six reals daily during his life, without any hope of earning more. The Tato, in the fits of rage of a bullying coxcomb, proposed to behead all the canons in the choir some evening and then to set fire to the Cathedral. And the bell-ringer, gloomy and scowling, said aloud, following up the course of his thoughts:

"And below so much wealth that is of no use to anybody—amassed from pure pride—thieves! robbers!"

Gabriel returned to pass his days by Sagrario's side. His disciples hid themselves daily more carefully in their isolation in the tower. Don Martin had his mother ill, and could not leave the convent.

Silver Stick felt quite satisfied with Luna seeing him alone, believing that it was he who had alienated his disciples, cutting short in this way his dangerous conversations so as to restore order in the cloister. One day he addressed him smilingly with a patronising manner.

"You will be rewarded for your good conduct, Gabrielillo, much sooner than you expect. Did I not say I would look out for something for you in exchange for the help you gave me in showing the treasury? Well, now you have it. From next week two pesetas daily will fall into your purse like two suns. Are you equal to staying all night in the Cathedral? The older watchman, the one who was a civil guard, is tired of it, and is going home to his own village. It appears that since his dog died he has taken a dislike to the duties. The other watchman is very poorly and wants a companion. Will you undertake it? If it were winter I should not say anything about it, as you cough too much to spend the night down there; but in summer the Cathedral is the coolest place in Toledo. What lovely nights! And by the time bad weather comes on we will have found you some better place. You are trustworthy, though your head is rather light; but you come of an honoured and well-known family, which is what is wanted. Do you accept?"

Luna accepted, declaring his intention to Esteban, when the latter objected on account of his weak health. He would only undertake the watchman's duties during the summer; besides, two pesetas a day were even more than Wooden Staff earned; the income of the family would be doubled, and it would be a pity to lose such a good opportunity.

That evening Sagrario spoke to her uncle praising the energy which prompted him to undertake any sort of work so as not to be a charge on the family.

They were in the cloister leaning on the balustrade; below was the dark garden with its waving branches, above a summer sky veiled by the heat haze which dulled the brightness of the stars. They were alone in the four-sided gallery. The lighted windows of the Chapel-master's little room threw a square of red on the opposite roofs. They could hear the harmonium playing slowly and sadly, and when it stopped the shadow of the musician passed and repassed over the square of light with his nervous gestures, which, enlarged by the reflection, appeared the most grotesque contortions.

The nocturnal calm and darkness surrounded Gabriel and Sagrario with a gentle caress; that mysterious freshness was falling from above which seems to revive drooping spirits and magnify old remembrances. The Church seemed to them as an immense sleeping beast, in whose lap they had found peace and protection.

Gabriel spoke of his past, in order to convince the young woman that his work in the Cathedral would not be very arduous. He had suffered much; there was no bitterness that he had not tasted; he had endured hunger, terrible hunger, in his peregrinations through the world. He did not know which were the most painful, his martyrdom in the dungeons of the gloomy castle, or his days of despair in the streets of crowded cities, seeing food and gold through the glass windows of the shops while his head was swimming with the dizziness of hunger. He could endure his misery while he wandered alone through the cruel selfishness of civilisation; but the most horrible days were those in which he shared his vagabond poverty with Lucy, his gentle and melancholy companion.

Gabriel spoke of the Englishwoman as of a dead sister.

"Had you known her, Sagrario, you would have loved her. She was a strong woman, a brave companion, united to me more by the community of thought than by carnal attraction. I loved her when I first saw her. I hardly know if it was love that we felt; poets have written so many lies about love, and have falsified it in such an exaggerated way, that I do not for certain know what it is."

He spoke to the young woman of love, explaining it according to his beliefs. Goethe had defined it as an "elective affinity," speaking as a man of science and not as a poet, using the term that chemistry gives to the tendency of two substances to unite and form a distinct product. Two beings between whom no affinity existed could meet through false laws of life in perpetual contact, but they could not mix or merge into one another. This happened more often than not between the individuals of different sexes who peopled the earth; a passing sentimentality could exist, or carnal caprice, but seldom love. The poor invalid Lucy was his affinity; they met and they loved. In their pity for human miseries, their hatred of inequalities and injustice, their self-abnegation in the cause of the humble and unfortunate they were equal; they were not only united by their hearts but by their brains.

She was plain, with a soft and sad plainness that seemed to Luna the supreme ideal of beauty in the midst of that struggling world of unfortunates and victims. She was the image of a woman of the people reared in the workmen's slums of great cities, anaemic from the mephitic air of the den in which she was born and from bad and insufficient food, with a wretched body, all feminine graces paralysed in their development by the rough work done in her childhood. Her lips, that great ladies paint red, were violet; the only beauty of her face lay in her eyes, those windows of sorrow, made larger by the cold nights passed in the street from horror of the scenes she saw in her childhood; her father, drunken, with the brutal wish of a workman to forget, who, after imagining that his tavern was a paradise, would become infuriated with the poverty of his home and beat the whole family.

138

"She was like all you women of the lower orders, Sagrario. Your beauty only lasts an instant; in fact, it can only exist in the first flush of youth. A woman of the poor cannot be beautiful unless she gets out of her class. Daily labour makes her lose all her freshness and strength, and maternity in the midst of poverty absorbs even the marrow in her bones. When her daily work is ended and she returns home, she has to sweep and wash, and shrivel herself to a mummy before the smoky kitchen stove. I loved Lucy for that reason, because she was consumed and drained by sweating, because she was the girl worker in all her melancholy decadence, born beautiful and made hideous by social injustice."

He recalled the unbending and deadly hatred with which that little woman spoke so quietly of the supreme vengeance of the fallen, of the revenge for long years of oppression. She showed herself more firmly rooted and fiercer in her illusions than Gabriel, and he would praise her daring as a propagandist, her perilous expeditions into the great towns, running the gauntlet of watchful police, carrying on her arm that old bonnet-box full of pamphlets that might have sent her to prison. She was the "miss" animated by evangelical propaganda, who travels over the globe distributing Bibles with a cold smile, fearless alike of the mockery of civilisation, or the brutality of savages; but what Lucy distributed were incitements to revolution; she did not seek out the happy but the despairing, in the factories and infected slums. The two endured hunger, finding themselves often separated by persecution and prison, but they met again, continuing their romantic career, till poverty and consumption ended her life.

Gabriel wept, remembering their last interview in an Italian hospital, clean and sweet, but with the frozen atmosphere of charity. As he was not her husband he could only visit her twice a week. He presented, himself ragged and downcast, seeing her in an armchair daily paler and weaker, her skin of a waxen transparency and her eyes immensely enlarged. He knew a little about everything, and he could not conceal from himself the gravity of her illness. She waited quietly for death. "Bring me some roses," she said, smiling to Gabriel, as if in the last moment of her life she wished to acknowledge the natural beauty of the world made hideous and darkened by man. The "companion" lived on dry bread, refusing the help of his comrades only a little less poor than himself, sleeping on the ground, in order to take her on his next visit a bunch of flowers.

"She died, Sagrario," groaned Luna, "and I know not where they buried her; possibly she may have served for a lecture at the school of anatomy; she fell into the common grave like those soldiers whose heroism remains in obscurity. But I still see her; she has followed me in all my misfortunes, and I think she lives again in you."

"But uncle," said Sagrario, gently, touched by his recital, "I cannot do what she did. I am an unhappy woman, without strength or will."

"Call me Gabriel," said Luna, vehemently. "You are my Lucy, who again crosses my path; I knew it from the first, and for a long while I have been searching my feelings, analysing my will, and I have arrived at one certainty—that I love you, Sagrario."

The young woman made a gesture of surprise, drawing further from him.

"Do not draw away, do not fear me. I am a feeble man, you are a weak woman; you have suffered much, and have bid good-bye to the joys of the earth, but you are strong through misfortune and can look the truth in the face. We are both wrecks of life, and the only hope left us is to wait and die quietly in the desert island which is our refuge. We are undone, rent and swept away; Death has laid his hand upon us; we are fallen and shapeless rags after having passed through the mills of an absurd society. For this reason I love you, because you are my equal in misfortune; elective affinity unites us. Poor Lucy was the work-girl enfeebled by sweating, weakened from her birth by poverty. You were the girl of the people drawn from her home by the attraction of the well-being of the privileged; seduced, not by love, but by the caprices of the happy; the girl offered as a sacrifice to the Minotaur whose remains were afterwards thrown on to the dunghill. I love you, Sagrario; we are two fugitives from society, whose paths must join; I am hated as dangerous, you are despised as an outcast; misfortune has laid hold on us. Our bodies are weakened and we bear the wounds of the conquered, but before death claims us, let us make our lives sweet by love. Let us seek for roses as did poor Lucy."

He pressed the young woman's hands, who, bewildered by Gabriel's words, knew not what to say, and wept softly. Upstairs, in the upper storey of the Claverias, the Chapel-master played his harmonium. Gabriel knew the music: it was Beethoven's last lament, the "Must it be," that the great genius sang before his death with a melancholy that made one shiver.

"I love you, Sagrario," continued Gabriel, "ever since I saw you return to this house, bravely facing the odious curiosity of the people around. I have spent weeks and months by the side of your machine, seeing how industriously you worked. I have studied you and read you. You are a sincere and simple creature; your mind has none of the doublings and hidden corners of those complicated and tortuous souls used to the artifices of civilisation. I guessed day by day, by your gentle glance and the attention with which you listened to me, your gratitude for the little I was able to do for you. I remembered the dark period of your life, your slavery to the flesh; and finding me always gentle with you, protecting you from your father's anger, your gratitude has grown and grown, till to-day you love me, Sagrario. You yourself have not realised it, you know not how to explain it, but your being responds to mine like those chemical substances I spoke of. That single and eternal love is a lying invention of the poets, of which facts often make a mockery. One can love several people with equal warmth: the indispensable thing is the affinity. You who formerly loved a man to madness, what do you feel for me? Have I deceived myself? You really love me?"

Sagrario continued weeping, with her head bent, as though she did not dare to look at Luna. He reassured her gently: she must call him Gabriel, speak to him as "thou." Were they not companions in misfortune?

"I am ashamed," murmured the young woman. "So much happiness disturbs me. Yes, I like you. No, I love you, Gabriel. I would never have confessed it; I would have died sooner than reveal my secret. What am I that anyone should love me? For many days I have not looked in the glass, for I should weep at the remembrance of my lost youth. And then my story—my terrible story. How could I imagine that you—or, I should say, that thou, wouldst read my thoughts so clearly? See how I tremble; the shock has not yet ceased, the surprise of finding my secret discovered. A man like you to descend to me, ugly and sick for ever. No, do not speak of the other man; I forgot him long ago. And am I going to remember him now that you give me the charity of your love? No, Gabriel, you are the greatest and best of men; you are like a god to me."

They remained silent a long while with their hands clasped, looking into the darkness of the murmuring garden. From above still sounded the lament of the genius at his fading life.

Sagrario leant on Gabriel as though her strength were failing, and as if terrified at so much happiness, she wished to take refuge in his arms.

"Why have I known you so late!" she said in a low voice. "I should have wished to love you in my youth, to be beautiful and healthy only for you, to have the beauty and charm of a great lady to soften the rest of your life. But my gratitude can offer you little, nothing but ill-health; the seeds of death are in me, and slowly I shall fade away. Gabriel, why did you set your heart on me?"

"Because you are an invalid, and unfortunate as I am. Our misery is the loving affinity. Besides, I have never loved like most men. In my travels I have seen the most beautiful women in the world without the slightest glow of desire. I am not of an amorous temperament. From my adventures in Paris when I was young I always returned with a feeling of disgust. My love for the unfortunate has mastered me to the point of blunting my feelings. I am like a drunkard or a gambler, who, obsessed by their passion, feel nothing before a woman. A studious man, buried in his books, feels very little the calls of sex. My passion is pity for the disinherited, and hatred of injustice and inequality. It has so entirely absorbed me, enslaving all my faculties, that I have never had time to think of love. The female does not attract me, but I worship a woman when I see her sad and unfortunate. Ugliness makes more impression on me than beauty, because it speaks to me of social infamies, it shows me the bitterness of injustice, it is the only wine which revives my strength. I loved Lucy because she was unfortunate and dying. I love you, Sagrario, because in your early youth you were a wanderer in life, one whom no one would love. My love is for you, to brighten what remains to you of life."

Sagrario leant on Gabriel's breast.

"How good you are!" she sighed; "what a beautiful soul!"

"Yours is the same, poor Sagrario. Your life has been a snare. You sold yourself through hunger and despair as do thousands of others; you thought to find bread in the false pretences of love. Everything is for the privileged of this world: the arms of the father, the sex of the daughter, and when those arms are weakened, or the youthful body loses its charms, they are thrown on one side and replaced. The market is abundant; I love you for your misfortunes. Had I seen you young and beautiful as in former times, I should not have felt the slightest attraction. Beauty is a bar to sentiment. The Sagrario of former times, with her dreams of being a great lady flattered by the words of youthful lovers, brightly dressed like brilliant birds, would never have thought of a vagabond aged by misery, ugly and sick. We understand each other because we are unfortunate; misery allows us to see into each other's souls; in full happiness we should never have met."

"It is true," she murmured, leaning her head on Gabriel's shoulder. "I love that misery which has allowed us to know, each other."

"You will be my companion," continued Luna, in a soft tone. "We will pass our lives together till death breaks the chain. I will protect you, although the protection of a sick and persecuted man is not worth much."

He passed his arm round the woman, raising her head with his other hand, fixing his eyes on those of Sagrario, which were shining in the starlight bright with tears.

"We shall be two souls, two minds who cherish one another without giving rein to passion, and with a purity such as no poets have imagined. This night in which we have mutually confessed one to another, in which our souls have been laid open to one another is our wedding night; kiss me, companion of my life!"

And in the silence of the cloister they kissed each other noiselessly, slowly, as though with their lips joined they were weeping over the misery of their past, and the brevity of a love around which death was circling. Above, the lament of Beethoven went on unfolding its sad modulations, which floated through the cloister and round the sleeping Cathedral.

Gabriel stood erect sustaining Sagrario, who seemed almost fainting from the strength of her feelings; he looked up at the luminous space with almost priestly gravity, and said, whispering close to the young woman's ear:

"Our life will be like a deserted garden, where amid fallen trunks and dead branches fresh foliage springs up. Companion, let us love one another. Above our misery as pariahs let spring arise. It will be a sad spring, without fruit, but it will have flowers. The sun shines for those who are in the open, but for us, dear companion, it is very far. But from the black depths of our well we will clasp each other, raising our heads, and though his heat will not revive us, we will adore him like a distant star."

CHAPTER X

In the beginning of July Gabriel began his nocturnal watch in the Cathedral.

At nightfall he went down into the cloister, and at the Puerta del Mollete, joined the other watchman, a sickly-looking man who coughed as badly as Luna, and who never left off his cloak even in the height of summer.

"Come along, we are going to lock up!" said the bell-ringer, rattling his bunch of keys.

After the two men had entered the church, he locked the doors from outside and walked away.

As the days were long, there still remained two hours of daylight after the watchmen entered the Cathedral.

"All the church is ours, companion," said the other watchman.

And like a man used to the imposing appearance of the deserted church, he settled himself comfortably in the sacristy as in his own house, opening his supper basket on the chests, and spreading out his eatables between candelabras and crucifixes.

Gabriel wandered about the fane. After many nights of watching, the impression produced when he first saw the immense church deserted and locked up had not yet faded. His footsteps resounded on the pavement, his strides shortened by the tombs of prelates and great men of former days. The silence of the church was disturbed by the strange echoes and mysterious rustlings; the first day Gabriel had often turned his head in alarm, thinking he heard footsteps following him.

Outside the church the sun was still shining, the coloured wheel of the rose window above the great doorway glowed like a luminous flower-bed; below, among the pillars, the light seemed overcome by the darkness; the bats began to descend, and with their wings made the dust fall from the shafts in the vaulting. They fluttered round about the pillars, circling as in a forest of stone; in their blind flight they often struck the cords of the hanging lamps, or shook the old red hats with dusty and ragged tassels that hung high above the cardinals' tombs.

Gabriel made his rounds throughout the church. He shook the iron railings in front of the altars to make sure they were securely locked, pushed the doors of the Muzarabe Chapel, and that of the Kings, threw a glance into the Chapter-house, and finally stopped before the Virgin del Sagrario; through the grating he could see the lamps burning, and above, the image covered with jewels. After this examination he went in search of his comrade, and they both sat down in the crossways, either on the steps of the choir or of the high altar; from there you could take in the whole of the church at one glance.

The two watchmen began by carefully putting on their caps.

"They will probably have ordered you," said Gabriel's companion, "to respect the Church, and that if you want to smoke a cigar you must go up to the gallery of the Locum; and that if you wish to sup you must go into the sacristy. They said the same to me when I first entered into the service of the Church. But these are only the words of people who sleep comfortably and quietly in their own houses. Here the principal thing is to keep good watch, and beyond that, each one may do as seems best to him to pass the night. God and the saints sleep during these hours; they really must want some rest after spending the whole day listening to prayers and hymns, receiving incense, and being

142

scorched by wax tapers close to their faces. We watch their sleep, and, the devil! we are surely not wanting in respect if we allow ourselves a little liberty. Come along, companion, it is getting dark; let us club our suppers."

So the two watchmen supped in the crossways, spreading the contents of their baskets on the marble steps.

Gabriel's comrade carried at his belt, as his only arm, an ancient pistol, a present to the Obreria which had never been fired; to Luna, Silver Stick pointed out a carbine, a legacy to the sacristy from the ex-civil guard, in memory of his years of service. Gabriel made a gesture of repulsion. It was all right standing there, he would get it if it were wanted; so he left it in the corner with some packets of cartridges, mouldy from the damp and covered with cobwebs.

As the night fell the colours from the windows above became obscured, and in the darkness of the naves all the lights from the various lamps began to shine like wavering stars; all the outlines of the church were lost, and Gabriel fancied himself once more sleeping at night on the open ground. It was only when he went the rounds with his lantern in his hand that the outlines of the Cathedral rose out of the shadow ever vaster and more mysterious. The pillars seemed to start out to meet him, rising suddenly up to the roof with the flashes of light from the lantern, the squares in the tiled floor seemed to dance with every swing of the light, and every now and then Gabriel could feel on his head the flutter of passing wings. To the screams of the bats were added the hooting of other frightened birds, who in their flight knocked against the pilasters; they were the owls who came down attracted by the oil in the lamps, and who nearly extinguished them with the sweep of their wings.

Every half-hour the silence was disturbed by the sound of rusty wheels and springs, and then a bell with a silvery tone struck; these were the gilded giants of the Puerta del Reloj, marking the passing of time with their hammers.

Gabriel's companion complained greatly of the innovations introduced by the cardinal for the annoyance of poor folks. In former times he and his old comrade, once they were locked up, could sleep as they pleased without fear of being reproved by the Chapter. But His Eminence, who was always endeavouring to find some means of annoying his neighbour, had placed in different parts of the Cathedral certain little clocks brought from abroad, and now they had to go every half-hour, open them and record their visit. The following day they were examined by Silver Stick, and if any carelessness was discovered he imposed a fine.

"An invention of the demon not to allow us to sleep, comrade. But all the same we might manage a nap if we help one another. While one sleeps a bit the other must undertake to check these cursed machines. No carelessness, eh, fresh man? The pay is short and hunger great, and we cannot afford fines."

Gabriel, always good-natured, was the one who made most rounds, looking scrupulously after the markers, while his companion, the Señor Fidel, rested quietly, praising his generosity. They had given him a good companion; he liked him much better than the old one, with his imperious manners of an old guard, always squabbling as to whose turn it was to get up and make the round.

The poor man coughed as much as Gabriel; his catarrhs disturbed the silence, echoing through the naves till it seemed like several monstrous dogs barking.

"I do not know how many years I have had this hoarseness," said the old man; "it is a present from the Cathedral. The doctors say I ought to give up this employment; but what I say is—who is to support me? You, companion, have begun at the best time. There is a coolness here that all those would envy who are generally perspiring about this time in the cafes of the Zocodover. We are still in summer, but you can imagine the damp which penetrates everything; and you should see what it is in winter! we must really dress up as maskers, covered with caps, shawls and cloaks. They have the charity to leave us a little fire in the sacristy, but many mornings they find us almost frozen. Those of the Chapter call the choir 'kill canon,' and if those gentlemen complain of one hour's stay in this ice-house, having eaten well and drunk better, you may just fancy what it is for us. You have had the good luck to begin in summer, but when the winter comes on you will just have a good time of it!"

But even though it was the best part of the year, Gabriel coughed much, his illness increasing from the dampness of the Cathedral.

On moonlight nights the church was strangely transfigured, and Gabriel remembered sundry operatic effects he had seen during his travels. The white tracery of the windows stood out against the blackness with milky whiteness, splashes of light glided down the pilasters, some even from the vaulting. These mocking spectres moved slowly along the pavement, mounting the opposite pillars and losing themselves in the darkness; those rays of cold and diffused light made the shadows seem even darker as they brought out of the darkness here a chapel, beyond, a sepulchral stone or the outline of some pilaster; and the great Christ, who crowned the railings of the high altar, glowed against its background of shadow with the brilliancy of its old gilding, like some miraculous apparition floating in space in a halo of light.

When the cough would not allow the old watchman to sleep, he told Gabriel of the many years he had carried on this nocturnal life in the Primacy. The office had some resemblance to that of a sexton, for he spent most of it among the dead in the silence of desertion, never seeing anyone till his watch was finished. He had ended by becoming used to it, and it had cured him of many fears he had in his youth. Before, he had believed in the resurrection of the dead, in souls, and the apparitions of saints. But now he laughed at all that. Whole years he had carried on this night work in the Cathedral, and if he heard anything it was only the scampering of rats, who respected neither saints nor altars, for after all they were only wood!

He only feared men of flesh and blood, those robbers who in former times had more than once entered the Cathedral, obliging the Chapter to establish this night vigilance.

He entertained Gabriel with the account of all the attempts at robbery which had happened during the century. In the Cathedral was enough wealth to tempt a saint, Madrid was near, and he much feared the "swell" thieves. But thieves would have to be clever and fortunate to get the better of them. Silver Stick, the bell-ringer, and the sacristan made their nightly inspection before locking up, Mariano then taking the keys away with him to the belfry. No one could think of breaking the locks and bolts, for they were of antique and extremely strong work; besides, they two were there inside to give the alarm on hearing the slightest noise. Formerly, by the help of the dog, the watching had been more complete, for the animal was so alert that no passer-by could approach the doors for an instant without his barking. After its death the Señor Obrero spoke month after month of getting another, but he had never fulfilled his promise. But all the same, without the dog, they two were there and that meant something, eh! He with his old pistol which had never been fired, and Gabriel with his carbine, which was still standing in the corner where his predecessor had left it. He plumed himself upon the fear he and his companion would excite, but, called back to reality by Luna's smile, he added:

"At any rate, in case of emergency we can reckon on the bell that summons the canons; the rope hangs down in the choir, and we have only to ring it. And just imagine what would happen if it rang in the silence of the night! All Toledo would be on foot, knowing that something serious was taking place in the Cathedral. With this and those cursed markers that will not let one sleep, one might say that even the king was not so well guarded at night as this church."

144

In the morning when the watch was ended, Gabriel would return to his house, perished with cold, longing to stretch himself in bed. He would find Sagrario in the kitchen, warming the milk he was to drink before turning in. His gentle companion still called him "uncle" in the presence of the household, and only used the loving "thou" when they were alone. When he was in bed she would bring the steaming milk, making him drink it with maternal caresses, smoothing the pillows; after which she would carefully close the windows and doors so that no ray of light should disturb him.

"Those nights in the Cathedral!" said she complainingly. "You are killing yourself, Gabriel. It is not fit for you. My father says the same. As it is certain there is nothing beyond death, and that we shall not see one another, do try and prolong your life by being careful. Now that we know each other, and are so happy, it would be so sad to lose you!"

Gabriel reassured her. This would not go on beyond the summer; after that they would give him something better. She must not be so sad; such a little thing did not kill one. He would cough just as much living in the Claverias as passing the night in the Cathedral.

After dinner he would go into the cloister, completely rested by his morning's sleep. It was the only time of the day in which he could see his friends; they either came to find him, or he went in search of them, going to the shoemaker's house or up into the tower.

They greeted him respectfully, listening to his words with the same attention as before; but he noted in them a certain air of proud independence, and at the same time of pity, as if, although grateful to him for having transmitted his ideas to them, they pitied him for his gentle character, so inimical to all violence.

"Those birds," said Gabriel to his brother, "are flying on their own account. They do not want me, and wish to be alone."

Wooden Staff shook his head sadly.

"God grant, Gabriel, that some day you may not repent of having spoken to them of things they cannot understand! They have greatly changed, and no one can endure our nephew, the Perrero. He says that if he is not allowed to kill bulls in order to get rich, he will kill men to get out of his poverty; that he has as much right to enjoyment as any gentleman, and that all the rich are robbers. Really, brother, by the Holy Virgin! have you taught them such horrible things?"

"Let them alone," said Gabriel, laughing; "they have not yet digested their new ideas, and are vomiting follies. All this will pass, for they are good souls."

The only thing that vexed him was that Mariano withdrew from him. He fled his company as if he were afraid. He seemed to fear that Gabriel would read his thoughts, with that irresistible power that from boyhood he had held over him.

"Mariano, what is the matter with you?" said he, seeing him pass through the cloisters.

"Much that is out of gear," answered his surly friend.

"I know it, man—I know it; but you seem to avoid me. Why is this?"

"Avoid you—I?—never. You know I always love you. When you come to my house you see how we all welcome you. We owe you a great deal; you have opened our eyes and we are no longer brute beasts. But I am tired of knowing so much and being so poor, and my companions are thinking the same. We do not care to have our heads full and our bellies empty."

"Well, then, what remedy have we? We have all been born too-soon. Others will come after us, finding things better arranged. What can you do to right the present, when there are millions of workers in the world more wretched than yourselves, who have not succeeded in finding a better way out even at the cost of their blood, fighting against authority?"

145

"What shall we do?" grumbled his companion. "That is what we shall see, and you will see also. We are not such fools as you think. You are very clever, Gabriel, and we respect you as our master, for everything you say is true. But it seems to us that when you have to do with things—practical things: you understand me? when one must call bread, bread, and wine, wine: am I explaining myself?—you are, begging your pardon, rather soft, like all those who live much in books. We are ignorant, but we see more clearly."

He walked away from Gabriel, who-was quite unable to understand the true bearing of this aberration among his disciples. Several times when he went up to the tower to spend a few moments with his friends, they would suddenly cease their conversation, looking anxiously at him as though they feared he might have overheard their words.

It was several days since Don Martin had been in the cloister. Gabriel knew through Silver Stick that the chaplain's mother had died, and a week afterwards he saw him one evening in the Claverias. His eyes were bloodshot, his cheeks thin, and his skin drawn as though he had wept much.

"I come to take farewell, Gabriel. I have spent a month of sorrow and sleeplessness nursing my mother. The poor thing is dead; she was far from young, and I expected this ending, but however strong and resigned one may be, these blows must be felt. Now the poor old woman is gone I am free; she was the only tie that bound me to this Church, in which I no longer believe. Its dogma is absurd and puerile, its history a tissue of crimes and violence. Why should I lie like others, feigning a faith I do not feel? To-day I have been to the palace to tell them they may dispose of my seven duros monthly and my chaplaincy of nuns. I am going away. I wish not only to fly the Church, I wish to get out of her atmosphere; and a renegade priest could not live in Toledo. You see this masquerade? I wear it to-day for the last time; to-morrow I shall taste the first joy of my life, tearing this shroud into shreds, such small shreds that no one will be able to use them. I shall be a man. I will go far away, as far as I can. I wish to know what the world is like as I have to live in it. I know no one, I shall have no assistance. You are the most extraordinary man I have ever known, and here you are hidden in this dungeon by your own free will, concealed in a Church which to your views must be empty. I am not afraid of poverty. When one has been God's representative on six reals a day one can look hunger in the face. I will be a workman; I will dig the earth, if necessary. I will get employment on something—but I shall be a free man."

As the two friends walked up and down the cloister Gabriel counselled Don Martin in determining the place to which he should direct his steps, as his thoughts wavered between Paris and the American republics, where emigration was most needed.

As the evening fell, Gabriel took leave of his disciple; his fellow-watchman was waiting for him in the cloister ready for locking-up time.

"Probably we shall never meet again," said the chaplain sadly. "You will end your days here, in the house of a God in whom you do not believe."

"Yes, I shall die here," said Gabriel, smiling. "He and I hate one another, but all the same it seems as if He could not do without me. If He goes out into the streets it is I who guide His steps, and again at night, it is I who guard His wealth. Good-bye, and good-luck, Martin. Be a man without weakness. Truth is well worth poverty."

The disappearance of the chaplain of nuns was effected without scandal. Don Antolin and the other priests thought the young man had moved to Madrid through ambition, to help swell the number of place-hunting clerics. Gabriel was the only one who knew Don Martin's real intentions. Besides, an astonishing piece of news, that fell on the Cathedral like a thunderbolt, soon caused the young priest to be forgotten, throwing all the gentlemen of the choir, all the smaller folk in the sacristies, and the whole population of the upper cloister into the greatest commotion.

The quarrels between the Archbishop and his Chapter had ended, everything that had been done by the cardinal was approved of in Rome, and His Eminence fairly roared with joy in his palace, with the fiery impetuosity of his usual feelings.

As the canons entered the choir they walked with bent heads, looking ashamed and frightened.

"Well, have you heard?" they said to one another as they disrobed in the sacristy.

In a great hurry, with flying cloaks they all left the church, every man his own way, without forming groups or circles, each one anxious to free himself from all responsibility, and to appear free from all complicity with the prelate's enemies.

The Tato laughed with joy seeing the sudden dispersion, and the agitation of the gentlemen of the choir.

"Run! run I The old gossip will give you something to think about!"

The same preparations were made every year in the middle of August for the festival of the Virgin del Sagrario. In the Cathedral they spoke of this year's festival with mystery and anxiety, as though they were expecting great events. His Eminence, who had not been into the church for many months, in order not to meet his Chapter, would preside in the choir on the feast day. He wished to see his enemies face to face, crushed by his triumph, and to enjoy their looks of confused submission. And accordingly, as the festival drew near many of the canons trembled, thinking of the harsh and proud look the angry prelate would fix on them.

Gabriel paid very little attention to these anxieties of the clerical world; he led a strange life, sleeping the greater part of the day, preparing himself for the fatiguing night watch, which he now undertook alone. The Señor Fidel had fallen ill, and the Obreria to avoid expense, and not to deprive the old man of his wretched pay, had not engaged a new companion for him. He spent the nights alone in the Cathedral as calmly as if he had been in the upper cloister, quite accustomed to the grave-like silence. In order not to sleep, he read by the light of his lantern any books he could get in the Claverias, uninteresting treatises on history in which Providence played the principal *rôle*; lives of the saints, amusing from their simple credulity, bordering on the grotesque; and that family Quixote of the Lunas', that he had so often spelt out when little, and in which he still found some of the freshness of his childhood.

The Virgin's feast day arrived; the festival was the same as in other years. The famous image had been brought out of its chapel and occupied on its foot-board a place on the high altar. They brought out her mantle kept in the Treasury and all her jewels, that scintillated kissed by the innumerable lights, glittering and flashing with endless brilliancy.

Before the commencement of the festival, the inquisitive of the Cathedral, pretending absent-mindedness, strolled between the choir and the Puerta del Perdon. The canons in their red robes assembled near the staircase lighted by the famous "stone of light." His Eminence would come down this way, and the canons grouped themselves, timidly whispering, asking each other what was going to happen.

The cross-bearer appeared on the first step of the staircase, holding his emblem horizontally with both hands so that it should pass under the arch of the doorway. After, between servitors, and followed by the mulberry-coloured robe of the auxiliary bishop, advanced the cardinal, dressed in his purple, which quenched the reddish-violet of the canons.

The Chapter were drawn up in two rows with bowed heads, offering homage to their prince. What a glance was Don Sebastian's! The canons, bending, thought they felt it on the nape of their necks with the coldness of steel. He held his enormous body erect in its flowing purple with a gallant pride, as if at the moment he felt himself entirely cured of

147

the malady which was tearing his entrails, and of the weak heart which oppressed his lungs. His fat face quivered with delight, and the folds of his double chin spread out over his lace rochet. His cardinal's biretta seemed to swell with pride on his little, white and shining head. Never was a crown worn with such pride as that red cap.

He stretched out his hand, gloved in purple, on which shone the episcopal emerald ring, with such an imperious gesture that one after another of the canons found themselves forced to kiss it. It was the submission of churchmen, accustomed from their seminary to an apparent humility which covered rancours and hatreds of an intensity unknown in ordinary life. The Cardinal guessed their disinclination, and gloated over his triumph.

"You have no idea what our hatreds are," he had often said, to his friend, the gardener's widow. "In ordinary life few men die of ill-humour; he who is annoyed gives vent to it, and recovers his equanimity. But in the Church you may count by the hundred men who die in a fit of rage, because they are unable to revenge themselves; because discipline closes their mouths and bows their heads. Having no families, and no anxieties about earning their bread, most of us only live for self-love and pride."

The Chapter formed their procession accompanied by His Eminence. The scarlet Perrero headed the march, then came the black vergers and Silver Stick, making the tiles of the pavement ring with the blows of their staffs. Behind came the archiepiscopal cross and the canons in pairs, and finally the prelate with his scarlet train spread out at full length, held up by two pages. Don Sebastian blessed to the right and to the left, looking with his penetrating eyes at the faithful who bowed their heads.

His imperious character and the joy of his triumph made his glance flash. What a splendid victory! The Church was his home, and he returned to it after a long absence with all the majesty of an absolute master, who could crush the evil-speaking slaves who dared to attack him.

The greatness of the Church seemed to him at that moment more glorious than ever. What an admirable institution! The strong man who arrived at the top was an omnipotent god to be feared. Nothing of pernicious and revolutionary equality. Dogma exalted the humility of all before God; but when you came to examples, flocks were always spoken of, and shepherds to direct them. He was that shepherd because the Omnipotent has so ordered it. Woe to whoever attempted to dethrone him!

In the choir his delighted pride tasted an even greater satisfaction. He was seated on the throne of the archbishops of Toledo, that seat which had been the star of his youth, the remembrance of which had disturbed him in his Episcopacy, when the mitre had travelled through the provinces, waiting for the hour to rise to the Primacy. He stood erect under the artistic canopy of the Mount Tabor, at the top of four steps, so that all in the choir could see him and recognise that he was their prince. The heads of the dignitaries seated at his side were thus on a level with his feet. He could trample on them like vipers should they dare to rise again, striking at his most intimate affections.

Fired by the appreciation of his own grandeur and triumph, he was the first to rise, or to sit down; as is directed in the rubric of the services, he joined his voice to those in the choir, astonishing them all by the harsh energy of his singing; the Latin words rolled from his mouth like blows upon those hated people, and his eyes passed with a threatening expression over the double row of bent heads.

He was a fortunate man, who had risen from place to place, but he never felt a satisfaction so deep, so complete as at that moment. He himself was startled at his own delight, at that orgy of pride that had extinguished his chronic ailments; it seemed to him as though he were spending in a few hours the stores of enjoyment of his whole life.

As the mass was ending, the singers and lower people in the choir, who were the only ones who dared to look at him, were alarmed, seeing him suddenly grow pale, rise with his face discomposed, pressing his hands to his breast. The canons noticing it, rushed towards him, forming a crowded mass of red vestments in front of his throne. His Eminence was suffocating, fighting against that circle of hands who instinctively clutched at him.

"Air!" he moaned, "air! Get out from before me with a thousand curses! Take me home!"

Even in the midst of his agony, he recovered his majestic gesture and his old soldiering oaths to drive away his enemies. He was suffocating, but he would not allow the canons to see it: he guessed the delight many of them must feel beneath their compassionate manner. Let no one touch him! He could manage for himself! So leaning on two faithful servants, he began his march, gasping, towards the episcopal staircase, followed by great part of the Chapter.

The religious function ended hurriedly. The Virgin Would forgive it, she should have a better solemnity next year; and all the authorities and invited guests left their seats to run in search of news to the archiepiscopal palace.

When Gabriel woke, past mid-day, every one in the upper cloister was talking of His Eminence's health. His brother inquired of the Aunt Tomasa who had just come from the palace.

"He is dying, my sons," said the gardener's widow; "he cannot escape from it. Doña Visitacion signalled it to me from afar, weeping, poor thing! He cannot be put to bed, for his chest is heaving like a broken bellows. The doctors say he will not last till night. What a misfortune! And on a day like this!"

The agony of the ecclesiastical prince was received in funereal silence. The women of the Claverias went backwards and forwards with news from the palace to the upper cloister; the children were shut up in the houses, frightened by their mothers' threats if they attempted to play in the galleries.

The Chapel-master, who was generally indifferent to events in the Cathedral, went nevertheless to inquire of His Eminence's condition. He had a plan which he quickly explained to the family during dinner. The funeral of a cardinal deserved the execution of a celebrated mass, with a full orchestra recruited in Madrid. He had already cast his eyes on the famous Requiem of Mozart; that was the only reason for which he was interested in the prelate's fate.

Gabriel, looking at his companion, felt the gentle selfishness that a living man feels when a great man dies.

"So the great fall, Sagrario, and we, the sickly and wretched, have still some life before us."

At the hour of locking up the church he went down to begin his watch. The bell-ringer was waiting for him with the keys.

"How about the Cardinal?" inquired Gabriel.

"He will certainly die to-day, if he is not already dead."

And afterwards he added:

"You will have a great illumination to-night, Gabriel. The Virgin is on the high altar till to-morrow morning, surrounded by wax tapers."

He was silent for a moment, as if undecided about Something.

"Possibly," he added, "I may come down and keep you company a little. You must be dull alone; expect me."

When Gabriel was locked into the church, he caught sight of the high altar, resplendent with lights. He made his usual trial of doors and railings; visited the Locum and the large lavoratories, where once some thieves had concealed themselves, and after he was quite certain that there was no human being in the church except himself, he seated himself in the crossways with his cloak round him, and his basket of supper.

He sat there a long while, looking through the railings at the Virgin del Sagrario. Born in the Cathedral and brought up as a child by his mother, who knelt with him before the image, he had always admired it as the most perfect type of beauty. Now he criticised it coldly with his artistic eye. She was ugly and grotesque like all the very rich images; sumptuous and wealthy piety had decked her out with their treasures. There was nothing about her of the idealism of the Virgin painted by Christian artists; she was much more like an Indian idol covered with jewels. The embroidered dress and mantle stood out with the stiffness of stone folds, and over the head-dress sparkled a crown as large as a helmet, diminishing the face. Gold, pearls and diamonds shone on every part of her vestments, and she wore pendants and bracelets of immense value.

Gabriel smiled at the religious simplicity which dressed heavenly heroes according to the fashions of the earth.

The faint twilight glimmering through the windows and the wavering flame of the tapers animated the face of the image as if she were speaking.

"Even as I am!" said Gabriel to himself. "If a holy person were in my place he would think the Virgin was laughing one moment and crying the next; with a little imagination and faith, behold here is a miracle! These flickerings of light have been an inexhaustible mine for the priests, even the Venus' of former times changed the expression of their faces at the pleasure of the faithful, just like a Christian image."

He thought a long time about miracles, the invention of all religions, and as old as human ignorance and credulity.

It was now quite dark. After supping frugally, Gabriel opened a book that he carried in his basket and began to read by the light of his lantern. Now and then he raised his head, disturbed by the fluttering and screams of the night birds, attracted by the extraordinary brilliancy of the countless wax tapers. The time passed slowly in the darkness; the silvery sound of the warriors' hammers re-echoed through the vaulting. Luna got up and visited the markers to record his visit.

Ten o'clock had struck when Gabriel heard the wicket of the Puerta de Santa Catalina open quickly but without violence, as though a key had been used. Luna remembered the bell-ringer's offer, but soon he heard the sound of many steps magnified by the echo as if a whole host were advancing.

"Who goes there?" shouted Gabriel, rather alarmed.

"It is us, man," answered from the darkness the husky voice of Mariano. "Did I not tell you we should come down?"

As they came into the crossways, the light from the high altar fell full upon them, and Gabriel saw the Tato and the shoemaker with the bell-ringer. They wished to keep Luna company part of the night, so that his watch should not be so wearisome, and they produced a bottle of brandy, of which they offered him some.

"You know I do not drink," said Gabriel. "I have never cared for alcohol; wine sometimes, and very little of that. But where are you all going to, dressed out as for a feast day?"

The Tato answered hurriedly. Silver Stick locked up the Claverias at nine, and they wished to spend the night out of bounds. They had been some time at a cafe in the Zocodover, feasting like lords. They had had all sorts of adventures, that was a night quite out of the ordinary way, more especially as all the town was in commotion about the Archbishop.

"How is he going on?" inquired Gabriel.

"I believe he died half-an-hour ago," said the bell-ringer. "When I went up to my house for the keys, a doctor was coming out of the palace and he told one of the canons. But let us sit down."

They all sat down, in their embroidered caps, on the steps of the high altar railing. Mariano put his bunch of keys on the ground, a mass of iron as big as a club. There were keys of every age, some of iron, very large, rough and rusty, showing the old hammer marks and with coats of arms near the bows; others, more modern were clean and bright as silver, but they were all very large and heavy, with powerful indented teeth, proportionate to the size of the edifice.

The three friends seemed extraordinarily happy, with a nervous gaiety which made them catch hold of each other and laugh. They cast sidelong looks at the Virgin and then looked at each other, with a mysterious gesture that Gabriel was quite unable to understand.

"You have all drunk a good deal, is it not so?" said Luna. "You do wrong, for you know that drink is the degradation of the poor."

"A day is a day, uncle," said the Perrero; "it delights us that the great ones are dying. You see, I esteem His Eminence highly, but let him go to the devil! The only satisfaction a poor man has is to see that the end comes also to the rich."

"Drink," said the bell-ringer, offering him the bottle. "It is a pleasure to find ourselves here, well and happy, while to-morrow His Eminence will find himself between four boards; we shall have to ring the little bell all day!"

The Tato drank, passing the bottle to the shoemaker, who held it a long time glued to his gullet. Of the three he seemed the most tipsy; his eyes were bloodshot, he stared stonily on every side and remained silent, he only gave a forced laugh when anyone spoke to him, as if his thoughts were very, very far off.

On the other hand, the bell-ringer was far more loquacious than usual. He spoke of the cardinal's fortune, at the wealth that would fall to Doña Visitacion, of the joy many of the Chapter must feel that night. He interrupted himself to take a pull at the brandy bottle, passing it afterwards to his companions. The smell of the alcohol spread through that atmosphere impregnated with incense and the smoke of wax tapers.

More than an hour passed in this way. Mariano had stopped the conversation several times as if he had something serious to say and was vacillating, wanting courage.

"Gabriel, time is passing and we have much to do and to talk about. It is a little past eleven, but we have still several hours to do the thing well."

"What do you mean to say?" asked Luna, surprised.

"Few words—in a nut-shell. It concerns your becoming rich and us also; we intend to get out of this poverty. You have noticed for some time that we have avoided you, that we preferred talking among ourselves to the pleasure of listening to you. We all know that you are very learned, but as far as things of this life go you are not worth a farthing. We have learnt a great deal from you, but that does not get us out of our poverty. We have spent months thinking how to make a lucky stroke. These revolutions of which you speak seem to us very far off; our grandchildren may see them, but we never shall. It is all right for clever people to look to the future, but ignorant people like us look to the present. We have employed our time discussing all sorts of schemes, to kidnap Don Sebastian and require a million of ransom, to break into the palace one night, and I don't know what besides! All wild ideas started by your nephew. But this morning in my house, while we were lamenting our poverty, we suddenly saw our salvation close at hand. You as the sole guardian of the Cathedral. The Virgin on the high altar, with the jewels that are locked up in the Treasury all the rest of the year, and I with the keys in my power. The easiest thing in the world. Let us clean out the Virgin and take the road to Madrid, where we shall arrive at dawn; the Tato knows a lot of people there among cloak stealers. We will hide ourselves there for a little while, and then you, who know the world, will guide us. We will go to America, sell the stones, and we shall be rich. Get up, Gabriel! We are going to strip the idol, as you say."

"But this is a robbery that you are proposing!" exclaimed Luna, alarmed.

"A robbery?" said the bell-ringer. "Call it so, if you like—and, what then? Are you afraid of it? More has been robbed from us, who were born with the right to a share of the world, but however much we look round we cannot find a vacant place. Besides, what harm do we do to anybody? These jewels are of no use to the bit of wood they cover, it does not eat, it does not feel the cold in winter, and we are poor miserable creatures. You yourself have said it, Gabriel, seeing our poverty. Our children die of hunger on their mother's knees, while these idols are covered with wealth, come along, Gabriel, do not let us lose any more time."

"Come along, uncle," said the Tato, "have a little courage. You must admit we ignorant people know how to manage things when it comes to the point."

Gabriel was not listening to them; surprise had made him fall into a reverie of self-examination. He thought—terrified of the great error he had committed—he saw an immense gulf opening between himself and those he had believed to be his disciples. He remembered his brother's words. Ah, the good sense of the simpleminded! He, with all his reading, had never foreseen the danger of teaching these ignorant people in a few months what required a whole life of thought and study. What happened to people stirred up by revolution was happening here on a small scale. The most noble thoughts become corrupted passing through the sieve of vulgarity; the most generous aspirations are poisoned by the dregs of poverty.

He had sown the revolutionary seed in these outcasts of the Church, drowsing in the atmosphere of two centuries ago. He had thought to help on the revolution of the future by forming men, but on awaking from his dreams he found only common criminals. What a terrible mistake! His ideas had only tended to destruction. In removing from the dulled brains the prejudices of ignorance, and the superstitions of the slave, he had only succeeded in making them daring for evil. Selfishness was the only passion vibrating in them. They had only learnt that they were wretched and ought not to be so. The fate of their companions in misfortune, of the greater part of humanity, wretched and sad, had no interest for them. If they could get out of their present state, bettering themselves in whatever way they could, they cared very little if the world went on just as it did before; that tears, and pain and hunger should reign below, in order to ensure the comfort of those above. He had sown his thoughts in them hoping to accelerate the harvest, but like all those forced and artificial cultivations, that grow with astonishing rapidity only to give rotten fruit, the result of his propaganda was moral corruption. Men in the end, like all of them! The human wild beast, seeking his own welfare at the cost of his fellow, perpetuating the disorders of pain for the majority, as long as he can enjoy plenty during the few years of his life. Ah! Where could he meet with that superior being, ennobled by the worship of reason, doing good without hope of reward, sacrificing everything for human solidarity, that man-God who would glorify the future!

"Come along, Gabriel," continued the bell-ringer. "Do not let us lose time it is only a few minutes' work; and then—flight!"

"No," said Luna firmly, coming out of his reverie, "you shall not do this; you ought not to do it. It is a robbery you suggest to me, and my pain is great, seeing that you reckoned on me; others rob from fatal instinct or from corruption of soul, you have come to it because I tried to enlighten you, because I tried to open your minds to the truth. Oh! it is horrible, most horrible!"

"What is the use of all these objections, Gabriel? Is it not a bit of wood? Whom do we harm by taking its jewels? Do not the rich rob, and everyone who possesses anything? Why should we not imitate them?"

"For this very reason, because what you propose doing is a suggestion of evil, because it perpetuates once more that system of violence and disorder which is the root of all misery. Why do you hate the rich, if what they do in sweating the poor is just the same as what you are doing in taking possession of a thing for yourselves—understand me well— for yourselves—and not for all. The robbery does not scare me, for I do not believe in ownership nor in the sanctity of things, but for this very reason I detest this appropriation to yourselves and I oppose it. Why do you wish to possess all this? You say it is to remedy your poverty. That is not true. It is to be rich, to enter into the privileged group, to be three individual men of that detested minority which desires to enjoy prosperity by enslaving humanity. If all the poor of Toledo were now shouting outside the doors of the Cathedral, rebellious and emboldened, I would open the way for them, I would point out those jewels that you covet, and I would say, 'Possess yourselves of those, they are so many drops of sweat and blood wrung from your ancestors; they represent the servile work on the land of the lords, the brutal plundering of the king's cavaliers, so that magnates and kings may cover with jewels those idols which can open to them the gates of heaven. These things do not belong to you because you happen to be the most daring; they belong to all, as do all the riches of the earth. For men to lay their hands on everything existing in the world would be a holy work, the redeeming revolution of the future. To possess yourselves of some portion of what by moral right is not yours, would only be for you a crime against the laws of the land, for me it would be a crime against the disinherited, the only masters of the existing——"

"Silence, Gabriel," said the bell-ringer harshly; "if I let you, you would go on talking till dawn. I do not understand you, nor do I wish to. We came to do you a good turn, and you treat us to a sermon. We wish to see you as rich as ourselves, and you answer us by talking of others, of a lot of people that you don't know, of that humanity who never gave you a scrap of bread when you wandered like a dog. I must treat you as I did in our youth when we were campaigning. I have always loved you and I admire your talents, but we must really treat you like a child. Come along, Gabriel! Hold your tongue, and follow us! We will lead you to happiness! Forward, companions!" The Tato and the shoemaker stood up, walking towards the railings of the high altar, the Tato seized one of its gates, and half opened it.

"No!" shouted Gabriel with energy. "Stop! Mariano, you do not know what you are doing. You believe your happiness will be accomplished when you have possessed yourselves of those jewels. But afterwards? Your families remain here. Tato, think of your mother. Mariano, you and the shoemaker have wives—you have children."

"Bah!" said the bell-ringer. "They will come and join us when we are in safety far away. Money can do everything—the thing is to get it."

"And your children? Shall they be told their fathers were thieves!"

"Bah! they will be rich in other countries. Their history will not be worse than that of other rich men's sons."

Gabriel understood the fierce determination that animated those men. His endeavours to restrain them were useless. Mariano seized him, seeing he was trying to push between them and the altar.

"Stand aside, little one," he said. "You are no use for anything. Let us alone. Are you afraid of the Virgin? Undeceive yourself, even if we carry off all she has, she will work no miracle."

Gabriel attempted one final effort.

"You shall do nothing. If you pass the railings, if you approach the high altar, I will ring the call bell, and before ten minutes all Toledo will be at the gates."

And opening the iron gate of the choir, he entered with a decision that surprised the bell-ringer.

The shoemaker in tipsy silence was the only one who followed him.

"My children's bread!" he murmured in thickened speech. "They wish to rob them! They wish to keep them poor!"

Mariano heard a metallic clatter, and saw the shoemaker raise his hand armed with the bunch of keys which had fallen on the marble steps of the railing, then he heard a strangely sonorous sound, as if something hollow was being struck.

Gabriel gave one scream, and fell forwards on the ground; the shoemaker continued striking his head.

"Do not give him any more—stop!"

These were the last words Gabriel heard confusedly, as he lay stretched at the entrance of the choir; a warm and sticky liquid ran over his eyes; afterwards—silence, darkness and—nothing!

His last thought was to tell himself he was dying—that probably he was already dead, and that only the last vital struggle remained to him, the last struggle of a life vanishing for ever.

Still he came back to life. He opened his eyes with difficulty and saw the sun coming through a barred window, white walls, and a dirty and darned cotton counterpane. After great wandering and stumbling, he could collect his thoughts sufficiently to' form one idea: they had placed the Cathedral on his temples—the huge church was hanging over his head crushing him. What terrible pain! He could not move; he seemed fastened by his head. His ears were buzzing, his tongue seemed paralysed. His eyes could see feebly, as though the light were muddy and a reddish haze enveloped all things.

He thought that a face with whiskers, surmounted by the hat of a civil guard, bent over him, looking into his eyes. He moved his lips, but no one heard a sound. No doubt it was the nightmare of his old persecutions returning again.

They looked at him, seeing that he opened his eyes. A gentleman dressed in black advanced towards his bed, followed by others who carried papers under their arms. He guessed they were speaking to him by the movement of their lips, but he could hear nothing. Was he in another world? Were all his beliefs false, and after death did another life exist the same as the one he had left?

He fell again into darkness and unconsciousness. A long time passed—a very long time. Again he opened his eyes, but now the haze was denser, it was not red but black.

Through this veil he thought he saw his brother's face, horrified and drawn with fear; and the cocked hats of the civil guards, those nightmares, surrounding poor Wooden Staff. Afterwards, more misty, more uncertain, the face of his gentle companion, Sagrario, looking at him with weeping eyes in terrible grief, caressing him with her glance, fearless of the black, armed men who surrounded her.

This was his last look, uncertain and clouded, as though seen by the light of a flying spark. Afterwards, eternal darkness and annihilation.

As his eyes were closing for ever, a voice close to him said:

"We have followed your scent, rascal; you were well hidden, but we have discovered you through one of your own. Now we shall see what account you can give of the Virgin's jewels, thief!"

But the terrible enemy of God and social order could give no account to man.

The following day he was carried out of the prison infirmary on men's shoulders to disappear in the common grave.

The earth kept the secret of his death, that frowning Mother who watches men's struggles impassively, knowing that all grandeur and ambitions, all miseries and follies must rot in her breast, with no other object than the fertilisation and renovation of life.

23801706R00087

Printed in Poland
by Amazon Fulfillment
Poland Sp. z o.o., Wrocław